The Depths of Her Soul

Highlander Heroes, Volume 4

Rebecca Ruger

Published by Rebecca Ruger, 2020.

This is a work of fiction. Names, character, places, and incidents are either a product of the author's imagination or are used fictitiously, and any resemblance to actual persons, living or dead, events, or locales is entirely coincidental. Some creative license may have been taken with exact dates and locations to better serve the plot and pacing of the novel.

ISBN: 9798677008931
The Depths of Her Soul
All Rights Reserved.
Copyright © 2020 Rebecca Ruger
Written by Rebecca Ruger

Cover Design by Kim Killion @The Killion Group

All rights reserved. No part of this publication may be reproduced, distributed or transmitted in any form or by any means, or stored in a database or retrieval system, without the prior written permission of the publisher.
Disclaimer: fflhe material in this book is for mature audiences only and may contain graphic content. It is intended only for those aged 18 and older.

Chapter One

North of Aberdeen, Scotland 1307

THE INTERIOR OF THE wagon was beyond anything Mari had ever known, as far as vehicles went. Not that she traveled often, or, well, ever. Save for seven years earlier, at age twelve, when she'd been sent down to her uncle in England on the back of a tanner's cart. She'd ridden hundreds of miles, by her reckoning, listening to that tanner's lad yapping endlessly about the unpleasant process of curing the pungent hides that had served as her seat. She could still hear the boy's nasal voice, could still recall wondering whether walking to England, had it been presented as a means of transport, might have been more to her liking.

As it was, her return trip now—home to Scotland—was as far different from the going as sugar was to salt. She had been retrieved that morning by her half-brother, Harman, and had been stuffed into this opulent conveyance. She still couldn't believe her good fortune, to be going home finally, and to be travelling in such luxury. Had her family's circumstances changed somehow over the last few years?

She ran her hand again over the tufted seat cushion covered in plum-colored velvet, and then touched once more the fine curtains draped over the arched dome of the wagon, which Harman had advised she keep drawn for safety. The long panels were fashioned of a decadent red silk, the likes of which Mari was sure she had only rarely seen, and certainly had never touched. Likewise, the frame of the vehicle was rich with carved wood, and the wheels themselves were made not of some roughly cut and shaped timber, but were smooth and perfectly round, allowing for a more comfortable ride. Never mind that with the curtains drawn, the vehicle was pitched into near darkness, and the air was close and smelled vaguely of old food and something even less pleasant.

They stopped around noon and Mari was jarred from a doze, having no one within the fine wagon to keep her company and thus, wakeful. She fussed with the drapes at the rear of the wagon and stepped out onto the solid ground of good, green Scotland. Mari let her eyes skim the immediate area, a thin forest of tall pines, whose lowest limbs sprouted well above her head. The midday sun fought to pierce the trees, triumphing here and there, dotting the forest floor with bits of light.

She found her brother, along with several of the dozen men in his company, taking respite on their backsides on the cool ground.

"We won't stop long," he said when he noticed her approach. "Take care of your business and we'll be off again."

Having no call for relief as of yet, Mari perched next to him, sitting on a bulge of dense roots directly under a particularly thick pine. Unabashedly, she stared at her half-brother, several years her senior, having not seen him in years. That morn, when he'd come for her, his pleasing but shocking news that she was going home had denied her the opportunity to consider him overlong.

He hadn't changed much, was still possessed of a thick mane of bright orange hair, with eyebrows several shades lighter and eyes the color of pale gray stone. They were of an equal height, which meant her brother cut a less than remarkable figure as a man, as he was similarly slim. He looked older, perhaps, than his twenty-six years, his cheeks narrower, while several lines seemed to have taken up permanent residency upon his forehead.

"Harman," she said, "you haven't told me why you've come for me. After all these years, why am I being returned now?" Truly, as the weeks and months had turned into years, Mari had begun to believe she was bound to spend the rest of her life with her mam's brother, Albert, and his sickly wife, Beatrice.

Harman plucked a small pouch from his belt and chewed with some exaggeration on the bread he pulled from it. He offered none to his sister, and she made no request for a share.

"Da' wants you home," was all he said, a shrug accompanying his words.

Mari grinned, hoping for more clarity. "Just like that, after seven years, he decides he wants me home, remembers he has a daughter?"

Someone snickered at this. Mari passed a glance around the men scattered nearby. Some met her gaze, as if they'd been watching her. Nervously, she returned her eye to her brother, uncomfortable with the leer of one man in particular, his brown eyes narrowed upon her with some hostile speculation, it seemed.

Harman shrugged again, still chewing. Around the food in his mouth, he said, "Time to wed. Da's arranged it."

Her eyes widened. "Wed?" Of course she knew she would wed one day, or rather had hoped she might. But she wasn't of a fine family, where arrangements were made for wealth and titles and land. Her father was naught but a farmer, and a poor one at that. "Wed to whom?"

"Walter," Harman said.

Mari blanched. "Walter?" Her shoulders fell while her stomach turned. "Walter Ramsay?"

Harman smirked, his face turned toward her. The smirk was ugly, made him more so. "You ken another Walter?"

No, she did not, more's the pity. Walter Ramsay was Harman's childhood friend. The son of a local landowner, from whom her father leased land, he was, or he had been when she'd known him, as awful as he was ugly. Mean and petty, he'd made her cry in his presence more times than not, had lived with a certain hunger for causing trouble, and one time had actually pulled old Meg Creech from her cart so that he might amuse himself with a joyride. Mari could still recall the damage he'd inflicted upon poor Meg's aged nag with a combination of his complete disregard for gentleness and the crop he'd quickly fashioned from the thin branch of a tree.

"Aye, he's been waiting on this day for years now," Harman was saying, his sneer intact.

"But shouldn't he be seeking an alliance with some noble family," she wondered desperately, "or at the very least, with a family of greater wealth?" This reminded her of her question about the costly vehicle that had been sent along to convey her home. "Has something changed in our circumstances, that we are to be aligned with the Ramsay family, and are now in possession of so fine a wagon?"

Several men within earshot of this snorted. Mari could not say whether this was in reaction to her obvious distaste and reluctance, or her mention of the wagon.

But Harman only lifted and dropped his shoulders once again. "Nae, Mari, we're still poor as shite. But Walter kens what he wants, always has. He willna be denied."

She feared the disagreeable sensation in her stomach, a rioting of her body, might become a permanent thing if she were to be married to that boy—man now, she supposed. *Walter kens what he wants, always has.* What on earth did that mean? Mari could make no sense of it. Perhaps she might talk her father out of this scheme. Her shoulders slumped further. Likely, she would know little sympathy from the man who had so easily sent her away, an extra mouth to feed being of greater import, apparently, than his love for her.

They stopped again just as the sun was beginning its final descent behind the jagged green and brown hills in the west. Finding Harman at the front of the wagon, she advised him that she would find relief in the strand of trees nearby. He nodded gruffly, busy with the poorly crafted shoe of his horse and whatever its trouble might be. Lifting the skirts of her plain brown kirtle, she picked her way over rock and around scrub brush and off into the trees.

Returning only moments later, having just cleared the last of the birch trees, Mari expected to find her brother and his men settling in for the evening, perhaps making a fire over which they might warm themselves, as the night air would grow cold, no doubt. This was not the scene. Men scrambled, some from spots upon the ground and some from other sections of those trees.

Harman was frowning, his light orange brows drawn down over his pale eyes as he stared off toward the south.

And then Mari heard it, a thunderous noise. She turned and followed Harman's gaze, but saw nothing but more trees, dissected by the sliver of a road upon which they'd just ridden. The noise grew louder, and it was only a split second before Mari realized it was horses. And plenty of them, galloping toward them at what must be a great speed, to have wrought such a booming commotion. The close movements of her companions then drew her attention. The men began to gain their saddles again, two of them already racing away, further north. Mari met her brother's gaze, her momentarily frozen feet moving toward him.

"Harman?"

Mari's brother raced toward his steed, ignoring her.

"Harman!" Panicked now, she turned and ran for the wagon, crying out when she noticed that the horse had already been relieved of its yoke, and that the man who'd driven the cart all day was leaping onto the bare back of the palfrey. He kicked the horse's flanks with a frantic zeal and rode away.

Stunned, Mari faced her brother again, the last man remaining. He'd gained the saddle and circled his mount around her, a grimace contorting his features.

Lifting her hand, expecting to be pulled up onto his horse, she heard instead, "I'm sorry, Mari." She jerked her gaze to her brother, while her hand remained arrested in midair.

The noise behind her grew louder still. Harman's gaze shifted, went over her head, and then back to her. "I canna be caught, Mari. 'Twould be the noose for me."

"Harman!" Mari screeched, his grimace explained. "Take me up!" she demanded. She lunged forward, but her brother moved himself and his horse out of her reach.

"I canna, Mari. I need you to stall them."

"Stall them?" Her throat clogged and her mind whirred. My God! What was he saying? "I—Harman, what—"

"It'll likely be over quickly, but you'll at least be alive when they're done. Wouldn't be the case for me."

Mari dropped her hand, only half understanding what he might be talking about. Certainly she understood that he cared naught for her, would leave her to whomever approached so furiously through the trees. She dashed forward, intent on climbing up onto his horse whether he liked it or not. But her brother, her only surviving sibling, gave another unsympathetic grimace, beat his heels into the animal's flanks, and was away.

She could only stare, gape-jawed, at her brother's departing figure. He charged straight up the lane, around the curve and out of sight. The empty road ahead held all her bewildered attention until the noise behind her became deafening.

Desperate now, tears threatening, Mari lifted her skirts and ran off the narrow road, thinking to hide herself in the trees.

LACHLAN MAITLAND PUSHED his steed up and over the last rise of Tyrebagger Hill and caught just a glimpse of a moving shape and flowing fabric headed into the woods. He called out harshly, "Utrid! Fetch that lass!"

In another moment, he flew past the place where the figure had disappeared, with the bulk of his men following him. They reached the spot where the well-trod path curved, affording them a fine view of a widened meadow and the Kirkhill forest beyond. The meadow was empty, naught to see but a patchwork of fields and grass and a lichen-covered yew tree, standing sentinel in the foreground.

Lachlan cursed roundly and slowed his mount. These were the reivers from Blackburn, he knew. He just knew it. Not true reivers, being so far north. True reivers were border folk, their land and homes destroyed by the ongoing feud with England, their location simply a matter of poor luck. Their homes and livelihood looted and burned in so many skirmishes with England had forced them to make their living any way they could. Raiding and wreaking havoc along the border, both in England and in Scotland, had provided food and monies they'd been robbed of by the war.

But this group, they were naught but opportunists—a band of unaligned thieves who made war on their own, claiming some protest to the continued battle with England, while their overdone violence suggested only bloodlust and greed as motives.

A muscle ticked in his cheek, another in his temple, as he clenched his jaw. They would pay, by God, when he caught up with them. Yanking hard on the reins, Lachlan turned his destrier and began to walk him back to where he'd sent Utrid off to recover the girl.

"We can catch them yet."

Turning to his left showed his captain, Murdoch, walking beside him. A heavy frown crinkled the eyes and forehead of his old friend.

Lachlan nodded. "Aye, we might have." Tipping his head to where Utrid was now dragging a screaming lass out of the woods, he said, "Should be easy to get the names of those we chase."

"Release me at once," the girl demanded of Utrid, scratching at the hand that circled her arm so tightly. "Did your mam raise you to manhandle women in this manner?"

Lachlan took note of her boldness as she upbraided the lad. He passed a glance over the abandoned cart—too fine a vehicle to have transported this lass in her rough-hewn gown—and drew conclusions about the leaving of the cart and the girl.

"Likely, she would scold you soundly," the lass went on, even as Utrid tried to ignore her—though his pinkened cheeks suggested otherwise—and delivered her to his chief.

Lachlan was presented with a slim figure dwarfed by a wealth of auburn hair, the mass of it a curtain around her face and shoulders. Her face was yet turned away from him as she continued to fuss over Utrid's hand on her arm. Settling his hands on the pommel, Lachlan met Utrid's aggrieved look and gave a nod, so that the lad removed his hand from her person. Utrid did not remain, but was off, back toward the trees, likely to collect the mount he'd discarded when pursuing the lass.

She turned and faced Lachlan.

"Oh."

The sound was not much more than a whimper, not at all unexpected. He was used to persons wilting before him when first they met him.

Lachlan lifted a brow at her, stalling, giving himself a moment to come to terms with the fact that whoever she was, whatever she was, she was absolutely breathtaking.

Eyes like that—bright blue under the golden setting sun, spiked by tears of panic—should rightly be outlawed, possibly had brought men to ruin, even as she appeared to have no more years than the lad Utrid himself.

Tossing his gaze briefly toward the bend in the lane, Lachlan said, "They left rather hastily." His words, as always, came unhurriedly, his voice deep.

Beside him, Murdoch added, "Left something behind."

She lifted her hand, turned the palm up, while the pale skin of her face turned white. And then, remarkably, the hand waved dismissively as she forced out a purposefully merry titter of a laugh.

"How silly of them," she said. "I was gone but a moment—" She stopped suddenly, as if the extent of her manufactured reasoning went only that far. "They'll be back." Her voice wavered now as she stared at Lachlan's unblinking gaze and did her best to not gape at the scarring.

"Will they?" he wondered aloud.

More false brightness. "But of course, just as soon as they realize they've...gone without me."

Lachlan nodded, digesting this, letting his silence unnerve her yet more. He kept hold of her frightened gaze, not at all immune to either her brave stance or the shape of her lips, full and bowed and temptingly pink. In reaction to his brash and hard perusal, she blinked rapidly and bit her bottom lip, creating a bracket of indents on either side of her mouth. *Jesu, dimples, too?*

Murdoch, ever impatient and bereft of any form of subtlety, chirped, "I dinna think so, lass. Fine friends you've got there, leaving you to fend for yourself."

"Fend?" she squeaked. But this, too, she waved off with further fabricated lightness. The dimples reappeared, "How fine of you to stop and offer aid to a weary traveler. But don't let me keep you gentlemen. Surely, my party will return anon."

Lachlan almost—almost!—barked out a laugh. The bonny lass had no idea how fortunate she was to have been found by him and his men. Many others...aye, they'd take what those lips promised.

"The men—the ones who just deserted you," Lachlan said, deciding the time for games was done, "who are they to you?"

Practicing a bit of her own stalling, she lifted a hand and pointed one slim finger in the direction of the bend in the road. "Those men?"

Aware that even the slightest facial expression intensified the grisliness of his scar, Lachlan smirked anyway. He leaned forward over the pommel. "Aye. Those men."

"They were—are—" she was quick to correct, "my escort." A small bit of silence preceded the addition of, "Home."

His grin widened. "I think not, lass. Home for you is not to the north. I ken an English lass when I hear her."

She frowned at him, which was amazing in that it detracted not at all from her beauty. "Half Scottish," she insisted, thrusting her hands onto her hips.

"When it suits you," he supposed in return, having no idea why he felt the desire to rile her. He sensed Murdoch's attention on him, as if he, too, questioned this response. "But aye, an escort is family or is hired. Which is it?"

Rather in a huff, fisting her hands as they dropped from her hips, she said, "Family, if you must know. Which is what assures me of my brother's return. Good day, sirs. I will await them at the wagon."

Lachlan watched her walk away, noticing the rigid set of her narrow back.

"Give her a few minutes to let her fear expand," he suggested when Murdoch made to follow.

With that, he dismounted and walked his destrier over to Rory, who'd taken charge of the horses when they'd stopped. He swept his gaze around the twenty men he'd brought with him to Midmar, in search of the devil wreaking havoc upon local villages. As if the war with England, as if their own king fighting for his proper crown was not enough turmoil to keep a chief busy, he had to contend with this lawless rubbish, some whelp of a boy—so said the reports—looting and pillaging at will up and down the coast north of Aberdeen.

"Charles! Niel!" he called out. "Get a fire going. We'll stay the night."

Murdoch, having likewise dismounted, was at his side again. "Do you not think we ought to head back to Hawkmore?"

Lachlan lifted a brow at him. "You have some need for a quick return?" He did not await a response but directed his steps toward the lass and her silly wagon, which was in all likelihood not hers at all.

She sat rather delicately upon the long and smooth timber of the tongue where it leaned from the front of the vehicle down into the ground, the neck yoke bereft of the beast who had pulled it. The low-hung sun, directly behind Lachlan's head, forced her to lift her hand to her brow as she measured his approach. Lachlan strode past her, to the rear of the wagon, and flipped back the silky curtain to peer inside. The curtain itself was much finer than the coarse linen of her plain gown. 'Twas empty inside save for one worn satchel, not even a lone trunk to say this girl's travel had been planned. Or, maybe all that she owned was just here, inside that worn satchel.

"Sir!" She'd followed him, had leapt from her perch and stood at his side, outraged at his intrusion. "What are—"

"'Tis a fine wagon," he commented.

"Yes," she acknowledged with some hesitation.

"So," he said, facing her, "you've been collected by your family, in a wagon that surely belongs not to you, and are being taken home, as you say. For what? Where have you been? Where is home?"

Curved brows of dark brown angled down over those blue eyes. Up close, Lachlan noticed the blue of her eyes was dotted with tiny spots of gold; the dense fringe of lashes surrounding these was a shade darker than her hair and brows. Freckles, slight and pale, dotted the skin across her nose and cheeks. Lachlan frowned.

"Sir, I am not sure that is any of your business."

They stood face to face, though Lachlan towered over her, while Murdoch hovered close. Other men, those without some chore to attend, gathered as well.

"Aye, but it is," Lachlan said. "We're hunting reivers, lass, and I've a feeling your brother and the party that deserted you are the ones we seek."

Those blue eyes nervously scanned the gathering crowd before settling on Lachlan once more. She couldn't help it, people never could, that her gaze was transfixed by his scar. The rate of her breathing increased, her chest rising and falling with greater speed under that drab brown gown.

"As I said, my brother came to fetch me home—I've been in England with my uncle for many years. I know nothing of any reivers." She bit her lip again, watching Lachlan still. When he said nothing to this claim, she added, "Apparently, I am to be wed."

This, then, was not to her liking, if her disagreeable tone and growing frown were any indication.

"To whom?" Murdoch asked.

"I'm quite sure his name will mean nothing to you," she answered, but revealed, "Walter Ramsay."

A collective clamor of disbelief sounded throughout the men. Murdoch whistled low to demonstrate his shock. Lachlan stared at her, watching her glance this way and that, around all the Maitland soldiers.

"Och, lass. You've made my day," Murdoch said, adding a chortle. Pulling on his long beard as he leaned toward her, he asked, "You ken who this man is, lass?" He flicked his thumb at Lachlan.

Her lips parted, worried now, and she dragged her gaze back to Lachlan. She shook her head, and Lachlan wondered briefly about what he considered a lack of the proper amount of fear on her bonny face; this would change with the introduction, he assumed.

"'Tis the Lord of Hawkmore, the devil himself, Lachlan Maitland, the Highland Hawk say some, proud defender of Scotland's freedom, and former confidante of the proud patriot William Wallace—may his soul rest in peace."

She turned her fabulous blue eyes from Murdoch back to Lachlan, completely unimpressed. Or dimwitted, Lachlan guessed. Or too long gone to England?

"Hawkmore? Is that anywhere near Newburgh? Perhaps you might escort me home—were you and your men headed home?" she asked, lifting her brow expectantly.

Lachlan and Murdoch exchanged another speaking glance, stupefied by her calm demeanor. Mayhap she was as innocent as she looked, mayhap she had no idea that the Maitlands and Ramsays had been grave enemies for decades.

Resisting the urge to roll his eyes, Lachlan said, "Nae, lass. We'll no' be escorting you home."

This answer seemed not to disturb her at all. "Very well, sir. I'm sure my party will return for me right quick." She followed this pronouncement with a beauteous and confident smile, which had many sets of eyes darting back and forth between the lass and Lachlan.

Lachlan ignored the growing befuddlement of his men and the bemused frown crinkling Murdoch's forehead.

"Saints preserve us," his captain muttered beside him.

"They won't return," Lachlan said firmly, wanting to be done with this nonsense.

The smile faltered and left her eyes, even as her pretty pink lips remained curved. "They will," she returned without an ounce of conviction.

Lachlan shook his head, holding her gaze.

She began to nod, as if the positive motion would make it true. Her bottom lip began to tremble while tears gathered once more in her captivating eyes. Glancing around nervously at the growing number of soldiers surrounding her, she swallowed and raised her chin. "And you won't help me, I gather?"

Shaking his head again, slowly from side to side, Lachlan answered, "Nae, lass. We've no plans to help you. We aim to kidnap you."

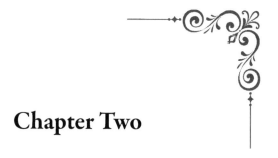

Chapter Two

Mari opened her mouth. Woefully, she hadn't the wherewithal presently to form even a proper gasp at this horrific news. She could do naught but stare at the very large man, too stunned yet to make anything of his hardened return gaze. If she didn't know better—if she knew this man at all, perhaps—she might have guessed that he was pleased to deliver such a frightful plan, as if he might delight in her fear.

She imagined she was expected to be horrified by his face, but of course this man could have no idea that her favorite person back in England, Gretchen, had a similar disfigurement that put this man's to shame. No doubt he enjoyed frightening ill-fated females with his visage, but she would not be one of them. True, she'd been shocked at first, having only just met the man, these scars being new to her. Yet, she'd learned years ago to always make eye contact with Gretchen to avoid any possibility of showing any reaction to the scars. This gave some relief to dear Gretchen, who was continually the subject of barbs and jests and pranks. It was only less than a year ago that Mari had swung her fisted hand into the foul mouth of Allard Bromley; he'd spoken harshly to Gretchen—not the first time—and Mari had had enough. There had been several witnesses to Mari knocking the boy on his backside, and she honestly believed Gretchen had been so much less abused in the months that followed.

Yet, this man's scars were no trifling matter. At one time, some sharp force had sliced down across his face, seeming to touch first above his left eye and then down and over his cheek and into the corner of his lip. The eye itself had escaped the blade. It must have been gruesome at the time, but was now only white and raised skin, slicing his eyebrow in two. Where it had carved his top lip, the skin was tight and drawn, not raised and puckered. Not gruesome at all.

But that was the pretty part of his face.

The right side of his face, like Gretchen's, had met with fire, Mari guessed.

This man's right cheek was similar to most of the left side of Gretchen's, red and white, sun-colored and then not, contorted and deformed. His right eye had not entirely escaped the injury, being narrower than the other, pulled by the puckered skin between the eye and temple. The mark covered most of his cheek and made a thick line down his neck, disappearing into his tunic.

If not for the scars, Mari would have considered him impossibly handsome, his eyes being the most unusual shade—hazel, she thought with outer flecks of blue. His hair was exactly the same shade as the wet bark of her favorite tree back in England, a magnificent yew whose trunk in the rain was all at once golden and amber and dark brown. It was brushed back from his forehead and curled with some charm around his ears but was short, not growing past the nape of his neck. His face was long and weathered with sun, the unmarred skin chisel-hard, his lips firm within a clean-shaven face. As most of the men in his party wore beards, Mari wondered if he kept his face free of hair because likely none would grow on his right side.

But no, his scars did not frighten her. His harshness and his plans for her, on the other hand, absolutely terrified her. And while his eyes were remarkable in color, the emotion of them, of some watchful and expectant severity, certainly did not put her at ease.

As he seemed to be awaiting a response, as did all who surrounded her, Mari cleared her throat and wondered, "Kidnap? Has this anything to do with me personally?" She recalled their reaction to the mention of Walter Ramsay. "Or is this about who I am to wed?"

The man grinned. And this, now, scared her. She was always fearful of persons who seemed to enjoy another person's terror. Some evil lurked in persons like that, she'd always thought.

And while her fear was large indeed, she'd never been one to back away from a fight. And having lived as friends with Gretchen for so many years, Mari had some inkling of at least one of his weaknesses.

"How came you by your scar?" She asked, assuming it to be fair game since he had employed it to intimidate her.

He frowned at her, as if he couldn't believe she dared. The complete stillness of those around them gave evidence that few had.

"It looks old," she continued bravely, "and not well cared for. Mayhap no one advised that woodruff and rose oil are essential for the care of burns."

She'd gone too far, she could see. His lips tightened and twisted while his nostrils flared. He stepped closer, standing an entire head taller and more. She held her ground, breathed sharply through her nose as he did, but was forced to tip her head back to maintain eye contact.

When the tips of his boots touched the hem of her gown, he said evenly in a dangerous voice, "This is a gift from your Englishmen."

"'Tis not my English—" she tried to defend, now regretting her foolish tongue, which frequently saw her in situations similar to this.

He ignored her. "They covered my beard in pitch and set it ablaze."

Mari widened her eyes and opened her mouth, still holding his very close gaze.

He shook his head. "No' for information, no' for Scots' secrets," he said, and grinned much as the devil himself might. "Just as entertainment."

This, then, would explain his desire for a clean-shaven face. Oh, but there was so much anger in him, so much pain. She lifted her hand instinctively, but luckily caught herself so that she only folded her fingers into her palm before she might have touched him. "I am sorry." And yet the practical side of her, the one that seized on solutions, compelled her to add, "It's not very old yet and likely doesn't pain you overmuch, but as years go by—if left untended—it will give you grief."

He frowned again, the smirk disappearing, and stared at her with some puzzled callousness.

"Mayhap no one advised, lass, that you dinna call attention to the very reason a man holds you and yours in such contempt."

It was Mari's turn to crinkle her brow. "I did not burn you." But she understood somehow that with this man, everyday someone must pay for the cruelty that was done to him. His jaw twitched again, and Mari thought it best to anger him no more. With a frustrated sigh, she said, "Fine. I'm to be a captive. Where are we off to, then?"

The older man beside him spoke up, his words halting. "Lass, you dinna seem to ken how these things work."

Mari turned to him. "Kidnappings? No, I have never been. But I'm hungry and I'm hoping that you will at least feed your prisoner. So, might we get on with it, and hopefully reach whatever our destination is by suppertime?"

The old man, whom Mari assumed might be a second-in-command, narrowed his gray eyes further. He was at least twice an age of Lachlan Maitland, but of an equal height, which meant that he, too, towered over her. He possessed not the same form of menace as his chief, showed no ticking cord in the muscle of his neck and could not lay claim to any visible battle wound, but was scary still. His hair was more gray than brown, thick but unkempt, as if it had not met a comb in many weeks; the gray eyes were used mostly for assessment and not for terrorization, she decided. Yet, she believed she would find little sympathy here, though she did imagine this man might bow more to rationale and practicality, as opposed to his chief who obviously was driven by anger and possibly a need for revenge.

Losing a bit of his frown, he explained, "We'll go nowhere this night."

Taking a step backward, away from Lachlan Maitland and his inescapable size and the aura of intensity that surrounded him, Mari aimed for a hopeful tone as she replied to the older man, "Then we are to eat soon?"

"Aye, and we'll get to that but—"

"I am Mari, by the by," she said to him. And then, including several other Maitland soldiers in a quick glance, she clarified cheerfully, "Marianna Sinclair, actually, though I've not ever cared for Marianna. Very formal, I'd always thought." She smiled at one soldier, who seemed to nod eagerly in agreement. And then to the older man, she wondered casually, "Am I to be chained or...such? Or do these things entail an honor system and the surety that it would be unlikely I could outrun any of you?"

Reacting to her politeness, and possibly her agreeableness, the man shrugged and announced, "Seems we might take your word you'll no'—"

"She'll be confined to her very fine vehicle," Lachlan Maitland cut in, a hint of impatience noticed, "with a man just outside every minute."

Maintaining an airiness that was better suited to visiting the rector's wife, she dared to press further, "Will the supper be delivered there?"

The man Lachlan snarled at her frivolous query and stalked away. Lifting her brows, Mari turned to his second and shrugged, as if she didn't understand why he might be upset.

The older man blew out a long breath and shook his head.

LACHLAN HAD LEFT THEIR makeshift camp, had taken himself off through the trees and down to the nearby loch. He'd sensed the water's closeness earlier, the rare heat of the day having brought to him the scent of green and wet things. He'd settled himself there and left the governing of the men to Murdoch, who knew that Lachlan most often preferred his own company.

He stayed quite a while that dusk had settled some time ago, with true night close on its heels. Lachlan had lain and watched the surface of the loch change from blue to green to gray and then black, though it shimmered tonight under the nearly full moon. With his arms under his head and his plaid draped about his waist, he considered the inky night sky now while his thoughts whirred. He wasn't in the habit of regularly lying to himself, but damn if he didn't want to disavow all the minutes he'd spent here thinking on that lass.

Too many minutes.

His only defense, so far as he could reason, was that he'd never met anyone quite like her. Beauty aside, she'd shown more daring in a quarter of an hour than most men might in their entire lives. He knew he cut an imposing figure; the combination of his great size and the sheer horror of his scars had seen lesser men fall to their knees in hysterics worthy of only a woman.

Save for this one, whom Lachlan had generously decided was not, after all, as daft as she would have liked them to believe.

Of course, it was all for show, Lachlan knew, the pretense of fearlessness, professing to care only if she were to be fed or not. However, the shaking of her hands, which moved often as she'd spoken, had not gone unnoticed. The lass was clever, he'd give her that. There must have been occasions in her life that called for such deception, hiding fear, that she had become rather adept at it. Likely it was only her startling beauty, which had compelled his steadfast gaze, that had allowed him to take note of the inconsistencies between her words and actions.

Even feigned courage required bravery, beyond what most men owned.

But damn, if she weren't about the boldest person he'd ever known, to experience fear that would shake your limbs and yet—

His musings were disrupted by a sound that was out of place in the quiet night, something borne not of field or loch or critter.

Reaching his hand to his side, his fingers covered the hilt of his abandoned sword just as he noticed the very clear silhouette of a figure creeping alongside the loch. He recognized immediately the figure as that of the lass—Mari, he recalled—and watched as she alternately scuttled many feet, further from the trees and their camp on the other side, and then crouched to invisibleness with any small noise that caught her ear. Intrigued, he watched without moving, still laying on the ground while she darted around in front of him, possibly having no idea that the moon glistening off the water outlined her every move, abetting him more than her.

With his head tipped forward onto his chest, he watched her scramble across his line of sight until she was completely gone from view. He didn't jump to his feet but rose and blindly fastened his plaid about him, knowing he would easily manage to stalk and re-capture her. He retrieved his dagger and sword, affixing both to his belt and started off after his prisoner.

This present pursuit had nothing at all to do with his intrigue, or her beauty, but everything to do with Walter Ramsay. He'd never imagined having his very own pawn in the on-going war with the Ramsays, but thanked God for throwing one in his path. Thus, he was not about to give it up without a chase.

Knowing far better than the lass how to creep silently about in the dead of night, he pursued her stealthily for many minutes. She'd gone around the small loch and had taken to the trees at the far side. At one point, Lachlan resisted the urge to rush to her when she cried out in fright. But as her cry was so quickly followed by a squeak of disgust and then a fairly annoyed huff, he guessed she might have only run into a spider's web. This gave him some pleasure, imagining her arms flailing and swiping frantically at her face. 'Tis only what she deserved.

When she'd traversed another few hundred feet through the thin forest of trees, Lachlan decided they'd gone far enough and began to close the distance between them. The light of the moon barely penetrated these trees, but he followed her moving shadow easily as she was not exactly soundless in her attempt to flee. He was aware of precisely when she realized she was being followed by another screech of fright and the hurrying of her steps.

He would have caught her anyway but her tripping and falling certainly did speed things up. Her shadow dropped from sight just as she cried out again. A moment later, he was standing above her as she rolled onto her back.

The bare light of the night showed her lifting one hand defensively while she propped herself up on her other arm. For this he was sorry; he needed her recaptured and securely held, but he had no desire to terrorize her.

"Who is it?" Gone was all her bravado, all her feigned courage. Her voice quaked and the raised hand shook violently.

"You dinna care for our company, lass?"

"Oh."

The relief he detected in her breathless response should have insulted him. Mayhap a greater fear *was* necessary to keep her well-behaved.

Lachlan grabbed her outstretched hand and hauled her to her feet, holding her very close to him. He ground out into her face, "I dislike having to chase something that now belongs to me."

So much for a little fear.

Outrage greeted his remark.

"I belong to no man, sir! How dare you—"

Lachlan yanked her hand, bringing her closer yet. "I dare. You are well and truly mine now, to do with as I please. Hence the term hostage."

"I'm not sure that merely the word hostage—"

"Jesus bluidy Christ, lass! Dinna come at me jousting words. You're a prisoner. I own you, until I decide that I do not and trade you for something of value."

Her mouth fell open, and damn if her pretty eyes didn't cloud with offense at his crudely worded statement, which suggested she had no value at all. And damn the moon that shone brightly in this one spot and allowed him to notice this.

Grumbling under his breath about dealing with whomever was responsible for this dereliction of duty, Lachlan turned and began to retrace his steps, tugging her along behind him, his fingers tight around her slim wrist.

"But please do not blame your man for any negligence," she begged in response to his muttering. "You won't, will you? Honestly, I'm quite clever and very quiet and his only crime appears to be that he sleeps so soundly." She had to skip quickly to keep up with Lachlan's angry pace and hence her plea came with some breathlessness, which had Lachlan feeling poorly again, as she sounded so fragile and pathetic.

She would beg for a life? For a man who'd been party to her own kidnapping. What manner of lass was this?

Lachlan sought to test it out.

"Carelessness can never be tolerated. He will be flogged."

Her response to this was one big jumbled and panicked mess. "No! Oh my heavens, no. But it was my fault. I've committed the crime, so to speak—which really is no crime, as it is my duty to escape, I would imagine. He had nothing—my God, are you so heartless? You've caught me. No harm was done—"

Lachlan stopped so abruptly that she all but crashed into him as he whipped around to face her. She lifted her hand to forestall the collision, her slim fingers landing smack in the middle of his chest.

"It *was* your fault," he said. "Mayhap you would volunteer to take his place?"

"Take his place?" She asked, confused, her chest rising and falling sharply.

Her hand remained upon him. Lachlan did his best to ignore it.

"For the flogging," Lachlan clarified. "You just said it was you who committed the crime."

"Aye, but...oh," she said. Whispered, really, and to great effect, as understanding dawned. Another whimper, combined with some unintelligible words followed, while Lachlan said nothing.

With a harsh deliberateness, he wrapped his free hand around the fingers at his chest and removed them from his person. But this seemed to escape her notice, her mind buzzing with the proposition he'd placed before her.

And then she did the most remarkable thing. Even as her entire person seemed to shake with dread, she lifted her chin and asked, "How many lashes?"

She actually considered it? His own frown shifted from anger at her near escape to disbelief over the fact that she was, or could be, real.

"Twenty," he said, his answer clipped, knowing five would maim her; ten would kill her.

She began to nod frantically, as if she fought some inner battle but needed to give her consent before the dread bade her change her mind. "And your man won't be punished for my ...recklessness?"

Clenching his teeth, Lachlan gave no reply, but turned and resumed stalking through the dark woods and back to camp, his prisoner in tow.

He found Edric asleep on the ground just outside the wagon and gave his hip a good kick. The lad jerked to a sitting position, his wakefulness coming fast when he recognized his chief and the lass and deduced the circumstance.

Edric scrambled to his feet, adjusting his plaid and belt. His mouth opened but no words came forth, his own dread not so very different from that of the lass.

"Get on with the others," Lachlan ordered, but otherwise ignored the man, who was quick to scurry away.

The wagon was only slightly separated from the group of men sleeping in varying positions around a dying fire. Lachlan whipped back the curtain at the rear and thrust the girl forward.

"Get in there," he said, releasing her hand. He spent a few moments making knots in each of the rear panels of silk so that a permanent opening was created. The girl scampered up onto the low step, the skirts of her gown brushing his arm as she climbed inside.

He paid her no more attention, gave no other instruction, but removed his plaid once again and made his bed in the spot Edric had vacated minutes before. It was a long time before his seething cooled.

And that was when he noticed her soft weeping. The sound of muted crying reached him, despite her attempts to muffle it. It was soft, fitful, and likely pressed into the rough wool of her sleeve.

It occurred to him that he'd never taken a female as a hostage. Many battles he'd seen that had brought a fair number of prisoners to him over the years—all men, all warriors, all understanding that they were at his mercy. He'd never given much thought to their fears or their expectations. His own harsh treatment at the hands of the English for seven long months had only served to make death, when necessary to any prisoner, quick and noble. He'd not wish upon any soldier, friend or foe, the atrocities that had been done to him. It wasn't human.

Of course, the lass was more a pawn than a prisoner, even if she had, for the time being, been robbed of her freedom.

The quiet crying continued, and Lachlan imagined he might not sleep much this night.

He sighed crossly. He had no business feeling sorry—feeling anything!—for a prisoner.

Instead, he concentrated on his plan for her. He would reach out to Ramsay when they arrived at Hawkmore. He would offer up a trade—the lass for her brother, the reiver. Ramsay would have his bride and Lachlan would get the reiver. His willingness to return the lass to Ramsay unharmed would buy him peace for Hawkmore, if only for a while. He didn't know Walter Ramsay personally, but assumed he might be one of the many sons of the miserable old man, Rannoch Ramsay. However, if Walter were a more distant relation, the value of the lass was diminished.

It was a long time before Lachlan finally slept, one of his last thoughts being that he'd rather be fighting the English in some grand battle than dealing with the toll her pitiful weeping took on him.

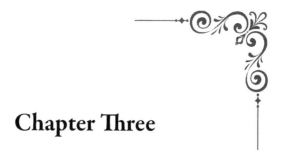

Chapter Three

Mari woke the next morning to a slow bustling around the camp. Stretching out onto her back, she threw her arm over her forehead and listened.

"Torquil! Niel! You'll ride rear today."

She recognized the chief's voice, rising above all other sounds of the camp being broken. He wasn't close, but the sharpness of his deep voice put Mari instantly in recollection of what was to come today.

Jerking upright, ignoring the cutting pain that lodged in her side, likely a gift of the hard floorboards of the cart, Mari stared at and through the opening in the curtains. She saw nothing but grass and trees, the greens and browns made more vibrant by the slight drizzle that greeted the early morn. Everyone was in front of the wagon, where their camp had been made and the horses had been tethered. She considered, and promptly dismissed, any idea to jump through that opening and run.

She'd be caught but quick, she imagined, and the day would only get worse.

And yet, she hadn't just now the nerve to exit the vehicle. Doing so might only hurry along the punishment that was to come. Mari closed her eyes briefly and willed herself to remain calm, wondering if she were to be lashed here and now, before they departed, or at some later time and place.

A thump on the sidewall of the cart elicited a strangled yip of fear. Opening her eyes showed the older man peeking his head inside the knotted curtains a moment later.

"Aye, c'mon now, lass," he said, his tone surprisingly pleasant. "Take care of your business afore we head out."

So, it was to be later. She would have many hours to dwell upon it, no doubt would be a puddle of pudding by day's end. But as this man hadn't yet been unkind to her, had indeed fed her yesterday evening, Mari scooted across the floor of the wagon and climbed out.

He pointed vaguely in the direction of the trees, the same path she'd taken yesterday in her failed attempt to escape, and advised, "Dinna make me chase you, lass. I'm old and I get surly fairly easily."

Unwilling to spare even a brief glance at the rest of the Maitland army, afraid she might meet the eye of the chief, Mari nodded and marched into the trees. She quickly saw to her needs and returned to the wagon, where the man waited.

"I don't know your name," she said, even as she didn't know why she might need to.

"Murdoch, lass." He'd waited at the side of the wagon, his arm thrown up over the siderail, his hands busy removing all the spiky leaves from a plucked thistle bloom.

Imagining he'd heard about her rashness of last night, she inquired, "That soldier won't be punished, will he?"

"Edric? Aye, he will, as—"

Mari frowned and cut him off. "But I said I'd take the lashes. That isn't fair. He said I could take his place and that no one else would be—"

"Whoa. Whoa," Murdoch said, straightening away from the wagon. "Now hang on, lass. What's this? Who said you could take whose place?"

Mari sighed heavily with her frustration and explained, "Your laird caught me, and I didn't want the man—Edric—punished for my trouble. He said I would be flogged in his stead."

Murdoch's gray eyes widened, but only momentarily before they narrowed, and his thick brows arched low over them. "You? Flogged?"

Mari nodded. As frightened as she was of what was in store for her, she believed she'd not be able to live with herself if an innocent man were made to take her punishment.

Murdoch glanced around her, off toward where the fire had been and then fixed his steady gaze upon her once again. "Lass, you canna be whipped. Would rip the skin from your back. Even a light touch would see the bone bared, I'm thinking."

Mari blanched, lifting her fingers to her mouth in shock.

Murdoch was undeterred or unattuned and went on, "The ends of the leather are knotted to gouge deep. I've seen more bone exposed by a flogging than I have in battle. You misunderstood, I'm thinking. The chief dinna say anything—"

She'd had nothing to eat but the small piece of bread and the pitiful gruel Murdoch had dared to call stew yesterday, but that didn't stop her stomach from heaving. With a horrified expression, knowing she couldn't stop it, Mari turned away and retched into the tall grass.

Her hair flopped around her head and shoulders until she managed to gather the bulk of it near her left shoulder, out of the way while she continued to vomit. Her eyes watered and her stomach roiled, the picture Murdoch had put into her mind causing such upheaval.

"Bluidy hell," she heard Murdoch mutter at her side.

Something touched her back while she remained hunched over. Mari startled until she realized it was Murdoch's hand, just as his words penetrated. "Och, now, lass. I've gone and jabbered too much. C'mon now, there'll be no flogging. We're no' heathens, you ken."

Her head swam even as her stomach seemed to quit its churning. Placing her hands on her knees, she remained bent over for another minute, making sure she would retch no more. When finally she straightened and faced Murdoch with a mortified grimace, she saw only compassion.

She swallowed tightly, holding herself in check. Being a hostage was exhausting and debilitating, she decided. Her humiliation forced her to raise her chin and admit only, "''Twas likely something I ate."

His frown took on a completely different mood, measuring her with those steely gray eyes.

The stem of the thistle had not left his hand. He lifted it and pushed it into the corner of his mouth, the deadened bloom dangling low. "Something you ate, eh?" At her rigid nod, he said, his tone no less kindly, "You keep pretending to be as fearless as you do, you'll have whittled yourself down to nothing by the time we reach Hawkmore."

Somehow, it did not surprise her that he'd seen through her bravado. She supposed then that his chief might have as well.

With an awkward smile, she asked, "Would you rather I wail and scream and keen all day?"

Murdoch let out a quick chortle, nearly grinning at her. "Aye, then keep it up with the show of courage, lass," he said. But after a quiet moment, while he only stared at Mari with some thoughtfulness, he changed his mind. "Nae, lass, you cry and scream and rail at all the unfairness of it. Otherwise, you keep all that locked up, you'll perish from the inside out."

She didn't know why, didn't understand how she surmised it, but she had a particular impression that this instruction somehow had something to do with Lachlan Maitland.

Perish from the inside out.

Mari sighed and nodded blandly, climbing once again back into the wagon.

OH, WHAT A MISERABLE existence, Mari thought with no small amount of self-pity.

She sat on the lone seat inside the wagon, bounced along as they moved further north. Last night, she'd been too upset to have been practical and had slept on the hard floor of the wagon as the seat was too short. Going forward, she would at least make use of the fine and thick cushion and move that onto the floor beneath her. She would still be without her cloak, which had accompanied her in her futile dash to freedom last night. Sadly, when she'd been startled by the Maitland chief and had tripped and fallen, the satchel with her few possessions had been flung away from her. In that next moment, faced with the huge man's controlled fury, she'd quite forgotten all about it. Later, when she'd been shivering inside the wagon, she'd been too frightened and too proud to have mentioned that she'd lost the satchel and the few precious items within.

Now, they were miles away, having driven for several hours. The rains had continued, bringing with it much cooler air that Mari felt the cold seep in to her bones, her mood then as gray as the day.

Yet, she'd embraced Murdoch's assurance that there would be no lashes for her, that they were not, after all, heathens, allowing his words to put her somewhat at ease. There was still fear—of the unknown, of her unfortunate circumstance, of that inscrutable leader, Lachlan Maitland.

She'd yet to see him today, for which she was thankful, saw not much more than what the bare opening of those silly silk drapes permitted her to see. They'd stayed primarily on or near that same road from yesterday for the first hour or so and since had drifted away, across a bumpy field and up and over a benign hill that surely was more rock than grass. The big horse they'd hitched to the front of her wagon had easily chewed up the ground beneath him, causing Mari to wonder fleetingly if the thin palfrey that had pulled the cart yesterday might have managed so effortlessly.

Two soldiers rode behind the wagon. For the first hour, if she dared to peek out at them, if she happened to make eye contact with them, they ignored her, holding to their purposefully solemn expressions. When she scooted back against the seat, and was out of sight, they relaxed, and Mari listened curiously to their infrequent conversations.

"You could no' peg a squirrel at fifty paces," said one at some point. "Twenty, maybe, but no' fifty."

"I could," argued the other. Mari imagined a shrug preceded his claim of, "I have."

"Using what? A stone'd no' fly so far. Would have to be larger, and I ken your skinny arm could no' send a heavier rock so far."

"Aye, and you should talk, Niel," returned the one who must be Torquil, if she correctly recalled the names the chief had assigned to this position. "I've seen you hurl the stones. Throw like a lass, and a wee one at that."

"I want to see it," challenged Niel. "When we get home, I'll put up a ha'penny says you canna peg *anything* at fifty paces."

Naught but boys, Mari deemed them, allowing a small grin for how un-warrior-like, how...normal they sounded.

As her brother's party had yesterday, this group paused around noon. The wagon came to a complete stop in a flat spot of grass and heather, once again very near to a loch. Mari was surprised to see the two men, Torquil and Niel, continue to move, presumably around to the front of the wagon with the rest of the party. She stared longingly through the opening, at the gray water of the nearby loch.

There was not a single tree or even any tall brush that might hide a person who might dare to run. No sooner had she thought this than the face of Lachlan Maitland appeared at the back of the wagon.

Instantly, her eyes widened and her chest tightened.

He flicked his hand at her, saying only, "Bring your belongings." His expression was similar to any she'd witnessed thus far from him, harsh and without a shred of kindness.

Mari obeyed, though didn't dare mention that she hadn't any possessions anymore. Scampering once again out of the wagon, she was pleased at least that the rain had not increased but remained only a slight and annoying drizzle.

He walked away from her as soon as he'd given his sparse instruction, around the front of the wagon, and Mari assumed she was to follow. Lifting her skirts, she stepped carefully, her leather shoes a hindrance on the slick ground. When she dared to lift her gaze from her careful footfalls, she saw that the entire surrounding area before them was peppered with thick outcroppings of gray and shiny rock. Most of them were taller than any man here. Their big destriers could likely traverse this terrain with relative ease but Mari wondered how the wagon might fare.

The entire party of Maitland soldiers waited, mounted still, grouped in a lazy circle under the dull sky and light rain. Lachlan Maitland walked into the circle and approached the lad who'd first caught her yesterday when she'd been abandoned by her brother.

"You'll ride with Utrid now," the chief said brusquely, and without a by-your-leave, lifted Mari up behind the young man.

Mari squirmed and tried to right herself, instinctively clinging to the plaid of the man before her. There was so much wrong with this situation, not least of all was the sour face she'd glimpsed on the lad. She'd been plunked onto the back of the horse, one leg on either side, that her kirtle rode up her legs, exposing most of her hose-covered calves and ankles. And because she sat directly on the horse, behind the saddle, all the linen of her undergarments that touched its coat were immediately soaked with the rain that had settled.

"Sorry," she murmured to Utrid, settling herself finally, fisting her hands into his tunic on each side of his waist, worried that the end of the horse was closer than was prudent.

The chief mounted again, and they moved on, Mari turning her head to watch the wagon grow smaller and smaller as it was deserted. It wasn't hers, and she hadn't known its luxury before yesterday, yet Mari felt some inescapable sadness to leave it and the shelter of it behind.

Hours later, Mari thought she couldn't have been more wretched. It was more difficult than she might have assumed to keep her seat on the slippery back of the horse. Her hold upon poor Utrid changed constantly, until finally she'd wrapped her arms completely around him. And when the sky finally opened and sent down a hard rain, Mari gave up her stiffness and her struggles to maintain some polite distance between them, and pressed her head onto his back, shielding her face from the torrent. Her teeth chattered and her entire form shook with her shivers, the coarse brown linen of her kirtle soaked through by now. She was sure that not one inch of her garments remained dry at this point. She was only thankful that they travelled at rather a crawl through the rough terrain, fearful that anything near a gallop would see her flying off the huge beast.

Utrid barely spoke, answering her few queries—about their destination and how much longer he expected they would need to travel—with as few words as possible. "Hawkmore" and "another day, maybe more," was all the information gleaned from him. And the cold had since given way to a near complete numbness that speech was almost beyond her, certainly not worth the effort for the terse replies.

They rode at the rear of the party, with only two or sometimes four mounted men behind them. Mari imagined it must be late afternoon when they reached a hill large enough that she prayed they might walk around it. Her misery continued however, when they did not stop but trudged up the side of the small mountain. She was forced to cling tighter and lean forward against Utrid and might have preserved her precarious seat if not for the horse itself losing his footing, jostling and twitching in such a way that Mari was sent off the back of the horse.

"Shite," she heard Utrid call as she sailed through the air.

Mari landed on her back and bum, but mercifully her head did not bounce against the hard ground. She didn't move, waiting for the pain to come. Possibly, the numbness from the cold and the difficult ride had wrought a complete lack of feeling.

Horses danced around her.

"Lass, are you—" Utrid began, his voice near frantic.

"Christ, Utrid! You dropped her," another voice chimed in, cutting off Utrid.

From her supine position, Mari watched the rain fall, felt it bounce off her cheeks and forehead. She decided she did not want to move and closed her eyes as more people gathered around her.

Leave me here, she begged silently.

And then she heard *his* voice and her entire body tensed.

"Bluidy hell!"

And while not one of the men who'd witnessed her fall had done anything other than prance their steeds around her, Lachlan Maitland was, in the next moment, on his haunches at her side.

Something hard and warm touched her skin. Mari opened her eyes to find his hand at her cheek. He was frowning down at her, which did not surprise her in the least. But under the heavily furrowed brow, in his more-blue-than-hazel eyes, Mari was sure she detected some hint of concern.

It stirred her not at all, not any more than his wondering aloud if she were harmed. What did he care, but that his hostage would serve no purpose if she were maimed or even accidentally killed?

"I do not feel anything," she answered weakly.

This only scrunched his brow yet more. He took her hands in his and lifted her upper body even as he asked, "Can you sit?"

Now upright, Mari noticed that her gown had ridden further upward and displayed to any and all her lower legs and much of her thighs. She hadn't the energy to manage a proper indignation over this even as the Maitland chief rather awkwardly yanked on her skirts to cover her limbs down to her calves.

He cursed again, "Damn it, Utrid!" before scooping her up into his strong arms, one hand under her legs, the other around her back.

Truly, she was too numb to bother with any stiffness and laid her head against his chest, closing her eyes against the watchful gazes of all those they passed. She opened her eyes when she felt a shift in their movement, just as he lifted his foot into the stirrup of his own mount and hopped upward, grabbing at the pommel with the hand under her legs, to hoist them both up into his saddle.

He settled her against him, her backside on the front of his saddle, both legs now thrown over his huge left thigh, and her head leaned against his shoulder and arm, lifted to work the reins.

Mari felt too wretched to protest. And, as she was immediately imbued with the warmth his body and this position offered, she was not about to raise a fuss.

"Christ, lass. You're soaked through," he grumbled, with less animosity than any previous words he'd given to her, just as he moved his destrier to resume their plodding trek uphill. "Have you no cloak?"

"I did," she replied before she thought better of it, and cringed, waiting for the inevitable question that must follow.

"Did? You lost your cloak?"

Perhaps it was her lack of sensitivity now, her complete despair that made her respond with some accusation. "I lost the satchel and all its contents last night when *you* chased me."

He cursed again. She thought his teeth might be clenched, which lifted her face to him. But from this angle, tucked into his shoulder, she saw only the bottom of his square jaw, her gaze riveted on the scarring that ran along his neck.

"You little fool. Why dinna you tell me?"

"I forgot about it," she lied, her tone tainted with both embarrassment and her own anger. But then meekly, "And by the time I remembered, we were too far gone."

He shook his head back and forth, his lips grinding in such a way as to suggest he wanted to say something but held back.

She didn't know what possessed her to charge, "It's your fault, anyway."

He lowered his face to her, showing her yet another scowl. "My fault that you're so muddled as to misplace your own belongings?"

"Your fault, indeed. You kidnapped me. You chased me and made me lose—"

"Of course I chased you!" He cut in with a grand amount of incredulity, his voice loud. "You shouldn't have run."

"It is my duty to try and escape," she shouted into his chest, turning her face away from the rain, which somehow still prevailed, grew stronger even.

"Hold these," he said curtly, shoving the reins into her hands.

Mari fumbled to gather the ribbons he'd thrust at her while he shifted and maneuvered his plaid, flapping out the length of it. He wrapped the entire piece of heavy fabric around both of them, collecting the reins once again to hold them and the edges of his plaid in front of her. Glancing up again showed Mari that part of the plaid extended beyond his shoulder, tented over her head. She sighed with less misery, sheltered from the rain now.

"You'll get yourself into more trouble," he continued, as if their argument had not been interrupted by his kindness, "if you persist with any foolish plans to flee."

"How much more trouble could I possibly know?" Her voice had lost its bite.

"You could get dead," he countered evenly. "That'd be more trouble."

She was too exhausted to argue that being dead would actually nullify any anxieties.

"I must try," she said.

"Listen, lass," he said, "it's a simple kidnapping for ransom. You'll no' be harmed, save by your own folly, and likely returned to your betrothed within a few weeks."

He tightened his arms around her as they navigated a particularly steep area of the mountainside. Mari felt the shift of her position and reached for and grabbed at the leather breastplate he wore over his tunic, hanging on tight.

"What do you get in return?" She wanted to know.

"The reiver," he answered. "Whom you've said is your brother."

"I'd said my escort was my brother. He is no reiver."

"He is. We've been chasing him for weeks."

The ground beneath them had leveled out as they'd reached a flat spot on the side of the hill, but neither Lachlan nor Mari loosened their hold on each other.

"I don't think my brother is the one you seek," she told him. "Honestly, I'd not seen Harman in seven years before yesterday, but I don't think he's clever enough to commit any crimes." And certainly not to elude capture for many weeks. Harman was, at best, a follower. He might well be guilty of certain petty crimes, she'd not put it past him, but he wasn't a leader of men. Never mind that Harman himself had taken off, telling Mari that if caught he'd likely hang.

"Did you ken that almost every clan, almost every farm or family, has their own unique design of horseshoes?" He asked, the fierceness of his tone in sharp contrast to the seeming banality of the question. "Aye, sometimes the farrier even puts his own mark on the shoes. And over the last few months, we've regularly come upon scenes of destruction, villages burned out and crops razed, people injured or maimed, livestock stolen—and each time, we've noticed the same print, left by the perpetrators. Every single time."

Sensing where he was going with this, Mari said nothing, but cringed inwardly. She didn't want to argue. She didn't want to pit herself against him. He said she'd be safe, and eventually released. Her head had begun to ache, and she wanted only to snuggle deeper into the heat of this angry man's body.

"Curiously," he went on in the same bitter tone, "those prints were identical to what was left by your *escort* yesterday. So you canna tell me—"

Drifting off, Mari nestled more closely against him, finding it hard to keep her eyes open suddenly. She let one hand fall to her lap while the other still held tight at his breastplate, her fingers curling around to settle between the leather and his tunic beneath. Once more, she tucked her head into the crook of his shoulder, only half aware that he'd stopped speaking.

LACHLAN QUIETED AS she burrowed against him. He glanced down to find her eyes were closed, her face void of all expression.

A wealth of emotions crossed his dark features, his gaze then trained on her thin fingers, wrapped inside his breastplate.

God, she was a mess, wet and bedraggled, her hair muddied from her fall, hanging in natty clumps all around her. Her gown was soaked and dirtied in more spots than not and the thin leather of her footwear was caked in mud and muck. And yet she remained uncommonly lovely.

Despite the rugged terrain, which should have necessitated his complete attention, Lachlan found himself again and again skimming his gaze over her sleeping face. Her dark lashes swept down across her cheeks, ridiculously long and arched to crescent-moon shape; her skin was generously sun-colored, highlighting the freckles, which only added to her allure; and those lips, moistened by the rain and shaped so sensually, truly tempted a man beyond reason.

He'd know her complete story soon, why she'd been sent down to England; why she appeared to be, as the pitiful gown told, of the peasant class and yet was set to marry a Ramsay, one of the richer clans in the north. He deemed it imperative that the swap with Ramsay take place sooner rather than later; Lachlan was fearful of absolutely nothing at this point in his life, but damn, if this disheveled lass sleeping so innocently against him didn't scare the bejesus out of him.

Chapter Four

The rain finally stopped early in the evening. Mari woke, needing only seconds to recall her circumstance. She stiffened, embarrassed by exactly how comfortable she'd made herself against the Maitland chief. For his part, he only acknowledged her wakefulness with a spare glance down at her before returning his gaze to the trail before them.

He said nothing and Mari was groggy enough that she pursued no conversation with him. She perked up soon enough, however, when she spied a swiftly moving waterway before them.

"Oh, please tell me we are not meant to cross that."

His chuckle, felt along her side and the top of her head, startled her, enough so that she jerked her gaze up at him, simultaneously understanding that she must have spoken her plea aloud.

"'Tis no' so bad as it seems," he allowed.

He reined in at the water's edge, while a soldier—Edric, she thought it might be—was sent to cross, testing its depth, she imagined.

Mari straightened yet more so that the back of her head bumped his chin. "Sorry," she said absently, her gaze riveted on Edric. He'd walked his mount into the water, the fingers of only one hand unaccountably loose on the reins. Very quickly, the water rose to the big destrier's knees even as he'd yet to cross so much as one quarter of the way.

Mari leaned to the left to see beyond Murdoch, who'd parked in front of them. She drew in a sharp breath when Edric and his steed were moved by the rushing water many feet to the right.

"Why does he not hold the reins more tightly?" She wondered of Lachlan.

"It's no' for Edric to navigate the river, but the horse," Lachlan answered at her ear. "The animal knows what's expected. A horse has better instincts than any human; he'll ken if he can do it. Being forced across is sure madness for both animal and man."

By the time Edric and his horse were halfway across the river, the water covered all six legs of man and beast and the animal appeared to be straining mightily against the raging current. Mari made faces and sounds with each misstep, and every time the horse seemed to lose his battle against the water.

"He's no' struggling," Lachlan said, "he's swimming. Takes a bit against the current. But see, he's almost there."

This relaxed her somewhat, even as she knew they must cross as well. More soldiers moved into the water even before Edric had made it to the other side. Mari's eyes widened when one horse seemed to seriously fight against the very idea of deep water and tried to buck and return to dry land.

The chief laughed again. "Aye, Davidh's horse never liked water." As more men and horses entered the water, Davidh's horse ultimately settled and began to follow all those crossing.

Mari didn't see the humor in it, and then less so as Lachlan steered their horse toward the water just as Edric was the first to reach the far bank. She wanted to turn sideways into him to better secure herself, but he slid his arm around her waist and drew her tight against his chest.

"Hold my arm and no' the horse," he instructed, holding the reins lightly in his other hand.

Mari obeyed, clasping securely onto his arm as the horse entered the water.

"Hope you can swim, lass," someone teased from behind.

She'd thought the chief's destrier to be the largest of all the Maitland horses but found herself re-evaluating this as the water quickly climbed up her legs. She knew exactly when the horse began to swim, aware of the loss of sure footing beneath.

"He's got us," Lachlan assured her.

Possibly Lachlan Maitland had done this a hundred times without misfortune; however, it was also possible that even her slight extra weight was just too much for the animal. Very soon, they were moving with the current, away from the steady line of horses crossing. Only the chief's calmness behind her kept her from panicking. He jerked at the reins, tugging them left to direct the animal but even Mari understood this was only reflexive, and went against what he'd told her about the animal's instincts only moments ago. Yet, the large beast was grappling without success to cross, his big head pointed skyward as the water covered so much of the animal and the saddle and the bottom halves of both Mari and Lachlan.

"Son of a..." Lachlan cursed lazily. "Aye, I'll have to swim."

Mari's eyes grew large in her face as he pressed the reins into her hands.

"No," she moaned, trying to push the reins back at him. "Do not leave me."

'I'll no' leave you, lass," he said firmly. "I just need to swim alongside."

She was beginning to panic now. "But what will I hang on to?"

"The pommel," he said, a lightness detected in his tone, as if he were amused. He began to slide out of the saddle, the security of his hand leaving her waist.

"Oh, no," she moaned. She didn't care about any previous instruction but used both hands on the reins, her knuckles white. "Oh, I hope you run fast. You're going to have to catch us further downstream, I fear." With the reins held securely though allowing a bit of slack, she wrapped her hands around the pommel for extra security.

She dared to look away from the horse's head, the only part of him above water, just briefly to see that Lachlan was fully in the water at her side. He didn't attach himself in any way to the horse, likely to add no more pressure to the poor beast, but grabbed hold of a fistful of Mari's skirts, which was unseemly in the extreme but offered her a tremendous amount of relief that he remained so close.

"Swing your leg over, lass," Lachlan instructed, spitting out the water that slapped angrily at his face. "Astride," he said when another rushing wave had passed.

Mari did as coached and was rewarded immediately with a steadier seat, for which she was thankful. She thought there'd have been a quicker recovery by the destrier once Lachlan's weight had been removed. A quick look left showed they were much farther still from the rest of the men and as of yet, not quite halfway across the river.

At one point the rushing water completely covered Lachlan's head and soaked her up to her waist; and for one terrifying moment only the long nose of the horse was seen. Mari instinctively made to reach for Lachlan, but he resurfaced quickly enough and gave a good shake of his head.

As nervous as she was, at no time did Mari believe she was in danger of drowning, or even being swept off the horse. The chief's firm grip on the fabric of her gown offered her plenty of assurance; his hold never loosened, not even as he was repeatedly dunked by the churning water.

Still, it seemed like so much time had passed before more and more of the animal's head was visible above the water as they passed the halfway mark. And just when she thought the danger was passed, a large bough of a tree crashed into them, pushed with such force by the water that all three, Lachlan and Mari and the huge destrier, were startled and banged up. A gangly branch, struck out from the main limb, slapped Mari's shoulder and nearly unseated her; Lachlan fought to push the thick limb away, momentarily moving his hand from her thigh to the rear lip of the saddle; the horse was spooked, twisting and bucking violently beneath her. Mari lost hold of the pommel and then lost her seat completely.

She was plunged into the water on the same side as Lachlan and was fully submerged in mere seconds.

Lachlan yanked on her wrist as she flailed underwater, instinctively kicking her legs. She surfaced, gagging and coughing, and then panicked when he let go of her hand. But it was only for an instant, dropping her hand to twist his fist into the neckline of her gown. With astounding strength, he yanked her toward him, while he'd somehow managed to retain his hold on the end of the saddle.

Mari scrambled, reaching out to him. He tugged more and she was brought against his chest. Still coughing up the mouthful of water she'd gulped down, she acted on impulse and wrapped her arms around his neck, pulling herself so close that her cheek and his were pressed together.

"I've got you," he said, the arm that had tugged her near now wrapped all the way around her waist. After another moment, he instructed, "Get back up there."

Mari shook her head against his. "I'm fine right here," she said in a shaky voice.

He held her closely for a few seconds more, while the horse still kicked his hooves beneath the water, and Mari could not deny the security she found just here, in his arms.

"C'mon now," Lachlan said, patting her back. "I need my hands free to finish the crossing."

She nodded and reluctantly moved her hands from him to the saddle. Lachlan turned, facing the horse now, and moved his hand around her back. He assisted her efforts to regain the saddle by grabbing a fistful of the back of her gown and propelling her upward. She took hold of the pommel again with one hand and swung her leg over when she was able, but refused to let go of Lachlan's shoulder, her fingers closing rigidly around his tunic. She didn't dare reach for the reins now.

Completely rattled, she looked around, saw the tree limb was already quite a distance away from them, further downstream and that the horse had, by now, taken them almost three quarters of the way across the river. Only when she felt the horse find his feet once again as they drew closer and closer to shore, did Mari glance down at Lachlan.

He was watching her, expectantly it seemed, his hands now on either side of the saddle, in front and behind her, letting the animal pull him along as well. She nodded shakily to let him know she was all right, even as she could not quite control the tremble of her lips and chin.

The water receded, covering only the bottom of her legs and then not any of her as the exhausted horse made his way toward the banks.

Only then did Lachlan let go and walk the remaining distance.

Horse and man walked up onto the bank at the same time. And while Mari imagined Lachlan might have liked to take a moment to regain his breath, as he bent at the waist with his hands on his knees, her panic was enlivened as the horse continued to walk forward.

Once again firmly set upon solid ground, she felt brave enough to reach down and retrieve the leather ribbons.

"Help," she cried to Lachlan, moving the reins this way and that, to no avail. "He won't stop."

"Pull them back into your chest," he called out to her, breathless still. "Hard."

Mari did, jerking the reins with greater force than finesse.

And finally, standing still, Mari collapsed, leaning forward over this brave and brilliant beast's neck, hugging him tight. "God bless you," she crooned to him.

In the next moment, several soldiers came to meet them, circling their wet steeds around both Mari and their chief.

THE DEPTHS OF HER SOUL

The young man she thought was Torquil stared at her with something akin to wonder. "You saved the Maitland."

"Me?" She sat straight and pointed a finger at her chest. "I did no such thing." She'd not even been able to hold her seat, let alone help Lachlan at any point. Had he not been watching? "How do I turn this thing around?" She asked Torquil. She wanted to see that Lachlan was all right.

Torquil grinned and moved his mount close to her, taking the reins from her hands, leading her back toward the river.

Lachlan Maitland had removed his leather breastplate, which lay on the ground at his feet with his plaid, and just now lifted his dripping tunic up and over his head. When he lowered his arms, he was talking to Utrid, telling him what Mari had suspected, that the horse had struggled with the weight of both of them.

Mari barely acknowledged this, couldn't say what Utrid's response was, her attention seized by the naked chest of Lachlan Maitland. She neither blinked nor, it seemed, breathed, her eyes scanning every inch of his bare flesh. She was a little nobody from nowhere, who knew nothing about anything, but she recognized her own breathless response to the raw beauty of the man. She ducked her head, even as her gaze remained on his person, afraid to be caught ogling the man who was yet her captor.

Lachlan Maitland was quite a specimen of a man. No softness dared to taint any part of him, it appeared. He was rock hard, impossibly lean for one so huge, his chest muscles moving provocatively as he sluiced water off his arms and stomach. The scar that had caused such damage to his face and neck did not venture beyond his collarbone. A smattering of dark hair peppered his chest, tapering down into a thin line that disappeared well before his breeches met his waist. For quite a long minute, she was intrigued by the moving parts of his huge arms as he twisted and wrung all the excess water from his tunic, muscles visible and then not, every motion rippling the cords up and down.

Only when she sensed his gaze on her did Mari remove her eyes from his astonishingly glorious form and meet his eye. She lifted her chin, trying to control her own breathing now, which wanted to burst forth with some declaration of admiration.

He continued to speak to Utrid, and now Niel, who'd sidled up near him as well, but he kept his gaze on Mari despite the crowd that shuffled around them. She was too mesmerized to look away, thinking that his eyes at this very moment were remarkably blue and...she didn't know what else. She could not name the emotion that flickered in them even as they remained with such steadfastness upon her.

When someone marched their steed between them, Mari blinked and blew out a noisy breath. Composing herself, she took the ribbons back from Torquil with a grateful but weak smile, unwilling to try and speak and discover that she could not just now.

Somehow when Lachlan finally approached her, she managed to feign complete oblivion, managed to pretend she had not just eyeballed him as hungrily as might a starved man when set before a feast.

"You did good, lass," he said.

She only glanced once at his naked chest just now before meeting his eye. She was pleased to be able to actually speak now, with him so close, and hoped to God he might attribute her pinkened cheeks to their near calamity. "I didn't though. I nearly got us killed."

Perhaps he would attach her breathlessness to their recent peril as well.

He shook his head, reaching up to take the reins from her hands. "You did fine, Mari."

He did not take his seat behind her on the saddle but led the horse by the reins he'd taken from her. They walked slowly, the entire group reunited and moving together. He had not donned his tunic but held that and his plaid and leather vest in his free hand. Mari managed to refrain from gasping aloud at his back but could not keep her lips from parting at the shock of it. His broad back, specifically the middle of it, was covered in dozens of scars, all bright white and raised, crisscrossing from just below his shoulder blades to just above his breeches. One spot showed a particularly ghastly pattern that Mari would swear was a brand, appearing to show the letter S.

His anger then was justified; any want of revenge she'd imagined from him had been frightfully earned.

In another moment, they veered off what appeared to be a well-trod path along the river and went deep within more tall and jagged rocks, which gave way to another clearing. Here, pine trees stood tall and thin, reaching for the setting sun, while their needles made for a soft floor beneath them.

As one unit, they reined in and dismounted, as if this were some agreed upon campsite, as if it might have been utilized previously. Lachlan turned and lifted his hands to Mari, who instinctively leaned forward into him. She touched her hands to his broad shoulders just as his hands circled her waist. And when she was set upon her feet, she was eye to eye with his naked chest.

She jerked her hands away from his warm and solid flesh. *Oh, my.*

"We are staying the night?" She blurted, rather loudly into the quiet between them.

He nodded, and only then pulled his hands away from her hips.

Practicalities would save the day, she determined. "How might I dry my garments?" She couldn't very well disrobe in front of one and all. And she hadn't anything to replace her sodden clothes.

"Would be nice to have a satchel about you, aye?"

Mari stepped around him, needing space between them, needing to think with a clear head. When his words registered a moment later, she whirled around on him, her gaze glancing off his chest once again before meeting his hazel eyes. She made a face at him for his quip, showing her lack of appreciation.

"Yes, we've already established I was foolish to have lost my own belongings, such as they were. But I cannot stay in these wet clothes. I'll be either frozen or taken with the ague by morning."

"Aye," he said and chewed the inside of his cheek, considering the dilemma. "Of course, there'll be a fire, which might dry them overnight, but I dinna know what you might wear in the meantime."

"Someone's likely to have a dry plaid," Murdoch called out, not too near the pair, but obviously close enough to have overheard, or eavesdropped, upon them.

Lachlan nodded and stepped around Mari to retrieve a leather saddlebag from the tired horse. Mari's shoulders drooped as he withdrew an extra plaid and tunic, both dripping wet, the bag having been completely submerged at some point.

"These won't be dry before morn," he said and tossed them into the pile with his other garments. But he appeared to have no solution to her dilemma and walked away, leading the horse to where all the others were tethered at the far end of the clearing.

Mari hugged her arms to herself, standing alone where the chief had left her.

The soldiers were busy. Utrid and Niel swept pine needles away from the remnants of an old fire pit. Another soldier approached, tossing kindling into the center of it before pulling a small axe from his belt and heading off into the trees. Torquil and two others rode away from camp, their destination neither stated nor questioned. Edric moved one end of a huge fallen tree so that it was laid out close to the fire pit.

Feeling conspicuous while everyone seemed to be about some chore, Mari addressed the pile of wet garments Lachlan had left behind. She lifted first the tunic he'd already wrung out and laid it across a flat topped stone that stood as high as her hip. The plaid was possibly twice the height of her, possibly weighed half as much as her, being soaked so thoroughly, which saw her rather wrestling with the dripping thing to arrange it over one end of the rock. She tried to wring out sections of it, but her hands were simply too small and barely any water was removed. Looking around her immediate location showed one solid branch of a pine maybe only a foot or two above her head. Thinking it might dry more quickly overnight if it were hung, she gathered the plaid and stood under the branch, trying to flip one end of the fabric over it. Several tries saw the heavy plaid reach no closer than several inches shy of the limb. She tried to jump up and toss it over but her own drenched skirts hindered any lift from the ground that this failed as well. Next, she attempted holding the length at one end and swinging the bulk of it around with a good twist of her body and a surge of strength for an upward swing. While this, too, failed, the twisting motion had shown her that many sets of eyes watched her futile endeavors.

Rather in a huff, she planted her hands on her hips and glared at all the watchers, which included Murdoch, who appeared to want to laugh; and Edric, who gaped at her with a scrunched up face that displayed so many of his teeth; and to her chagrin, the chief, who seemed if he might have been busy with something in another saddlebag until his attention was caught by her antics.

"Gawking at me won't get this thing hung over that branch," she charged while no one said anything or made any move to help her.

Murdoch's face creased in a weathered grin. Edric glanced sideways at the soldier next to him, as if looking for direction. And Lachlan Maitland, with a look that Mari interpreted as disgruntled, walked his naked chest over to her and took the plaid from her, shoving this dry saddlebag into her hands.

Of course, it took him only one try to flip half the length over the branch. Mari was quite satisfied, though, when he bothered to stretch the thing out so that it was not bunched and folded and might actually stand a chance of drying before morning.

Mari reached down for the leather breastplate, thinking he might as well swing that up over the branch as well. It didn't budge, the weight of it unexpected.

"Dear Lord," she said and tugged again. "No wonder we almost drowned," she groused as Lachlan stepped around her and lifted the thing up onto the rock next to his tunic. A better idea, since it would likely have snapped the limb from the tree. "How is that so heavy?"

"Waterlogged," he answered with a shrug. "And the metal plates inside the leather aren't light."

"Why do you wear that? It must be terribly uncomfortable."

He glanced down at the piece, as if he'd not ever known any discomfort from it. "Kept me alive more than once."

Mari wondered, "But won't the leather shrink now?"

"It may, a bit, but the metal plates will help it retain most of its shape. Might be snug for a day or two, then will relax again."

He took the saddlebag from her and dug inside to produce yet another plaid.

"Donal's stayed dry. You can cover up in this while you hang your own gown and..." he waved a hand around between them, staring at her waist, "other things."

Mari's jaw dropped. Her hands found her hips again. "You want me to remove all my clothes and parade around in this?"

His brows fell, as if he didn't see a problem with this arrangement.

"You understand that I am soaked through to the skin, so that everything would have to be doffed?"

He nodded and lifted a hand, turning it palm up, silently wondering what the trouble was.

Mari rolled her eyes and yanked the plaid from his hands. She really hadn't any other choice. She stalked off in a direction opposite than any other man had taken.

When she was far enough removed from the clearing and all the Maitlands, she did remove her gown and her kirtle, and her shoes and her hose. She unfolded the plaid, thankful now for the length of it and wrapped it around her shoulders.

Oh, bother. This wouldn't do. True, it did cover all the important parts, but wrapping it sideways left her bare from the knees down.

Glancing around the tree and wall of greenery that separated her from the camp, she saw that none had followed and removed the plaid to rethink how best to utilize every inch of this warm wool to show the least amount of skin.

Good Lord, how mortifying.

This was all Lachlan Maitland's fault.

Chapter Five

Lachlan stared off where the lass had disappeared. After enough time had passed that he began to think she might again be trying to flee, he headed off into the dense trees. A few grumbled *ughs* reached him that he realized the lass was yet near, and obviously struggling to wear the plaid.

"Lord love a sinner," he heard muttered in the next minute from perhaps a dozen feet away, behind a copse of wood-moss and a thick-trunked rowan tree. Lachlan leaned his back against a scratchy barked pine and waited.

"You can cover up in this," she said next and Lachlan nearly barked out a laugh, all good humor returned, as she'd mimicked him, deepening her voice and infusing his earlier suggestion with no small amount of derision.

Crossing his arms over his chest, he grinned at her sass. If nothing more, the lass was certainly entertaining.

But there was more. So much more.

It would be a long time before he forgot all about her gaze on him only a short while ago. A very long time. It had already been ages since anyone had looked upon him with anything other than revulsion. But she...she had set her fabulous blue eyes on him for quite an intoxicating moment, almost as if she liked what she saw. He didn't know what to make of wee Marianna Sinclair, who after her initial shock, had seemed or acted as if she were oblivious to any of his scars. Hell, he still sometimes caught Murdoch gaping at the ravaged part of his face, nine years later.

As it was, her gawking had rattled him. He didn't like being unnerved, didn't like surprises, as in a fairly remarkable but obviously innocent lass staring at him with something that looked an awful lot like longing. Something was wrong.

It was only his utter confusion about the way she'd regarded him earlier that granted this brief conjecture over the entire matter now. He wouldn't allow himself the luxury of revisiting how she'd felt in his arms in the river, how she'd clung to him as if she had no doubt he would keep her safe—there was no confusion about any emotions attached to that happenstance and he determined he would do himself no favors by reexamining it.

She muttered more behind her cover of trees and brush, which lifted Lachlan's gaze.

"At least the near drowning cleaned my shoes," she said to herself, sounding still put out.

She showed herself to Lachlan, coming out from behind the tree but did not yet realize his presence as something caught her attention. With a softer, "Ooh," she darted several feet north and knelt to pluck at some weeds.

Lachlan straightened away from the tree, unfolding his arms, and could only stare.

He squinted at her, trying to determine how she'd managed it, as she wore the plaid from the top down. It appeared she'd laid the center of it over her right shoulder, much as he did every day, letting either side fall down her front and back. Because she was so small, both ends of the plaid reached nearly to the ground. And then she'd wrapped those sides securely around her, possibly several times, and fastened it with—was that a vine?—around her waist, holding everything in place. Save for the fact that her left shoulder and arm were completely exposed, the skin creamy and unblemished, she was covered from head to toe.

Actually, her feet were not covered, he noticed, as she sat on her heels, the tips of her toes visible beneath her nicely rounded bottom.

Lachlan cleared his throat, drawing her gaze to him. Her loosened hair, lacking any device to hold it together, swung damply over her plaid covered shoulder. Her sour mood evaporated as she lifted her hand and happily showed him a cluster of green leaves with small, drooping berries that were nearly black.

He nodded, expecting that he was to be impressed, or at least know what was so promising about the plant. But he couldn't yet give attention to anything but the plaid she'd donned so ingeniously. She stood and walked toward him, the woolen fabric lovingly hugging her curves, curves the shapeless brown kirtle had failed to adore.

While she stood before him and prattled something about *black currants* and *boiled* and *stave off the ague*, Lachlan clenched his teeth and fixed his gaze on her naked shoulder and collarbone, admiring the line of it, and how smooth and delicate her skin appeared.

Not even bothering to pretend he'd paid her any heed, he said, "You've made good use of the plaid," needing this, right now, to be his focus.

She glanced down at her front, moving the skirt of her costume a bit. "It's ridiculous, of course," she said, lifting the gorgeous shoulder in a negligent shrug. "But it's dry, so I won't take you to task *too* much for first, losing my belongings and then, soaking what few I still possessed."

These words certainly penetrated, despite her proximity.

Lachlan shook his head. This lass hadn't any idea about how basic abductor-and-hostage matters were done; being polite when she needn't; not grousing at all about their harrowing river crossing, though he'd suffered a small death when she'd been flung into the water; laying out his clothes to dry, as if her captor's comfort should be of any concern to her; ogling him as if she thought him handsome when he knew he was not.

She was the absolute worst captive he'd ever known.

MARI WALKED WITH LACHLAN back to the camp site. She spent a few minutes arranging her wet garments on the same big rock as she'd laid out the chief's tunic, keeping her hose and long chemise on the side of the rock furthest from the men gathering round the fire.

"They'll no' be dry by morning, lass," Lachlan said, "unless you set them close to the fire."

"I am not about to hang my...undergarments in the midst of all your men—"

"Even if it means a wet bottom come the morrow?"

"Even then," she assured him. As she had no wagon in which to retreat, she leaned against the edge of the big rock, happy to maintain this position, away from the soldiers, sure they didn't want her company any more than she did theirs in her current state. She rather wished she had one more plaid to cover her bare shoulder. She backed her feet up, arranging the draped plaid over her toes.

Lachlan was digging through his wet saddlebags. He withdrew a short length of rope and tossed it to her.

"I dinna trust that vine to hold for you, lass," he said by way of explanation.

She wasn't sure she did either and accepted the rope with some relief, affixing it to her midsection, having to circle it twice around, knotting it tightly at her front.

The chief walked over to join his men, most all sitting or reclining in some form around the fire. Awkwardly, Mari simply sat on the rock, perhaps thirty or so feet away, deciding that these Maitlands must not take many hostages. They seemed fairly careless about the whole situation. She might have escaped successfully last night if not for the chief, and today, had she the wherewithal, she might have kicked her heels into his horse when they'd completed the crossing and simply ran, far, far away. Even a few minutes ago, if not for the sorry state of her undress, there would have been none to know if she had run off, certainly not before she might have gotten a good distance away.

She glanced upward, beyond the trees to the sky, darkened past dusk to a milky nighttime blue. She gave some thought to Harman, wondering if he spared her any thought. Improbable, she decided, and found herself uncharitably hoping her father at least gave him grief for abandoning her. Crossing her legs, she placed her elbow on her knee and her chin in her hand.

She considered it a fair assessment to imagine that not even Uncle Albert and his wife, Beatrice, would bemoan her present circumstances, if they but knew of it. She had rarely been mistreated by either of them, but her position in that tiny house, with their own four children, had been made clear very early to her: she was there to work—for them, and often in their stead.

She was charged with the care of the children, as Beatrice left her bed so infrequently. She was tasked with the laundry and the cooking and the maintenance of the small number of livestock, which shared the rear of the house with them. She sold eggs in the village and worked in the fields at harvest to earn extra coin, which was given directly to Albert. Only in the past few years, when the children had been taught some duties, had she been relieved of the very minor chores of sweeping and squirrel hunting and sometimes fishing.

She hadn't hated it, not always. However, if not for the children, the oldest only eleven now, she might have lamented her situation more. Yet, she'd dreamed for years that either she might be returned to her own family and Scotland, or that she might meet a boy who would take her to wife and give her a home of her own.

She'd been so excited by Harman's arrival, not averse at all to leaving England or even her cousins. But that excitement had been short-lived, the news about her betrothal to Walter Ramsay causing her to wish she were back with Albert and Beatrice.

And now what had she to look forward to? Lachlan Maitland had said she would be traded back to her family, back to their plans for her—in exchange for something of value, he'd said, she recalled with a sweeping bitterness.

Such marvelous choices: a prisoner of one man who saw her as insignificant, worthless even; or married to another, for whom every memory she'd retained was tainted with aversion.

The only thing she had going for her just now was her belief that Lachlan Maitland meant her no harm, physically at least. She didn't think he would mistreat her, was quite sure he'd only threatened the lashes to frighten her into compliance—she might yet berate him for terrifying her unnecessarily. He'd cursed Utrid for dropping her from the saddle, had shown concern—for her, the object; not for her personally, she knew—but had still taken charge of her himself. Why else would he do so, if not to directly be assured of his pawn's well-being?

She was little disturbed by the return of Torquil and the other two soldiers, glancing up only to see Torquil proudly holding a handful of rabbit ears, their bodies dangling lifelessly beneath his fingers. One of the other men returning made no boast of his success at hunting, simply tossed three dead rabbits on the ground close to the fire.

Before turning away, Mari caught the eye of Lachlan Maitland. He stood next to Murdoch, listening to the older man's speech. Murdoch's conversation, whatever it was, saw him lifting his hands and making a shape in the air, as if denoting the size of something. The Maitland chief nodded, though his stare was fixed on her. The golden light of the fire set his eyes ablaze, imparting a certain dark and inscrutable mood that unnerved Mari.

Quickly, she averted her gaze, letting out a big sigh.

Fifteen minutes later, she was invited to the fire by Murdoch, who called out that if she wanted to eat, she'd be wise to get some before it was gone.

Having no intention of walking amid all those men garbed as indecently as she was and made irritable again by her own deliberations of moments ago, Mari declined.

"Thank you. I'm not very hungry," she called back, grateful now for the darkness and her position, away from the fire, which kept her in shadows. She slunk off the rock, feeling her belly growl in protest at her denial of food, and settled her bottom onto the ground, softened by the fallen pine needles. She ran her hands up and down her arms, feeling the chill of the evening on her bare skin. Leaning her head back against the rock at her back, which now separated her from the rest of the party and saw her facing the opposite direction, she closed her eyes and wondered if she might be able to sleep.

The meal put the men into finer spirits, the din of their many conversations growing louder and more boisterous as time went on. She was hungry and cold but allowed herself to be lulled into sleepiness.

Sometime later, a blaring chortle burst forth from someone, startling Mari out of her doze. She jumped, her eyes flying open.

Lachlan Maitland sat before her.

Across from her, really, seated and slanted against the trunk of a pine many feet in front of her, his face tinted gold by the fire. The glow did not highlight his scars to eeriness but softened them to a blur. His chest was covered again, possibly having borrowed a tunic from Murdoch or Torquil, either of them being close in size to their chief.

He lifted his hand and pointed toward the ground at her side. "Eat."

She saw that he had placed a hard chunk of broken bread, covered with bits of meat, on a section of her borrowed plaid where it draped onto the ground. She did not demur but took the small feast into her hands.

"Thank you," she murmured and lifted her knees to balance the food atop them. She knew he continued to stare at her while she ate and could only hope that the rock behind her kept most of the light away from her face, kept her in shadows. "They seem to be quite jolly tonight," she remarked, referring to more laughter from his men.

"The closer to home a soldier gets, the merrier he becomes."

She supposed that made sense. "How long have you been away?"

"Since winter."

The meat was overcooked, and cool even, that Mari wondered if he'd waited to bring it to her, or if he'd sat and watched her for a while. "Where were you?"

"Near Ayrshire for a time, and then Galloway."

"What's in Ayrshire or Galloway?"

"English."

Mari's fingers stopped picking at the bread. "English? Were you in a battle?"

"Several."

"Are we winning, then?"

"We?" He leveled her with a hard but curious stare. "We, England, or we, Scotland?"

Mari frowned, but supposed her accent, more English than Scottish in the last few years, had prompted the question. "I was born and raised—mostly—in Scotland. But my mum was English and when she died, my da' was a bit...well, he sent me off to my mum's brother down in England."

"Where you learned some English sympathies?" He'd picked up a stray pine cone and began to snap off the scales, one by one.

She ignored his intimation that she was not a loyal Scot "I learned," she retorted, "to weave wool and churn butter and change nappies and winnow the grain *and* to cook rabbit better than this." She held up the last piece of meat.

Lachlan tossed the remnants of the stripped pine cone off to his left. "We fare better than we did a year ago," he said after a while. "Robert Bruce wants to—"

"The king? Do you know him?"

He found this amusing, his mouth turning up on one side. "Aye, I ken him. Was he that led us at Loudon Hill and Glen Trool this year."

"It's said that his sister, Mary, hangs from a cage at Roxburgh Castle."

"And his good friend, the Countess of Buchan, is subjected to a similar fate at Berwick."

"How awful," she commented, finishing off the last of the bread, swiping her hands against the plaid.

"They've committed greater atrocities," he murmured heatedly, and clarified, "the English."

This brought to mind the fate of the patriot, William Wallace, and so recently, the brothers of Robert Bruce, who'd been executed most awfully. And, of course, seated before her, bearing wounds you might not wish upon an animal, Lachlan Maitland. "Yes, I suppose they have." She leaned her head back again.

"I've stated my plans to you," he said, his tone even now, "that I hope to trade you to the Ramsays for the one who's been pillaging and plundering all around Aberdeen—"

"Who is not my brother, I assure you again."

Ignoring her interjection, he wondered, "Will they deal for you?"

She couldn't say. Shrugging, she only allowed, "I haven't been home in seven years. I have no idea what the present condition is, or if the old Ramsay is still even alive."

"Aye, he is. But your own family...?"

"Are naught but peasants, farmers," she admitted, adding, "not very prosperous, thus insignificant."

"Then how came you to be betrothed to a Ramsay?"

Another shrug preceded the only understanding she had of it. "I'm not sure. I only learned of it yesterday. We grew up with Walter, leasing the land from his da. He was quite bothersome as a lad, filled with his own importance, supposed everything was his for the taking."

"Including you?"

Mari sent her gaze back to him, at this softly worded query. She didn't comprehend what he was asking. "My brother only said that Walter has always wanted this. I wouldn't have guessed, hadn't known."

"Is Walter the son of Rannoch?"

Mari nodded. "One of four, if I recall, second oldest, I believe." She dared to ask what had been troubling her since yesterday. "But if they do—for some unknown, inexplicable reason—place more value on me and actually agree to the trade, what will become of my brother?"

It was Lachlan's turn to shrug. Without great sympathy, he acknowledged, "His crimes are punishable by death."

Mari stared at him, frightened by his tenacity in this regard, even as she was beginning to understand that Lachlan Maitland was the type who would see wrongs righted and criminals prosecuted and likely, see every single English person driven from Scotland, by his own hand if he could.

Closing her eyes for just a minute, she pictured herself enveloped in his arms so closely as she had been for an all too brief moment earlier. It was a shame that so much security was found in those arms, the same that would send her off without so much as a by-your-leave, when it suited him.

A shame then, too, that she must escape, as she had no desire to see her brother hang.

MARI WOKE SHIVERING many hours later. The ground beneath her was cold, her bare shoulder felt every cool waft of air that glided over it, and she was reasonably sure her own chattering teeth might have been what had woken her.

She sat up, still near the large boulder that had served as her seat hours ago. Somehow she was not surprised to see the Maitland chief sleeping where he had sat earlier, stretched out under the same tree against which he'd leaned.

In sleep, there was nothing frightening about the huge warrior. Gone was the seemingly perpetual frown, gone the intense gaze, but then hidden as well, his striking hazel eyes or any chance of just one glimpse of that rather remarkable crooked grin.

Escape.

Mari's jaw dropped as this came to her with all the force of a sudden summer storm. She held her breath and listened to the quiet all around. They were all asleep.

To test this, she cleared her throat. The golden light of a surely dying fire showed no movement at all from the Maitland chief, only several yards away from her. She repeated this, a bit louder now. Lachlan Maitland didn't flinch.

It was amazing how quickly her heartbeat accelerated, simply by her daring thought to flee. She sat for a moment, hoping her pulse would settle but it only grew in intensity while she considered what must be done to make this effort successful.

Very slowly, she reached up and behind her, pulling down her hose and shoes, one at a time, her eyes never leaving his face, watching for even the slightest sign of wakefulness. Inch by inch, she dragged her chemise and gown off from the rock, over her shoulder and into her lap. He'd been correct, in that nothing was dry. In her lap, she bundled everything save her shoes into her gown and tied the bundle into a knot, her gown now her satchel.

She sat still then for several minutes, watching, waiting.

He'd yet to move. Over the thundering of her heart, she heard his low and even breathing.

Carefully, she slid her foot into one shoe and then the next, tying the ribbons tight, supposing the wet leather might prove slippery if she were forced to run. She stood, simultaneously moving the bundle behind her back, should he waken now and confront her.

He did not. Mari took one painfully cautious step away from the rock but stopped when she moved the other foot to join the first. She should not take the same path she'd used earlier to change into this absurd plaid gown. When he found her gone, he'd chase that route first.

Backing away then, step by step, Mari soon found the entire camp visible to her, saw all the bodies scattered around the fire, heard more than one man's heavy snoring. The fire indeed had dwindled to naught but orange and red coals. When she'd backed all the way into the trees, further and further from all the slumbering forms, she turned and skittered away.

At first she moved carefully, conscious of each step, keeping her footfalls light, almost bouncing on her toes. When there came no cry of alert, no call for a chase, when she was sure she must be a hundred yards away from the Maitlands, Mari lifted the silly plaid up to her knees and ran for all she was worth.

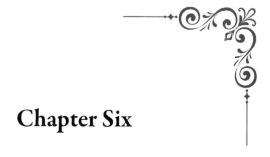

Chapter Six

Lachlan scratched his hand along his jaw, ducking under a low hanging limb. He clucked to his mount, keeping the pace steady and fairly quick for this area, which was dense with undergrowth and plenty of scrub brush.

Possibly, he would have ground his teeth down to nubs by the time they found the lass, for all the clenching and grinding of his jaw.

If they found her.

He'd woken shortly before dawn and had only needed a half second to realize that the lass had not simply wandered off to take care of any personal need. Her clothes were gone from the rock, the pale gray of the stone still darkened with the wet mark left behind.

He'd given a quick and angry whistle, alerting the entire unit of trouble. It had taken less than a quarter hour for all of them to rise and mount and head off after her. Sadly, it had been almost an entire hour more before he'd reined them in, determining that the little brat must have run in another direction, as surely they'd have overtaken her if she'd truly been headed east.

So now they were anywhere from two to five hours behind her, by his reckoning, their only advantage being that they were not on foot and they had Utrid for the tracking. Alas, her slight weight and the fact that so much of her flight would take her across an endless floor of forgiving pine needles made any attempt at trailing her fruitless.

Some noise behind him had Lachlan turning to see Niel dismounting. The lad kept his attention on his steed, who was clearly favoring a front leg. The horse shifted and snorted and slowly lowered himself to the ground. Niel followed, kneeling at his side. He didn't inspect what trouble might have come to his aging horse but rubbed his hand gently along the animal's jowl and muzzle.

Cursing, Lachlan faced forward again and marched on.

An hour later, having by now scoured miles and miles in three directions—she couldn't have gone south, back across the river—Lachlan was far ahead of his men, his need and his reasons for wanting to recapture her far greater and infuriatingly more confounding than any other Maitland.

It was then he spied a spot of movement, darting and dashing through the woods ahead of him. Pressing his heels into the horse's flanks, he sped up, maneuvering the big destrier quickly around the downy birch and through the tall grass of this woodland.

It was her, he realized for certain in the next minute, gaining on her. Her frenzied movements told him she was aware of his pursuit. Still garbed in the black and red and gold of the Maitland plaid, she couldn't hide, was easy to keep track of.

He closed the distance quickly enough, feeling his blood boil for the trouble she'd caused. Lachlan leapt off the horse even before he'd reined him in fully, swinging his leg around the rear of the beast. It took him only a half dozen angry strides to reach her, clutching onto her still bare arm as she ran, grabbing so much of her flying hair in his grasp.

She cried out when he touched her.

As he spun her around, she swung her bundled bit of belongings up at him. Lachlan's free hand easily met and deflected the attack, growling at her at the same time she demanded, "Let me go!"

"You little fool!" He shot back.

MARI RETURNED HIS SIMMERING glare, showing him her own fury and exasperation. For one moment, they only seethed and glowered at one another, his hand upon her arm keeping them close.

How, in the name of all that was holy, had he managed to find her?

He yanked at her arm, drawing her nearer still. Her thigh pressed against his from her hip to her knee. He lowered his face to her and ground out, "You just cost us half a day and one horse worth more than all of you."

"I don't care." The words sounded reasonable, not at all imbued with any of the fright that shook her limbs just now. "I warned you I would try. I told you it was my duty."

"I dinna give a rat's arse about your duty."

"Fine. But I'm not taking your place!" She hollered back at him, lifting her face to shout directly into his. His hazel eyes were very dark now, stormy, glistening with his anger.

He backed off, putting a slight amount of distance between them that their breaths barely touched. With the darkest frown she'd seen as of yet on him, actually staring at her as if she were babbling incoherencies, he questioned, "Taking my place?"

Employing a haughty sense of supremacy that she certainly did not feel, she sneered at him. "Taking your place for the flogging. I believe that was you in charge of my captivity last night when I escaped." It took every ounce of boldness she possessed to level upon him a look of utter smugness, letting him know what a churl he was for having lied to her, for having frightened her as he'd done yesterday.

Well, now she'd gone and done it. A muscle ticked in his forehead. Another, inside the mangled scarring at his temple, seemed to course bright red and blue. His eyes narrowed yet more, his gaze moving from her own wide eyes to her lips and back again. He closed his mouth, livid now, the breath from his nose bringing its own heat. He looked at her lips again.

And then he marched her backward, still curling his lip at her, until she collided with a tree behind her. But he didn't stop, just kept coming until he'd crushed his mouth to hers.

Stunned, Mari panicked, having some sense of being attacked, lifting her hands to thrust between them and push. This moved him not at all away from her. His hands left her arms and slid into her hair as he leaned into her, his mouth grinding against her lips. She was caught off guard and terrified—and dimwitted apparently, that it took her many seconds to realize that she was being kissed.

This dawning of understanding came with its own conflicting horde of emotions, ones she could neither identify nor investigate at the moment.

Lachlan Maitland was kissing her.

Her fingers curled into the linen of his tunic, but she stopped pushing against him. And somehow, for some unknown reason, Mari's shoulders relaxed. Indeed, her entire body seemed to slither downward, melting, even as he held her, and she clung to him.

His kiss was as hard and unyielding as the man, his mouth brutal and punishing—until Mari began to kiss him back. Of course, she didn't know how, had only the ten second prelude to her acquiescence to instruct her, but some frantic and dancing knot in her belly demanded that she kiss him, too. So she pulled at his tunic and moved her mouth and lips as he did. Some harsh sound escaped him at her consent, originating in his diaphragm and coursing up his throat and out. He opened his mouth to release it and Mari followed suit, which seemed then to serve as a certain invitation to his tongue. He licked the inside of her lip and then pushed further, meeting and joining with her tongue. She gasped against him, thrilled by the thrumming of her heart that surely now sat much higher in her chest that its beating was felt in her ears.

He slanted his head and molded his body against her, pressing her further against the tree. His lips were warm and firm, his tongue probing and delightful. Mari sighed into the kiss, wanting it to last forever.

But then he was gone.

He backed away, jerked away from her really. Breathing heavily, he stared at her as if she'd pounced on him, and not the other way around. He swiped his hand angrily over his mouth, leveling her with an accusatory glare.

She processed this, she really did, but not entirely, her mouth and brain and heart so taken with the wondrous thing he'd just done to her.

Cloaked within the daze of her own reaction to her first kiss, Mari pushed away from the tree and stepped forward, wanting to feel his lips on her once more.

She smiled at him.

LACHLAN STEPPED BACK, held his hand up in front of him, between them, pointing a finger at her. He swallowed hard and glared at her with considerable recrimination that certainly had nothing to do with this latest attempt to flee.

Closing his eyes just for a moment, he tried to steady his breathing. Upon opening his eyes, he found her waiting, anxious, her smile intact but wobbly.

He clenched his jaw against the annoyance rising at her reaction—did she not see his scars?—though admittedly a greater part of his present anger was reserved for his indefensible misstep.

"God's blood, lass, now dinna be smiling at me," he warned in a dangerous voice.

She tried to hide it. She rolled her lips inward, but this only served to highlight her dimples.

Lachlan further grumbled heatedly to her, "You dinna smile at a man who kisses you like that—who kisses you at all!" He managed to douse these words, as ridiculous as they were right now, with all the irritation he felt, that he should not have kissed her, that he absolutely should *not* kiss her again.

Perhaps it was his stoniness that wrought such confusion, and that wounded frown. "Why did you...then why did you kiss me?"

"I'll be damned if I ken," he answered promptly, though with less hostility. Truly, the vexation was directed solely at himself. She deserved none of it.

"But I liked it very much," she proclaimed, startling him with her candor, even as it was given with much hesitation. "You didn't enjoy it." A statement, a guess. "Did I do it wrong? I've never been—"

"Just stop talking," he bit out, feeling his head swim with everything that was wrong with their present circumstance, and *Jesu*, everything that was so very right. "Forget about kissing."

She clamped her lips, appearing all at once injured and still so damn bonny.

He needed to get himself back on proper footing with her. "What the hell were you thinking, running off like that?"

Every emotion displayed related to the kiss disappeared. Her brows angled down again over her eyes.

"What do you imagine I was thinking?" She returned hotly. "I was thinking you have no right to take my freedom, and you have no right to nearly get me killed, and you have—ugh," she spat out, throwing up her hands. "Why are you staring at my mouth? How can I forget about kissing if you still have that—"

He kissed her again. He couldn't *not*, it seemed. Some force inside him, some voice that assured him she was possibly as genuine and warm and real as she seemed moved his feet back to her. He slid his hands into her hair again, his palms at her perfectly pinkened cheeks and saw just of hint of excitement crease her kiss-swollen lips before he touched his own to her. He didn't need to back her into any tree so that there was no escape. Mari wrapped her arms around his middle and tipped her face up to him.

She really was the worst captive he'd ever encountered in his life.

But he continued to kiss her, entranced and enslaved by her willingness, by her very untutored but extremely provocative response. She tasted of some forest found berry, her lips soft and yielding. He tipped her head to the left and his to the right and exerted even more demand and more pressure, honest to God, with some half-arsed attempt to scare her off. She needed to be frightened of him, of his kiss. However, it was also possible that the present severity was just need, and a desire borne of her beauty and her person and exaggerated by her apparent inclination to see beyond the scars, as no one had in so many years. Still, he'd just shown her that he could not control the impulse, his own sudden and inexplicable want for her. It was necessary that she control it for him, for them.

She did no such thing, showed no corresponding fear. She neither demurred nor cried out against his assault but clung to him as if her own longing might be equally as damnable and vexing. This weakened Lachlan, softened his hands and his mouth upon her so that his kiss was now only a caress. She moaned deep in her throat, enflaming Lachlan but further compounding the already disastrous problem of this kiss.

A noise disturbed them.

Lachlan dragged his lips away from her, acknowledging the movements of his men as they finally caught up with him, though they were yet hundreds of yards away.

He stepped away from her before their embrace might have been noticed through the trees, needing to unwind her arms from him as she seemed disinclined to do so herself. He should apologize, he thought, but only for a moment before he discarded such a pointless notion. She was staring at him again with a similar expression as she'd shown after their first kiss, some combination of wonder and astonishment and pleasure.

"Damn it, Mari, quit with the grinning," he said, his voice thick. "I mean it," he said as his men drew nearer. "They'll no' take kindly to you looking so damn happy after the inconvenience you've brought to them." He thought only some of his men might notice that she appeared well and thoroughly kissed, her lips puffy and reddened, her eyes bright, brimming with liveliness.

But his words sobered her instantly. She looked left, from where came the Maitlands, closing in on them to less than twenty yards. Her shoulders dropped and her lips parted while she watched. She stood before him, draped still in the Maitland plaid, her hair as disagreeable as if she'd wrestled with some many-pawed and angry critter; he saw that there were scratches on her left hand, at least half a dozen, caked with the little blood that had oozed; she looked tired and cheerless suddenly, and for the first time Lachlan knew some small bit of remorse for her present unkempt and unhappy condition.

She turned and faced his men while Lachlan collected his steed.

Murdoch led the charge, reining in only at the last minute, sending grass and mud skidding up onto the bottom of her legs. Murdoch's pinched expression informed Lachlan that he'd done it purposefully, miffed at the girl for the trouble she'd caused. Others followed suit, gathering around Murdoch and showing a unified perturbance.

"Ye done now with being a nuisance?" Murdoch wanted to know, his tone craggy and cranky.

Lachlan stopped behind her just in time to see her slim shoulders straighten with her indignation. Apparently, a man could kiss her brutally and deliciously and be rewarded with a wee hopeful smile, but one would not be allowed to get away with calling her on her misdeeds, which she believed were justified.

"No, I am not," she answered pertly. She lifted her lean, bare arm and jabbed her forefinger toward Murdoch, either unaware or untroubled that she stood before all of them so scandalously attired. "You have kidnapped *me*. You have inconvenienced *me*. You have taken *my* freedom and it is only *my* fortitude that sees me now unharmed, for you Maitlands are not very good at keeping your prisoner protected." She swiveled her head as she lectured them, including one and all in her rant. "Good grief, is this your first kidnapping? You do not know how to keep me from harm and you clearly have no idea about how to keep a captive from running off. *And*, not one of you has yet to offer me even one drop of water or ale, that if not for the rain and the river, I'd have had no liquid sustenance at all."

Some stared gape-jawed at her. Some removed their gazes, their cheeks colored with shame. Murdoch had clamped his lips, shocked by her daring, it seemed. A shuffling of horse hooves took place as someone started to move, but she was not done yet.

"And another thing," she went on, planting both her fisted hands onto her hips, which Lachlan was beginning to think was a regular pose of hers. "I'll tell you what I told him." With this, she raised her hand and thrust her thumb over her shoulder in Lachlan's general direction, as he was the only one behind her. "I have an obligation to try and escape. I'm sure you're all very nice men, but kidnapping is a crime, and what you're doing is wrong. I have a good mind—"

Utrid interrupted, his words less harsh in tone than accusation, "Reiving is a crime as well, lass." Several men muttered their accord.

She returned quickly, "You are either suggesting that I myself am a reiver or supposing that one crime should be answered with another. Great. You understand that makes you no better than the actual reivers, aye?"

Lachlan himself was slack-jawed now. Less so for her words and her defense—he'd been treated to fragments of this already—but more so for the sheepish, suddenly awkward expressions of his men. These were the same men that had fought alongside their chief and Robert Bruce at Loudon Hill, where he saw Torquil near cleave a man in half with an ear-splitting warrior's cry, where Murdoch had taken a sword to the thigh but had managed to rise up and over an English whelp half his age, slicing his head from his body. Just now, Murdoch chewed the inside of his cheek, showing some hesitation, as if he were seriously swayed by her words; Torquil couldn't meet her eye, finding great interest suddenly in the mane of his large steed. And Utrid, who'd dared to challenge her, with what had seemed a sound argument, looked at her blankly, his expression inscrutable, but certainly not steeped with any enmity.

Lachlan walked his horse around her. "Have you finished?" He asked tersely. If it killed him—and it might—he needed to remind her of their roles.

She nodded tightly.

He told himself to completely ignore her quivering chin and her white knuckles, her fingers bunched now into the plaid at her thigh, showing him exactly what it had taken for her to brave so much.

"I should make you walk back," he said darkly. This whole day had been shite since he first opened his eyes. As soon as this thought entered his brain, some loud and challenging voice inside his head brought their kiss to mind. Lachlan staunchly refused to acknowledge it.

"That should make for a nice slow return to Hawthorn," she threatened, apparently still imbued with whatever boldness had seen her call out him and his men for their ill-treatment of her.

"Hawkmore," someone corrected. Lachlan thought it might have been Donal, who rarely spoke.

Lachlan ignored all of this. "Let's no' leave your belongings this time," he said, pointing to the bundled heap on the ground, near the tree where he had kissed her only a few short minutes ago.

It would have served him better to have her taken up by someone else, anyone else. Likely, it was a bad idea to have her so close, essentially in his arms, with their kiss still so fresh in his mind, the memory of it overshadowing her outburst and possibly many other things in the near future.

She retrieved her knotted and still damp clothing and returned to Lachlan. And now she was uneasy, hugging her bundle to her chest. The returned wariness of her magnificent blue gaze suggested that mayhap she felt some regret for her boldness.

He grabbed her clothes and attached it to his saddlebags, giving her previous knot a good tightening.

"C'mon," he urged then, a sigh detected in his tone.

She stepped toward him and Lachlan lifted her up into the saddle, his motions utilitarian, cool even. He climbed up behind her, pulling her back against him that they might better fit on the saddle. Her plaid covered legs sat next to his left thigh, her head reached just to his chin. He arranged his arms around her to hold the reins in both hands, settling his forearm on the top of her legs. She held herself away from him, her back as stiff and straight as a board. She sat sideways but faced forward, staring out in front of them.

They rode away, following his men, in silence.

Casually, when they were fifteen minutes gone from the spot where he'd caught her, he wondered, "Where'd you learn to scold like that?"

And all her stiffness evaporated. Her shoulders relaxed and she turned her face slightly toward him. "I was charged with the care of four younger cousins in England," she told him. And then, with more pertness, "And my uncle was sometimes a tyrant. I'd learned early on that he'd walk all over me if I didn't stand up to him."

She lifted her plaid covered arm and moved some of her disheveled hair away from her face. It was then Lachlan noticed the bruise around her left wrist, the fair skin mottled purple and red and blue, nearly a complete circle. Immediately he understood this was likely caused by him yesterday when they'd crossed the river or at any other time when he'd yanked on her arm with such negligence.

For the next several minutes they were quiet again, the only noises heard were the occasional snort of a horse or the repeated *tupp-tupp* call of several crossbills. Lachlan wrestled with no tiny amount of guilt for the lass's wretched condition. But then, he reminded himself that there were always casualties in war, indeed in life, and that this was sometimes necessary to set matters right.

Mari Sinclair would only be one more, a little worse for wear by the time she might be returned to her kin or her betrothed, but neither broken nor seriously misused.

Scowling now, he resisted any urge to recollect their kiss with any magnificent detail, only entertained an inner debate that examined whether or not the kissing might fall under the category of *seriously misused*. With a heavy sigh, believing the lass might be more trouble to him than her sweet kisses could possibly be worth, Lachlan determined that when they stopped next—and going forward until they reached Hawkmore—he would charge someone else with her supervision.

Because right now, with the taste of her kiss still fresh on his lips and with her nestled so enticingly in his arms, he wasn't sure he would be able to contact Ramsay and make any trade at all. Not for peace, not for dangerous reivers, not for anything.

Chapter Seven

Mari spent the remainder of the day holding back tears, of frustration and of exhaustion. While she wouldn't allow herself to be plagued by any ruefulness for her attempt to flee, she'd had no such luck in her efforts to be less afflicted by a certain shame over her reaction to Lachlan Maitland's kiss. Perhaps she might have found more success in this endeavor if not for the fact that during a brief stop, he'd transferred the responsibility of her to Torquil.

He offered no explanation for the move, gave naught but a thickly instructed, "Go on now with Torquil," when he'd removed her from the horse. It was possible she'd managed to hide both her shock and her initial distress over this. Torquil's seeming agreeableness helped only minimally.

Thus, she sat before Torquil—thankfully not behind—and soon gave up any attempt to not relive the kiss, or how little it must have meant to him that he'd so eagerly and at first opportunity passed her off to another. However, she could make no sense of anything, her experience with kissing akin to that of being kidnapped. She didn't know how these things worked, wasn't sure of what anything meant, or even if she had done anything that should have her feeling so poorly and conflicted.

By the time they stopped for the night, she convinced herself she was better off far away from the Maitland chief. He was all kinds of dangerous—too powerful, too confident, too angry for her to ever hope that she might not be harmed in some way if she poked that bear.

Torquil awkwardly asked of her, when he'd dismounted, "Do you need to—that is, do you have a need that...needs taking care of?"

This returned some of her good spirits. Torquil was easily twice her size and his face was not what anyone would call handsome in that his natural expression saw his brows bent angrily over button hard brown eyes and his thin lips inside a scraggly not-quite-a-man beard were often turned downward; and yet he'd stumbled awkwardly over these words about any personal need she might have, obviously having taken her earlier scolding to heart.

She smiled at him with some thankfulness, for acting like a human, for treating her as one. "I do."

He looked around and pointed to a thicket of denser brush, in which she might find the required privacy. And then he stared at her, while Mari lifted her brow, hoping it wasn't expected that she leap from the horse to the ground, so far below. Maybe she might slide off, she considered.

Torquil caught on. "Och, lass. Sorry." And he stepped forward and swept her off the steed and plunked her firmly on the ground.

"My thanks," she murmured and faced the direction he'd indicated.

"Aye, but you keep up a good hum, lass," he cautioned, lifting one thick black brow, which eased his expression not at all. "I'm no' intending to be the one you get away from."

This was not unwarranted, she allowed, and began humming to satisfy him as she walked away.

Returning to the party minutes later, she once again found herself in that awkward position of not knowing what to do or where to go. She saw that Torquil now held her belongings, likely handed over to him by his chief. She accepted these with a thin smile and untied the knot, not without difficulty, to assess the progress of the drying. They were mostly dry, though not completely.

"Fire'll help that," Torquil said, watching her flap out her gown.

Yes, it would. She supposed her reservations about this same idea last night were pointless now, as every man had had a good long look at her appalling present attire while she'd lectured them earlier.

Therefore, thirty minutes later saw Mari sat 'round the fire, cross-legged on the ground between Murdoch and Utrid. In front of her, to her great unease, hung her gown, close to the heat but not the flames. Torquil had rammed the ends of two broken and stripped branches into the ground and then had split the tops of the limbs and shoved a third branch horizontally between them, which served effectively as a bar to hang her clothes. She'd not been brave enough to unfold and likewise hang her hose and chemise, but then Murdoch had laid a flat stone against the outer rim of the fire pit and advised, "Just lay 'em up on there, lass. The heat'll get to the stone eventually, dry your stuffs."

Tonight, it was Donal and another man who'd seen to the hunting, returning with more rabbit and squirrel and even two brown feathered pheasants. These were quickly and efficiently plucked and skinned and readied for the fire. While they cooked on spits fashioned from more chopped tree limbs, the men all gathered around the warmth of the blaze.

Save for the chief. Mari had made a point not to follow his every move with her eyes and thus did not know where he might have gone off to.

Soon enough, with their bellies filling and ale flowing, conversation became more robust, sounding much as it had last night. Murdoch shared his leather flask with her, which she accepted gratefully, taking several sips of the warm ale. Utrid inquired if she preferred the critters or the bird and cut off several pieces of rabbit when she'd chosen that, imagining that the pheasant might be more in demand by most persons. Edric stepped near the fire and unloaded a bumpy burlap bag onto the ground, so that several chunks and pieces of hard bread bounced and rolled on the carpet of soft green grass.

"And that's the end of it," Edric advised. "No more bread until we're home."

"No worries there, lads," Murdoch announced. "Be home at this time tomorrow."

Mari bit her lip as Murdoch handed her a reasonably sized portion of the strewn bread. "What will become of me at Hawkthorn?" She wondered.

"Hawkmore," three people corrected.

While Murdoch looked unsure, Niel called across the fire, "It's the dungeon for you, lass."

The brawny captain shot Niel a dark scowl. "Go on wit' you, Niel. Dinna be frightening the poor girl." To Mari, he shrugged and said only, "We'll see what the Maitland says, but dinna fuss, lass. It'll be fine, aye?"

Aye? How could she know that?

She slept that night where she'd sat, as did so many of the men, just moving from a sitting to reclining position when the night grew old and the fire dwindled to embers. She woke several times, cold and uncomfortable, twice feeling at her hanging gown to find that it was still damp and could not yet be of any use to her. Curiously, she did not think of escape now, though all the men around her were sleeping so soundly, loudly almost. She curled more tightly into a ball, hardly imagining she might not actually freeze to death before the morning came.

And when she woke either the fourth or fifth time, it was to find that another plaid had been laid over her. She sat up, clutching happily at the generous gift, just in time to see the shadowy but unmistakable figure of the Maitland chief walking away from the fire, away from his men. He moved off into the trees and disappeared completely.

IN BETTER SPIRITS, if not great, the next day, Mari awkwardly approached Lachlan Maitland just before they set out the next morning. She'd folded his plaid neatly and pushed this out to him when he realized her presence next to him as he tightened all the straps and buckles around his horse.

"That was very kind of you," she said, not quite stiffly but then neither brimming with cheeriness, despite the fact that a pleasant tone had been her intent.

Still facing and attending the gear on his destrier, he only turned his head and looked her over head to toe but showed no obvious opinion that she was once again returned to her own clothes. She made particular note that he did not meet her eye, not at all. She'd already returned Donal's plaid to him, still not quite sure what to make of that lad's expression which had demonstrated some confusion, as if he'd forgotten it was his plaid she'd been traipsing around in for more than a day.

Lachlan reached out a hand to receive his plaid, thumping it onto the saddle and returning both hands to his task, seeming to dismiss her with naught but a gruff, "Aye."

A little surprised by this present crustiness, when he'd done that kindness for her last night, Mari sighed loudly and turned and walked away.

She returned to Torquil as most had or were mounting up. Smiling up at him with some self-consciousness, she asked, "Am I to be your burden yet again today?"

Fairly agreeably, he stretched his hand down to her. "No' too much a burden." And he winked at her, which was done awkwardly as if he rarely did such a thing, employing so much of his cheek and mouth in the motion.

Mari laughed and took his hand, swiftly hauled up in front of him as if she weighed no more than a small child.

The day was not horrible then, she decided. There were no steep mountains to climb nor any raging rivers to cross. She was warm under a clear sky and bright sun and her clothes were dry.

SHE REALLY WAS A VERY adaptable person, Lachlan thought, listening to her question Torquil about a myriad of things in the morning. He rode several lengths in front of them, but could hear, as he supposed many did, their discussion. It was unusual at first, as he and his men rarely talked much as they rode, needing to be so alert to their surroundings and any possible trouble or threat that might come their way. But this was close enough to home, the area well-known that their talk posed little expected danger to them.

"What do you do when you're not in service to your king?" She asked Torquil.

"We are always in service to our king, lass," Torquil answered, possibly not understanding her exact query.

"But when you are at Hawkmore," she pressed, "you are not actively involved with the pursuit of Scotland's freedom. So what do you do?"

"Aye," said Torquil, comprehending now. "Then we train to be ready to defend our freedom."

"Oh." And then a moment later, "Is that it?"

Torquil was offended, but not angrily so. "Lass, it takes a lot of time to hone skill, to sharpen reflexes, to train on different weapons."

"Different weapons? I see naught but swords and only a few spare bows."

Edric, riding close, chimed in. "Soldiers use daggers and axes and pikes as well. And every man, whether an archer or not, needs to know how to wield and effectively use the bow."

"But not all of you have bows or arrows."

"Not in this unit," Torquil enlightened her. "The archers and the rest of the foot soldiers were sent home weeks ago. Most of the cavalry, too."

THE DEPTHS OF HER SOUL

"There's another thing to train on," Edric advised. "A man's got to be able to ride and maneuver in close combat."

"But how can you prepare for that?" She asked.

Edric answered promptly, though differently than Lachlan might have. "We have mock battles, charge at each other. Sometimes we take up to the hills near Hawkmore—those trails are challenging. If you can navigate those with ease, you can likely hold your own in battle."

She laughed then, an enchanting sound that inexplicably curled Lachlan's brows down over his eyes. "So you train, you say, but it's really just men being boys. Like my young cousins having pretend sword fights with whittled sticks?"

Silence then. Lachlan grinned, imagining the lads' faces screwed up at her for such disrespect. Even Lachlan understood she was teasing them, could detect the playfulness of her tone.

Defensively, Edric grumbled, "It's very important work."

"I know it is," she was quick to say. "Very important, indeed. But what else do you do all day when you are home? Or is that it?"

Torquil answered. "There's always work to be done 'round the castle. And now Hawkmore has been short a hundred men for most of the year, there'll be things that need attention. Harvest is coming, too, so it'll be every man, woman and child working."

After a moment, Torquil said, as if he were happy to continue this conversation with the bewitching lass, as if he thought she might like it, too, "There's also hunting and putting up stores for winter. Everyone needs to contribute something."

"Are there many people at Hawkmore?"

"Aye, hundreds in the village and dozens more in the castle itself."

Edric wondered, "Did you no' live in or near a castle, lass?"

"I did when I was small. The big Ramsay castle cast its shadow over all of Newburgh, but I never had occasion to actually go inside the castle or the keep. In England, we lived in a small cottage in a village that was miles away from the landowner's manse."

"Aye, but you'll like Hawkmore," Torquil said, seeming to forget that she was but a prisoner, and that she'd not be in residence long enough to develop any opinion of it, like as not.

They were quiet for a while, seeming to have exhausted their interest either in talking or getting to know each other, whatever tiny worth that might have.

Halfway through the day, they crossed a small and unthreatening stream, calm now that the rains had ceased. Lachlan reined in before crossing, letting everyone go by. They might as well break here, he decided, letting Murdoch know as he passed. Edric and Niel and Donal followed, with Torquil and the lass bringing up the rear.

He saw that Mari was asleep, nestled into the crook of Torquil's shoulder. This would account for the silence over the last hour, Lachlan guessed. Her shiny auburn hair tumbled around her head and shoulders, her face nearly unseen but for the left side, her closed eyes and pretty lips completely at ease. Lachlan clenched his teeth, unwilling to examine thoroughly his reaction to this, though he did acknowledge some dastardly negative emotion attached to the sight of her sleeping so peacefully in the arms of another.

THE DEPTHS OF HER SOUL

They nooned only briefly, their food gone but for what ale remained and the few berries found and plucked from low-growing bushes near the water.

Wakeful once more, the lass entertained the gathering, less intentionally but possibly without any fondness for the silences that so often dogged their journeys, certainly more so when they were tired and hungry.

"Have you a wife and bairns at home, Murdoch?" She asked, turning to squint up at the captain. The sunlight highlighted her face, emphasizing the blue of her eyes and underscoring each dot of a freckle—rather to distraction, Lachlan determined from across the open space between them.

"Nae, I do not," Murdoch answered. "Never did meet a bairn I liked," he added with a hearty chuckle at his own humor.

"Mayhap you just haven't met the right ones," the lass insisted.

"Would I ken it if I met it?" Murdoch wondered, lifting his brow at her.

"I should imagine. I have four cousins, all much younger than I. I liked...most of them," she admitted with her own charming grin directed at Murdoch. She made a face and amended, "Possibly only some of them."

"Half?" Utrid guessed.

"Aye," she said, "but only sometimes. Honestly, the older ones were occasionally very difficult."

"Wasn't your problem though, aye?" Torquil guessed.

She turned toward Torquil, on the other side of her. The sun glinted off what appeared to be true red streaks in her thick wavy hair. "But it was," she said. "My aunt was very sickly, which rarely saw her out of bed." Almost as an afterthought, she added flippantly, "I might have pretended an illness as well, if those were my bairns."

A few chuckles greeted this.

Utrid dared, his toothy grin flashing, "Did you scold them the way you done us?"

She smiled still, accepting her due, being called out on her rant. "Gentlemen, that was barely a scolding. Was more a stern mother chat, reminding you of what good manners your own dear mam might expect from you." She gave this some thought, staring only at her hands, her bonny face light and cheery. "Of course you have to be wily to contend with four not very well-behaved children. I used to play games with them to keep them busy and to retain what little was often left of my sanity."

"Like get-'em-out-of-the-house games?" Edric wondered and invented, "A prize for the first lad to bring me the rainbow tail of a unicorn?"

Mari laughed fully, the sound surprisingly throaty and sweet. "No, but I sure wish I'd thought of that. I employed fairly simple games. *Who can be quietest the longest?* was used often. But by far my favorite was, *Who wants to style my hair?* This particular game insisted upon one hundred strokes of my hair before any design could be attempted."

"That's no' a game," Murdoch accused with a loud chortle, though it seemed he was clearly impressed with her cunning.

Mari displayed not one ounce of guilt for the deception she'd engaged in with those cousins of hers. "Well, it was, until the little hooligans figured out that the benefit was all mine."

More laughter followed this, many gazes sent in her direction, seeing her in the same new light Lachlan did. Murdoch passed his flask to her again, shaking his head at her wit.

Lachlan stared, a bit removed from the entire resting party, intrigued and admittedly enchanted but mostly, disbelieving.

She couldn't be real. It wasn't possible. She was supposed be cowering and quaking before them, mayhap wailing away, threatening a great reprisal from her betrothed. Not sharing flasks and plaids and telling amusing anecdotes that made her captor really want to kiss her again.

He vowed right then and there this would definitely be his last kidnapping. The lass was bonny for certain, but she was tearing him up inside. He was by turns angry and amused and then both skeptical and desirous. And that was all before noon. So often while he wrestled with the undeniable attraction to her, he resorted to browbeating himself for all the trouble it had thus far and would continue to cause, if left unchecked—or God's blood, pursued.

They made good time the rest of the day, Lachlan's heightened and frustrating emotions spurring him to adopt a fairly treacherous pace. This was abetted by long stretches of agreeably level ground across the vast meadows and woodlands between them and Hawkmore.

When they were but a quarter mile from home, he could swear he heard the faint and low chime of the supper bell and smiled. His mother would be pleased to see him, he knew. The smile widened but was quickly interrupted. That sound was not the supper bell, he realized, the noise longer and lower than the higher pitched call to sup. He glanced to his left, where rode Murdoch, and touched his finger to his ear to alert his captain.

Murdoch's perpetual frown deepened as he said what Lachlan had just surmised.

"That's the alarm."

Lachlan's frown thrust his eyes into shadow, and he dug his heels into the big black's flanks just as Murdoch called out loudly to all those behind them, "High-tail it, lads. The alarm is sounding!"

They emerged from the last of the woods before Hawkmore to see thick gray plumes of smoke rising from the front corner of the yard of the keep, where no fire should be.

MARI CLUNG TO TORQUIL'S hand around her as they raced toward the keep.

She'd heard Murdoch's cry that the noise sounding out across the valley that led to Hawkmore was an alarm and now saw for herself the fat wafting smoke rising above the red stone of the outer curtain wall.

Torquil was yelling in her ear, "If there's trouble within—more than fire—you take the steed and make for the village to the west."

She nodded against him even as she was sure she would do no such thing, convinced that she was yet unable to manage one of these big destriers by herself.

The castle was immense, the curtain wall being several stories high. They rode in at the same elevation so that only the top two floors of a massive keep were visible above it. As they neared at a breakneck speed, Mari saw that the huge gate, made of wood and iron, was lowered over a depression in the ground. People scurried and screamed inside, running back and forth, in and out of sight through that open gate.

They charged over the lowered gate, the hooves of the party clopping noisily over the planks, above the clamor of screams and cries and the still wailing alarm horn. Lachlan was the first through, Murdoch close on his heels. They dismounted instantly. Torquil followed them, leaping off from behind her, not even taking a moment to transfer the reins to her.

Holding the pommel to keep her seat, Mari turned toward the front, southeastern corner of the bailey. It appeared several bales of hay and a huge stack of chopped wood had caught fire, and was burning out of control, threatening now a wooden structure near the open gate and steps mounted against the wall, leading up to the battlements.

The small Maitland unit that had just arrived crashed onto the scene, each man leaping from his horse to assist in the efforts to douse the fire. The soldiers wasted no time, asked no questions, but hopped into the line of people running back and forth from the well in the middle of the bailey and back at the fire, tossing their impossibly small buckets of water on the huge and growing blaze.

There was so much noise, but Mari frowned when she heard above the ruckus the unmistakable shriek of a child. She saw, on the left side of the open gate a child, not more than a toddler, set or abandoned on the ground away from the fire.

Instinct kicked in and Mari scrambled to dismount, never having done so by herself. She swung her leg around and hopped off, the distance far greater than she'd imagined without the assistance of a soldier's hands. She landed poorly, using her hands to stop her face from meeting the ground and quickly charged through the moving line of peasants and serfs and soldiers to grab up the distraught babe.

Holding the child close, she cooed and bounced the bairn against her chest, moving away from the bustling people, away from the fire, toward the far interior of the bailey.

"Get these horses out of here!" She heard Lachlan call, his voice rising above all other noises.

With her back to the keep, Mari cradled the still crying babe and watched their efforts. It was not getting smaller and the lower two rungs of the stairs were now ablaze. Two young boys, mayhap stable lads, took hold of the newly arrived destriers and moved them out of the yard, two and three at a time.

She searched for and found Lachlan, needing him to be unharmed, giving some brief thought that he charged back and forth from the well to the blaze without any fear. As if he'd never himself been set on fire. He moved quicker and went closer to the actual blaze than any other man. He shouted orders and called encouragement all the while. Murdoch had grabbed a rake and was pulling the unburnt hay away from the flames and tumbling the stacked cords of chopped wood down and away as well, to prevent fire from spreading further.

Only then, the small blaze, which might have grown and wreaked so much havoc, was reduced and after another few minutes, extinguished completely.

She continued to console the frightened babe, deciding she was a girl, her pretty blue and glassy eyes fixed on Mari even as she continued to cry. "You're fine, love. You're safe." She bounced her smoothly, the motion not unknown to her, and pressed her forehead to the babe. "The fire is all gone now."

She was startled from her care of the bairn by Lachlan's voice calling out, "Where is she?" Mari lifted her face from the sweet babe and saw Lachlan pivoting to search every direction, every corner of the yard. It dawned on her that he was speaking of her, looking for her.

He was nearly frantic, his movements jerky and rigid.

"Where is she?" He hollered. "Mari!" He shouted.

Startled, she stepped forward away from the wall, where several people had gathered, those who weren't directly involved in the dousing of the flames.

"I-I'm here," she called out, her voice catching, alarmed by his behavior.

His gaze found her. And he seemed to breathe again, a great rush of breath blowing out of him.

Mari's lips parted, watching him stride toward her with great purpose.

He was...he'd been afraid.

But for all the fright he'd just displayed, and for how powerfully he'd just stared her down as he stalked over to her, his arrival was then anticlimactic. He only stopped in front of her, did not touch her as her mind had imagined he might, did not take her up in his arms.

"You are unharmed?"

She nodded, didn't trust herself to speak, only cuddled the child closer even as she forgot about her, the intensity of Lachlan's gaze so riveting...so enlightening.

The day was warm, the fire even hotter, that he was bathed in perspiration. One trail of sweat, dripping from the corner of his forehead down over his scarred temple left a gray streak of soot and smoke and sweat in its wake. Mari lifted her hand from the child's back and gently wiped away the grime, over his clear forehead and down across his scar until it was gone.

Belatedly, she realized what she'd done, how she had touched him. She might have felt some awkwardness for her boldness, but that he did not shirk away from her touch. Indeed, he took a step toward her.

He stopped when a distinctly feminine voice called out his name.

"Lachlan!"

Mari turned and saw a woman running toward them. Eyes widening, Mari was quite sure that this woman was the most glorious person she had ever beheld, beyond beautiful and garbed so regally Mari thought she must be a queen.

"Mother," Lachlan said, turning slightly away from Mari.

The tenderness of his tone, one she had for certain not ever heard, dragged Mari's gaze back to him. Something pleasing and warm filled her as she watched him.

It was the first time Mari could honestly say that she saw true happiness in his eyes.

Chapter Eight

The very first thing that Mari noticed about Lachlan Maitland's mother was that she was absolutely gorgeous, so much so that Mari stared rather breathlessly at her. She was easily more than twice Mari's age—must be, to have a son Lachlan's age—but appeared still splendid and youthful. Her skin was enviously creamy and pale, not a freckle or blemish to mar it, and showed only tiny lines to announce her age, in the corners of her eyes and at either side of her mouth. Her hair, shiny and mayhap a shade lighter than Lachlan's very dark brown, had been attended well, neatly secured in a serviceable chignon at the back of her head, but with stray wisps of curls framing and softening her face.

Absently, Mari continued to rock the little girl, though her gaze was riveted on this reunion, recalling that Lachlan had said he'd not been home in many months.

His mother pushed back from his arms and took his face in her hands. "Oh, but you look well, my dear."

"Advancing Scottish freedom agrees with me," he quipped and pecked a kiss on her cheek once more.

Stepping back, though she held his hand still, his mother said with a shake of her head, throwing her gaze toward the now snuffed fire, "And arrived at a perfect time." And then, with a severity that lifted Mari's brow, she said, "I'll have Easton's head for this. I've told him about his pipe and that hay."

Lachlan frowned. "How do you ken it was Easton?"

Mistress Maitland answered without hesitation. "Because he sits there, at the bottom step and smokes his pipe. Every day. I've warned him."

"Aye, I'll look into it."

Seeming then to notice her presence for the first time, Lachlan's mother turned toward Mari and smiled. "And who have we here?"

"This is Marianna Sinclair, Mother," Lachlan said, with some hesitation, as if he might wonder why, or whether he should, introduce his captive to his mother.

Her eyes were the same blue-hazel as her son's, her lashes just as dark and thick, and her smile was possibly the most welcoming thing Mari had ever seen.

Mari sketched an awful curtsy, the child in her arms precluding her best effort.

"Oh, but you're absolutely lovely," said his mother.

Mari's eyes widened. In no way could she compare to this woman. Her gown alone, a fitted wine colored tunic of fine combed wool over a long-sleeved kirtle of pale blue, put Mari and her shapeless and travel-worn ensemble to shame.

"It is a great pleasure to meet you, my lady—"

"We'll have none of that, my dear," she broke in with yet another warm smile. "The Maitlands have yet to be granted the nobility they deserve, so you will simply call me Diana."

Mari determined she would likely die before showing any such disrespect.

"Is this your daughter?"

"Good grief, no," Mari blurted and quickly explained. "I found her over there by the wall, crying while the fire burned."

Diana Maitland laughed and swept the child from Mari's arms. "I thought she bore a striking resemblance to Adam's bairn." And she turned toward the crowd of people, still gathered near the entrance and the remnants of the fire. "Adam Painter!" She called. "Did you misplace something?"

Several heads swiveled toward them, but only one man's countenance gave any indication that the child was his, making a face that informed that he had indeed forgotten about the babe.

"Aye, Mistress," the man called back and trotted over to retrieve his child. Diana Maitland handed over the girl, displaying not a shred of grief for the damage done to her gown by the child's dirty and snotty hands.

Facing Mari again, she clapped her hands together and said, "Let's get you inside, my dear. You'll no doubt want a nice long bath after being on the road. And we'll keep a trencher warm for you—what?"

Mari had sent a frantic glance to Lachlan. He'd scratched his jaw and stared back at her. She could almost see a debate waging inside him, what to tell his mother.

Their exchange had not escaped the older woman. She smiled again, looking at Mari and then at Lachlan. "What is amiss?"

Mari and Lachlan spoke at the same time.

"Aye, Mother, I'll see to—"

"I'm actually a prisoner—"

To her credit, Diana Maitland only blinked once, obviously caught off guard, but recovered with a certain enviable poise.

"Oh." And to her son, "She'll still be wanting a bath. We're not so boorish to—"

This was interrupted by Torquil, who bounded over to them. "Good evening, Mistress," he said to Diana, but did not await a reply before turning his attention to Mari to wonder, "Lass, how'd you get down from the big black?"

"I had to jump," she confessed and was not ashamed to admit, "Nearly fell flat on my face."

"None the worse for wear," the lad said with a shrug and a neat grin. He seemed to have no other purpose for having approached them, but then was quickly shooed away by an almost imperceptible tip of Lachlan's head. "Aye," he said, pivoting to take his leave.

"Thank you, Torquil!" Mari called after him.

Facing the chief's mother once again, she was surprised to see that now her brow was lifted and that she stared at Mari with some greater regard, more than she'd shown when she'd learned that Mari was her son's captive.

Mari bit her lip. *Oh, bother.*

MARI FOLLOWED LACHLAN'S mother into the hall, the door being very close to where she'd stood only minutes ago, holding the child. As she'd said to Torquil earlier in the day, she'd not ever been inside a massive keep, or any home that was larger than three rooms, one of which was reserved for the family's livestock. The home in which she'd been born and the one she'd shared with her mother's family had been naught but thatched cottages, the main room serving all at once as the kitchen and gathering area and some bedrooms.

She glanced upward first, as soon as her foot crossed the threshold, her mouth forming a small *o* for the grand size and height of the ceiling. 'Twas made of timber, the wide planks stacked side by each and met in the center by a thick chunk of board that ran the length of the room.

Mari gaped, discovering at the opposite end a wall of stone behind a raised table and huge ornate chairs. The stone of the wall was dark but decorated with hanging drapes of gold velvet trimmed in black and red. Several shields and banners, most bearing the similar image of the head of a howling wolf in profile, adorned the stone of that wall.

The room was busy, as a group of lads moved carved trestle tables and benches away from the wall and into two rows across one half of the room. Her gaze was drawn upward again, taking note of the numerous windows perched high on both of the longer walls. The windows were tall and narrow, letting in only a sparse amount of light. Mari thought they might even be too narrow to allow her arm to squeeze through. From that fabulous timbered ceiling hung two huge metal rods, about ten feet in length, and from the end of these, spaced at either end of the hall, sat what looked like an enormous round wheel on its side, save that these wheels were stacked with a dozen thick tallows each, giving the entire hall a not unpleasant golden hue.

The lads had finished arranging all the tables and benches and disappeared around the far stone wall, which Mari just now grasped did not extend to either long wall, but showed an opening on either side, beneath the shields and banners.

"Marianna?" Diana Maitland called from the center of the room.

Mari skipped ahead, not realizing that she had stopped to gawk at what was surely the finest keep in all of the highlands.

"Apologies, my la—Mistress," she corrected and caught up.

Lachlan had not waited for her but had walked all the way to the longest table at the front of the room, the only one covered with linen, and sitting on a raised wooden platform. He poured some liquid from a pitcher into a goblet at one of the place settings and downed the drink in one gulp.

"Really, Lachlan," his mother scolded, but without any harshness. "Supper is less than an hour away." She then called over her shoulder, "Come along, lass."

They did not stop near the table as her son had but continued past it and through the opening the lads had taken. Behind the wall were several different corridors and a set of stone stairs, which leaned directly against the wall. Without pausing, the lady of Hawkmore lifted her fine gown and walked up the stairs with Mari following closely.

THE CHIEF'S MOTHER hadn't stayed long with Mari but had delivered her to a chamber on the third floor. The room was airy and light, furnished with a bed that was elevated off the ground and draped in what appeared to be a sumptuous coverlet of beige cotton; a tall cupboard of some dark wood stood in one corner and opposite that, a table, complete with ewer and basin, stood at the ready. The table sat beside a window, this one much wider than the ones seen in the hall and flanked by a fine tapestry depicting yet again that howling wolf.

Standing yet near the door, having allowed Mari to pass, Diana said, "Consider this your dungeon, I suppose."

Mari whirled around, wanting to see if her expression was as lighthearted as her tone. It matched almost perfectly.

"Your son doesn't actually kidnap many people, I'm guessing?" She wrung her hands in her skirts, being reminded, as she was, about her position.

"No, Marianna, he does not. Least, not any that have ever been walked into the keep, their hands unbound." The words themselves might have been what sent Diana's gaze to Mari's hands. She frowned instantly and marched across the room to her, lifting her hand and pushing back the sleeve of Mari's brown kirtle. Mari had only noticed the discolored bruise earlier this morn, thought it must be the cost of Lachlan having plucked her so forcefully from the violent water of the river when she'd been dunked.

"Oh, that's not anything at all," Mari was quick to defend, the lady's scowl not inconsequential in the least as she ran her fingers over the mark on Mari's wrist.

"Not anything at all? Did my son cause this damage?"

"He did, but it wasn't his fault," Mari was quick to defend. And while the lady appeared to await some explanation, Mari said, "He was trying to save me, had to hold tight...." She didn't think she was expected to recount the entire tale of their river crossing.

Accepting only this small explanation, Diana Maitland patted the top of Mari's hand and announced, "I'll send the lads up with the tub and the water." She held up her finger, forestalling Mari's nearly spouted refusal over such a luxury. "I'll hear no fuss. Now, I don't suppose my son was so chivalrous as to allow you to pack a change of clothes for your own kidnapping?"

Mari couldn't help but smile at his mother. "I did have belongings, as I was heading home, but they've since been lost—again, through no fault of your son."

The woman rolled her eyes at Mari, which in turn widened Mari's blue eyes.

"And that will be the last defense you give him, do you hear?"

Mari nodded, but only because she felt it was expected, not that she understood why the woman should care. She'd thought the woman might want to have her own son exonerated from so many misdeeds.

Perhaps she read Mari's confusion; she turned at the door, holding the handle and explaining, "He did kidnap you, not the other way around?" At Mari's hesitant nod, she said further, "He is responsible for you then, for any harm that comes your way, for your person and your possessions, and for every aspect that must ensure a safe captivity." Pointedly, in what Mari could only assume was a frustrated mother's tone, she finished, "And he knows that."

Thus, an hour later, Mari sat on the surprisingly firm mattress of the pretty bed and waited. She'd been bathed by two giggling lasses, who'd informed her that normally they worked in the laundry and kitchens. Mayhap they'd been instructed to curtail any robust conversation with the prisoner, as they offered only replies but did not instigate any dialog. Mari didn't care, the bath proving a luxury she'd not expected, the water warm and scented with heather and lavender. So delighted was she by the godsend of the bath, she did not even let any nervousness plague her overmuch about disrobing before two strangers. The lass named Edie handed a hard ball to Mari, telling her to sniff it. Making a face, thinking it might be some kind of trick, Mari did so haltingly. Her eyebrows shot up into her forehead.

"Scented soap," the girl confirmed with a wide smile and bright eyes.

"Oh, how lovely," Mari couldn't help but coo, sniffing it again and again until Edie giggled and took the hard soap from her hand and applied it to a soft cloth of linen.

When the bath was done and Mari was dried, Edie slipped a soft linen kirtle over her head followed by a frock very similar to what these girls wore, a plain gown of gray wool with a rounded high neckline and a thin rope belt. Fiona handed over a pair of cotton hose, finer than any hose Mari had ever known. She donned these and added her own shoes and then sat patiently while the girls combed through the snarls and knots in her hair, each girl taking one side of Mari's head. They spent quite a bit of time on her hair, most of which saw them trying to dry so much of it, rubbing it mercilessly between the linen of the bath sheet.

So she sat now, the girls gone, having been given no instruction to leave the room, not even daring to test the door to see if any latch had been set. Diana Maitland had said she might as well consider this her dungeon so that Mari could only hope some tiny supper might be brought to her. She couldn't believe the woman would have any plans to deny her food.

She touched the hair at the back of her head, where Florie had taken up two thick sections from the sides and pulled them back, tying them to each other at her nape. It felt awkward but then luxurious, to have her hair unbound but still out of her way.

A knock at the door startled her. She jumped up, expecting to open the door and find a supper of sorts. Instead, the door opened before she reached it and Lachlan Maitland stood on the threshold of her dungeon.

Good heavens! She thought, and almost, nearly said that aloud.

Oh, but he was handsome, striking even. Freshly bathed himself, his hair had been washed and brushed back away from his forehead, save for one lock that insisted on curling downward. He'd shaved what little stubble had grown in the last few days and sported a clean tunic just the color of wheat and breeches a shade darker. He wore different boots than the road-worn ones and he'd donned another belt, this leather newer, neither creased nor faded. His sword and scabbard, which she supposed only rarely left his hip, had met with some polish as well, shining neatly in the bright room. And his plaid, which she imagined was never far from his person, was pleated perfectly and draped over his broad shoulder and wrapped around his waist.

She'd not quite looked her fill, but his very presence alone had taken some of her breath already. Mari lifted her gaze to him, biting her lip, supposing he'd caught her staring at him.

His eyes were on her lips.

HE'D ENGAGED IN SOME brief reflection as he'd climbed the stairs to fetch Mari that for all the time he'd spent thinking about her over the last few days, he'd not once given thought to what might be done with her once they reached Hawkmore. Thus, he'd been happy to leave her caretaking to his mother when they arrived. Still, he'd been a little surprised when he'd come to the hall for supper and his mother had advised that he should bring down the lass to eat as well.

When he'd responded to this suggestion with a heavy furrowing of his brow, his mother had waved her hand airily and insisted, "She's not a criminal, Lach, that she needs to be treated impolitely."

So here he stood.

And there she was, bonnier than ever.

"We'll go down to sup," he said, appreciative of the way her eyes brightened with this news. The lass did like to eat. Stepping back out of her way, he lifted his hand, indicating she should precede him through the door.

She did not, but held up her hand as well, palm forward and knuckles locked.

"Can we first establish some...rules or something? I do not know what is expected of me, or what is allowed, or even prohibited and it makes me nervous because I wouldn't want to anger anyone or get myself in...more trouble."

He shouldn't ever touch her. Not ever again. But her present unease wrenched at something inside him. He circled his fingers lightly around hers.

"Dinna try to run anymore."

Her eyes, which had found great interest in his chin when she'd spouted all those words, lifted to meet his watchful gaze. She tilted her head at him. "That's it?"

He couldn't claim to know Marianna Sinclair very well, knew not much more than that she was betrothed to his greatest enemy and that her kiss was not something a person could easily forget, despite his best efforts, and that her eyes were impossibly blue and showed every single emotion. The only other thing he could claim to understand about her was that she cared about people, cared what they thought, and what they thought of her.

Having met his mother, who in all probability could have charmed Christ off the cross if only she'd had the chance, Lachlan felt confident that Mari Sinclair would not in a million years do anything to upset her.

But he sighed. Mari would need a greater explanation than *dinna run anymore*.

"It's as I've said, lass. You'll no' be harmed. You'll be returned to your family in short order. So dinna do anything that leaves me with no choice but to lock you up." Another thought occurred to him and he knew he was not above playing on her compassionate nature. "Mari, think of the good you'll do. Even if I dinna collect your brother—the reiver," he corrected before she might have needlessly argued this point, "returning you to the Ramsays could end decades of feuding, years and years of senseless fighting between the Maitlands and the Ramsays. All because of you."

She nodded, her acquiescence nearly instant, as he'd suspected.

He led her out into the corridor.

As they started down the stairs, she tipped her face up to him and asked, "Can I tell you one more thing?"

Lachlan stopped and faced her, imagining he wouldn't be able to stop her. She'd paused as well, one stair above him so that she was nearly eye level with him.

"Your mother is...she is remarkable. She is so warm and has been so kind to me," she said, twisting her hands in front of her, though Lachlan could not decide why this present conversation should be making her nervous. "She did not know me before this day, and then she finds out I'm, well, essentially your captive, and her attitude changes not at all. She is absolutely the most perfect person I've ever met. Of course, you probably already know that...but I wanted to tell you I think she's lovely."

He smiled. He wouldn't argue, couldn't argue, since he agreed. His mother, and only his mother, was the reason he did not fall into despair when he was returned from England. She was the reason he'd abandoned his long-held dreams of vengeance, that which he'd planned and hoped for every day while a prisoner of the English. It was she who'd redirected his purpose and she who'd pushed him to return to the war, though surely it broke her heart to see her only child ride off again toward the English.

"She is a good person," he concurred. "Remarkable, actually."

For his accord, Lachlan was rewarded with one of Mari's smiles. This one was nice, as if she'd somehow expected her statements to have been challenged and then was especially pleased that they were not.

Her lips were made to smile, he decided. They lost none of their fullness, seemed only to widen and stretch happily over her even white teeth, and could so easily beckon a man to recall how they felt pressed against his.

Sadly, the smile faded while he continued to stare at her mouth.

Lachlan lifted his gaze, met her rapidly blinking eyes, but showed no remorse for having been caught in the act, so to speak. He clenched his jaw and wondered if his surely dark countenance just now told her what he was thinking.

She swallowed visibly, answering that question.

If she'd moved on, if she'd just continued down the stairs, maybe talked more—she liked to talk, he knew—maybe spoke further about his mother, she'd have been spared. But she did none of these things. She only stared back at him and he understood fairly quickly that while he put up an admittedly half-arsed internal fight, she was only waiting.

So he kissed her.

Later, he would tell himself that she'd brought it on herself, for not running, for bringing the scent of a lavender field to him, for owning eyes that stared at him without so much as a grimace, for having lips that could be so perfectly molded against his own.

And it might have only been a short kiss, but that she leaned into him, putting her hands onto his shoulders when he touched one of his to her hip. She opened her mouth almost immediately, sending her tongue out to meet his. It was so far different from their first kiss, her response now knowing and eager, yet no less scintillating. He liked her boldness, liked that she leaned into him, didn't shy away from him. It heightened the hunger he'd worked so hard to deny. But for just this moment, he didn't care. He would deny it again, but later, not now.

Lachlan moved his hand against her, found the rope belt at her waist and drew her even closer. Her hands slid over his shoulders and around his neck, her fingers sliding into the hair at his nape, and he knew if he were a lesser man, if he'd not learned at the hands of the English to keep any seriously joyous emotions well in check, that he'd have wept for the beauty of those movements, for how sweet she was and felt and tasted.

A loud crash, perhaps a metal tankard falling onto the stone floor in the hall below, took her lips away from him. She stayed close, glancing over his shoulder and down the stairs, and the moment was gone then.

Straightening, while her hands slid out of his hair and off his shoulders, she looked up at him. And then she said, in her frank and curious way, even as she was as breathless as he, "You've kissed me twice now, so that now I recognize that...look that comes over you just before you do. But this one—the expression that comes after you've kissed me, is harder to understand."

Lachlan had some sense that if he spent any great amount of time in her company, he might regularly be well entertained. He had to ask, "What do you mean?"

"Well, before you kiss me, it appears that you really want to even though your expression is quite dark—I can't explain it," she answered. The frankness obviously didn't come without some apprehension, that she absently plucked at a thread on the shoulder of his tunic, then smoothed her hand over the fabric with some distraction. "And then you kiss me but...after you do, it looks as if you're sorry you did."

While she didn't appear exactly forlorn, she did seem to be troubled by this.

"I should no' be kissing you."

"Then why do you?"

Because lips like yours should no' be neglected, could no' be ignored. Because you see me, just me. Because you're good.

He met her eye, kept his features bland. "You'll be returned soon to your family. You're to wed the young Ramsay. I've no business kissing you."

Maybe she looked a little forlorn now.

Her hands fidgeted, while she contemplated only his chin. "I know there's more, that comes with... after kissing, and that needs to be...saved for my husband, but..." she lifted her gaze to him, all bright-eyed and sweet, rushing out the remainder of her thoughts, "kissing by itself is not wrong and I don't see how that alone should cause any—"

Lachlan covered her mouth again. And God's truth, he'd not even been staring at her lips this time, had been coerced so beautifully by the fact that she'd just essentially given him permission to continue kissing her. He ground his lips against her, felt her shuddering, happy response as she clung again to him.

Jesu, this lass!

Chapter Nine

Diana Maitland set the tray of sweetbreads on the head table and turned just as her son and the lass entered the hall. She hadn't been married to two different but equally awful men and lived to tell about it by showing so many emotions, but it was certainly difficult to keep her eyes from widening at the sight of the pair. *Oh, my*.

In truth, her glance only skimmed over the girl, quickly taking in her pretty blush and the way she stared up at Lachlan. Diana turned her eye to her son, saw him give a reserved grin before he responded. He set his hand on the small of the lass's back, guiding her into the hall. Diana watched him watching her, as Marianna sent her glance around the now-bustling room. The lass's eyes lit up as she pointed to Wilbur and Nellie, set in chairs near the huge hearth, playing the rebec and the dulcimer. Marianna's excitement was palpable, but Diana was more interested and keenly aware of Lachlan's response to it.

He looked happy.

As he had not in so many years.

She gave more consideration to the lass. She was bonny for sure, the loveliest thing Hawkmore had ever seen. Possibly, she was made so pretty in Diana's eyes for how she stared at Lachlan. It made her heart weep with joy to see Marianna Sinclair so unaffected by his scars. True enough, and to her utter disgust and dismay, there had been too many lasses that had looked at her son as if he were a monster. In the beginning, when he'd first returned, Diana had once witnessed a trio of girls in the village crossing to the other side of the road to avoid walking near him and being so close to his ravaged face. She'd hated those three instantly with a mother's fury, and ever since.

Lachlan and Mari paused to talk to Adam Painter, holding his bairn. Likely the man was giving his thanks to the lass for the care she'd shown to his child. And then, while Lachlan and Adam exchanged a few words, Mari initially followed the discussion, her gaze moving back and forth between each man, until it settled and stayed with Lachlan.

Amazed, Diana watched as her pretty hazel eyes moved over all of his face while his attention was taken with Adam. She neither frowned nor sneered, but bit her lip, her face alive with some secret pleasure. Diana's heart flipped for how softly and contentedly her gaze remained on Lachlan. And then Lachlan turned to her, mayhap sensing her prolonged watching, and—Diana wouldn't have believed it if she hadn't seen it with her own eyes—he leaned toward her and said something low, to which Mari's eyes brightened and a smile came, beauteous and for him alone.

And Lachlan smiled back at her. It wasn't huge or miraculous—he did occasionally still smile—but good heavens, Diana thought, he was teasing her or sharing some secret, she could see by the mischievous glint in his eye.

Prisoner, indeed!

Diana's thoughts began to whirl, seeing her son so absorbed by the lass, and apparently pleased to be so. She didn't know who this lass was or what the complete story was surrounding her current circumstance as she hadn't had time to investigate it fully, but Diana comprehended fairly quickly that she was not merely a captive. She was much more than that. She could spare no more seconds to evaluate much else as the pair walked toward her now but knew it would be easy to make a few changes at supper so that she might learn more about what was going on between them.

Diana yanked at Florie's sleeve as she passed and whispered to her, "Add another high-backed chair to the head table."

She smiled when the pair stood before her and took note of how Lachlan schooled his expression into flatness in front of her. Very telling, thought his mother.

"You look invigorated," she said to Mari. 'Twas no lie. The lass was uncommonly lovely that even the drab kirtle could not diminish this.

"The bath worked wonders, thank you," said Mari.

"Won't you help bring out the platters?" Diana invited.

Mari nodded, eager to be of use, and followed Diana around the wall and through the right-most corridor into the kitchens. "The return of their chief has brought so many more to sup than we would normally see," Diana explained. "And we've only Edie and Florie and Robert to deliver the food."

Inside the large, high-ceiling kitchen the air was thick with smoke and grease and the very distinctive, fantastic odor of garlic. A long counter sat in the middle of the room, filled with platters to go to each table. The cook, Marjorie, was busy at the tall ovens and spits along the outside wall. Edie darted by, carrying two trays of food at once. Diana grabbed up the nearest ready platter and handed it to Mari, who sighed and breathed in deeply the wafting steam from the roasted pheasants.

"Take that to the head table, lass," Diana instructed and lifted another tray herself. She followed Mari back to the hall, passed by Florie and the lad, Robert, who, like Edie, would run back and forth possibly a dozen times to see the entire meal delivered.

Once Diana and Mari had set down their laden platters at the head table, Diana pointed to a chair on the dais behind the table and told Mari to sit and then walked around the table and took the seat next to her. If the girl thought it odd that she, an outsider—a prisoner, even—was seated at the family table, she gave no indication.

When people noticed that Diana had taken her seat, they followed suit. Lachlan turned away from his conversation with Murdoch and several other soldiers in the middle of the room, his tankard stopped from reaching his mouth by the sight of the lass at the table.

Diana met his questioning gaze and smiled innocently at her son.

Little by little the people settled down. Murdoch stepped up on the platform, grinning like a fool when he noticed Mari. He walked behind her and leaned down to the lass. "Better eating than anything we'd give you on the road, lass," he promised.

Mari turned her head on her shoulder and flashed a magnificent smile at the Maitland captain. "That's not saying too much, Murdoch," she quipped.

Lachlan took the chief's chair next to his mother while Murdoch sat at his left. Diana pretended not to notice her son's glance across her to Mari, wondering if he had any idea how unsubtle he was. Mayhap it didn't matter; the girl was so entranced with all the goings-on and the feast laid before her that she did not notice Lachlan's attention.

Hawkmore's steward, Oliver, sat in his usual spot next to Murdoch, with Edric next to him at one end of the table. The next highest-ranking officer, Utrid, took the chair next to Mari, filling the table.

It was rather expected that any returning warrior give a good accounting of his travels and his deeds at the first gathering upon his return. In her day, when either of her husbands had returned from long absences, there would have been absurd feasts, which neither man had ever earned, by her understanding. Sometimes the feast would last for days, for which she was mostly thankful as it had kept both men, at different times, inebriated enough to leave her alone.

Lachlan was different, of course. His return from his very first foray into war had seen him broken and battered. It was one of the rare times he'd ever raised his voice to his mother, shouting that he had no need and no liking for any feast in his honor. She'd gotten used to his anger since then, though she'd wept initially for what had become of her carefree boy.

As it was, it was mostly Murdoch who told any tales of their exploits nowadays, Lachlan so reluctant to put himself on display before all his kin.

So when all the people were seated and the hall quieted completely, Murdoch pushed back his chair and stood. He tapped his fingers thoughtfully on the rim of the tankard before him as he began.

"I ken some of you are sorry to see us returned," he began cheekily, drawing an enthusiastic bit of laughter. With more seriousness then, he continued, "When I look out over all these familiar faces, known for many years, I think to myself, I'm rather sorry to be back as well." This time he laughed robustly at his own jest. "Aye, aye, now, I'll get to it." He sipped from his tankard then and went on. "So we met with the king himself down near Turnberry and you ken he was fighting mad, his brothers betrayed by that damned MacDouall—"

"Curse the name!" Someone shouted.

Murdoch nodded, pulling on his long beard. His tone sober now, he said, "He weren't in a good place, the king. Wanted vengeance, wanted every English head on a pike, and who could blame him? But he's settled down, made to reason, understands we haven't the numbers to make a stand, but damn if that bastard Pembroke isn't on his tail, swinging close. And the king decides that we've no choice but to use our own beloved soil to help us fight these mongrels. Soon enough now, we set up near the crags of Glen Trool and damn if I thought the king had lost his mind when he said, *aye, we'll charge from here.*" Murdoch often used his hands to talk, threw them up now to express his disbelief. "Charge from here, he says, and I'm looking down a steep incline of seven hundred feet, wondering if he believed the horses were unicorns, and flying ones at that." He tipped his head, acknowledging, "Ye ken, there's only one way across to get where they're going, and it's the glen below us so, aye folks, here's what we do: we wait until all the hundreds of English are within the glen and we push off these huge boulders, maybe a dozen of them. Each one is bigger than me, takes ten men to budge it, fifteen to send it down the hill. They roll right over a good thirty or more English, too daft to get out of the way. And then Bruce calls the archers and while they're scrambling below, watching for more rocks to roll over them, here come hundreds of arrows, and there goes another quarter of their army." He took a sip of his ale and picked up where he'd left off, his audience rapt. "So, the glad thing is, ye ken, the king ain't mad at all, and down we go. But I promise ye, ye ain't ever pissed yourself from fright until ye ride a horse down the side of a mountain, 'bout as steep as Donal's nose—Jesus, look at that beak." Murdoch waited until the laughter died down to continue. He put his two hands together, showing a perpendicular angle. "God smite me here, aye lads? It's like this and I still dinna ken how we managed it—only lost maybe half a dozen to the tumbling, but there ye have it. And we charge right into the English, like as no' pissing themselves for what they see coming and it's done in minutes. And that's Glen Trool." He glanced to Lachlan and confirmed, "Aye, but we lost sweet William—he was a good'un. And Alan and Simon fell as well, God rest their bonny fightin' souls."

"And Gilbert," Lachlan said in his deep voice, "who fell bravely, good enough to take two English with him."

"Aye, Aye!" was called in recognition for these men.

"Now I'll tell ye all about Loudon Hill," Murdoch promised, "but no' today. My belly's rumbling so loud I canna hear my own words."

Some shouted out protests to this, but Murdoch lifted his hand to quiet them.

With some reflection, his tone somber once more, Murdoch said, "A true Scotsman doesn't hie with any dissention. 'Tis our land, our freedom, our lives we fight for. Aye, the king's made mistakes—plenty over the last decade to be sure. But I tell ye now, as I stand here, Robert Bruce is committed to our freedom, he's committed to wrestling us out from under the English noose." This was greeted by a chorus of happy cheers. "As committed, I tell ye, as Wallace ever was, as our own proud chief ever shall be." Another cheer, which quieted quickly when Murdoch finally raised his tankard for the toast. "As always, to our freedom—may we know it in our lifetime."

They cheered and drank and banged their cups on the wooden tables. Murdoch was just about to sit when someone called out, "But, captain, where'd ye find that wee bonny lass? You've told us nothing about her."

Enlivened again, pleased to address this, Murdoch waved a hand toward Mari.

"Aye now, this lass is Marianna Sinclair. But I ken she dinna like her own name, so we just call her Mari." He turned to grin at the lass. And then, to the people of Hawkmore, "Now she's done no harm to no one and bears no ill toward any, but we did kidnap her, aye, dinna we?" Murdoch sent out a hard frown to settle down the clamor that arose from this news. "Ye dinna need the particulars but I'm telling ye now, she's to be treated fairly and kindly or you'll answer to me and mine." He patted the hilt of his sword to introduce *mine*. "Aye, and just ignore all those English sounds that come out of her mouth, 'cause she's half-Scottish, too. She dinna ride so well and she canna swim, far as I can tell, but still, if ye see her running, give us a shout, aye?" This brought much laughter, including from the lass herself. Her cheeks were bright pink for the attention upon her, but she took it all in stride and with good humor, making a face at Murdoch that wrought a good chortle from the old man. "Ye ken how sassy she is? Och, but I'm serious, she had no choice in the matter, being taken an' all, but she'll come in right handy so let's no' lose her."

"I volunteer myself to be her personal guard," called out someone.

Frowning, Diana identified the blacksmith, Edane, as the voice behind the words.

"Will she stay long enough for a courting?" Asked another.

Diana recognized Anthony's booming voice and decided she would wring his neck later. A chance glance at Lachlan showed his teeth clenched and his knuckles white around his tankard.

"I'll shackle her to—" someone else began.

Murdoch cut this off with a terse and very angry, "You'll stop that right now. *Jesu*, I've just said the lass was to be treated kindly. What kind of arse are ye, showing disrespect and the words barely out of my mouth?" He shook his head with no small amount of disgust. And then, all good humors gone, he drilled it into them again, "I catch any one of ye causing any trouble with the lass, the good Lord Himself won't save ye from what I'll bring down upon ye."

Poor Mari, Diana thought. The girl bit her lip and stared at the linen covered table, likely embarrassed for the trouble she'd so inadvertently caused. Knowing fully what weight her own opinion carried, Diana covered the girl's hand with her own and smiled at her so that everyone could see. She leaned over and whispered to her, "Lads being lads, that's all."

Mari responded as Diana hoped, smiling with her thankfulness for this support. Possibly half the room witnessed this exchange, which would go far to keep the lass from being harassed by any such foolishness.

Finally they began to eat. Of course, 'twas only a Maitland gathering and not some royal court affair, that everyone happily served themselves. Robert and the kitchen lasses would make the rounds with the pewter pitchers, refilling ale as needed, but that was the only service this hall would see.

Mari only moved after others had first, watching Diana and Utrid and those at the table directly in front of her before copying those actions, though she only served herself very small servings of only a few dishes.

This did not go unnoticed by Diana. "I cannot imagine that you are not hungry, Marianna."

The young woman blushed and quickly explained, "Oh, I am, Mistress. I'm just not sure—beyond the pheasant—what anything is...or how much I am allowed."

It was Utrid who responded to this, and happily so. "Aye, lass, these are the sweetbreads," he said, showing Mari the warm cake in his hand. "Melt in your mouth is what they'll do."

She had already added one of these to her plate and sampled it delicately, under Utrid's watchful eye. Her eyebrows shot up into her forehead and she giggled at Utrid, covering her full mouth with her hand. When she swallowed the tasty confection, she said to Utrid, "Oh, my. I might want to live on these."

The lad smiled back at her. He was sufficiently handsome when he smiled, Diana thought. She would have to keep the lass away from him as best she could.

Utrid embraced his role, however, and pointed to the vegetables on her plate. "Course, that's just leeks and onions, but Cook adds something, not sure what, makes 'em right tasty. And you've got a bit of the wild boar," he went on, chuckling over the face Mari made in response to this. "That there is cheese, but you ken that. Och, but you dinna get the pork pie." The lad then spooned some of his own onto Mari's plate. "I dare you, lass, to tell me you've had it better?"

Diana was quite sure she could hear her son's teeth grinding and might have smiled but that her boy was feeling poorly.

After a few more minutes, Mari asked of Diana, "Is this a festival then?"

Diana smiled at her. What a strange, sheltered girl. "This is supper, my dear."

"But it's so...lively," Mari countered, "and fun." Her pretty eyes darted all around, appreciative of the joyous atmosphere and the sweet music, her smile rather a permanent thing. Diana was sure her foot tapped under the table to Wilbur and Nellie's jaunty music.

When the meal was done, Torquil and Niel approached the table, begging Mari's company from Diana. "I want her to meet my mam and sister," Torquil explained.

Diana nodded, and watched as the lass excused herself, grinning with excitement as she stepped away from the table to join the lads. She was almost immediately swallowed up by the crowd as so many had risen from their benches to visit with others.

Diana sat back, folding her hands across her waist and watched Lachlan without turning her head. Her son sipped slowly from his tankard of ale, said nothing—he rarely did unless in the smaller company of his officers and men—but followed every move Marianna Sinclair made. He must be feeling some terrible disagreement, Diana decided, as he appeared to *chew* his ale. Nae, he was only tightening his jaw, repeatedly and harshly while he watched the lass.

Intrigued, Diana said, in as casual a voice as she could manage, "She's very lovely."

She'd startled him, she thought, or mayhap he'd forgotten his mother still sat beside him. Turning toward her, his expression quickly shuttered, he said only, "Aye, and she'll get us the peace with the Ramsays that we've craved for years."

"She's set to wed one of the Ramsays, I understand," she said. Lachlan gave her only a brief lift of his brow, having learned by now that Diana Maitland knew how and where to get information.

He nodded. "Was returning from England, where she's been for many years, I gather, for her own wedding."

"That's a shame, then," Diana lamented. At Lachlan's look of inquiry, she said, "Waste of a good lass, I'm thinking, giving her off to a Ramsay."

"Hmm," was all she was given before he returned his gaze to the lass.

HOURS LATER, ALL HER duties attended to for this evening, Diana Maitland strode with great purpose through the hall and out into the night. She crossed the bailey with some haste and pushed open the door to the gatehouse, which was also the main door by which to enter the soldiers' barracks.

Young Edric, climbing the stairs to the top of the wall, turned, showing his surprise to find the mistress here. He was several steps above her but stopped suddenly, tipping his head politely at her. She didn't wait for him to inquire what she might be about but said, "I'm looking for your captain."

"Murdoch? Aye, he's up top, Mistress."

"Would you be so kind as to send him down?"

"Aye, ma'am." And he was gone, further up the stone steps on the inside wall.

She paced back and forth along the stone and gravel ground but was not kept waiting very long.

Murdoch lumbered down the steps, his frown and his question coming even before he'd reached the ground floor.

"Aught amiss, Diana?"

The Maitland captain was the only person, other than the castle steward, who actually took her up on her invitation to call her by her given name. Likely this had more to do with longevity—both Murdoch and the steward, Oliver, had lived in this keep and served the Maitlands for as long as she had, had indeed seen her through two marriages, the birth of her son, and the loss of other bairns.

She rushed him as he came off the last step. "Murdoch, what is going on with the lass and Lachlan?"

"Going on? With Mari?"

She nodded eagerly, her voice a hurried whisper. "Aye. Please tell me it did not escape your notice how he chews her up with his gaze when she's not looking."

Her old friend chuckled at this. "Nae, it has no'. Sometimes the lad dinna even wait until she's no' looking." His frown returned then. "But what of it, Diana? She's been kidnapped, bound for the trade that we finally get our hands on those reivers and some peace."

"Reivers, humpf," she said dismissively. "Lachlan can catch them anytime, or likely would have anyway. He needn't give up the lass simply because—"

"Whoa, Diana," Murdoch cautioned, lifting his hands, palms forward, intent it seemed on curtailing what he guessed might be coming. "That lass is betrothed to a Ramsay and we've got enough trouble from them without adding to it. Heard just this evening about all the poaching and thieving of livestock they've been getting up to. Anyhow, you canna steal a man's bride."

With great petulance, such as only Murdoch might ever be witness to, Diana cried, "But Murdoch, she's perfect for him."

His look told her so much before he spoke again. He shook his head slowly, his gray eyes keeping with her anxious gaze, while his lips firmed with some discomfort for what she was proposing and must be thinking.

"Jesu, Diana, the lad can shoot sparks from his eyes all he wants, maybe he'd even go further with Mari, but it would change nothing—you ken it as well as I. He'll no' ever wed, thinks himself a monster," he reminded her and was quick to add when she looked about to argue, "and you ken also he will always put the castle and the clan above anything else."

"Which is ridiculous," was her reply to this. "But Murdoch, what if she's the one to change his mind? You spend an inordinate amount of time with him, so much more than I—it's different, is it not? The way he looks at her."

Somewhat hesitatingly, Murdoch nodded. "Aye, it is at that. I swear the lass could swipe at him with his own sword and he'd no' move, no' give her any grief, still be sure she's safe and warm."

Diana's eyes lit up. "Oh, it's very different indeed then," she said, thrilled with this further insight.

It was a rare mother who ever met a woman perfect enough for her own son, she knew. Oh, and the lass was no such thing, not perfect at all. She was lowborn and obviously untutored in so many areas; she would likely never understand the societal system, would possibly speak to one and all as if the entire world were classless; she was perhaps *too* innocent, too naïve, to not ever cause Lachlan trouble; and Diana had a suspicion that she might well be one of those impetuous girls, who acted and reacted from the heart and not the mind. All in all, she was far from ideal. But then, that might just be what made her perfect for Lachlan.

Murdoch lifted and dropped his shoulders. "Make no difference in the long run, Diana. He'll turn her over to the Ramsays, hang her brother, and be a wretch for weeks, months maybe—and what would you be thinking that you or I might do to change that?" This, posed with a tone suggesting the answer could only be *nothing*.

"I haven't figured that out yet, but I promise you, Murdoch, I am not about to let her get away," Diana vowed, "*or* be sent away."

Chapter Ten

Mari woke the next morning and gave herself up to a lazy feline stretch. She took a quick inventory of her present circumstance: a blue dawn sky greeted her through the window; the bed and pillows beneath her were plump and cozy and there weren't four little bodies squeezed in here with her; the borrowed nightrail was of soft cotton and fit her fairly well; and she would see Lachlan today. She could have cried with joy for how pleasing each of these things were.

She reminded herself that it was only temporary, that this wasn't real life, not hers, that she was promised to Walter Ramsay and would be forced to kiss him, and not Lachlan Maitland, for the rest of her life.

Her good mood nearly flew out the window. She saved it only with the very promising notion that Lachlan Maitland might want to kiss her often while she *was* still here.

Some light noises reached her that she supposed others were rising as well. She climbed from the bed and dressed quickly in the same frock she'd worn last night, anxious to make good use of every minute she would be allowed to remain at Hawkmore. She tried to replicate the design Florie had made with her hair yesterday but found no success so that when she bounced down the steps a few minutes later, her loose hair swayed and danced about her back and shoulders.

The hall saw only a few people sitting about the lone trestle table still standing. She found Murdoch among them and approached him, not without some sense that she didn't yet know how she might go about here, what might be expected of her.

"Good morn, Murdoch," she greeted as she stood beside the table where he sat.

He turned, surprised to see her, she thought, if the lift of his thick brows was anything to go by. "And to ye, lass. But what are ye about, risen so early?"

She shrugged, thinking it unlikely that any would believe the captive Mari Sinclair was excited to be here. "I was hoping to find Mistress Maitland and be of service to her."

"And hoping to fill your gullet, if I ken ye," supposed Murdoch in good humor.

Mari did not demur. "Well, yes. That, too."

"Aye, then, ye sit yourself down here," he patted the bench next to him. "This here is Edane, he's the smithy but ye dinna wanna keep company with him," he said with a wink at her while Edane rolled his eyes. "And ye ken Donal, from all his chatter on the drive here."

Mari couldn't recall if she had ever heard the man speak and smiled at how amusing Murdoch always was. She slid onto the bench next to him.

"Aye, go on then, Donal," Murdoch said to the young man. "Lass wants to break her fast. Get on to the kitchen and make that happen."

"Oh, my, no! I can see to my own meal—" She began to rise again but Murdoch's hand, heavy on her shoulder sat her back down.

Donal was already up and away then.

"Let him go, lass. He's done naught but churn my ear with his yapping already and the sun's still groggy."

"So," Edane said, drawing Mari's attention across the table, "kidnapped, eh?"

"Um, yes," Mari said. And then because he only stared at her, rather grinning like a simpleton, Mari thought uncharitably, she added brightly, "My first time."

"Dinna encourage him, lass."

Utrid and Torquil entered the hall, joining them at the table, pleased to find Mari there.

"What will you get about today?" Utrid asked of her as he sat on the bench next to her.

With some excitement, Mari confessed, "I was hoping to be helpful to the chief's mother, if I could, but honestly, I'd like to explore the castle and keep." She turned to Murdoch on her other side. "Do you think that could be arranged? I understand I'd need an escort," she said, and then playfully imitated Murdoch's scratchy voice when she added, "*since I dinna ride so well and canna swim.*" The captain turned his head and grinned at her. Mari continued, "But I'd really love to see it all."

Murdoch seemed to consider this, his grin hanging on. "Aye, but ye take up with the mistress first. You'll have to earn it."

"I will," she was quick to agree, having no idea what he meant. "I promise."

Donal returned, followed by Florie and Robert, the former smiling a greeting at Mari, which warmed her just as much as these fine men accepting her presence at their breakfast. Florie set a trencher before Mari and another in front of Murdoch and returned to the kitchen, no doubt fetching more food for Utrid and Torquil. Robert set a pitcher of ale in the middle of the table and departed as well.

Mari stared greedily at the feast before her, the bread trencher filled with eggs and ham and fruit and cheese.

Torquil's chuckle lifted her gaze to him. "Calm down there, lass. You'll never fit it all inside ye anyhow."

"But is it really all for me?" She looked over at Murdoch's fare, which equaled hers. "It is! Oh, I wish I'd been kidnapped a long time ago."

She was halfway through her meal, thinking Utrid might be right—she couldn't possibly eat all this food—when Lachlan Maitland strode into the hall. He came from outside, suggesting he'd risen much earlier and was already about his day. At his side was a short bald man in a floor-length tunic of dark gray, his hands barely seen beyond the wide and long sleeves, holding several ledgers and parchments.

She straightened herself and wiped her mouth, hoping Lachlan noticed her.

He did, almost immediately, but his countenance as he neared only seemed to darken, his perpetual scowl expanding while he stared at her squeezed between Murdoch and Torquil.

He gave only a tip of his head as a general greeting to the table, not her specifically, and said to Murdoch, his eye given to his captain, "Let's get 'em out in the field before noon, and I want a full day's training. Set up the archers near Killin Hill and let the fletcher ken I want a thousand more before month's end. And I'll no' stand for warped arrows, not one."

"Aye," said Murdoch, his eating knife paused and hovering over his trencher.

And that was it. With one last glance at Mari, which she would have called blustery, he pivoted and left the hall, his companion following suit.

Mari hadn't been awake long enough to have angered him today, so she imagined his sour mood had something to do with the little bald man at his side, the one who'd taken his supper at the family table last night in near complete silence, so far as she could tell.

And when Florie returned and announced the mistress requested her presence in the kitchens, Mari tapped at Utrid's side to get him to scooch off the bench so she could slide out, eager to be made useful to the mistress and hoping Lachlan's mood improved before she saw him again.

DIANA MAITLAND WAS just as lovely today as she'd been yesterday. She was gowned in a long tunic of soft plum, this one showing a bit of wear and age, the long sleeves thinned a bit at the elbows. It was still very pretty, embroidered with several different colored threads along the neckline and hem. Her beautiful hair was completely covered with a gauzy linen wimple that Mari decided must be terribly uncomfortable in any rare heat or humid weather, seeing how fully it was wound around her neck.

"Good morn, Mistress," Mari greeted, sadly finding the lady to be in much the same mood as her son.

Diana turned those familiar hazel eyes to Mari and let out a frustrated sigh, her returned greeting rather curt that even the cook raised a brow, lifting her eye from the dough she was kneading on the long counter.

Mari bit her lip, which had Diana shaking off her sourness. "Apologies, Mari. It's been one calamity after another this morn."

The cook frowned at this, as if she'd not been aware of any mishaps thus far.

"I'd wanted to spend some time with you today, get to know you," Diana explained. "But I'll be knee deep in one issue after another, which would be terribly unfair to you."

"I can help," Mari said earnestly.

"No, my dear," Diana said with a quick shake of her head. "'Tis all dreary castle business and would bore you to tears. I thought we might spend time together tomorrow, but for today could you possibly find your own way? Mayhap seek out Lach and insist upon a tour or a nice ride to the village?"

Recalling his exact brusqueness of only minutes ago, Mari was hesitant, "Um...all right. But are you sure I can't—"

Diana lifted a hand, forestalling any further argument. She grinned ruefully at Mari. "Truly, it will be easier if I can attack each problem head-on and without any distractions."

"Of course," said Mari, seeing now that the cook was staring at her mistress with skinny eyes, confused, it seemed.

Mari excused herself and returned to the hall, dismayed to find Murdoch and the others gone from the table, replaced by several people she did not know.

Essentially having been given authorization to leave the keep and find Lachlan, Mari stepped outside.

The bailey was huge and bustling. She spied Edane in his smithy's shed across the way, busy hammering a glowing piece of metal. Two women stood at the well, hands on hips and chatting away while their filled buckets awaited them at their feet. Three lads ran by, screaming something about a monster chasing them. Mari smiled, thinking she recalled those boys from last eve in the hall.

And then she saw Lachlan. He was directly across from her, near the gate, which put him a good hundred or so feet away. He was on his haunches, his back to her that she recognized only his shiny crop of dark hair and those very broad shoulders. She walked toward him, seeing that he was addressing the steps that had been burned so badly in yesterday's yard fire.

"Good morning," she called even before she reached his side.

Lachlan stood as she reached him. Mari gave him a cheery smile, very appreciative of the sun's efforts, which colored his eyes more blue than hazel and glinted off his hair.

He glanced around, yet another frown evident, this one likely elicited by the fact that she was, for all intents and purposes, wandering around by herself.

"Your mother was too busy and refused any help from me," Mari explained, assuring him, "though I did try." Her smile grew and she told him, not bothering to hide her hopefulness, "She said I might find you and beg a tour or a ride to the village."

He sent a look over her head toward the keep, as if some confirmation of this might be forthcoming. He didn't look at her again, but turned back toward the stairs, where Mari saw there were two freshly cut boards waiting to replace the burnt planks.

"I've got this to finish."

"Can I help?"

His head turned on his shoulder, though not actually far enough that he looked at her. "Nae, lass. Take me no time at all."

"Then you'll be free?"

"Nae, then I'm off to the field for the training." He picked up one of the boards and a hammer that had leaned against them.

"Can I go with you? Just to watch?" She pictured him frowning, though she couldn't know as he kept his back to her. He did not answer immediately that Mari thought to fill the awkward silence between them. "You won't even know I'm there."

He shook his head. "Training is no place for a lass."

"Oh."

"They're no' allowed on the field." He squatted again, his back to her, and began to rip the burnt boards away from the staircase.

Disappointed, Mari lifted her skirts and meant to turn away, but he stopped, his forearms on his thighs. He looked over his shoulder again, barely, that conceivably he saw not much more than the hem of her kirtle.

"I've sent off word to Ramsay."

Oh.

Mari stared at the back of his head and the sparse profile he showed her, the scarred side of his face angled toward her.

It was a long time, or seemed that way, before she said, "I see."

And a moment later, when his shoulders relaxed with a heaved sigh and he stood and turned around, Mari was gone.

LEFT TO HER OWN DEVICES, Mari did as she pleased. If no one seemed very concerned that the prisoner was wandering about as if she were free, she would not argue and perchance have the freedom taken from her.

She returned to the keep, and explored the second floor, finding only more bedchambers and one locked room and then a lady's solar that the mistress likely used to entertain female visitors if this remote place saw any such thing. The rooms were tidy and clean, some better appointed than others, but truly held little interest for Mari.

She left the keep again and thought to explore beyond the walls. Utrid hollered down to her from the battlements when she passed through the open gate. Mari turned and lifted her hand against the sun, walking backwards away from the castle.

"Where you off to, lass?"

"Just exploring," she called back to him. "I was told I could if I stayed close." She smiled up at him and another unknown soldier, who stood next to Utrid and peered down at her as well. She felt no guilt at all for her fib.

Utrid nodded and gave her a wave and Mari turned and marched on.

All the land before her and the castle was a tall-grassed meadow dissected by a well-worn path. It stretched quite a distance, Mari recalling it had taken them many minutes upon racing horses to cross it. Beyond that, a very pretty line of birch trees sat on the horizon and behind them, at some higher elevation, purple, gray, and green mountains sat majestically, shrouded yet in a bit of fog.

Mari remembered that yesterday Torquil had said the village was to the west, so she set her course to the right of the castle, though she acknowledged to herself that west and east, north and south meant nothing to her. In this direction there stood another copse of trees, not plentiful enough to be called a forest, though it was a pleasant woodland, shaded and quiet within. She walked under tall pines and more skinny birch trees, noticing a trail of sorts underfoot. She followed this and very soon the quiet was overtaken by a rumbling noise Mari could not identify.

Walking faster now, her curiosity piqued, Mari followed the noise, getting closer to its source she thought, as the low rumbling became louder, filling all the woods with the hum of it. There was sunshine ahead, she saw, and ran toward it.

She came to the edge of the trees and gasped, catching herself before she might have tumbled down an embankment of rock and heather.

Mesmerized, Mari could only stare.

All thoughts of Lachlan Maitland, very few of which had been kind, fled from her mind.

The trees were all behind her now and before her, beyond the decline at her feet and beyond a great expanse of white sand, was the sea.

She was made thoughtless by the sight of it, could not form any coherent idea for several minutes. Dark blue water, topped occasionally by white-capped swells rushed in with a great savagery, smashing onto the shore in large curling waves. They rolled up high into the sand and barely had time to swim back to the sea before another crashed over it.

Mari closed her eyes and breathed in the scent. Salty air. She'd heard the phrase, and now knew its fascination. She stepped forward, felt the wind was wild here at the shore and couldn't for the life of her understand why no one had told her about this. Her hair whipped around her face, her skirts were pressed to her thighs and made to fly sharply out to her right.

She looked left and then right but did not see any better place to make her way down and closer to the magnificent water. Stepping forward, she discovered it was not terribly difficult at all to hop from one jutting rock to the next. She laughed out loud for her joy and for what the wicked wind continued to do to her hair. Her arms flailed about, trying to steady herself but it took no more than a minute to navigate the embankment and press her feet, for the first time ever, into sand.

She dashed forward only to be sent away by the furious waves, again and again. She twirled about and cried out with delight, catching sight of Hawkmore, further down the beautiful beach and set way back from the sea, atop a slight terraced berm.

A spot of gravel and stones, swept against a raised dune of sand and sea grass, caught her attention for all the pretty baubles captured within. Mari sank to her knees, the sand dry here, removed from the water, and studied each stone and shell and unidentified item, making a pile of her favorite finds.

She was quite happy to explore every nook and cranny of the beach, which stretched forever it seemed and was flanked by dunes and trees and the raised castle. At one point she lay down in the flat sand and spread her arms wide, staring up at the wispy clouds lazily drifting about the blue sky. She never dared to step into the water, having no idea of what it might do, but supposing its power to be great.

Mari gave no thought or had any sense of time, but understood she hadn't felt joy like this in, well, forever. She'd never been allowed such freedom, to idle away an entire day, and had never a destination such as this in which she might want to get lost.

She explored the beach and the dunes and the trees and watched gulls and other birds fly overhead, imagining they, too, loved the solitude and the liberty. Eventually her adventure brought her nearly in front of the castle itself. Shielding her eyes from the sun which hovered over Hawkmore, Mari looked at the wall, not elevated so much that she couldn't make out soldiers patrolling the battlements, but far enough away that she could not identify any faces.

She waved happily, scissoring both arms above her head in her excitement, wondering if anyone even noticed her presence down here.

They must have, she decided with a happy laugh, hearing a distant volume of shouts erupt from the castle. Maybe Utrid or Torquil might join her and frolic about the beach with her.

She waited and watched bodies moving almost frantically about the wall. It looked as if they were pointing at her. And then the noise quieted, and the soldiers disappeared that Mari thought they must not have noticed her after all. Shrugging, she continued her scavenging, having learned that the gravel beds and any piles of stones held many treasures.

She was on her haunches, bent over a very small pile of stones when a noise that was neither water nor wind penetrated her soft and happy humming. Mari rose and turned back toward Hawkmore, eyes widening when she spied two galloping horses charging her way.

They were upon her in seconds, Utrid and Torquil.

Mari blanched, thinking something awful must have happened, their faces filled with dread. Utrid extended his hand out to her, his features tight.

"C'mon, then, lass," he said, even as Mari had rather unconsciously put her hand into his. He hauled her up before him. "Chief's been looking everywhere for ye."

Mari grimaced and glanced at Torquil who rode beside them back up the shallow hill.

"Shite, lass," Torquil said, "he's in a rage."

Her stomach bottomed out, the look of sympathy Torquil had given her only adding to her sudden disquiet.

SHE STOOD IN THE HALL, glum and well-chastised, her head bowed, as both Lachlan and his mother took turns scolding her for going missing for so many hours.

"I had twenty men out searching for you!" Lachlan roared, throwing up his hands in disgust as he paced in front of her.

Diana Maitland was less demonstrative but no less angry, it seemed. "Did you give no thought that we might be worried about you? Did you not think to tell even one person where you were off to?"

"Half a day wasted that would have been better served by training, but we're out looking for you!"

"Going forward, Mari, I suggest you not leave the keep or yard."

"Nae, she'll no leave the keep ever again! Should've locked her up as soon as we arrived."

"But you never said—" she tried to defend.

Lachlan spun around and shouted, even as he put his face so close to hers, "I never said to go missing for five hours!"

"But I only wanted—"

"I told you no' to run, to stay close!"

Mari clamped her lips, beginning to see that any defense would not satisfy him. But as he continued to sputter and spew before her, her hackles did rise. When he turned on her once more, preparing to bark out yet more harsh scolding, Mari fisted her hands and yelled at him instead.

"Then *you* should have taken me to the village! Or you should have taken me with you to the training! I asked, didn't I? Nearly begged and you couldn't give me even half an ounce of your attention. You gave me no instruction at all." To her own ears, her voice sounded pitiful and weak, when contrasted against Lachlan's booming shouts. But she might have startled him by daring to challenge him, that he only stared, so she continued in an indignant voice, "You told me yesterday all I had to do was not run away. Well, I didn't. Here I am. Your precious pawn is safe. Your bargain with the Ramsays is not harmed. I'm still here, to be bartered away for a bunch of people I don't even know or like, and why? Because I was in the wrong place at the wrong time? Because my brother was so cowardly to leave me behind, hoping I might make for good sport and keep whoever was chasing him well occupied so he could make his escape?" Now that she'd gotten going, she couldn't seem to stop it. All the injustice of the last several days crashed into her, and she continued to shout. "Lachlan Maitland, I swear if I were a foot taller, I'd punch you right in the face. You're a bully. And you've been nothing but mean to me and I don't deserve it. I've done nothing to you. I'm sorry I am betrothed to a Ramsay! I'm sorry you think my brother is a criminal! I'm sorry you assume me guilty of only God knows what by my bare association to either of them! And I'm sorry my half-English blood sets you off so easily even as I find it so curious that it doesn't seem to bother you anytime you are kissing me!" She ended with a rafter-shaking flourish, the veins in her neck protruding and angry.

She seethed and shook with the violence of her outburst, realizing she'd lifted herself up onto her toes to rage at him. Angrily, she swiped at tears that fell while her lip and chin quivered.

The pair before her were aghast, eyes bulging and rigid with shock. Diana Maitland's mouth hung open as Mari was very sure it never had before.

Mari tried to unscramble her brain, tried to recall all that she might have just shouted with such vulgarity at the pair.

Sweet Jesus, what have I done?

She sent a pleading look to his mother. "I'm so sorry. I didn't mean—I wasn't talking about you when I said—" she stopped abruptly, certain there was no way she could hold back the tremendous sob that threatened her just now. Spinning around, Mari ran from the hall, her shame increasing tenfold when she noticed what she hadn't before, that Murdoch and Torquil and Utrid stood just inside the door. Their matching incredulous expressions confirmed that they had witnessed the entire outrageous debacle.

Chapter Eleven

Lachlan could not recall a time in his life he'd been rendered speechless. He stared at the spot where she'd stood and had raged so passionately at him. God's blood, he'd known she had spirit, but he'd not ever expected such anger. And he couldn't yet wrap his brain around what she'd revealed—not deliberately, was his guess—about her brother, and his leaving her.

My God.

"Lachlan," his mother's voice interrupted his wretched musings, "good heavens, is what she said true? Did her own brother leave her behind intentionally?"

Blowing out a huge sigh, Lachlan turned and faced his mother, and saw that Murdoch and the lads had moved further inside the hall. He shrugged, lifting his hand to Murdoch, asking him the same question. "Did he?" He couldn't think straight.

Murdoch pursed his lips thoughtfully before saying, "Bastard never did come back for her."

Florie entered the hall at that moment from the kitchens. With greater impatience than she'd ever displayed toward any of her servants, Diana waved her away with a stern, "Go on, now. Leave us."

When a flustered Florie had retreated, Utrid chimed in, regarding the debate. "Seemed strange, they took the time to take the horse from the silly wagon she'd been using but dinna remember the lass."

Torquil added, "But aye, they might've set loose the mare for their stop and then here we come and someone panics and hops on the nearest horse."

Murdoch sent Torquil a challenge, "Ye ever *hop on* the wrong horse, lad?"

"They never did return," Lachlan repeated. "Not even for his own sister."

Silence surrounded them while this sunk in.

Murdoch proposed, with some hopefulness, "Suppose it dinna help the poor thing that we *dinna* make sport with her?"

Diana rolled her eyes. "Oh, didn't you?" When no one dared respond, she charged, "How exactly would you categorize kidnapping then, Murdoch? I swear, if I ever meet a man with an entire brain in his head and any thought for a person who is not his own self, I'll drop to my feet and know the Lord has come. That poor girl is right—you've terrorized her as well. You're no better than her brother and any other with cruel or negligent intentions."

Begrudgingly, while Diana drew breath, Utrid admitted, "She did say that much to us."

Murdoch sent him a withering glare, for confessing this.

Diana jumped all over it. "Oh, dear Lord. You were schooled by the very victim of your crime and still didn't set it right! Why she smiles at any of you, how she can stand to look any of you in the eye without smacking you," she railed and sent a derisive look at her son, "and why on earth she would let you touch one hair on her head is beyond my ken." She marched over to her son and met his scowl with her own, wagging her finger at him as she said, "You'd better fix this, and fix it fast. And if you think for one moment that fixing it means sending her to the bluidy Ramsays, I'll tell you right now—"

"I've sent the message already."

"Bluidy hell, Lachlan!" His mother cursed, as she so rarely had cause to do.

"We need the peace!" He argued hotly.

Diana's chin trembled with the force of her anger, in the very same way Mari's had only minutes ago. She looked as if she wanted to rail yet more, had more charges to lay against him. Instead, she composed herself and asked, "Which do you suppose you might need more, Lach? The peace or the girl?"

LACHLAN STORMED OUT of the keep and made his way across the yard and up the steps he'd fixed just this morning. He took the stairs two at a time, up to the battlements, ignoring everyone he passed, walking all the way around to the eastern side. He set his palms upon the stone, between the embrasures, and snorted heavy breaths through his nose.

He stared out across the angry blue sea, its violent churning a fine match for his own disgruntlement.

He had no idea where to even begin, with all the thoughts spinning about in his head. The first thing he'd need to address, of course, would be Mari's complete and sudden disenchantment with him. Mayhap *disenchantment* was too mild. Mayhap *sudden* should have been expected. Whatever it was, he supposed even he was not so cold-hearted to not understand that at some point he needed to offer an apology.

Her anger was warranted. Likely the exact depth of *his*—his reaction to her disappearance —was not. He closed his eyes for a moment, cursed his sometimes reckless rages. He understood they hadn't any place near her. It was a defense, he saw, had known for some time now. He'd been stung, thinking she'd run again, that she'd left him. His response was unreasonable, certainly in light of how coolly he'd treated her this morn. Again, his fault. Only moments before he had found her in the hall so happily ensconced with his men, he had dictated to Oliver the missive that needed to be sent to the Ramsays. And when it had gone, when Oliver had done as he'd asked and had seen to the delivery, Lachlan had chewed himself raw on the inside, wishing it back, even as he knew he couldn't keep going off to Robert Bruce's side with so much unsettled and hostile between the Maitlands and the Ramsays.

She had to go to her betrothed. He had to show his good faith to the Ramsays. He didn't even care about her brother, the reiver, anymore. Or rather he hadn't as of this morning, hadn't even mentioned him in his demands, had asked only for a truce for her safe return.

But then, that was before he'd learned that her own flesh and blood had left her to whatever fate might have come her way when she'd been abandoned. Discarded, really.

And he was no better. He'd known how innocent she was and he'd kissed her anyway, had put those silly notions in her head that they might only kiss and nothing more, imagined himself capable of some formidable store of willpower that he could resist, time and again, the damnable and still growing desire for her.

That was what had made him so angry this morning. Not with her, though he'd surely taken it out on her. He'd been angry with the entire circumstance. And with whatever weakness lived inside him that he'd wrestled with first, actually giving those instructions to Oliver. As if a lass's bewitching smile and heart-pounding kiss should hold any weight against the peace between two Highland clans. As if he had naught to consider but his own self, and the way she made him feel when she was so foolish as to suggest he should indeed continue to kiss her.

Bluidy hell.

And then—he cursed soundlessly—he was ashamed of his weakness as he could truthfully say his only experience with jealousy in all his life had only ever been connected to meeting and knowing so many people who were not deformed and not so damnably unfit for public viewing. But wasn't that him, last night and again this morning, his jaw clenched so tightly as to bring pain, suffering a fool's madness as he'd watched her so happily embraced and entertained by so many men that were not him? Since she'd given the lads a what-for at the time of their very first kiss, each man had made an about-face, tripping over themselves to be of use to her and kind to her, making her laugh and including her—damn, introducing her to their family!

He should be thrilled that she'd been so well received, that she would not be harassed or harmed, but he couldn't quite get past the violent jealousy that came with each word, every smile, and any of her time she gave to another and not him.

Lachlan sighed and cursed himself a fool. Even he understood that any of this was no justification to treat her poorly in the morning.

MARI DETERMINED SHE would never leave these chambers again, too mortified to face anyone. She'd retreated here last night and had neither been called to or collected for supper, which she'd rather expected. Edie had delivered a tray, a hearty meal contained within, the girl's sorrowful glance suggesting either word had travelled or possibly some had eavesdropped on the disaster in the hall this afternoon.

So now today, Mari stared out the window, watching rain pour down from an angry black sky. She'd not even combed her hair, despite the fact that she'd spent so much of the wretched and wakeful night scratching at all the sand she'd brought back to these chambers and the bed.

When a knock sounded on the door late in the morning, Mari stiffened, unwilling to see another living soul just yet.

Diana Maitland poked her head around the door as she pushed it open.

Mari couldn't immediately ascertain if Lachlan's mother was angry yet or not, the woman's expression as inscrutable as her son's often was.

"Come along then, you can help with the mending."

Mari groaned inside but stood and followed her out the door and down the corridor.

Diana Maitland spoke very little to her initially, setting her up in one of the two chairs in her private sitting room and placing between them on the wooden floor a basket of garments that needed attention. She was given needles and threads as provisions and put to work.

Mari began with someone's chemise, presumably the mistress's as it was too long to fit any other female in the household that Mari had met.

When Mari could stand the silence no more she set her hands and the work into her lap and faced Diana across the small table that separated them.

"I really am very sorry for my outburst, Mistress," she began, knowing it would take many words and great explanations, and likely the woman to be in possession of a huge and forgiving heart, for Mari to be pardoned. "My conduct was grossly inappropriate, and I am deeply ashamed that I behaved in such a fashion."

Diana kept her head bent over her own needlework. Mari only knew she'd heard the words by the pinched look that came over her features.

"I just get so angry," Mari explained, wondering what else she might say to earn any forgiveness. "It's not fair."

With this, Diana slapped her needlework into her lap, and shared her pinched expression fully with Mari. "While we live, only breath is guaranteed, not one other thing."

"Yes, ma'am," Mari said, expecting another full scolding to come her way.

"Marianna," Diana said, and inhaled and exhaled sharply, "I am not so much angry with you as I am with...men. All of them."

Mari didn't move, having not expected the direction her words seemed to be taking.

Diana scratched with some annoyance at her wimple covered head. "You were wrong to behave so crassly, but I can see that much of it was warranted. I cannot extend such tolerance to either your brother or my own son. And Murdoch, he should know better."

"My brother?" Mari asked, confused.

The lady lifted a brow to Mari. "Did you or did you not admit that your own brother sacrificed you for his own selfish reasons?"

Mari lifted her fingers to cover her jaw dropping. "Did I say that?"

"Yes, you most certainly did. Among many other truly enlightening things."

Slumping in her chair, wishing for the floor to swallow her whole, Mari groaned. "I don't think I care to know what else I might have said."

"And we needn't discuss it all today, but it will be addressed, and soon."

Having given great thought to what statements and accusations she did recall of her tirade, Mari said now, "Mistress, I should tell you I spoke unfairly at times. Honestly, I dislike being treated as only an object—that people can kidnap you, take your freedom simply because it suits their purposes. They gave no thought to my wants or needs, or how unjust it was, and yet I must say that while I was frightened initially...and dreadfully, they did not once harm me or treat me poorly."

Diana challenged softly, having returned to her needlework that it seemed only a casual statement, "But you specifically said to Lach that he was a bully, that he'd been mean to you."

She had, she knew. "Ma'am, your son is a very angry person. I think my very English-ness sets him off. He appeared to enjoy, to some degree, making me afraid." She clarified hastily, "At first. Of late, he just seems to enjoy being angry."

Diana sighed. "He does have mountains of fury inside."

"I don't blame him."

Diana shook her head, even as she asked, "Can you defend him?"

"It's not unjustified, his anger...for what was done to him, but mayhap he should learn to reserve it for people deserving of his rage."

Diana seemed to chew on this a bit before she said, "He wasn't at all like that before.... He was arrogant and impetuous, completely unafraid—thought himself untouchable, immortal, as most lads do. But he was also kind and lighthearted. Oh, how he used to make me laugh."

Mari thought of Murdoch's perennial good humors and jests but could not imagine Lachlan behaving in such a manner. But then, she hadn't known him before.

"You said he should save his anger for those deserving of it," Diana recalled. "Did you mean your brother?"

Mari considered this, considered how to answer. "I'd told Lachlan I couldn't believe Harman could be the person he sought simply because he's not a very clever sort. Since then, I have to wonder how well I really do know him. I haven't seen him in many years. The fact that he would—did—leave me behind suggests he's not the same person I'd known all those years before."

Seeming satisfied with this, Diana change the subject. "And Walter Ramsay? Are you familiar with his character?

"Not at all, save what I recall from my childhood. He was spoiled and rotten and not very nice. For my own sanity, because I've been pledged to him, I keep hoping and trying to imagine that he has changed for the better."

"It's a rotten thing to be born a woman," Diana concluded, still harboring her own stiffness and anger. "Chattel is all we are, our lives governed by unfeeling men, with no thought for any soft thing such as happiness. Bartered and traded and sold for their own good, not ever for ours. But who's the stronger sex? Think men could bear up as we do? Taking on miserable husbands, birthing and burying your own children, holding their whole damn world together while they gallivant around, doing exactly as they please, answerable to none but their king, whoever he be this month or this year."

Mari's eyes widened with each bitter word spat from her mouth. Diana stopped jabbing the needle so angrily through the poor fabric of the hose in her hand and glanced up.

"Your husband was not like Lachlan, then? Not a good man?"

Diana burst out laughing, startling Mari, causing her to wonder if she might be a bit touched in the head. Through her laughter, she said, "Make up your mind, Marianna, is he good or is he not?"

Mari understood now, her statement of a moment ago contradicting what she'd accused him of yesterday. Rather sheepishly, she told his mother what the woman surely already knew.

"Of course he is. He's just so...pardon, ma'am, he's very maddening."

"Does this have anything to do with the kissing?"

Mari moaned with embarrassment, not having forgotten that she'd exposed this in all her righteous anger, but clearly wishing that his mother might have.

"I plead to you in earnest, can we please not talk about that?"

Diana's smile stayed, was soft. She finally answered Mari's question. "No, Lach's father was not a good man, and neither was my next husband." At Mari's stunned expression, Diana said, "I've buried two husbands, both happily." She finished this with a pert grin.

It was Mari's turn to laugh. "Oh, I hope we will talk about *this*."

Diana shrugged but said, "It's as you might imagine. First my father selling me for horses and sheep and a few hundred acres—that was to Lachlan's father. And then good King Edward and some groveling nobles of Scotland thought Hawkmore should make a favorable forward base for resupplying the English this far north and bade me marry Nigel Walie. He was a wretch but at least had the good grace to succumb to the sweating sickness before the English could advance their objective here. And no, I did not personally kill either one of them, despite my fervent desire to. But the burials were cause for great celebration."

She went on to explain that only Lachlan's coming of age, declaring himself and all the Maitlands for Scotland, and taking back his own castle from the few English garrisoned here, shortly after Walie had died, had saved them from the English designs.

And then Diana shocked her by asking outright, "Marianna, are you truly not bothered by the scars?"

Mari's brows crunched over her eyes, not in any consideration of the question, but that his mother had asked it. Forgetting herself, she asked heatedly, hardly believing it could be true, "Do they bother *you*?" Even as she asked it, she understood her perception of Diana Maitland hinged on how she responded.

There was only one answer that would satisfy Mari, only one that would confirm her good opinion of the woman.

"Of course not." Her tone was indignant. "Save that I wish he'd not have suffered such torment and horror."

That was the correct answer, thankfully. Mari had thought for a moment that she might have had to excuse herself from the woman.

She breathed easier, and answered, with a bit of a blush. "Honestly, Mistress, I'd thought fairly early on that it was probably a good thing he was scarred—like as not, I'd have made a bigger fool out of myself around him for all his beauty."

Diana grinned again, her eyes shining with pleasure for this response. "Very well," she said and stood up, placing the piece she'd been working on back in the basket. "That's enough of that. I really do not enjoy the mending. Let's play with finer things." She went to the corner of the room and opened a pretty carved cupboard, returning to Mari holding a stack of fabrics, silks and velvets and unbelievably soft cottons.

Mari sighed with pleasure, watching Diana sift through the pile to withdraw a gorgeous silk of soft blue. Diana handed it to Mari, who ran her hands lovingly over the beautiful thing.

"But where do you come by these?" Mari wondered, her tone reverent.

She was quite sure the glorious woman blushed. "I have an admirer. I do not see him very often as he is a MacBriar and resides down at Swordmair. But when he does visit, he brings the most fabulous fabrics—spoils me, really."

"I think I want an admirer," Mari decided, smoothing her hand over the luxurious silk.

Diana giggled like a woman of fewer years. "Oh, but my dear, you have."

Mari jerked her gaze to the woman.

The mistress shrugged, her grin intact, lifting her perfectly arched brows. "So let's talk about that kissing."

A great heave of a sigh was Mari's primary response. "I'd rather we did not."

The chief's mother considered her for a moment, hugging the remainder of the fabrics to her chest. "Very well. I will ask just one question."

This sounded reasonable, a fair compensation for not having to discuss the matter in detail.

When she nodded, Diana said with some practicality and a great deal of perception, "I will not insult you, Marianna, but I will say what has become obvious to me, that you are not very worldly. And while you are very lovely and surely had your admirers wherever home was, somehow I still get the sense that you may have never been kissed before."

Mari was positive her reddening cheeks answered before she opened her mouth. "That is true."

"So my question is," Diana continued, "did you mind when Lachlan kissed you or do you wish he had not?"

Mari needn't consider the question as the answer was so easy, but she did give some thought to how cleverly the woman had actually asked more than one question.

She decided she would simply deliver the truth, straight-faced and as succinctly as possible. "I don't mind it at all. Truth be known, it was me that convinced him that kissing was fine so long as that was all we did. I rather had to talk him into it." She didn't think it was necessary to add, *since I am betrothed to an-*

other. Undoubtedly, his mother needed no more examples that might confirm she was a complete ninny. She also thought it unwise to tell his mother exactly how much she enjoyed and craved Lachlan's kisses.

Diana's eyes glittered, her curving lips widening as Mari spoke. "Oh, but you've said so much just there."

"I have?"

"Yes. To start—"

A knock at the door interrupted any fabulous insight that might have followed.

Florie poked her head around the door. "Mistress, they're calling for ye in the village. Bernie's bairn is coming."

Diana lost all lightheartedness, adopted her lady of the manor posture and tone and advised she'd be along directly. When Florie left, Diana said to Mari, "You may *not* hide in your chambers at all. I won't have it. Go on then, find Murdoch or one of the lads, and keep yourself tied to them and out of trouble."

"Yes, ma'am."

Diana held up her finger, hinting at one more thing, and dipped her hand into the basket that contained all the sewing notions, including threads and yarns and ribbons. She pulled out a short length of wide blue ribbon and passed it over to Mari. "Fix your hair, Marianna."

Chapter Twelve

Hovering at the bottom of the stairs, only the wide wall separating her from the hall, Mari first tried to listen to the few people gathered there at this hour of the day. Before showing herself, she'd really like to know that Lachlan wasn't in the hall, not quite prepared to face him.

She recognized none of the low voices but then heard Murdoch's, coming closer as if he might be entering the hall from the yard.

Peeking around the stone, Mari saw that indeed he was, his back turned as he continued to address someone in the yard. She raced forward and was standing near when he turned around.

He gave an exaggerated start, pretending to be frightened, chuckling at her when she rolled her eyes.

And very kindly, he asked, "Ye getting by, lass?"

She nodded, truly warmed by his fatherly tone and concern. "I spent the morning with Mistress Diana but she was called away. She advised that I should find you or maybe Torquil or Utrid and keep close and not get myself in any more trouble."

His shaggy brows rose as he said, "It's a good plan, lass."

"Have you time for me? Or can I help you with something?"

The look he gave her was filled with sympathy.

"I'd really rather you didn't pity me, Murdoch. I caused the trouble, I'll get through it...eventually. But I am a hard worker. I can be helpful if someone would let me."

"Aye, lass, I dinna doubt it. I'm bound for the beach, there's fishing nets need some attention. Ye can help me with that."

Mari perked up. The beach and industry and Murdoch. It was perfect.

Murdoch had a few tools and items to fetch but rejoined her soon enough. They left the hall through the kitchens which put them in the rear yard and then used the same man-sized gate Mari had been driven through yesterday when she'd so ignobly been returned to the castle by Utrid and Torquil.

This decline toward the sea was not very steep at all, the raised tongue of land on which the castle sat being set back so far from the water and the beach.

Mari bounced happily behind Murdoch. The rain must have ceased some time ago that only the spots of the ground shaded by the taller dunes of swaying sea grass were still wet.

About halfway down the slope, Mari noticed what she had not yesterday, three wooden boats, tucked into a valley between two softly mounded dunes. They were all facing belly down, one leaned upon the next. They were not huge, but easily twice the length of the big captain. When he reached the last stacked boat, Murdoch flipped it over and wedged the centered keel into the sand and grass.

He then collected a big hemp heap that was clearly the net, from the ground where it had been stored under the boat. He tossed that into the bottom of the boat and climbed inside himself, sitting on a crosspiece of wood, pointing to the only other seat. "Aye, ye sit there, lass. We'll keep good company while we work."

Mari climbed inside herself, with less ease than Murdoch and his much longer legs had known, and perched herself on the second board, facing Murdoch. He set all the items he'd brought with him between them and then lifted the net and handed some of it off to Mari.

"Just run it all through your fingers," he instructed, "and find the tears and holes, and then we'll fix 'er up nice and tight."

She found her first tear and waited for Murdoch to do likewise. He then cut off pieces of the spare hemp lines he'd brought and showed her how to weave it into the net, replacing the tear or sometimes simply using the cut pieces to join two parts together.

"Now I'll be wondering, lass," Murdoch said when she'd been well instructed and they'd worked quietly for several minutes, "will we talk about yesterday or no'?"

It was a fair question, a polite question, one that did not surprise Mari. "I've already had one very awkward discussion with the mistress." She showed a wince to Murdoch, eliciting a chuckle. "But I owe you an apology—among others."

"Ye dinna owe me a thing, lass. Ye dinna say anything that weren't truth."

"But how I said it—"

He leaned forward, which stopped her speech, his elbows on his knees, and peered up at her. "I ken sometimes the volume is necessary that ye might be heard."

"Nevertheless, Murdoch, I bear you no ill will. You are and have been very kind to me. I truly mean that."

"No' too kind, I hope. Makes a man weak, ye ken."

"My uncle used to say it made one vulnerable."

"Nae, lass. That's no' kindness. It's all the feeble kin of kindness that make a man vulnerable."

Mari grinned and returned, "Spoken like a man. I assume that by *feeble kin*, you refer to such wasted sentiments as empathy, compassion, indeed *love*—"

"Aye, and soft-heartedness and hope, desire and jealousy—I can keep going."

Her head down that it seemed she spoke only to the net and the rope, Mari said, "Murdoch, you're not leaving too many things a person might feel and not be made vulnerable."

"Well now, you girls can feel all you want, but dinna be expecting a man to return the sentiments. Dangerous things to a man, 'specially a fighting one, those emotions are."

She lifted her gaze, but found that he was attending the rope, so she could not read if there was, or should be ascertained some thinly hidden message here.

But she thought of something else she'd wanted to say to Murdoch. "You gave a fine speech that first night, Murdoch. You're a wonderful storyteller. Is that trait a requirement to rise to the position of captain, that you spin a good yarn?"

He was bent and frowning over his work, his fingers surprisingly nimble upon the hemp. "Chief's job, of course. But you ken, Lach'll no' draw any undue attention to himself."

These words brought Mari's hands and fingers to a halt. *Oh.* And yet...that shouldn't have surprised her either, she supposed. He was very miserly with his words.

Her stillness had drawn Murdoch's attention. Gruffly, he said, "Aye, and there it is. That look right there is what'll get you in trouble."

Mari misunderstood and defended her expression instantly. "I wasn't feeling sorry for him."

Murdoch gave her a knowing look and said slowly, with great enunciation, "Feeble kin."

Mari gasped.

His gaze lifted over the top of her head. His hands still moved, even as he looked at something beyond her. "Erase that look now, 'ere he comes."

"Lachlan?" Mari stiffened, didn't dare turn around.

Murdoch met her nervous gaze. He knit his brows again and groused, "And lose that expression as well. He's no' planning on having you as supper."

Still, she braced herself, embarrassed still, knowing she must make amends, and not entirely sure he wouldn't yet holler more at her.

She saw his sword first, or the glint of the sun off it, as he came to stand at the side of the boat. She saw his hand then, his palm pressed over the hilt of his sword. She lifted her gaze, trying to keep her eyes from widening when she noticed he wore a sleeveless tunic under his breastplate—he must just be coming from the training field—and every one of his glorious muscles was highlighted by the adoring sun, gleaming off the sheen of perspiration about him.

The sun truly did revere him, shining so bright as to stroke everything with a soft and hazy brush, diminishing the severity of each crease and divot and line of his scars.

Mari rolled her lips inward in some effort to keep them from drooping with appreciation. 'Twas naught but a pair of bare arms, she scolded herself. And then she met his eyes, or would have, if he'd been looking at her. He was not, his gaze upon neither she nor Murdoch, but on the net between them.

Mari threw a look at Murdoch, who was staring with some expectancy at his chief, before he rolled his eyes when no words were immediately put forth.

"Can I have some time with the lass?" Lachlan finally said.

Mari tucked away the giggle that wanted to come at Murdoch's response, which showed him extending and wiggling all ten fingers with some drama, as if to say, *Yay! He speaks*! which was pretty close to what Mari had been thinking.

"Aye, and you're welcome to her," Murdoch said, rising and sending a wink down to Mari before stepping out of the boat.

She thought Lachlan might take Murdoch's spot and turned toward him with some question when he did not.

"Let's walk," he said instead, and extended his hand to her.

She hesitated only a moment, heartened by the fact that his mood appeared more somber than angry just now. She set her hand into his and climbed out of the boat, having to lift her skirts high to get her leg over the side wall, same as she had earlier.

He released her hand and walked ahead then, down toward the beach.

When they'd reached the level ground where only sand lived, they walked side by side along the shore, keeping many feet away from the highest rolling wave. It was not half as stormy as it had been yesterday, but Mari was still glad for the ribbon Diana had given to her. She'd tied the delicate silk around the bulk of her hair at her nape, which meant even today's light breeze did not throw any tangled tresses into her face.

When Lachlan didn't speak directly, Mari amused herself gathering the stray shell or stone she came upon, bending at the waist to pluck them quickly. In no time at all, she had nearly a handful of tiny treasures and wondered if he had any intention of making conversation with her. Or was it merely his intent to confound her more?

They'd walked very far from beneath the castle, almost to where Mari had first come upon the beach yesterday, when finally Lachlan stopped and faced her. Mari had just bent once more to fetch another beach bauble when she saw his boots unmoving and aimed at her. She snapped upward, giving him her attention.

"I'd meant to apologize for my behavior of yesterday," he said after a long and slow inhale.

Somehow, she imagined that any teasing query about whether he *meant to* or whether he would, might not be well received by today's very serious and enormously aloof Lachlan.

She did feel sorry for him, imagining it wasn't often he found himself in the position of having to tender any apology. But knowing she would submit to her own act of contrition before him—in all likelihood a more verbose one—she was not about to let him off so easy. She stared up at him, waiting for him to expound upon that very bleak and trite apology.

He pivoted, facing the water and the cloud speckled sky.

"I thought you had run," he said to the sea. "I was angry—" he stopped and shook his head. "Nae, I was...it wasn't anger. I thought you enjoyed—despite everything—Hawkmore and...the lads, and Murdoch, and no doubt my mother."

And there went her heart, breaking in two, for all that he said and all that he hadn't. She hushed Murdoch's voice in her head, *all the feeble kin*, and added what Lachlan had not. "And you, of course."

His head swiveled toward her, a question in his mesmerizing gaze. He seemed to hold his breath.

It was amazing to her that she was so often nervous and anxious in his presence, but now in this moment of such great vulnerability, she found her courage.

"Possibly you most of all," she said. However, the courage came not without its own unease yet attached that she rushed on, "But I didn't run, and I won't. And...I am grateful to you for your apology...and your honesty."

He nodded tightly, as if he still processed her words, might be thinking about how to reply.

Mari gave him no chance, beginning to regret her fantastic revelation. "I apologize as well, for more than merely the volume of my upset, but for the things I said to you. And I'm very sorry that I announced so much in front of an audience; that was inexcusable. I was hurt, if we're being honest, that you dismissed me so easily in the morning. Be that as it may, I really did lose all notion of time down here. I was so happy to have discovered this paradise, I just...well everything else fled my mind. Still, the crux of it is that it was wrong of me to have spoken so sourly. You—and your men—really have been very fair to me." Hoping to infuse some lightness, hoping to ease the drawn lines of his brow, she added jauntily, "As far as kidnappings go, this is by far my favorite."

He grinned, looked surprised to find himself doing so, and Mari's heart melted.

"You give so much to your apology, lass, speak so eloquently. It's got me thinking you've had quite a bit of practice with these things."

With these words, his teasing, something she absolutely knew he did but rarely, Mari was fairly certain she might be in love.

She was giddy and not quite sure the fluttering in both her chest and her belly would not be fatal, yet she wanted so badly for him to tease her more and look at her with that intensity he showed just before he kissed her.

He nodded, the conversation apparently concluded to his satisfaction, and tossed his gaze back up to the castle. She thought he might want to return, possibly had more pressing matters to contend with, but she said to him, "Stay with me."

He faced her, beautifully scarred, bitten by anger but genuinely good, hard and cold with kisses that made her want to know so much more with him. He was perfectly formed, tall and rock solid inside and out, and in possession of the most compelling hazel eyes just now, turned more blue than not, courtesy of the sea and sky, and Mari knew this was the image she wanted to take with her when she was gone. He wasn't frowning at her, daylight kissed his hair, his arms and face were shaped by the gods and colored by the sun, and she wanted so badly to beg him to not trade her back to Walter Ramsay.

She smiled, a bit ruefully. She would never dare. Bravery had its limits.

He surprised her yet more by not refusing her outright now. He tipped his head at her and asked, "Stay and do what?"

"Anything at all," she answered, hopeful, sensing consent in his tone. "Walk with me. Run. Swim. Talk." She held up her filled hand. "Collect sea treasures."

"Would you swim, lass?"

"Me? Heavens, no."

The corner of his mouth lifted at this and he began to unlace the front of his breastplate. "Aye but let me have a quick dunk to wash away the grime."

Lachlan removed his belt and sword, not laying it on the ground but stabbing the point of the unadorned scabbard into the sand. Then he lifted the loosened shield up and over his head and his tunic followed. Mari was conflicted by hoping he did not remove his breeches as well, while alternately wanting to suggest to him that she'd not be offended if he did.

He left his breeches untouched and spared a moment to remove his boots. He plopped them next to the other discarded pieces of clothing and walked toward the surf.

Mari stared, and happily so since his back was to her. She moved closer to the water as did he, wanting to be near, wanting to see it all clearly. She stopped just before the water might have gotten her shoes wet. And when the water reached to Lachlan's knees, he turned back toward her.

"Are you afraid of the water? That why you willna come in?"

She nodded, her eyes on his chest.

"It's calm today, the rains gone," he said, coaxingly.

She grimaced and shook her head, hugging her hands to her chest.

"I'm fine," she assured him, wishing he might resume his entry into the water. It was very difficult to ogle him if he were looking directly at her.

"I'd stay near, Mari," he promised. "I could teach you to swim, enough at least to lose the fear."

She knew he could. She didn't doubt this at all.

She wanted to, she really did. She wanted to be close to him. But—

Just as he waved his hand, beckoning her, daring her, she called out, "I can't strip down as you have."

This seemed to perplex him but only because the answer was so obvious to him. "You leave your underthings on. The lasses do it all the time."

"Oh." While it seemed so innocuous to him, Mari was both scandalized and intrigued. Then she remembered that she'd spent almost twenty-four hours with him while garbed in naught but a plaid.

She nodded then. "All right. Wait for me." An equal measure of excitement and dread built inside her.

She sat in the sand and set her beach finds into a neat pile at her side. Hardly believing what she was about to do, she put her hands under her skirts without revealing any skin and removed her garters and hose and shoes. A quick glance at Lachlan showed him scooping up water and splashing it onto his arms and face. Mari stood and turned her back to him to untie the gown at the back of her neck and lift it over her head. She breathed, her back to the sea and Lachlan, and didn't dare to look down and see what the sun might reveal through her linen kirtle. Lastly, she removed the ribbon from her hair and was thankful that when she bent to lay it on her discarded gown, her hair swung over her shoulders and covered most of her chest.

Bravely, she walked toward the water and promptly squeaked when it covered her toes. "It's cold!"

Lachlan laughed and that alone was worth…everything.

He strode toward her and reached for her hand, folding his strong fingers around hers. "It's the sea, lass, no' your nighttime bath. Course it's cold."

They walked until the water skimmed his knees once more but was higher on Mari's thighs.

"Now the smart thing is to dunk all at once," he told her. "You'll feel the cold less." He glanced back at her, being a step ahead of her. "Aye, and obviously you ken to hold your breath, aye? Good. I'll go first, then you come to me." He let go of her hand.

Mari nervously reached to grab him back to her but missed. He took a few more steps and pointed his arms up, his forefingers nearly touching each other as he dove forward, hands then head cleaving the water. He disappeared completely for several seconds, his head popping up many yards away.

Mari walked toward him until the water reached her hips.

"Hold your breath, push forward and kick your feet nice and smooth and aim straight out toward me."

Wanting so badly to please him, she tried. She started and stopped twice, and Lachlan was kind enough not to laugh. And then she copied his movements, or tried, but feared it was possibly the most graceless entry into water the world had ever known.

She slammed her eyes shut and dived head first, panicking as soon as she was completely submerged, flailing wildly instead of kicking smoothly, and taking water in through her nose. She came up sputtering and coughing, her hair covering all of her face, her feet scrambling to find the bottom.

She heard his chuckle and in the next instant he was at her side, helping her to stand and brushing the hair out of her face. "I forgot to tell you no' to breathe in through your nose."

When she stopped choking, she asked, "Anything else you forgot to tell me?" And then she screamed and jumped. "Something touched my leg!" She lurched toward him, pulling herself up against him with some instinct toward preservation, simultaneously lifting her feet away from the sea floor.

He grinned devilishly at her, his arm encircling her waist. "Aye, there's fish and crabs and mussels in the sea."

"Ew," she groaned but quickly calmed herself, swiping more of her hair off her face. She took a deep breath and gingerly lowered her feet again. "Very well. I'm here. Now what do I do?"

She had a feeling he found her vastly amusing, his handsome grin a rather permanent thing these last few minutes. She was aware of some feeble kin sweeping over her.

He pulled away from her, walking backwards, his hand drawing her further into the sea. Mari discovered that the deeper she went, the more difficult it was to step normally; she could only bounce her toes off the squishy sea floor to move herself forward. She was still leery of the water, climbing higher over her, but for Lachlan's fingers entwined with hers and how primly the water covered her scantily clad body.

"Swim," he said in answer to her question, letting go of her hand and floating off on his back, his arms spread wide, his face tipped up at the sun.

He turned, she didn't know how, that his face and front were under water, and then he disappeared again. Mari watched for him, standing in water deep enough to cover her chest, looking for disturbed water that would indicate his location.

Something touched her leg again and she screamed once more, kicking her feet. And she found Lachlan, who surfaced immediately in front of her, chuckling at his own little fun.

Mari smacked his shoulder and decided she might swim every day, against all her fears and ineptitude, just to see him smile.

"C'mon, I'll take you swimming," he said and turned his back to her. "Put your arms around my neck."

Hesitantly, she touched her hands to his sleek and broad shoulders, keeping a foot of distance between their wet bodies. Lachlan reached up to grab her wrists, pulling her arms further around him and joining her hands at the front of his neck, forcing her closer.

"Hang on," was all the warning he gave before smoothly gliding into the water, pushing off with his feet, heading deeper into the sea.

Mari hung on, essentially lying on his back, clinging to him. Her initial scare evaporated quickly, with Lachlan so sure and steady beneath her. He stretched his arms forward, pushing his hands through the water in front of him and sweeping them back until they were completely extended at his side. Then he sluiced his hands under the water, under his chest, to bring them back up in front of them and the motion was repeated. With his first kick, Mari had lifted her legs, letting them float along the surface as she could, while he swam them around the sea.

Occasionally, he ducked his head under water for the length of a complete stroke, but he did not once dunk Mari's.

Hanging on as firmly as she was, her face was immediately to his right, sitting on his shoulder. She said in his ear, "I like this swimming. It's fairly easy."

Actually, she liked it very much. It was outrageously indecent, with naught but her thin and wet kirtle between her breasts and his back. But he was warm and solid, and she was acutely, wonderfully aware of every movement of every inch of muscle and skin beneath her.

He responded initially to her quip by spewing forth water into the air before them, the stream arced like a sickle, which made Mari giggle, and next he told her, "Aye, but you've got to do the swimming on the way back in."

She knew he was teasing. "We're doomed, then, I'm sorry to say." She was slightly concerned though. He was not breathless, not exhausted, but his breathing certainly reflected the effort expended thus far. "You're going to run out of energy before we make it back." He was still swimming lazily away from the shore, his movements smooth and rhythmic.

She felt him shift beneath her. "Loosen your hands."

She relaxed her grip but did not release him. He turned and faced her, lowering his legs so that Mari's drifted beneath her as well, and they were upright in the water.

"Lachlan, there's no bottom," she said with some anxiety, her feet swaying but not touching anything but his shins. She pulled herself closer to him.

He'd been holding her at her hips with one hand, tightened his fingers to show her this. "I've got you."

Made a bit breathless by the depth of the water, she asked, "Are you touching the bottom?" but she knew he wasn't, could feel his legs moving back and forth against hers. His one arm moved constantly with his legs to keep them afloat.

With some lightness, incompatible with her mounting anxiety, he said, "Now stave off the panic for a wee bit more, lass, 'cause you ken I will no' let you sink, and look behind you."

She did, turning her head on her shoulder.

A slow smile came for the unexpected sight. Suddenly without any fear for how far they were, she took in the beauty of the shore, so different from this perspective. The castle was there, much further to the left, small and chunky upon the ledge. The beach itself looked tiny. And she noticed just now that the sound was different here. She could see the small waves rolling in but could barely hear them. Fascinated, she realized the only sound out here was the water lapping lightly against them.

She faced Lachlan, happily showing him her appreciation for both the amazing view and the way his dark lashes were clumped and spiked around his eyes. "This is incredible. Oh, but I'm very sorry that you'll not have a moment's peace until I'm gone now. I'll want to swim every day."

"And by swim, you mean lounge about my back while I slave beneath you," he supposed, his good humor uninterrupted by the hard exercise he'd just had.

"Absolutely," she said easily.

He turned and waited for her to latch on again. "You can soak in the view all the way back."

"I know. I'm so excited."

Chapter Thirteen

They returned to the shore at about the same pace that had taken them so far out, Lachlan's strength seemingly limitless, his arms and legs in perpetual motion.

Her concerns over her wet kirtle returned as soon as Lachlan put his feet onto the rippled sand under water and they walked back to shore. First, Mari had to lift the heavy fabric up out of the water, the wet linen so weighty that it hindered her every step. When that issue was resolved by coming up onto the shore, she looked down and was made aware of exactly how revealing the linen was now, that she saw the entire globe of her breasts and even the pink tipped nipples were completely visible. Reflexively, Mari pulled the gown away from her, thankful that Lachlan walked a half-pace in front of her. With the fabric plucked away from her skin, she assured herself that her modesty was preserved for the moment.

Lachlan ran his fingers through his hair, and shook his head several times, spraying water in all directions. He stopped where their piles of clothing sat and scooped up his tunic, using that to dry off his arms and chest. But he did not then don the long shirt but laid it out in the sand and sat down. He bent his knees and slung his forearms over them and stared out at the sea.

It occurred to her that he might have done this to afford her some privacy to make sense of her own condition and garments. He'd laid the tunic out and now sat several feet in front of her, closer to the water.

Of course, she could not don her gown just yet as her kirtle was still dripping but thought there might be a way to sit next to him and allow the sun and trifling breeze to dry her undergarments. She laid out her dry gown within a foot of where Lachlan was and sat down on the sun-warmed linen. She crossed her legs, her feet tucked in at the juncture of her thighs, and pulled the wet linen taut over her knees, which happily tented all the fabric away from her breasts and covered every inch of skin from the neck down, save for her hands.

She was cold now but hadn't any plan to complain about this and run the risk that he would want to leave the beach.

"Do you spend much time down here?" She asked. "You must have, to have mastered swimming as you have."

He turned his head on his shoulder, giving some consideration to her kirtle and how she'd arranged it, and said, "I was here all the time as a lad. All year long, couldn't be kept away by foul weather even."

"What is it like in the winter, though?"

His lip curved. "Like this, only colder."

"So enlightening."

The grin expanded, but he did add, "It's wilder in the winter as we tend to have more storms, but roaring waves that reach as far as the boats up there hold plenty of temptation to a lad."

"The boats are for fishing?"

"Aye."

"Who does that? Does Hawkmore have regular fishermen?"

"Mostly lads, too young for the sword. No' everyone can stomach the sea, though. On a rough day, those boats can be recklessly tossed about. Think how that river—a hundred times smaller than this sea—moved us atop the big black. Now picture that tiny boat caught in a fierce gale, or even a strong wind."

"Have you ever lost anyone to the sea?"

"Aye, happens more often than you'd think." His brow furrowed, while he thought on this. "I'm thinking last ten years, we've lost six or seven lads."

"But then why would anyone want to dare, simply for fish?"

"The winters can be long," he told her. "If we get a bad one, and if we've not been able to put up enough stores from the harvest, the food runs out. Fish never leave and we have to eat." However, he clarified, "But we've lost lads in the summer as well. Aye, the storms in summer come out of nowhere at times. You might leave the shore under clear blue skies and by the time you've reached good fishing waters, a storm is directly overhead."

"Are you ever party to the fishing?" Was this something she needed to worry about as well?

"No' for years now," he said. "I'd just reached fourteen summers when Da' was killed. Becoming chief meant I lost so much freedom, had to give a greater care to staying alive."

"Do you like being chief?"

He shrugged. "I figure I'm well suited to the commitment it requires."

Mari glanced sideways at him and asked cheekily, "Is this now, all these replies, more words than you've ever strung together in one sitting?"

His shoulders shook as he dropped his head between the arms hung over his knees. When he raised his head, he sent her a wry glance, not averse to her teasing. "Aye, like as no."

He stretched out his legs then and reclined onto his side facing her, supported by one elbow pressed into the sand. His free hand plucked idly at small stones half-buried around him.

"You think you'll miss your English kin?"

"No," she was quick to answer. "Truly, I haven't any idea how my uncle could possibly have been kin to my dear mother. She was day to his night. And my Aunt Beatrice was just absurd, and I never thought for one minute she wasn't taking advantage of me and my circumstance. The children, however—though they could be troublesome—I will miss. Maybe. No, I will. Well, some of them."

Lachlan grinned and tossed a stone toward the water. "How'd your mam find herself wed to a Scotsman?"

"She told me he found her, that he'd been down to Hallamshire and came upon her moving the sheep from the pen to the meadow. She said he was handsome and glib and within a month she was returning with him to Scotland, against her parents' wishes. She also told me, in one of her more miserable moments that she regretted it almost instantly, but she was so quickly with child—me—that she stuck it out."

"Was she bonny as well?"

Mari turned to him, pleased by the inference, but he was staring out to sea.

"Everything and everyone paled in comparison when anywhere near my mother. She was...she was just perfect."

He turned now toward her, a bit of a frown hovering. "Your brother must be fairly young then, if you were the firstborn."

Shaking her head, she admitted, "Harman is only my half-brother. Da' never told mam until they'd arrived in Newburgh that he'd been wed before, that he had two children. But the eldest, William, died young. I don't recall him at all."

They sat quietly for a moment, Mari lost in memories, Lachlan charting the flight of a loud gull overhead.

She didn't want to ruin this enormously pleasant interlude, this time with him, but she was curious about something he'd said yesterday. "It's probably too soon for you to have heard back from the Ramsays?"

His hand, the one that had continued to move, swirling a small stone to make paths and grooves in the sand, stilled. After a bare moment, he flung this stone aside.

"Aye, no word."

And now the silence was uneasy, hampered by this matter hanging between them, and Mari was sorry, after all, that she'd been the one to thrust it between them here and now.

But then Lachlan asked, "You in a hurry to leave, lass?" He scratched his jaw against his shoulder, facing her, and waited.

Mari leaned close and shooed a fly from his hair. "I hope it takes forever." This, given softly as she moved her gaze to the soft swells of the sea.

"You dinna want to marry Ramsay?"

He misunderstood. "I don't want to leave Hawkmore." *Or you.*

She couldn't explain it. She'd known him but days. He was, in effect, her enemy. He had threatened her and raged against her, had stolen her freedom, had kept her safe and had kissed her senseless. It made no sense, but she wanted to be near him, never far away. She bit her lip and stared straight ahead, until she felt his gaze so long and silent upon her that she looked over at him.

Lachlan rolled forward toward her and tugged on the ballooned front of her kirtle, pulling her toward him.

She went willingly, closing her eyes even before his lips touched hers.

This kiss in no way resembled any of his prior kisses, this one taking neither of them by surprise, this one being so soft and light. His lips barely grazed over hers, every motion slow and reverent. A different kind of fire built inside her for this version of his kiss, a want of more, a need to be closer. Mari leaned further down into him, intent on having more. She put her hands on either side of his face, two completely different textures felt beneath her palms, and opened her mouth against him. She gave him her tongue and received his, that now familiar giddy delight lighting a fire in her soul.

Lachlan breathed a throaty noise and rose up over her, molding his lips against her while pushing her backward until she lay upon the cool sand. Mari gasped with pleasure when he laid his body against her, wet and warm and hard. The kiss swiftly became hungry and their embrace more intimate. Lachlan set his hand onto the side of her face and slid it down over her jaw, his fingers splaying out over her neck and throat and moving lower still, sweeping down over the middle of her chest. Every fiber of her being reacted, nerves firing, heart thumping, belly fluttering, in some great anticipation. And then he moved his hand over one breast and molded his fingers around the whole of it. She neither froze nor pulled away but sighed against his mouth with her joy. His fingers moved, tracing over her nipple and her sigh became a whimper of desire. The nipple hardened immediately at the enticement of his fingers. Mari arched upward and Lachlan abandoned her lips to rain suckling kisses along the same path his hand had taken, down the exposed column of her neck and onto her chest until finally his mouth settled over the wet fabric of her chemise. He pulled at her nipple with first his mouth and then his teeth, and every reaction to this was centered between her legs. Heat and tingling and need stirred there, and Mari moaned for the new and dizzying thrill.

He moved his hand, grasped hold of the fabric at her shoulder and she wanted so badly to cry, *Yes*. She wanted it gone, wanted nothing between them.

He did not rip the silly thing away, but stopped completely, his breath sharp and hot against her chest.

"We've got to—we canna do this."

"Yes, we can," she insisted, her voice shaky and filled with desire.

Lachlan shook his head and sat up abruptly. The hand that had so lovingly caressed her breasts sat unmoving on her belly. He looked down at her, his eyes stormy, filled with his own longing. Mari's body was pudding. She tipped her head a bit on the pillow of sand and lifted her hand to caress his strong arm. She didn't know how to plead for more, thought only that he fought some inner battle and she needed to await the outcome.

He turned and faced the sea, sitting as he had earlier, his knees lifted and arms hung over them. And Mari understood that whatever fight had taken place inside him just now, she had not emerged as the victor.

"But can we stay?" She implored, then suggested, "We can talk more." She sat up.

Lachlan blew out a breath and pulled his boots between his legs. "Lass, at times it's the talking that...brings on the kissing."

She liked this statement, didn't know why, but it pleased her. But then, "And other times?"

He concentrated on putting one boot on and then the other, though he did admit, "Mostly, it's your mouth, those lips taunting me."

This, she understood. There hadn't been many moments in his company since that first kiss—even when he'd been yelling at her—that she hadn't given some attention to his mouth, hadn't recalled how it felt against hers, hadn't longed to know more.

When he'd finished lacing his boots, he only dropped onto his back and stared up at the sky. Mari sat very still, wondering what it was that too often ended their kissing.

"Is it because I'm half-English and...does it remind you of what they did to you?"

He sighed loudly. "It should be, I sometimes think."

Mari waited, hoping he would expound on all the parts of the question she didn't ask.

After a while, he said, "It's like I said, Mari. I've got no right to take something that is no' mine." He sat up again, his back to her. "No matter how badly I want it—you. Aye, you say we can kiss and no more, but Mari, I canna...I dinna think I can keep resisting." He chuckled. "And lass, you're no' much help."

She felt no shame for her desire for him.

When it seemed he would say no more, Mari sighed and pulled her shoes toward her, unrolling her hose to put them on. Since he'd just touched her and caressed her so intimately, had indeed so delightfully taken her breast and nipple into his mouth, she saw no reason to employ any great pains to shield her legs from his view. She was tying the garter of the first one around her thigh when he stood, and she felt his heated regard.

"*Jesu*, lass, but did you plan to entice me this way?" he said with a fair amount of irritation.

Mari lifted her attention to him, found his brilliantly fiery gaze on her hose-clad leg and the bare thigh above it. She was yet woefully untutored in all these matters, but she knew immediately that she very much enjoyed the hunger she read in his eyes. It didn't do anything for the awkwardness that came with his chastisement and she did quickly cover her legs, but she smiled as she reached for the second hose.

"I'm still going to want you to kiss me," she said, and then imitated his voice, "*I dinna think I can resist.*"

LACHLAN GRINNED AT her.

It was both a magnificent and a regrettable fact that there wasn't anything about her, not one damn thing, that he disliked. He donned his tunic and breastplate, tying the hard leather laces only loosely. He recovered his belt and sword and secured these around his waist, low on his hips. His wet braies and breeches had done little to dampen his desire for her, his erection only decreasing in the last minute or so. He had the rest of the day to figure out from where came the strength to stop what he'd started.

God, how long had it been since he'd held a woman like that? Touched a lass so wonderfully? How long had it been since he'd wanted to?

He'd been home a year from his captivity in England, bitter and angry, before he'd even begun to think about his physical needs. And his bitterness had only escalated when he'd discovered that the days of lasses falling so easily into his arms were gone, and that he, the lauded chief of all the Maitlands, would have to pay for it like a common beggar if he wanted a woman's company.

Until Mari.

Sometimes he thought he might wave his fingers before her and ask her how many he was holding up. More than once—he was loath to admit—he'd considered she must be practicing some form of self-preservation, appearing compliant and oblivious with some fear that he would visit serious harm onto her if she expressed disgust over his scarring.

He knew this wasn't true; she was neither blind nor feigning. She'd touched his face now more than once and had not recoiled or winced or startled. He contemplated what his mother had once said to him, when he'd insisted he would never marry, that no woman would have him. She'd given him a stern look, and had told him, "You're being ridiculous, of course. Your scars set you apart no more, no differently than a man with a limp or a crooked nose or a pocked face."

He'd scoffed at this at the time.

But now...he turned and waited while Mari finished lacing her shoes, the plain gown returned to her person, though he supposed it was uncomfortable now with her kirtle still wet beneath it. She must have sensed him watching, lifted her head to him. He eased his expression, lest she think he was imbued with impatience. She smiled magnificently in return.

Hope hadn't lived within him for so many years that he'd failed to recognize it immediately, forcing its head from whatever hole he'd buried it in. But he saw it for what it was now, every time she smiled at him or kissed him, touched him or reached for him.

Hope was a dangerous thing.

Shite, Mari was a dangerous thing.

He should never have kidnapped her, should never have...done anything with her.

"You're doing it again," she said, some hesitation in her tone, as she came to her feet.

Lachlan focused his gaze on Mari, dismissing the haze that had been his thoughts.

He needn't ask to what she referred, recalling her accusation after his last kiss.

"Because nothing has changed," he said.

"It could," she suggested in a very small voice. Absently, she brushed the sand from the back of her gown.

He watched her now with fresh eyes.

She was braver than he would ever be, he guessed, not avoiding hope for the fear of so much disappointment. She embraced it, even though she clearly understood disillusionment had an equal chance of success, as revealed by her tiny voice.

But he would not be the one who expanded her hope; he had enough guilt to contend with.

He made it about him that she might feel less disappointment. He ticked off items on his fingers. "I've already kidnapped you. I've nearly drowned you. I've taken liberties I shouldn't have. I canna keep adding to this."

To his amazement, her eyes darkened, and her brows crinkled.

"That sounds like a bunch of rubbish."

At his stupefied expression, she explained, "The kidnapping—while wrong, to me personally—was justified if it gets you the reivers and peace between clans. As *you* yourself explained. Also, I don't truly believe I was ever in danger at the river; I knew you wouldn't let me drown. And I'd, well, I did tell you that I enjoyed your kiss so naturally you were going to do it again." He remained speechless, his own frown incredulous at the defense she'd given, so that she taunted with a fantastic impishness, "Of course you could not withstand how charming I am, how very persuasive I can be."

For a moment, he could only stare. Then he laughed, slowly, just a harrumphed sound at first until it grew and he let it come, loud and unexpected. Not that it wasn't entirely true what she said, but he laughed for how spirited and bold she was to have uttered these words, to have included that haughty little shrug, to have shown him her dimples when she was done.

She wanted only peace between them, he understood, wanted no regrets or overthinking. Her time was limited, she desired that none of it be wasted. He was suddenly of the same mind, and to hell with how much more difficult it would make her departure then.

"You are, by far, the most infuriating and brazen and troublesome person I have ever kidnapped."

The dimples deepened in her cheeks. "Lachlan Maitland, I've suspected for quite some time now that I might be the *only* person you've ever kidnapped."

That was entirely true as well, actually. Plenty of warring Englishmen he'd taken as prisoners of war over the years, but he'd not ever once actually kidnapped a person, male or female. Possibly this was evident to any who might be watching, for the freedom she was allowed, for the things he wanted to do to her, with her.

They returned to the keep then, Lachlan pausing only a moment to upend the boat he'd found her and Murdoch inside earlier. A lifetime ago, it seemed.

"You'll want to change," he suggested when they stepped through the rear gate near the kitchens. He led her around to the front of the castle, that she might find her chambers quicker.

"Yes. It's very cold now." And then she made a moue of her face. "Oh, I left my treasures again down at the beach. That's twice now."

Assuming she meant the shells and debris she'd collected along the shore, he said, "I'll take you down tomorrow to fetch them, if the tide hasn't swallowed them back up." He hadn't the heart earlier to tell her that one piece she'd plucked from the sand, the one that had enthralled her most, was naught but a piece of an eel's backbone. He pushed open the door to the hall.

The grateful look she gave as she passed him was riddled with some beaming confidence that supposed if they were to visit the beach again, there likely would be more kissing.

He might have teased her about this, her mood infectious and his willing to be contaminated, but that his mother and Oliver were seated at the family table, going over accounts it appeared.

"Quit the grinning, lass," he whispered playfully at the back of her head, harkening back to the first time he'd kissed her.

But she was Mari, so naturally she turned and smiled even more at him for this happy recollection. And since both Oliver and his mother's gaze were somewhat intent upon them as they approached, it was unlikely either of them missed this.

Only yesterday, his mother had asked that most amazing question—which he needed more, Mari or the settlement with the Ramsays. He had yet to examine what she might have been insinuating—was it as simple as it was obvious, that his own mother thought he should pursue something with a lass pledged to another, to a Ramsay?

Mari stood before the table and bobbed a needless curtsy at his mother, who inclined her head in return and couldn't exactly manage to keep some pleasant surprise from her gaze, possibly in reaction to this complete change in circumstance, from when last she'd seen the pair together. For his part, Oliver only seemed to be getting his first good look at Mari, his head slowly moving up and down while he assessed her as she asked of Diana, "The birthing is done?"

"Not yet," Diana answered, "but Bernie was comfortable and in good hands, as the healer had finally been located and is now at her side. It will be many hours yet."

Mari nodded and informed the pair, possibly unnecessarily as so much of them was yet damp, "We've been down to the beach."

"So I see."

"Might I be excused then to change?" Mari asked.

Diana nodded. "Of course. And you'll be delighted to find that Edie and Florie had scrounged up some more garments for you to try. They're in your chambers."

Mari's lips formed a small *o* at this kindness. She expressed her gratitude to the mistress and excused herself, throwing one last smile over her shoulder at Lachlan as she walked away.

He watched her leave, happily so, enjoying the sway of her hips beneath the rope belt. He'd thought he'd only watched for a second, thought the couple at the table shouldn't have noticed, but turning back to them showed two brows, one of his mothers and one of Oliver's lifted in conjecture. He believed his mother was trying not to smile. He didn't know what to make of Oliver's interest.

Then the steward lifted his ledger from the table and set four wrinkly fingers onto a wax-sealed missive that had been hidden underneath and pushed it forward toward Lachlan.

"This came, but an hour ago."

Possibly, Hawkmore received two or three letters a month. Always, once a month, came a letter from Diana's sister on the Isle of Skye. Occasionally, he'd be given a furtive missive from other loyal Scotsmen, detailing plans or giving updates about the king's movements and expectations.

He would wager this was the first time any missive had arrived bearing the blood red wax of the Ramsays, the image of a boar's head set in the middle of the hardened drop of wax.

His mother's jaw dropped, possibly recognizing the stamp. "So soon?"

His mood darkening, Lachlan swiped angrily at the note and snapped the seal. He skimmed quickly over the words, his lip curling further with each sentence read.

"Lachlan?"

He looked up at his mother. "They'll sign a truce."

"For the return of Marianna?" his mother guessed.

Lachlan nodded. To Oliver, he asked, "You have a record of every infraction? Each crime against Hawkmore and the Maitlands perpetrated by the Ramsays?"

He tossed the missive back onto the table. Diana picked it up immediately and read it herself.

"Aye, lad," Oliver answered promptly, earnestly. "Has its own journal, pages and pages."

He thought for a moment then said to his steward, "I want it all listed, written into the truce settlement."

Oliver only showed surprise at the request and not any annoyance for how long it would take him to transfer the notes to the peace contract. "Of course, lad. Will need a few days. But don't wait for me, lad. Go on and schedule the appointment with Ramsay to sign the papers."

"Nae," Lachlan said, which raised his mother's gaze to him. "I want the bishop to sign off on it. And I want it recorded, beyond Aberdeen. Send it down to Glasgow to Bishop Wishart and get his approval."

His mother gasped. "Lachlan, you cannot circumvent Henry le Chen in Aberdeen."

"He'll get no sympathy there, mistress," Oliver explained.

Lachlan further told his mother, "Bishop le Chen will no' give any assistance to a supporter of Robert Bruce, being kin to Comyn and having sworn fealty to Edward. Shite, he'd been put in charge of the Aberdeen sheriffdom and heard many of our complaints against Ramsay. He did nothing, knowing my loyalties lie with Bruce and Scotland. He'll no' help us now."

Possibly, she'd latched on to Lachlan's other reason for wanting Wishart's consent and not the Aberdeen bishop's. "That will take weeks, Lach."

"So be it."

Chapter Fourteen

Mari felt like a princess. She'd not ever been one to give much thought or have desires for fine garments, but she was not so silly to have no appreciation for what had been delivered to her borrowed chambers. 'Twas only two gowns, but one was lovelier than the next, the first being a saffron yellow wool sleeveless tunic with a finely sewn hem decorated with a line of embroidered doves. The other was a muted red wool, sleeveless as well, with no decoration save the neat seams of creamy linen thread. Two kirtles had been left as well, both of linen with fitted long sleeves and one with a gathered ruffling at the neckline.

Mari opted to wear the red tunic over the ruffled-neck kirtle, the latter rising slightly above the scoop neckline of the former. She found on the bed where the pieces had been laid a belt of wooden beads. She marveled over this, running her hands over the smooth round beads, each one painted the same creamy white as the linen shift and having been drilled individually and strung together with a stout piece of yarn. She applied this to her waist, interlocking the beads at her middle as a knot. She ran her hands over the front of the gown and down the soft linen of the kirtle, smiling with her excitement.

Florie and Edie had left the combs they'd used on her hair previously and Mari made good use of these, though it took some time to work out today's tangles. She might have fussed longer with her hair but that she was so excited about the day thus far and her new outfit that she left it loose and swaying in waves down her back. She wouldn't let it fall over her shoulders as she was pleased to have her fancy neckline on display. She wanted to return to the hall, to see if Lachlan remained, or if people were already gathering for supper. She couldn't wait for Lachlan to see her in this darling ensemble.

When she reappeared in the hall, having only been gone an hour or so, people were indeed starting to file in. She bid good day to the always quiet Donal and then Florie as she passed, finding Murdoch and Utrid and Niel at one of the low tables. Neither Diana nor Lachlan were yet in attendance.

Mari skipped the last few feet toward the table and happily twirled before Murdoch and the others, lifting the skirt of the red wool for their inspection as she spun around.

"Look what I have. Isn't it fabulous?"

"Verra fine, lass," said Utrid agreeably.

Niel added quietly, with some small appreciation, "The red is nice."

Murdoch was Murdoch and said, "Aye now, ye needn't another swooning over ye. And stop with the spinning, you're turning my belly and I haven't even loaded it yet."

Mari stuck her tongue out at him. "You're just jealous that you haven't a pretty new gown to wear."

He chuckled now, discarding the pretense of annoyance to say, "Aye, that must be it."

She took a deep breath and said to Utrid, "Might I beg some of your time?"

Murdoch, surely understanding what she was about, said with some crustiness, "I told ye, lass. You dinna need to—"

"I do, Murdoch. For *me*."

This raised Utrid's level of interest. Mari waved him near and pulled him even further from the table when he'd stood and come to her side.

When they were far enough away to not be overheard, which put them near the wall several feet away from the main door, Mari said promptly, "Utrid I am sorry for my behavior yesterday. It was impolite and uncalled for and I regret it deeply. I wanted you to know that I do know that you have been very kind to me, more than was necessary under the circumstances and that I actually consider you my friend."

He appeared not to care.

Scowling, Mari turned to see what had captured his attention, that he was not looking at her, but darting glances over her left shoulder.

Ah, a lass. And a pretty one at that. A girl stood talking to Florie, the resemblance to the sweet servant uncanny enough that Mari supposed they must be sisters. The one who'd caught Utrid's eye was of average height with bright blonde hair and an incredibly ample bosom, which widened Mari's eye for a moment.

For his inattention and for her own fun, Mari stepped to her left, hindering his sight line and his very rapt perusal of the girl, whom Mari had never before noticed about the keep.

This brought Utrid's attention to Mari finally.

"I thank you for accepting my apology and how kind of you to do so with such considerate mercy."

He had the grace to blush, and before he caught himself, asked, "Apologize for what?" possibly not realizing that this confirmed he had not heeded one word she said.

Mari laughed and waved it off. She moved right again so he could ogle once more the bonny lass. "What's her name?"

He answered absently, "'Tis Elesbeth."

"Florie's sister?"

"Aye."

"And you like her?"

He tipped his head, his gaze locked on the unsuspecting girl. "Aye, verra much."

"Then why are you standing here talking to me?"

This removed his attention from Elesbeth finally. He faced Mari, giving her a scowl for what was apparent to him but not to Mari. "I canna talk to her."

Mari giggled at this foolishness. "Why ever not?"

"What would I say?"

Shrugging, Mari offered, "Ask her how her day has been? Tell her she's bonny. Invite her to walk with you on the beach. I don't know. Good grief, Utrid. How long have you been watching from afar, too anxious to approach her?"

He shrugged and blew out a breath. "I dinna ken. Forever, I guess." His gaze jerked sharply to Mari. "You could talk to her for me, Mar," he said quickly.

She was not opposed at all to another shortened version of her name...but, "Me?" Mari jabbed her finger at her chest. "How would that help you?"

Embracing this fresh idea, Utrid straightened and said to her, "You could. Maybe get a notion what she thinks. Maybe, I dinna ken, tell some tales of me, make me sound good."

"Utrid! That is—dear Lord, I will not do that. You needn't have any tales invented for a person to see how good you are."

He dismissed this, correcting his idea, "Make me sound brave and fierce."

"I will do no such thing."

His face fell and Mari felt poorly. She decided, "Fine, I will introduce myself to her and mayhap learn some things about her that might be useful to you—things she likes and stuff like that so you have some idea of what to talk about with her. But I won't make up tales to build you up in her eyes. You're perfect just the way you are and if you talk to her and she doesn't realize that, then you needn't give her any notice."

Pleased with her agreement, even though it wasn't all that he hoped, he told her, "She watches us on the training field almost every day. I dinna ken why, or what she thinks to see that brings her out every day, but she hides by the big yew true north of the field. She ken the chief would no' have women near the field. You could find her there tomorrow." This last, given with a fair amount of hopeful expectation.

Mari nodded, actually pleased to be of service to him.

It was decided that Utrid would make an excuse to return to the keep after the noon meal, since Elesbeth always came to watch in the early afternoon.

"I'll ride ye back down, and drop you near to where she hides, and get on back to training then."

Mari agreed and they returned to the table where Murdoch and Niel were sat. Torquil and Donal had joined them. She only stood at the end of the table and listened to their usual ribbing on each other.

"Murdoch," implored Torquil, "tell the wee lad he'll no' ever be able to best me on the field."

He must be speaking of Niel, since he was the only man who scoffed at this declaration. Torquil listed his accomplishments. "I ride better and run faster. I'm undefeated in hand-to-hand and no one has ever managed the quintain so well as I. Niel, on the other hand, sometimes requires help lifting his own sword."

"You're speaking out your arse—" Niel began to defend.

Murdoch groused about this. "Aw, c'mon now, the lass is standing right here, Niel! Are ye blind then as well as daft?"

"Pardon, lass," Niel said but went right on arguing with Torquil, though Mari didn't know why. Even she understood that Torquil was only trying to goad him.

Mari completely stopped listening when Lachlan entered the room.

Her heart sank. Something must have happened, something awful, from the time she left him with the steward and his mother, until now. His countenance was dark again and though he was yet halfway across the room, she easily recognized that all too familiar tightness about his beautiful face that suggested he was gritting his teeth.

Oh, bother.

He greeted the people he passed with naught but a nod of his head, his gaze having yet to find her. And when it did, there was no lightening of his features.

He was still in glorious form, she allowed, unabashedly raking her eyes over him. He'd changed again, fresh breeches and linen tunic and his plaid was once more returned to his shoulder and around his lean waist. Mari made a face, dismayed that they'd shared that magnificent interlude earlier—which she imagined was as close to bliss as she might ever come—but that she had not touched him enough. She'd been too engrossed in what he'd been doing to her.

This, to her, seemed a horrific tragedy.

As he strode toward her, she imagined it would have been impossible for him to have missed how hungrily she stared at him. He didn't frown though, which she thought a great step forward, so much so that when he stopped next to her at the table, and his gaze was so rapt upon her as if he, too, might be recalling what they'd shared this afternoon, she stood up on her toes and whispered to him, for his ears alone, what she had just been thinking. "I wish I had touched you more today."

She shocked him, she decided fairly quickly. She lowered herself off her toes and waited for him to make of it what he might. She rolled her lips inward, seeing disbelief and then some finer reception to her statement flicker in his eyes, dark hazel under the golden haze of the chandeliers.

When he spoke, the surprise was still evident, though it was painted with pleasure, "You ken there's a better time and place for that revelation." His voice was deep and low, nearly intimate, and roused the butterflies to dance in her belly.

"I do," she admitted freely, her cheeks heating rapidly. "But I didn't want to forget."

"I'm no' about to let you forget, lass."

"Oh, thank you."

And there it was. Just that easy. His mood, whatever had soured him, was gone. Mari smiled cheerfully.

"Feeble kin," she heard muttered at her side.

Mari gasped and turned to Murdoch, closest to her. They'd captured the very rapt attention of every man at the table, she noticed, maybe others in the hall as well, but Mari exposed her mock censure to only Murdoch. "Hush up. And leave off about all those relatives. I happen to enjoy their company."

This elicited a monstrous shout of laughter from Murdoch. He laughed so hard his eyes watered. He put his elbows on the table and his head in his hands, trying to control his mirth.

Mari sensed a general quieting of the hall, while so many persons glanced over at this table, trying to figure out what had Murdoch in such a happy uproar. She looked around and settled her gaze at Lachlan, who was still watching her intently. Shrugging, as if she didn't know what to make of it either, she told him she would hie to the kitchens, where likely his mother was, and see if she might be of some help.

THE NEXT DAY, WHILE she waited for Utrid to come for her, Mari leaned against the wall of the keep, her hands pressed behind her, flat against the warm stone. She'd taken note of the slow bustle about the bailey when she'd first come out, but just now, she was delighted to close her eyes and lift her face to the sun, thinking about last night.

She had to suppose it was just another ordinary supper at Hawkmore, this one seeing fewer people than the first one she attended. But Mari had loved every minute of it. The food was fine and the company excellent. Lachlan had been, while obviously not demonstrative, very cordial during the meal. At one point, he'd even beckoned with his fingers—across his mother between them—for her plate, saying that she should try Cook's pork and almond milk pie. He'd filled her wooden trencher and watched her sample the fare, smiling at her when she'd nodded with the expected enthusiasm.

Mari hadn't missed the look Diana had given her. She still didn't know if she'd interpreted it correctly, but it certainly had appeared as if she were satisfied.

And when dinner was done and his mother had excused herself to speak with Oliver, Mari had turned sideways and leaned across Diana's empty chair, her own tipping, that she might talk with Lachlan.

She'd told him first that she was going to hold him to his pledge to return her to the beach to collect the treasures she'd left behind.

He'd nodded and told her that red was a good color on her. Which was silly, that she'd needed to be reminded by him of her new gown. She'd been so excited for him to see it, but all thoughts save one had fled her mind when she'd first spied him.

"I have an assignation with Utrid tomorrow," she'd told him next, swaying slowly back and forth on her tipped chair.

He'd frowned at this, of course, until Mari had clarified, "It's nothing untoward. I cannot tell you what it is yet, but I will be leaving the keep for a bit. I will be with Utrid and Florie's sister, Elesbeth." And, as explanation for her explanation, she'd said, "I only tell you so that you don't send out a search party should you find me not within the keep."

"That's verra cryptic, lass," he'd said, the furrowed brow lingering.

"And you may not harass Utrid about it, it would only embarrass him. Likely, I'll be able to tell you afterward."

"But you'll no' get up to no good," he'd said, as instruction and not a question.

"Sir, I'm not sure why or how you could possibly imagine that I might be the type to *get up to no good*."

"Then you're wanting that I start listing the examples?"

Aside from his kiss, and being in his arms, and knowing his touch, she'd never adored anything more than the smile that hovered in his warm gaze at that moment.

The clippety-clop of a horse's hooves, sounding over the planks of the laid-down gate, interrupted her delightful musings. She opened her eyes to find Utrid had come for her.

"Ye sure ye dinna mind, lass?"

"I'm sure," she promised.

As they rode out through the gate and off toward the field, Utrid ticked off a list of dos and don'ts.

"Now, dinna be too obvious. But dinna forget what you're about. And whatever you do, dinna say that I asked you to talk to her. Act natural, pretend you're out to make a friend. Maybe no' too friendly, that might raise suspicions."

Feigning complete innocence, she said, "I'm going to march straight up to her and ask her point blank: do you or do you not have any interest in Utrid? He wants to know."

His reaction to this was immediate and severe. "Aw, Jesu, lass. That's no' how you go about it. Aye, but this was a bad idea."

"Utrid, I was jesting. Only jesting. Please have some faith in me, I will not betray your interest."

He settled then— "Aye. All right. Aye." —though obviously, was still a worried wreck.

When the tall yew he'd mentioned came into view, still beyond some straggly pines and birch trees, Utrid reined in.

Mari slid from the saddle, her hand in Utrid's as he let her down.

She told him once again, "Please don't worry. Really, the worst that can happen is that I actually do make a new friend, though it would be all for naught as I shall be gone soon, I think."

Utrid nodded jerkily, his nerves still on edge apparently.

Mari turned and began walking toward the giant yew, waving over her shoulder, sending him off.

Elesbeth was indeed where Utrid had supposed, leaning against the thick trunk of the yew, with other tall brush and greenery hiding her position from the field before her.

Debating her approach, Mari walked closer. When she was but a dozen feet behind the girl, she said, intimating some surprise, "Oh, maybe I'm not the only one who likes to watch the training."

Elesbeth startled, swirling around, her hand at her chest.

"Sorry. I didn't mean to scare you."

Elesbeth shook it off. "Nae, ye dinna." Plenty of hesitation in her voice.

"I snuck out," Mari lied and did know some guilt for starting a conversation with a seemingly kind stranger this way. "Hopefully, no one will notice I've gone."

"You're the one they kidnapped."

"Aye," Mari admitted as she crept closer to the lass, as if she wanted the cover the tree and brush would provide. She introduced herself. "Mari."

"Elesbeth."

"You must be Florie's sister," Mari said. "You look just like her."

The lass smiled and nodded. Elesbeth's smile was gorgeous, even with the wide space between her top center teeth. It rounded her cheeks and brightened her eyes and Mari decided she might be, actually, sweet enough for Utrid.

Curious, Elesbeth asked, "You...come out here to spy?"

With a conspirator's grin, Mari acknowledged, "I think Lachlan Maitland is very handsome." No hardship here, delivering this truth.

Elesbeth's pale brows rose into her forehead "The chief? But he kidnapped you."

Mari shrugged innocently.

"But he's...dinna he frighten you?"

Mari was all set at that moment to dislike her straight away. If she made any mention of his scars, she vowed she would turn and walk away and tell Utrid she would not ever allow him to take up with such a mean-spirited arse.

"He's so angry all the time," Elesbeth said when Mari hadn't answered her.

Oh, well, that made sense. He was—until yesterday—mostly a very angry person.

"But I still think he's very handsome," she confessed, pretending to peek through the greenery now.

Elesbeth grimaced but allowed, "He might be, if he'd ever stop scowling."

Mari remembered she wasn't here to debate Lachlan's beauty or even his permanent scowls. "But who are you here to watch? Anyone caught your eye?"

A blush instantly stained Elesbeth's cheek.

"Him," she said and pointed.

Mari looked out beyond the shaggy rowan bush but didn't know why she bothered. *Him* was a little vague, as there were forty *hims* grouped together on the field while Murdoch paced in front of the line of soldiers, giving some instruction.

The training field, she learned just now, was a vast meadow of light brown grass, surrounded on three side by a thick woodland. Mayhap the tall grass would have been greener if there had been more rain of late. The soldiers were all unmounted, the large group of horses tethered on one side of the field. The men stood attentively in front of Murdoch while he made several jabbing motions with his foot long-dagger. Mari found Lachlan quick enough, well removed from the large group, in discussion with a lad she did not recognize, his hand upon the boy's shoulder as he spoke to him.

"Does he have a name?" She asked of Elesbeth.

"Utrid."

Oh, thank God.

Elesbeth turned to Mari, each of them hovering at one side of the giant yew. "But didn't I see you talking to him yesterday in the hall?"

"You did. I had an apology to tender for my poor behavior."

The girl turned a quick frown on Mari. "You were mean to Utrid?"

Mari smiled, possibly having all the answers she needed for Utrid. She could tell him, with sound assurance, that he was right to favor Elesbeth with his attention.

"I was...moody and expressing some frustration, which poor Utrid sorrowfully had to witness," Recalling her objective, she added, "Of course he was wonderful, his forgiveness instant. He's such an amiable lad."

Elesbeth turned sharply to Mari. "He's a man now, no more a lad," she asserted.

"Quite so. In fact when I was first...captured, it was Utrid who chased me down."

This drew the lass's fervent interest.

Mari continued, "He was neither mean nor even heavy-handed, but you can imagine how terrified I was, he being so...burly," she said hoping that was the right word to make Utrid sound strong and brave. No, Elesbeth's expression only showed confusion. Mari tried again. "He was very powerful." Yes, that was it; Elesbeth looked very pleased, seemed not to mind that Mari might have been terrorized by Utrid running her down like a hound to a fox.

Pleased by this news, Elesbeth said, "I ken he must be brave and fierce."

"Aye. It'll be a lucky lass who ever claims his heart, I'd wager."

Elesbeth nodded, digesting this with a slow and contemplative nod.

They returned to their positions, hugging each side of the tree, spying on the training, Mari considering her work here done.

And then Elesbeth screamed. Shrieked, really, and jumped away from the tree.

"Elesbeth!" Mari cried, turning just in time to see the girl stumbling and falling to the ground while a long and leathery snake slithered away from the brush near the tree.

Mari rushed to her. "Did it bite you?" She asked, going to her knees beside Elesbeth.

Shaking her head, blowing out a relieved breath, likely because the creepy creature had slid away, Elesbeth said, "Startled me, that's all. Och, I hate snakes."

THE DEPTHS OF HER SOUL

Mari helped her to her feet, just in time to hear the unmistakable sound of dozens of charging horses.

"Oh, bother."

Elesbeth's eyes widened, realizing what her scream had brought to them.

Quickly, Mari said, "Let me handle this."

"But they'll...they'll kill you."

Sweet St. Andrew. "Of course they will not. Let me be the one to speak," she instructed harshly, not wanting Elesbeth to get into trouble. With Elesbeth's frantic nod, Mari threaded her arm through her new friend's and turned to face the coming horde.

They came around the tree, on either side, reining in sharply, likely not having expected to find anyone just here, behind the yew.

Mari spotted Lachlan immediately and focused her gaze on him. His initial surprise at finding her here was tempered by some twisting of his face that both recalled the advance notice she'd given him last night and showed a decidedly long-suffering irritation, implying a query of, *What have you done now*?

Mari was quick to explain, and led with, "Before you start shouting, let me just say that I wasn't aware that you prohibit females to watch the training." This lie only served to darken his glower. Mari spared a glance at Murdoch, immediately to Lachlan's left, and made note of his lop-sided grin, as he showed not one ounce of shock to find her somehow connected to the scream and the disruption. Utrid was next to Murdoch, his eyes wide, possibly waiting for her to reveal his part in this present misfortune. Mari found Lachlan's angry gaze once more and said, "Elesbeth was kind enough to instruct me proper and was just now insisting she should see me back to the keep."

Murdoch could barely keep the chortle from his question. "And ye shrieked as if the devil pinched your bottom because you dinna like being told what to do, eh, lass?"

Raising her chin, she levelled a good glare at him and explained, "It *was* the devil, in the form of a snake, which wrought the scream." Weakly, she added, "It's gone now."

Lachlan hadn't said a word, just sat there leaning over the pommel where his hands were set. By now, of course, she was all too familiar with the ticking cord in his neck and what it meant.

With a bit more repentance, she said to Lachlan, "I am very sorry for having disrupted your training. It will not happen again."

He nodded, extremely displeased, she decided. But he only said, "Nae, it willna. Go on then, get back to the keep."

"Yes, sir," she conceded hastily, hardly able to believe she'd escaped so easily. She tugged at Elesbeth's arm, catching sight of the girls' stunned expression, and turned her around to leave.

"Oh, dear," Elesbeth muttered as they scurried away. "Oh, Mari."

She seemed to have no other thoughts or words to give but these, the *oh, dear* repeated several times as they trekked back to the keep, until Mari assured her that if she were going to know more trouble for that small calamity, the chief would have given it to her already.

At least, she hoped this was true.

Chapter Fifteen

Walter Ramsay sat in the chair next to the bed. His ailing father slept now, that Walter didn't bother to hide his contempt as he regarded him. Would that the old bastard might die already. How breath still managed to move in and out of him, Walter would never know, only wondered if mayhap the devil was afraid to come collect him.

A cough roused the man, though he was too weak to sit up and address it sufficiently, that it sounded as if he might choke right there in the bed. Walter didn't move, just sat in the chair, his elbows on the carved arms, and watched his miserable father fight for the upper hand against breath that didn't want to come. He won—he always did—but slumped back onto the blood and mucus stained pillow, having only passed one snarling glance over his son before closing his eyes again.

Walter didn't even move when ol' Fowler came into the room. He sat with fingers steepled under his chin while the woman tidied around the room but did little for the patient just now, save for laying her hand briefly against his forehead. It was generally understood that Fowler was a woman, but Walter had yet to see evidence of this. She stood a head taller than an average man, had been a part of Gershouse for as long as Walter could remember, uttered words deeply and sparingly, and tortured people with her glowers and meaty fists. As a lad, he'd not escaped the brutality of the woman; her paw would swipe without warning, sending a lad a third her size into the next week. To this day, he did not know what her official title was, but knew that she had served his father faithfully, as healer and housekeeper, as henchman and conspirator.

Walter supposed his father had tossed some tidbits to her over the years, mayhap had swived her occasionally to keep her complacent. She had no fear, and that was the only means his sire understood to effectively control a person and garner their promise of loyalty, that Walter had often wondered about her continued—and seemingly freely given—allegiance.

"Ye get it out, then?"

Rannoch Ramsay's scraggly voice pulled Walter's attention from Fowler taking leave of the room, having not acknowledged his presence at all.

"Aye, sent the missive," Walter answered, dropping his hands to the arms of the chair again.

"Good," said his father, "and God damn those Maitlands, getting above themselves." He coughed and sputtered, brought his hand to his mouth. A crumbled piece of linen cloth in his hand received whatever bits of himself he spat into it.

Walter's lips curled.

His father continued, "Let them be pleased with themselves, let them pin their woeful hopes on a treaty. Bah, I'll roll three times in the ground before a Ramsay ever signs a treaty with a Maitland." He closed his eyes briefly, staved off another coughing fit, and then said, "Aye, but they've given you fine validation to lay siege to Hawkmore—"

"I am not about to bring war to a castle in which my betrothed is held," Walter inserted vehemently.

Walter's face, what some might call unfortunate, was only made fouler by his fervor. It appeared he was possessed of too much skin that it sat rather thickly upon his face and neck, giving him a jowly appearance. His eyes, brown and mostly thinned with displeasure, seemed only to have been plunked into his face as an afterthought, too small and too close together for his broad face and head. Contrarily, his mouth was too large, his lips appearing inside-out, ever bright red and glistening with moisture.

Rannoch lifted and dropped his hand on the bed, the gesture meant to be dismissive. "Wedding the Sinclair lass was only ever going to get you that acreage 'round the loch returned to us, and if you were lucky, bairns that bore no resemblance to you. That was all. You'll find another to take to wife."

Walter said nothing. His father might well be about to take his last insufferable breath, but the man still held the reins of Gershouse tightly. If Walter openly opposed him, Rannoch would call out for that detestable Fowler or that hatchet-faced bailiff of his, Merton, or any of his other hovering goons. Walter would be forced to submit to his father's will, or hence be dismissed, and have no say or awareness at all of the plans and maneuvers regarding the Maitlands and the recovery of Marianna. As it was, he'd agreed with the Maitland chief to a meeting to sign the peace accord that he would regain his betrothed, that was all he wanted.

He still couldn't quite imagine whatever fortune had favored him that his request for Marianna Sinclair's hand had not been dismissed with only a snarl from his sire. Sure, he'd stared at him, all those months ago, as if he'd spoken in tongues. But when his father had been first, reminded who she was, and next, reminded that her father farmed—industriously, if not successfully—hundreds of acres, the old man had perked up. He'd said simply at the time, "Get her da' to agree to it, her dower being the return of half his acreage, and you can have the wench."

It had been no hardship to convince Mari's father to give his consent. He, too, was likely not long for this earth; his back and heart and hands weary of laboring for naught but a leaky thatched roof over his head, and a son who was more a hindrance than a help.

He'd agreed gruffly but swiftly, likely supposing his daughter, once lady of Gershouse, might extend some ease to her sire, as he was getting on in years. If it pleased Marianna, Walter imagined he would allow it.

Marianna Sinclair had been a child when last he'd known her. Until only weeks before she'd been sent down to her kin in England, Walter had barely given her a thought, but that he sometimes got about with Harman, causing trouble, and Marianna was his sister.

On that occasion before she'd been sent away, she'd come upon Walter and Harman at the loch near the Sinclair house. They'd been slicing legs off frogs when Mari had approached. She'd screamed at them, telling them they were evil. She hadn't been more than twelve or thirteen, but her outrage had been spectacular. She'd scolded them harshly, had even picked up a stone and flung it at Walter, had asked him how he liked it. It had glanced off his cheek, her throw remarkably accurate, leaving a deep gouge in his cheek. And her anger had vanished instantly. She'd gasped and covered her mouth with her hands, her anguish instant. She run to his side and apologized swiftly and profusely, her remorse genuine.

He didn't know what it was at the time that made him play it up, but he liked her attention just then. He'd pretended the wound was greater than it truly was. She'd fretted and cooed over him, had wiped his blood with her scratchy sleeve. In her eyes, he'd found something he'd not understood at the time. Compassion, he'd realize later. The lass was full of it. At twelve years of age, she'd been fierce and fiery, protective of lesser beings, and not at all averse to conceding her own wrong-doings. And when she'd laughed, trying to ease the tension, teasing that she would help him invent some grand tale to attach to the scrape on his cheek, "so the lads dinna give you any grief for being walloped by a lass", Walter had known some other emotion. It had seemed misplaced at the time, her being so young, but he'd not ever forgotten how she'd made him feel.

Her mam died shortly after that, and she'd been sent away. Harman had told him it wasn't forever, she'd be back one day, and Walter had known he would wait for her. He might have requested her hand sooner if not for the war with England that had seen him, at his father's behest, straddling a very precarious fence between the two countries. Straddling, as in playing both sides, waiting to see who might emerge as the victor.

But the playing both sides had served a purpose to Walter as well. It had seen Walter on two occasions over the last few years, sent down to England, once with half the Ramsay army which he'd delivered to the Earl of Lincoln. He'd not wanted any part of the fighting, had only been tasked with the job at the death of his older brother, and was happy then when he'd been party to none. And once he'd been sent to deliver a missive personally from his father to the Earl of Pembroke, which his sire had not trusted to any regular courier. Walter hadn't cared to inquire of the specifics of the missive, had only thought he might again seize upon the opportunity to find Marianna Sinclair. Harman had unknowingly given her direction, under Walter's subtle questioning, that the house of Albert de Beaumont was just at the edge of Hallamshire. He'd ridden half a day out of his way to find her both times. He'd not approached her, unable to think of what he might say, how he might explain his presence to her. He'd been content to spy upon her from afar, and then more than pleased to realize that whatever promise the very young Marianna had shown years ago had come wonderfully, amazingly to fruition over the years. She was striking, beyond so even, and Walter knew he must have her. He'd yet to have much success with the lasses, none that hadn't been acquired by coin, that he devised his best strategy was not for him to woo her or court her, but for the arrangement to come from his sire and hers.

She would, as his wife then, naturally grow to love him. It was, he'd convinced himself, simply how she was made, loyal and kind and compassionate.

He still couldn't believe, that after all these years, she would finally be his.

But for that bloody Harman, and that bloody Maitland!

With a great sigh of refreshed frustration, Walter let his gaze roam once again over his sire. Walter had never known a more miserable, violent, or nasty person. He could imagine no redeeming qualities inside the man, could recall not one kind word ever uttered to his second child—or any other person, for that matter. He'd known nothing but anger and disdain from Rannoch Ramsay, had only been taught more of the same. The elder Ramsay was not held in esteem, not lauded, or even liked, was feared and loathed and reviled, seemed to revel in it.

And while this had never seemed to bother the old man—indeed, he'd seemed to court such hatred—Walter had no plans that this should be his own legacy.

He knew he wasn't a good person, but he thought Marianna Sinclair could make him so.

While his father slept, knowing that one of these times he would not waken, Walter left the room and the keep. He crossed the rain-muddied yard of the bailey and entered the cylindrical stone tower in the northern most corner.

Inside, he inclined his head to William Wedast, who acknowledged his coming with only a grunt. All seven feet of William stood beside a large wooden frame, raised off the ground at an angle. William's hand, the size of a small ham, paused on the ratchet mechanism at the top of the frame. The ratchet was part of a roller assembly, one at each end of the frame, the connected chains pulled taut, about to be made tighter, Walter assumed.

He waved his fingers at William. With great amiability, he said, "Pray, carry on. Do not let me interrupt you."

Walter approached the frame and smiled gently at Harman Sinclair, whose four limbs were attached to the four chains of the rack.

"You ken this had to happen, aye?" His tone was friendly.

Harman whimpered and then groaned weakly as William worked the ratchet. Likely, he would have howled with pain, but that he was so weakened by the four days of interrogation and torture that he hadn't the strength to do so.

A gruesome popping noise was heard, and Harman did now scream.

"Bloody Hades," Walter said, feigning a wince, "that dinna sound very good." He looked up at William. "Is that bone or cartilage being disengaged?"

"Dislocated joints," the big man answered. "He'll scream for death when the cartilage breaks."

"I see," Walter said, as if he discussed something so mundane as the weather. To Harman, he said, still congenial, "A sister is a thing to be cherished. She is not something to be sacrificed, to be left to the mercurial whims of that madman, Maitland. I'd given you one job: fetch your sister. Bring her to me. That was all you had to do." Pursing his lips, he ran his gaze over the length of his one-time friend, taking in the dried and fresh blood, the tattered tunic and breeches, the two missing fingernails, his bruised and bloody face. Walter lifted his finger, happy to point out, "It will be fine, of course. The Maitlands have agreed to return her. Now, Harman," he said, leaning over the terrified man, "I'm willing to give you a reprieve just now, until the trade is made. And here's my plan: if your sister is returned to me, whole and unharmed, I will arrange for your death to be merciful." Harman cried. Or tried to. He hadn't the will or the energy or the saliva for much else. Walter straightened and waved his hand in front of his face. "Jesu, lad, you reek." He walked to the door and pulled at the handle, turning back to add, "On the other hand, if Marianna has been ill-treated in any way, any way at all, these last few days will seem only a pleasant interlude before the true pain begins. Do you understand? Your death will be neither swift nor kindly."

The pathetic whimpering that followed was silenced as Walter closed the door behind him.

THE DEPTHS OF HER SOUL

LACHLAN FOUND MARI in the corridor, between the kitchen and the hall, shortly before supper.

Mari was brought up sharply, biting her lip as she stared at him, waiting now for his reprimand, hoping it wasn't awful, hoping it didn't send them back two paces again. Strangely, he held up his hand, as if to keep her at the present distance of half a dozen feet.

After a moment, he said, "I'm waiting, Mari, very patiently, for your explanation."

She nodded nervously. His voice was low and controlled.

"Very well. First, please consider that I wasn't actually or specifically *on* the training field, just to be clear." His response to this hair-splitting, a more severe tightening of his jaw, told her this helped her cause not at all. She then told him quietly about Utrid's infatuation with Elesbeth, warning, "But you cannot tell him I've divulged this secret." She explained about her and Utrid's plan to learn more about the lass. "So, while I *was* there, close to the training, it was in the service and advancement of another. And I didn't want to embarrass either Elesbeth or Utrid by telling you right there what I was about."

Sadly, this seemed to have little impact on his brutal scowl.

"Lass, I'm no' sure why you would risk my wrath for such a trivial purpose—"

"Ugh," she gasped, insisting, "there is nothing trivial about matters of the heart. You need to stop talking to Murdoch."

For just an instant, he appeared perplexed, but quickly shook his head and plowed on, "You lied to me, in front of many witnesses. I'd told you the training field was no place for a lass. Mari, I'm trying verra hard—how can you possibly be smiling now?"

"Because you're not shouting at me even though I think you really want to," she told him, immeasurably pleased. And before he did start yelling, which seemed yet to be an imminent threat, she dared, "I did take a risk, but only because I was sure—hopeful, anyway—that you'd not risk *my* wrath and consequently not be allowed another kiss."

It was becoming more of a regular thing, the befuddlement she caused in him.

"You are the worst captive ever," he reminded her, falling back on this mild offense.

Her smile grew. She closed some of the distance between them, slowly, one step at a time. "That is your doing, I'm sure. You shouldn't have ever kissed me."

"And dinna I ken it."

"But you will kiss me now, yes?"

"Aye."

She rushed the last few steps, holding his gaze, which was overtaken by a heat that hadn't anything to do with anger. Their lips met but briefly, her hands on his chest, before Murdoch's snarly voice was heard just inside the hall, on the other side of the wall.

"I dinna care if the sweet Mother Mary herself told ye to do it that way, lad. You'll do it as *I* instructed or be the worse for it."

Mari pushed away from Lachlan reluctantly as Murdoch's now quieter grumbling grew closer.

"Lad must believe I was birthed just yesterday."

She would normally have grinned at the captain's grousing, but her bright eyes were locked on Lachlan and his on her. When

Murdoch showed himself, coming around the wall, he saw only the chief and Mari staring at each other in the dim corridor, a respectable distance between them. Mari's anxiously flexing fingers were hidden behind her back.

To cover the awkward silence, and while Murdoch stared back and forth between the pair, quite obviously comprehending he'd walked into something, Mari invented, "Murdoch, would you teach me how to wield and use a knife, as you did today on the field?"

"No, he willna," came from Lachlan.

"Now why would ye be needing to ken that?" And this, from Murdoch.

Mari huffed a bit, the all-too-brief kiss momentarily forgotten. "Why shouldn't I learn to defend myself?"

Murdoch chortled and claimed, "You're a wee bit too dangerous already, lass."

Warming to the idea, Mari argued to Lachlan, "Why would you say no? I might find myself in danger one day or put upon by wastrels, or heaven forbid, attacked in some manner when—"

"I will keep you safe." Lachlan growled, possibly offended that she suggested otherwise.

"—when I am no longer at Hawkmore," she finished pointedly.

This effectively silenced their arguments.

Murdoch threw a sidelong glance at Lachlan and after a moment of beard scratching decided, "Aye, I'll teach some basics." To Lachlan, he offered, "Canna hurt that she ken how to protect herself when she's gone."

Mari wasn't sure whether it was Murdoch's taking her side or the reminder that her present condition was only a temporary one that sent Lachlan stalking away.

Chapter Sixteen

"Can you do it again, but slower this time?" Mari asked of Murdoch.

This was her second day of training with the small dagger, half the size of Murdoch's but still an unfamiliar instrument in her hand. They'd started yesterday and continued today with the basics he'd promised her. Presently this meant that he wanted her to know how to hold, turn, wield, and maneuver a knife. He'd just used his long dagger to demonstrate what he called practical handling. Holding his blade by the slim hilt, he'd flicked his wrist and tossed it into the air. Mari had watched as it spun several times, end over end, several feet straight up. Three times in a row, Murdoch had caught it, each time at different heights, when gravity pulled it back down. And each time he'd caught it by the hilt and not the very dangerous blade.

"Why do I need to know this? Seems only a fancy trick for some street performer."

"Aye, and I'll tell ye why. Two things. First, it gets ye comfortable with the blade and ye ken the weight and handling of it. Next, I've rarely seen a short blade brought into a fight that it wasn't knocked out of a man's hand. So you better be able to catch it."

This made sense to her. She hadn't really doubted Murdoch's teaching method, had only failed to understand how this exercise, particularly, could be helpful to her. Now it made sense and Mari threw herself into mastering it.

Murdoch watched as she tried to replicate his movements.

Her first toss went forward and not up.

"Aye, lass, look here," Murdoch said when she'd recovered the blade. She faced him and he demonstrated again only the flick of his wrist. "Dinna move the whole arm, just the wrist."

Mari nodded and tried to ignore all the notice they were drawing here in the bailey, inside the gate. Lachlan had left Hawkmore yesterday on some castle matters, she been told, which meant that the soldiers were getting a reprieve from training, since about forty men had gone with Lachlan and because, as Murdoch had said, there was work about the castle and fields that needed to get done.

So yesterday and today she and Murdoch had stayed right here in the yard, tucked against a side wall to be out of the way. But the unusual sight of the captain teaching their very own prisoner how to properly brandish her new small weapon had drawn a considerable amount of interest. Presently, three small lads sat atop the wall above—with Murdoch's permission; they wouldn't normally be allowed up on the battlements, but the captain had thought it safer for them while Mari was yet untrained. Edane, the smithy who'd fashioned her new dirk, stood leaned against a pole near his work shed, quiet but observant. Utrid had stopped by to ask something of Murdoch, then remained to observe, giving Murdoch and Mari a wide berth as to be unobtrusive. Mari had been thrilled to see Elesbeth approach Utrid and shyly ask, with a pretty blush, what was going on. She'd stayed next to

Utrid even after he'd answered and Mari had thought there really had been no need for her intervention, such as it was; she'd said as much to Utrid when she'd merrily delivered her opinion to him that Elesbeth might also be sweet on him, reminding him that garnering the courage to speak to her for the first time only needed to be done once. Also in the bailey were two women from the village, who'd come to fetch the leftover bread that was free to any who needed it every day and had stayed to watch Mari's training as well. Mostly, the audience remained at a distance, which was kindly and had Mari feeling much less self-conscious than she might have if they were all gathered around so close.

"When will Lachlan be returned?" She asked of Murdoch, flipping the knife over and over again under his watchful eye. She was showing some success, catching it almost every third time.

Murdoch stood close, his feet braced apart, his arms folded over his chest. "When his business is done."

"Where did he go?"

"Ye dinna need to ken that, lass. He's off and about the work of God and country, and that's all I'll be telling ye."

"Ooh. That sounds very gallant," she said, keeping her eye on the hilt as it spun round and round as Murdoch had directed.

"Lass," Murdoch said, shaking his head, "I could tell ye the chief is riding roughshod over the land, cleaving the heads off all the bairns in a hundred mile radius and I'm thinking you'd find some redemption for him in even that." His tone was not gruff, but amused. "Dinna hold your fingers so stiff," he instructed. "Loose and easy will give ye better reactions."

Mari relaxed her fingers, trying to steady herself that she didn't immediately follow the knife and its path, not reaching to grab for it while it was still ascending, but waiting, as Murdoch had done, to pluck it from the air on its descent.

"You're getting it," Murdoch praised.

"That's three in a row I've caught now," she said with no small amount of pride.

"Aye, now toss it with a little more speed, which is only a quicker flick of your wrist and no' more power. You dinna wanna send it over the wall. That's it. Perfect."

"Aye, lass, you're a natural."

She recognized Torquil's voice and smiled, though she didn't dare turn to acknowledge him. Still, she failed to catch it that time, reaching too quickly that she would have only grabbed the blade and not the hilt. She bent and plucked the dirk from the ground and began again.

She caught the knife many times in a row and then heard Torquil. "That's six, lass. Now seven. Keep going."

Soon, the younger boys atop the wall, their feet dangling above Mari's head, began to count out loud with Torquil, calling out the number of each subsequent catch without drops.

"Nine," the boys called.

"Ten!" Torquil's voice continued with them.

"Eleven!" Mari heard more voices chiming in, did not recognize all of them, her concentration steadfast.

She made it to seventeen and when she missed and the blade fell to the leafy, dried dirt at her feet, a collective groan of dismay was heard all around her. This was quickly followed by a unified cheer for how well she had done. Mari laughed and picked up the knife, turning and curtsying to the crowd with a great flourish, as if she were indeed a street performer.

When she straightened, she saw Lachlan.

She saw nothing else and no one else, just him, standing with several soldiers who'd gone away with him, many yards behind Murdoch and Torquil. Her smile softened, the knife and her accomplishments forgotten, while he regarded her with a piercing gaze. Her heart thumped and she would never believe otherwise, that just then, for one magnificent moment, Lachlan Maitland looked very happy to see her.

The other returning soldiers began to file into the keep, save for Edric, who'd just returned as well and walked over to stand near Torquil, amused it seemed by what he'd just witnessed.

Lachlan winked smoothly at her and turned to follow his men inside.

Mari's smile remained even as Murdoch said, "That's impressive, lass, but now we'll try it while walking."

MURDOCH KEPT MARI BUSY for twenty more minutes, which she truly did not begrudge. He was kind enough to be teaching her, first of all, and also, Lachlan would have matters to address immediately upon his return. Possibly he would have no time to spare her, but as soon as Murdoch released her for the day, she tucked her knife into the small leather sheath now attached to her belt and dashed into the hall.

Lachlan was seated at the head table upon the dais, eating heartily of Cook's veal tarts in cream, which they'd dined on last eve. Oliver, the quiet steward, stood at his side, pointing at a parchment he'd set before his chief. Lachlan was nodding as he perused the paper and listened to Oliver's speech about the matter.

When Mari had moved close enough before the table, but still only halfway across the hall, Lachlan lifted his head and wiped his mouth with his hand. He said nothing to her, just returned her regard while Oliver continued to talk at his side. Mari waited patiently, unwilling to interrupt. Very soon, Lachlan said to Oliver, "We'll be fine if we get the two crowns for every ten sheep sheered. Let's finish this tomorrow morn."

"Aye, lad," said the older man. He gathered the papers into his ledger, noticed Mari and nodded, and moved away from the table in his usual serene manner.

Mari let her smile come then and rushed forward with some excitement. She did not step up onto the wooden platform but leaned her hands and her chest against the edge of the table, directly in front of him.

"I am very delighted with your return," she said.

Lachlan continued to eat. There was no hardness about him, none that she saw. He seemed relaxed, at ease. She decided just the whiff of a smile hung about him, ready to expand if she could make it so, if he would allow it.

"Because you wanted to show off your handiwork with the pretty blade?"

"No, even though I am rather amazing," she said without hesitation, knowing that he only teased her, her understanding of this guided by the lightness of his gaze. "Because you owe me a trip down to the beach. Cook claims her knee says it's going to rain soon. But you're home now, we can go today, before these phantom rains come."

He smirked while chewing, not quite a smile yet. And then he set down the dull silver spoon and straightened in his large chair. Holding her eye, he reached under his plaid and into his tunic just above his waist, withdrawing a small lump of dyed blue linen. He tossed it on the table before her.

Curious, Mari picked it up and stretched out the wadded thing. She made a happy moue when she realized it was a small linen pouch, with a drawstring cord, just about the size of her hand.

"For your beach finds," he said casually, as if he had not just done the most astonishing thing.

Mari gaped at him, cradling the bag to her chest, cherishing it instantly. "Truly?"

And now he smiled, at her overwrought reaction. "Aye. You keep the strings around your wrist and you'll no more leave your finds behind."

Her eyes watered with her joy.

He finished off the remainder of the veal and caught her still staring at him. He chuckled. "It's a bag, Mari, neither made of gold nor filled with coins."

"But it's a gift then?"

He shrugged, a frown threatening. "I saw it at a market. Thought you would make good use of it."

"I will," she promised, keeping at bay all the feeble kin that wanted to blanket her. She sensed her pleasure somehow made him uncomfortable. Thus, she probably shouldn't tell him she'd never received a gift from another living soul in all her life, or that she might very well keep this on her person all her days until she was put into the ground.

Lachlan pushed back from the table and stood. "Aye, I see you're chomping at the bit. Let's get you down to the beach."

At that moment, Mari was quite sure her joy was unrivaled in all of Christendom.

HE WAITED AS LONG AS he could.

They'd walked down to the beach—Mari had actually bounced, he thought—and strolled along the wild shore, closer to the dunes really as the waves covered so much of the beach proper today. She'd collected this shell and that stone, exclaiming over several to him before dropping them into her new cinched pouch.

He watched her, unable to ignore how she made him feel, how he'd missed her though he'd been gone but a day. He didn't know any words to describe or classify what he'd felt when she'd noticed his return in the yard; the regard of those fabulous blue eyes warmed him as he was sure nothing else ever could.

Lachlan suspected that he should not still be robbed of breath at only the sight of her, but he was. The wind ripped shorter strands of her glorious hair from the ribbon at her nape and sent them dancing around her face. Her eyes were bright and blue and smiling, having no equal, he somehow knew. Her fingers were slim and blue-veined, delicate upon the stones; she skipped or floated or ran and every movement was lithe and graceful.

Aye, he'd waited long enough, he decided when they were far from the castle, close to where they'd sat days before. She darted all around and then ran toward him, howling with laughter, chased by a wave, her hand waving whatever new treasure she'd claimed before the sea had.

Lachlan marched forward, met her, slammed into her, claimed her lips as jubilantly as she'd claimed her silly stones and shells. And his beautiful Mari took his hungry kiss, all but leapt up into his embrace, flinging her arms tight around his neck. He held her tight, both arms wrapped fully around her to crush her to him. He thought her feet might be lifted off the ground, felt the water roll over his boots. He devoured her, with lips and tongue and hot breath, wild and needful.

They kissed forever and then not enough. Still aching for her, wanting so much more of her, Lachlan slid his hand between them, cupping her breast from the underside, lifting it, his fingers searching for her nipple through the layers of her kirtle and gown.

He yanked with some savagery at her shoulder, the wide scoop neckline abetting his efforts to free her breast to his hungry hands. She whimpered several times in quick succession when he touched his mouth to her and took her hardened nipple between his teeth. Three passionate moans, one after another and Lachlan's cock grew tenfold. He suckled at her nipple and Mari arched against him, her fingers threaded into his hair, holding him tight and close.

He pulled her hand from around his head and placed it over his erection, closing his eyes at the sheer beauty her initial touch brought to him. He moved her hand up and down against him, teaching her how to torment him. She squeezed her fingers around him, over his breeches and drawers, making out the complete and still growing size of him. Lachlan gave attention to her arched neck, laving his mouth and tongue upwards, back to her lips.

She kissed him violently, greedy and breathless, her hand still between them, driving him wild. Unable to bear it, he moved her hand away, then uncovered her other breast to feast there.

Mari whimpered. Lachlan groaned.

God, how he wanted—needed—to drive into her right now. Damn!

"I willna be able to stop, Mari," he said thickly to her, against her lips once more.

"I don't want you to stop."

He pulled back, stared at the sharp rising and falling of her glorious chest, both breasts bared to his worshipful gaze. "But then, there's no turning back."

Silence for a moment, until she wondered, her voice husky and breathless, "But will you feel poorly, will you be angry at yourself for not stopping?"

He blew out a tortured breath, "Not until we're done, when regret comes."

He did not mistake the sound of anguish in her voice when she asked, "Why would you regret it?"

He kissed her again, letting all his desire for her be felt in the harshness of it, as wild as the sea. But the answer that came in his head to her pitiful query, *Because you are not mine*, would not go away, would not be still.

If he did this, he would never let her go. He absolutely knew that to be truth right now.

A sorrowfulness shook him as he pulled up her kirtle and gown, covering her breasts. Whatever took hold of her in response to this made her jerk away from him, her hands clutched over her bosom as if she had now her own regret, for having given him so much of herself, so freely.

"Then why do you keep doing this?" The anguish continued. "Why kiss me at all?"

"I canna help myself," he admitted feebly.

Bitterly, she decided, "It's wrong, then, what you're doing to me. And wrong, of me to allow it. I should have struck you the first time you kissed me, would've saved me so much torment. I wish you'd never touched me." With pinched and trembling lips, she turned and walked away. Gone the breeziness, gone the merriment, gone all traces of the wild passion that had gripped her.

Lachlan thrust his hand on his hips and watched her leave him. Her arms swung angrily with each strident step she took to be away from him.

He'd cried once while in captivity. Only once. Not for the pain or the taunting or the fear that he might die. But for the hopelessness. It had done him little good, had only made him feel more pathetic, weaker, had erased even the last small shred of hope he'd clung to.

He couldn't remember that he'd ever cried before then, knew for certain he hadn't since.

Just now, he felt he could weep for this current despair.

SHE WASN'T ANGRY AT him. Though she had no experience at all with things of this nature, some part of her understood his continued refusal to ravish her completely. Splendidly, she was sure.

Maybe she only understood it a very little bit. It had something to do with honor, she believed, having witnessed the battle he fought with himself. She didn't believe it had anything to do with a lack of want, of desire. It was all about the battle. He wanted to, but he wouldn't let himself. And that was the extent of her understanding.

If only he loved her as she did him.

Mari gasped.

So there it was. She'd said it. Granted, only in her mind, but there it was.

I am in love with Lachlan Maitland.

Ah, but she knew that.

Mayhap that was why she couldn't be cross with him; she loved him and thus could not hate him for breaking her heart.

And yet she would leave him—be sent away—and she would become his enemy in name when she married Walter Ramsay.

All this and more spun around in her mind the next day while helping the cook in the kitchen. Florie had sliced her finger—not badly, she'd been assured; but then, "We dinna want blood in our beans and carrots," Marjorie had said with a jowly grin. Thus, Mari had been tapped to finish the preparation of the vegetables. She sat on a low stool near the hearth, a bowl in her lap and one again at her feet. She snapped off the ends of the beans and dropped them into the second bowl, happy for her position near the many fires of the wall ovens and spits as Cook had been right about the rains. They'd come this morn, and with them a blast of cool air that Mari felt all the way to her bones.

She was happy she'd not avoided supper last night, though she'd been sorely tempted. Only her prevailing hunger and the aroma of garlic and onions and bacon, which had greeted her upon her return from the beach, had advised that she wouldn't want to be absent from the meal. And she'd been quite proud of herself. She'd managed clever conversation with Diana, had made time to deliver the apology to Torquil that she'd owed him yet, and had even exchanged small and meaningless words with Lachlan as if she didn't ache inside for so much more from him.

And so it went, day after day.

Even as she knew it would only make the eventual leave-taking that much more difficult, Mari was happy to carve out a happy little spot here at Hawkmore. There wasn't a person she disliked or a chore she bemoaned or a minute she regretted. She continued her training with Murdoch, which he'd moved to late afternoon to accommodate his returned schedule of being at the training field in the morning. Always, a crowd watched, that Mari began to think people were beginning to plan their day around this hour. Murdoch was ever patient, sometimes silly, and Mari was absolutely in love with the inspiration that came with each little bit of knowledge she acquired. She felt empowered with this small ability to possibly be able to defend herself, if need be.

Murdoch had twice now taken her out rowing in one of the boats. They had no purpose, no chore to be about, "just idling, lass", Murdoch had said. She loved the boat and being upon the water almost as much as she'd loved swimming with Lachlan. Murdoch had said one day he would teach her to row, and she'd pretended some excitement over this, but she'd thought sadly she would be gone from Hawkmore before that day ever came.

As days passed, it became a regular thing to see Utrid and Elesbeth keeping company with each other. Elesbeth's charming blushes and Utrid's nervous manner of swiping his fingers repeatedly and quickly through his hair whenever she came near told one and all that a genuine courting was under way.

Mari spent a fair amount of time with Diana, whether in the kitchens where she now regularly helped out, or in the solar, where mending seemed to be never-ending. They traded tales, of Mari's early years and her memories of her own dear mother, and then of Diana's youth as the only daughter of a great landowner. They tackled the job of giving the hall a thorough cleaning, walls scrubbed, hearths emptied and whitewashed, floors swept, and rushes replaced. That had taken two whole days, and only with Florie and Edie laboring alongside them.

She saw Lachlan regularly of course, even if only at supper every evening. He was polite but distant and Mari allowed him to be so. She wanted more but didn't think she could endure any further rejection from him, no matter the reason.

She told herself she was still happy to be here at Hawkmore, knew she didn't ever want to leave. It was just that she was also heartbroken at the same time. Somedays she did not even recognize herself and her brooding moods. It was a very difficult thing, to accept that they had no chance, that he could not, would not, ever be hers.

When a week more had passed, Mari found herself restless and unable to settle after supper was long done. It was late but it was also summer, which meant the sun had yet to disappear completely. Mari wrapped herself in the Maitland tartan, a gift from Diana—not quite as large as a man's plaid, but large enough to serve as a fine and cozy shawl. They'd spent one afternoon sewing a frivolous fringe of lace onto it, in which Mari had delighted and which Diana had assured her was not at all disrespectful.

Tonight she was particularly beset with some misplaced anger at Lachlan, that he wasn't of the same mind as she, that he didn't ever think, *to hell with the whole world, I want her.*

She wandered outside and around the rear of the keep, glancing up at the wall to see who had duty tonight. Edric waved to her, interrupting his conversation with another soldier.

"Edric, am I allowed to go to the beach at this hour?" She called up to him. "I'll stay directly below the keep."

"Aye, lass, go on down," he called back, waving his hand with permission.

Mari smiled her thanks and exited the yard through the man door. Edric called out to her from the other side, once she was amid the dunes. She couldn't hear him now, he so high above and the surf singing so joyfully below. It couldn't have been terribly important as he disappeared from view then.

She was not quite halfway down the slope when she saw that she was not the only one to seek the solace of the sea. Ahead of her, where the fishing boats lived, was Lachlan.

Mari pulled the tartan wrap more tightly about her and debated, for many long seconds, if she should stay or go.

Chapter Seventeen

He didn't know what opened his eyes. Mayhap that sixth sense upon which soldiers relied so heavily. He'd come only for the solitude, had sat first on a dune near the boats for a while before giving in to the luxury of using part of his plaid as a pillow, stretching out with his arms under his head and crossing his feet at the ankles. He'd closed his eyes and let the constant and soothing rumble of the surf lull even his thoughts into quietude.

Lachlan opened his eyes now, glanced up to find Mari standing above him, huddled in the Maitland tartan, her regard wary just now, likely awaiting his reception.

"You canna sleep, lass?" He had some idea that she was usually abed before this time of night, usually up with the first of them in the morn.

She shook her head, her hands, burrowed inside the wrap, lifting it up against her chin.

"Plenty of room here," he said, by way of invitation. "Though you'll quickly be chilled, despite your new wrap."

She sat down, not very close but still along the slope of the same dune, unusually quiet. She crossed her legs under her kirtle and gown as he'd seen her do before and faced the sea, gave it all her attention, pleased to do so it seemed.

"I dinna recall them weaving the tartan with lace," he commented, curious about her mood that had rendered her speechless.

She glanced down to the hem of her shawl and smiled in response to this. The smile was slight, lacking any tiny bit of her normal cheer. "Your mother helped, said it was all right."

He nodded, but she didn't see, had returned her gaze to the darkening sea.

After a few minutes, when he didn't push for conversation, she turned slightly and said, "I was out the other day with Florie and Elesbeth, gathering herbs and seeds and whatnot. I found some rose plant and hypericum. I gave them to Cook and shared the procedure for steaming and seething them to make oil." Staring straight ahead once again, she added, "If you ever had need."

Lachlan digested this, all that was revealed in so few sentences. She got on well with the lasses, with everyone, but he'd known this. She'd given additional thought to one of the first things she had ever said to him, about his scars and the pain. She offered the instruction to Cook—*if ever you had need*—because she would be gone soon.

"I only have pain near my eye," he was surprised to hear himself tell, "the rest—the cheek and neck—dinna bother me at all."

"Very sensitive skin, there at the eye," she said softly.

"Will I smell of roses, then?" He asked lightly, wondering if she would smile—for real—at all this night.

She shrugged, "Like as not."

Aye, he did not care for this Mari, this silent and stingy and melancholy Mari.

And yet, he understood. He was sullen as well, truth be told.

"The first whole day after I was burned, I didn't feel a thing."

This admission—where it had come from he could not say—drew more of her regard, that she turned her face and laid her chin on her shoulder, watching him.

"A day after that, and I was wishing they would just finish it. The pain was unbearable. Worse than the flail or the rack or anything else they'd tried. I was always amazed that not one of them, not at any time over all those months, ever showed any misgivings for what they did to us." He chewed the inside of his cheek for a moment, considering this again, still watching the gently rolling waves of late evening breaking over the sand. "I've done my fair share of interrogations, have witnessed so many more, and I canna think of a time at least one softbelly dinna turn away from the methods used. But no' those English. They held some special hate for us."

"How long were you held?" Her voice was slight and low, her chin barely moved.

"Seven months."

"How did you—did you escape?"

Lachlan harrumphed softly. "I could no' even walk at the end, could see my own ribs. Nae, they'd moved us up to Hawick, getting ready for a trade of prisoners. But the MacBriar, who was to make the trade, having a dozen Englishmen, decides he willna be trading naught and storms the keep—Hawick House, maybe, I dinna ken. In and out in less than a quarter hour, the six of us who'd survived carried out like bairns. There had been twenty-three of us when we were taken." Thoughtfully, he added, "The MacBriar's son was with me the entire time, from the time we were taken captive. I found out later the MacBriar was so enraged over the barbarism visited upon us, he took out every one of his English prisoners that night. Sliced their throats, just like that."

"And evil begets evil," she concluded.

"Aye."

"Is that why you have such difficulty making peace with what happened to you, because of what happened to those Englishmen?"

"Aye, it's part of it. Nightmares are the other part, won't let me forget for too long."

A bit more silence, until she said, "I'm sorry that happened to you, Lachlan."

Her tone was sad, but joined by something else, something that gave him pause. "You're sorry but then you're wondering how can I possibly visit harm upon any person—you, now, with the kidnapping—knowing how it destroys a person?"

She did not demur, kept her gaze steady on him, but she said nothing.

"I'm tired of the war, tired of warring. Aye, it was selfish, but the idea of putting the Ramsays out of my mind held great appeal. I ken you'd no be harmed, thought I might eke out a wee bit of peace until the great war calls again."

That was the truth, but he had some suspicion that she was not satisfied.

But she stayed, did not dispute the silence that fell between them. This was a tragedy, he realized, and wondered what screamed inside her now, for he knew that while she might not be speaking aloud just now, words still moved within her.

"What do you hear in the quiet between us?" he wondered.

He watched, his head tilted on his arms toward her, as she lifted her gaze to the night sky. She didn't chase the stars around the sky or sigh at the moon. But then, she didn't answer him immediately. First, she stood and pulled the tartan more tightly about her.

She stood near, her feet not too far from his. "I hear your demons, Lachlan." She let only a second pass after this delivery to add, "I'm glad you'll have your peace with the Ramsays."

That was it, and she walked away.

THE NEXT MORNING, LACHLAN was summoned to Oliver's tiny office at the back of the keep, tucked between the garderobe and the larder. He found his mother and Murdoch already there and frowned over the three of them until Oliver delivered a missive to him. Red wax. Boar's head smashed so violently into the wax as to be almost unrecognizable.

Jaw tight, he broke the seal and read the thickly penned, angry words.

He cursed with vehemence and said to Murdoch, "He found the lads we left watching him."

Murdoch's curse was twice as fiery as Lachlan's. He began to pace, his arm lifted, fingers tapping at his forehead.

"What lads?" Diana was eager to know.

"We set up a watch near Gershouse," Lachlan confessed, "wanted to make sure he dinna try to come at us, while I stalled."

"Three lads," Murdoch supplied, "Charles and Edmund and Niel."

Diana covered her mouth with her hands.

Oliver, who'd retrieved the letter from Lachlan, advised, "Wants the trade anon, this Saturday. Every day after that, he'll send bits of the boys back to Hawkmore," he said, paraphrasing. "He's promising war here, lad."

Diana cried out, "Lachlan! Those poor boys! Why did you infuriate him? Why anger him by stalling—"

"I was trying to figure out a way to keep her here!" He finally shouted, raising brows and the rafters.

After a moment, while they digested this admission, while they considered the anguish on his face, Murdoch said sorrowfully, "The lass was never gonna be tortured or killed. Those lads will."

"The last thing I wanted was for you to give her to the Ramsays," Diana said, about to weep it seemed, "but Lachlan, you must."

"I ken that," he barked out. "I've always ken that."

Collecting herself, Diana asserted, "I will tell her."

Lachlan met his mother's teary gaze. He shook his head. "I will tell her."

MARI WAITED FOR MURDOCH in the corner of the yard, practicing what he'd taught her yesterday. She liked the footwork part least of all, but Murdoch had promised she would understand the necessity of it soon enough. She coupled this with the few strike and jab motions of her bladed arm that she'd just learned, keeping the forearm of her free hand held up horizontally at chin level as she'd been shown.

"Mari."

She startled and turned to find Lachlan and not Murdoch. Lowering her hands, she bit her lip with acute embarrassment, knowing how silly she looked practicing her technique and not knowing how long Lachlan had watched.

But her discomfiture faded quickly, his solemn expression and eyes that would not quite meet hers telling her why he'd sought her out.

"It's time," she guessed. "You're going to send me away."

Lachlan nodded, now lifting his intense gaze, to gauge her reaction. "They've threatened to bring war to Hawkmore."

Mari swallowed, felt her chest tighten. "I understand."

She hadn't yet spent too many years on this earth, and she wouldn't have said that the majority of them had been kind to her. Still, she did not often wallow in self-pity and had only sometimes wished for something better to come to her, to happen to her. Just now, though, she really wanted to rail against the unfairness of it all, that something better had come for her, but that she could not stay with him, or keep with it. A strange bitterness engulfed her and, too, a resentment directed at Lachlan, that he would not fight for her or for them or for all the hope that she'd attached to this sometimes wonderful thing between them.

As if he read her thoughts, he said darkly, "It's no' just you and me I've to consider. All of Hawkmore, all the Maitlands, the village—we canna have war here."

"I understand."

"Mari, you've said that now twice, but I dinna think you do. You're angry."

She was quick to shake her head. She wasn't truly angry. "I'm sad, Lachlan. I don't want to leave you. I don't want to marry him."

He said nothing though his jaw worked as if fighting words that wished to come.

Truly, she couldn't bear to see him torn up over this. "It's all right. I've known this from the start. I really do understand."

"If I could—if there was some way—"

She gave him a stiff smile and brushed this off, not interested in hearing any falsehoods from him just now even as she felt almost as sorry for him as she did for herself. "When?"

"Two days."

Oh.

Tucking her short blade back into its sheath, she said, "I think I'll take advantage of my prisoner status now and retreat to—my chambers." She'd had all she could do not to call it a dungeon.

She brushed past him, ignoring his simple plea of, "Mari...." she strode toward the keep.

She hadn't lied to him. Her first instinct had been to seek the solace of her chambers and cry her heart out into her pillow. This would not do, of course. There were so many people she loved here, and she wanted to be with them now. They wouldn't need to know her sorrow, wouldn't need to know these might be their last moments together. But she needed it, wanted to tuck away all the perfection that was Hawkmore, and every person inside. Shaking herself, lest the barely contained tears spilled, she found the kitchens, and happily, Diana and Florie and Edie within, all busy helping Marjorie with preparations for supper. Immediately, she offered to help.

Florie's pretty face, so like Elesbeth's, minus the space between her teeth, lifted from her task. She waved a hand vigorously before her while she stood in the middle of the long counter. It seemed her eyes were watering.

"Onions," she groaned. "And I'm sorry now my finger is healed."

Mari grinned.

Diana turned to her, her gaze questioning. She moved sideways at the end of the counter, making room there for Mari. "Edie's slicing the sweetbreads—"

"And only eating every third piece," Edie said saucily, tossing a small bit into her mouth.

Diana shook her head, showing a bemused face and not any chastisement, and said, "Marjorie has all the fish and eel under control, but you're welcome to help with the bacon and cabbage."

Mari stood next to Diana and reached toward the center of the counter, into a short crockery jar that held various knives and implements. She picked up where Diana had left off, slicing the cabbage into chunks and strips, while Diana began trimming the pork belly into smaller pieces, pushing all the fat off to one side.

"Will the onions be cooked in the fat?" She dearly hoped so.

"Aye," called Marjorie from the fireplace and all the racks of seafood filets. "Otherwise, what's the sense of eating 'em?"

Mari's stomach growled. Cabbage and bacon and onions, all mixed together, was one of her favorite dishes.

"Mari," Florie said, "I'm going home on Saturday—just off to the village—for a wee bit to help me mum with some chores. Won't you come and meet her?"

"I would love that—oh, but...I don't know...if I'll be here then." This last bit emerged with some awkwardness, her situation so very recently brought to the fore once more. To cover the ensuing unease—hers and theirs—she said with feigned sass. "I'll have to speak to the powers that be."

Florie and Edie grinned.

Marjorie called over her shoulder, "And good luck with that!" And she chortled merrily.

"Have you not spoken to Lachlan today?" Diana asked.

Something in her tone, the question asked almost too casually, had Mari understanding Diana had already been made aware of the news her son had delivered to Mari.

"I have." She continued chopping with the big kitchen knife but turned sideways to consider Diana's unsubtle expression. She was sorry as well, giving Mari a heartfelt pout.

Mari shrugged. Mayhap they would talk about it, she and Diana, but not now.

Edie asked of Diana, "Is it true what I heard? That Niel and Charles and that skinny lad, Edmund, were taken by the Ramsays?"

Mari gasped.

All eyes turned to Diana, who was glowering, tight-lipped, at Edie. Obviously, this was not general knowledge.

"What has happened?" Mari was desperate to know.

Aggrieved, and exhaling a heavy sigh to show as much, Diana said curtly. "That is not for common consumption, Edie." At the lass's baffled look, Diana said tersely, "The whole damn keep doesn't need to know." Her hands stilled in front of her while she composed herself. Even Marjorie stopped what she was doing to listen. "It is true," Diana said, eliciting gasps, "but they'll be returned in two days' time, as part of the...exchange of prisoners."

Florie covered her mouth with her hand, her eyes wide. Marjorie wrung her hands in her apron, her horrified gaze settling on Mari, while Edie stared slack-jawed at Mari.

Silence reined. Mari pinched her lips and lowered her head. But then she resumed her chopping and avoided all the sympathy aimed her way. With false brightness, she said, "Of course, I'd always known my time here was to be of a short duration." She forced a laugh, "Who'd have thought I'd not actually want to leave?" Her misleading attitude begged any to imagine an *isn't that silly?* question might have followed.

No one said a word.

And she couldn't stand it. And she couldn't pretend anymore.

"Excuse me," she said shakily and set down the knife. She bit her lip to keep from crying out as she raced from the kitchen.

In the corridor, well away from the kitchen, she leaned her back against the wall and took long breaths to calm herself. For a moment, her own unfortunate situation was forgotten, replaced so swiftly by concern for Niel and Charles and Edmund. Of course, she knew Niel well enough, but the other two only by sight. Still, she prayed to God that they were unharmed, treated as kindly as she had been.

She considered this, brought to mind Lachlan's scars and hoped the Ramsays practiced no such savagery. Oh, but if—

Her musings were interrupted by voices on the other side of the wall, inside the hall. They sounded close enough to suggest they might be sitting at the head table.

Lachlan and Murdoch, she recognized immediately. Possibly, they'd been there all this time, had been talking even, but Mari's upset had overshadowed the sounds.

"—dinna matter," Murdoch was saying. "we've hundreds here, raring to go. I'll send half them off tomorrow night, have them stake out the field."

Lachlan said, "I'd like to think he wouldn't dare try anything, not when we've got his bride, but I dinna trust any Ramsay."

She pictured Murdoch shaking his head. "Aye, just 'cause we dinna bring harm to her dinna mean they will no' to them. And ye ken that."

"Aye, they were entirely too eager to accept the terms of the peace. But I swear to God, if those lads are roughed up beyond...I'll kill him with my bare hands."

"Would be Rannoch, no' the boy, giving that order, I imagine," Murdoch supposed.

After a few seconds, Lachlan said, "I just dinna like it."

"But Lach, like or no', trust him or nae, ye still gotta turn her over. It's the only chance those lads have."

"I get that part," Lachlan barked out, then lowered his voice enough that Mari couldn't hear, but that he ended with, "...if they're even still alive."

Mari had heard enough. Her stomach flipped and flopped, with what their conversation intimated. She tiptoed away from the wall and found the stairs, hiking up her skirts and skipping up to her chambers.

She couldn't process it all, couldn't make sense of any of it. But she understood Niel and Charles and Edmund were in danger, possibly might be killed.

She must do something.

WALTER RAMSAY STORMED into his father's chambers, his fury unchecked, and then escalating yet more when he saw that Rannoch was actually sitting up in the bed. *Jesu*, but why wouldn't he die?

"Is it true?" He spat, uncaring that Merton and Fowler stood near the bed. "Are you planning a siege of Hawkmore? When we're only days away from having Marianna returned?"

In a surprisingly strong voice, Rannoch groused, "Get out of here while we speak of higher matters than that bluidy wench!"

"She is my betrothed!" Walter roared, his face as colored as his sire's was not. "I will not have her harmed—"

"She's dead, you fool!" Rannoch hollered. "Likely been dead since they found her. Used her good and slit her throat. Why do you think they've been stalling? Pretending some want of Wishart's signature on a formal treaty? Horseshite! Put their scouts out on our hill, just the forward party before they strike, that's all." He paused but only long enough to hack up more blood and disease into a kerchief. "And I'll be goddamned if I'll sit here and play dumb, while they plan to draw us out to Loch Liddel under the guise of signing papers and trading prisoners they've probably already killed."

"But what if she's not dead? We've our own prisoners to offer now. Should we no' meet them as planned and see if—"

"It's a bluidy trap, you fool!" Rannoch roared. He coughed more, his face now colored sharply with the toll this took on his frail body. At his side, holding a cup of some liquid, Fowler favored Walter with a disdainful glare, as if his presence or his argument had wrought this attack.

When Rannoch could speak again, he growled, "If you're done playing God with that waster, Sinclair, give those Maitlands to Wedast and let him earn his keep for real now."

THE DEPTHS OF HER SOUL

Walter was not at all against persecuting the Maitland soldiers, but he'd be damned if he would do so before they might prove useful. He wasn't sure where his father had gotten his information, but he felt Mari was still alive, and he wasn't about to dispatch the only securities he had at his disposal to make sure she came to him, finally became his.

Merton explained tersely while Rannoch's began to cough again, his sickly face turning from light red to bright red, "We figure they'd stalled to plan for and coordinate an attack at the meeting place, will lie in wait for us. But we'll get to Hawkmore a day before, before they might depart for the loch." Merton watched Walter, awaiting his reaction, seeming to expect a further dispute of this.

Rannoch finally regained his composure, blowing out several careful and even breaths before lifting his contemptuous gaze to his son. "The siege is already in motion. You can lead them, like a true Ramsay, or you can sit here like the weak child you've always been and leave the avenging of your honor to greater men."

MARI'S ABSENCE FROM supper was duly noted by many people, certainly all those seated up on the dais. At this table, unlike most of the hall, the mood was somber throughout the entire meal, barely any words spoken.

When Lachlan had eaten half of what he'd served himself, he pushed his plate away with a hard jerk of his hand, as if the meal itself had offended him. He downed the remainder of his ale and refilled his tankard.

"Lachlan," his mother said beside him, "You cannot blame your—"

"I really dinna want to have this conversation, mother."

He didn't want to talk about anything, or to anyone, if it didn't relate directly to some plan to save the lads and keep Mari with him. But his mother read well his mood, indeed his spinning reflections. Guilt chewed him up. First, Lachlan knew that he, as their laird and commander, was to blame for the lads being taken. He didn't know what to do with that guilt. Given the same circumstances again, he would have made the same decision, to send off watchers to Gershouse. It had to be done. He didn't trust the Ramsays. Not one bit.

Next, he was beginning to feel really lousy about how miserable he'd made Mari. Not for the first time, he reflected that he should have never kidnapped her, should have never been so short-sighted to have only considered at the time what benefit she might bring to him and to Hawkmore, giving no thought at all to her fright and her wants and damn, to her wee hopeful heart. It was no consolation at all that it was wholly possible Walter Ramsay might make her more miserable yet, might prove to be a worse person to her than Lachlan was.

No consolation at all.

And of course, in addition to all that remorse, he had his own bitterness to contend with, his silent fury that she could not be his. When he came to the end of his life, he might well have lived tens of thousands of days. How devastating it was to know that only a very tiny number of those days would have been spent with Mari, near her, kissing her. Murdoch had said something earlier that had given him pause, something that Lachlan hoped to be able to embrace in the coming weeks and months and years. He'd said, rather philosophically for the old man, "Ye canna see it now, Lach. But one day, maybe no' too soon, you'll be able to understand—to ken—that you'd no' wish away these days. Better only this than never."

Better than having never known her.

He wasn't ready to completely give up, was even now tossing around some idea in his head—he'd yet to infuriate Murdoch by sharing it with him—that maybe after a little while, maybe after the lads' release was secured, when the Ramsays felt safe and undisturbed once more, maybe he would simply charge into Gershouse with his army and claim what rightfully belonged to him.

She *was* his.

He needed her in his life, not merely as some memory that might only ever torture him.

For just a moment, he closed his eyes. When he opened them, he breathed slowly and deeply to calm himself.

And then he wondered what Mari Sinclair did with her bitterness. She'd shown her anger and had raged at him; she'd known fear but hadn't let it get the better of her, had sought to do something about it, had tried to escape him; she'd known joy, even since he'd kidnapped her, he liked to think, was pleased to share it and spread it—had given him so much. But what did she do with her sorrow and her bitterness? Lachlan had some idea that these emotions did not sit well with Mari, whom he sometimes believed might have been put on this earth merely to smile radiantly at damaged souls, one and all. Still, he didn't imagine she suffered sorrow well, didn't imagine she suffered it at all, if she could help it.

This line of thinking had dogged him for quite some time after she'd left him earlier, with some nagging but unspecified concern in his head that Mari wouldn't take this lying down.

Thus, he was not entirely surprised when Utrid stepped into the hall, remaining just there at the door. He inclined his head slightly and when he received Lachlan's return nod, he disappeared again.

Lachlan stood at the same time Murdoch did, the captain had witnessed Utrid's coming as well. They removed themselves from the table and left the hall together, Lachlan very thankful that he'd regarded his earlier instincts, and had set up a detail of soldiers to watch her every move today.

Utrid shook his head, a bit of a grin hovering. "Aye, she's off. Gone to the beach, sat for while, but on the move now. Luckily, Mar thinks herself quite clever—and unnoticeable—that it was fairly easy to keep an eye on her."

"Who's with her now?"

"Edric and Torquil have her, keeping their distance," Utrid answered. "They'll wait for your call—I told 'em to listen for the goshawk—and then they'll back off when you're ready to pounce on her."

Murdoch grinned at this, at the lad's wording. Utrid gave Lachlan more specific directions to her last known location before Lachlan thanked him and dismissed him, and he and Murdoch crossed the yard.

Inside the stables, leaning against the post near the stall where Lach saddled his big black, Murdoch said, "Suppose this'll end up being the last time ye do have to chase her."

Lachlan dropped the saddle in place and stilled, considering this. He nodded, staring at the leather and not at Murdoch for several seconds. When he lifted his gaze, he saw that Murdoch himself wasn't too pleased, either, that she would be bartered away.

"I dinna—I dinna ken another way." But they'd talked about this already, earlier today most recently.

"Nae, lad," Murdoch said, with some sympathy, exonerating Lachlan. "You've no choice in the matter. I ken how it's feeding on your gut, and I'm sorry for that." Then, hurriedly, as if he was displeased with himself for his soft-heartedness, Murdoch said, "But ye chase her down, once more for ol' times' sake, and ye have a nice last few days with the lass, aye?" He grinned at himself, didn't seem to mind that Lachlan did not. "I'll keep close here, send out some lads for ye if she comes to her senses before ye find her."

Fifteen minutes later, having screeched a competent imitation of the goshawk, Lachlan met first with Edric, who was smiling as Utrid had been, despite the nuisance she was being once more.

"It's a good thing we did follow her," Edric said. "She dinna even look behind her ever. Lass has no idea about the dangers of wandering around like this by herself. But she's definitely on the move, chief, walking at a good clip." He explained further, "Once she left the beach, she high-tailed it up to the forest and has been heading northwest ever since."

Lachlan nodded, receiving this, wondering if she were headed for the Ramsays land, and how she might have known in which direction to travel.

Edric lifted his arm and pointed, locking his elbow. "Straight, that direction, you'll find Torquil, couple hundred yards ahead or so."

Another nod and he was off, keeping to a light and quiet canter through the trees. Even as he called for Torquil, he already had caught sight of her much further ahead.

"Aye, I see her," he said when Torquil drew back to him.

"She's all yours," Torquil said in a low voice, smirking with good humor when he passed, heading back to Hawkmore.

Lachlan kept his gaze on her and made note of what Edric had said, which was sadly correct, she never took her gaze off her path, had no idea what might be around or close to her.

He followed her at a distance, this chase reminiscent of the previous one, he upon horseback and watching her dart about the woods. After a bit, he began to close the distance between them.

When she quickly dashed out of sight, behind a tree, Lachlan decided she was aware of his presence. Walking the big destrier close to her and then stopping completely, he called out, keeping his voice level, "C'mon out, Mari."

She did and with a huff, but he could not say that the huff came with some disgruntlement for having her exodus discovered, or because it was he who'd found her.

She faced him, her hands on her hips. He couldn't read her expression, couldn't know if that were mild annoyance or some hint of determination that colored her gaze and tightened her lips. But there was no fear.

"Lachlan, do not try to stop me," she warned, showing not one wee little bit of shame for what she was about.

Determination, then, he decided.

"I dinna ken what you're doing, lass, or where you're going, so I'll no' stop you until I do."

She rolled her eyes at him, which lifted Lachlan's brow.

"I'm going to the Ramsays, if you must know," she answered and began walking again, away from him. Her stride was quick, her arms folded at the elbow and moving back and forth to abet her efforts for speed. "To Walter Ramsay, specifically," she called back to him. "I plan to turn myself over—beg, if need be—so that Niel and the others are not killed."

Lachlan nudged the steed with a heel to his flanks and began following her, closing the space between them that he walked nearly beside her.

"I've heard worse ideas, I imagine," he grumbled, and then wondered if that were actually true. "Mari, why would you think they might be killed?"

She glanced up at him, favoring him with a look of irritation. "You said it yourself. I heard you talking to Murdoch earlier."

He supposed that answered his next question, how she'd learned of the lads' capture.

"You think you'll be able to convince Walter Ramsay? Actually, it's more likely you'd need to plead your case to the old man, Rannoch Ramsay, for any consideration."

"I'm sure I can reason with them."

Her tone oozed with both confidence and purpose. If he were a betting man, he'd put his money on her—that is, if he weren't personally aware of how the Ramsays conducted themselves and what methods they might employ to bring harm to the Maitlands.

She stepped to the left of a fat-trunked yew and Lachlan went right, meeting her on the other side.

"How do you even ken where you're going, which way to Gershouse?" He wondered.

"I cannot tell you," she answered pertly, but relented quickly enough. "Fine, I'll tell you but Lachlan, no one did anything wrong." At his nod, she explained, "A few weeks ago, Murdoch and I were out on the boat and there was some discussion about how you know where you are, when land is not in sight. And that led to some talk about travelling on land, and well, basically Murdoch taught me how to use the sun for direction." This was clarified, as she added, "Of course, that was after he taught me the directions themselves. Naturally, I didn't think I would ever need to know these things, but you know how interesting Murdoch makes everything, that it rather stuck with me."

"But how'd you ken where Gershouse is?"

"Oh, well that knowledge came just as inadvertently. I was asking Oliver about what other possible benefits Hawkmore might know having the sea at its back, aside from as a food supply." She stepped over some protruding roots. "He's not nearly as interesting as Murdoch, but he did explain the benefit of the location of Hawkmore in regard to the sea, and explicitly if there were to be a siege. And that led to some discussion about neighboring clan lands and he just stood there in the yard, pointing fairly precisely in each direction, naming the clans who lived where. Thus today, I only needed to recall the direction and basically, I just followed where he pointed."

"Take you about a day on foot, I'm thinking," he said.

Afforded a view just now of only her profile, he was still able to detect a quick frown.

"I'll walk faster then," she said, suiting her actions to her words. "Lachlan, I do thank you for not jumping all over me and dragging me back to Hawkmore."

"Aye, my pleasure," he said agreeably. However, he wasted no time enlightening her, "Of course you're no' going anywhere near Gershouse."

This brought her up short. She stopped and tipped her face up to him, scowling, her blue eyes darkened. "I just knew you wouldn't understand."

"I understand your wanting to help."

"So then you—"

"It's no' safe," he interrupted, just now his tone beginning to find the edge of anger, which simmered constantly beneath the surface. She was about to argue so that Lachlan continued, "Mari, listen to me. You going to Gershouse will almost assuredly result in their deaths."

She gasped at this and began to argue, "If Walter Ramsay wants to marry me so badly, I'm sure he will listen to—"

"He'll have what he wants," he interjected sharply. "Right now, you are the only bargaining chip we have, so what then would prevent him from executing the lads once he has you?"

Her mouth opened and closed several times while she digested this. "Oh, dear Lord." She then covered her mouth with her hand, her dawning of understanding coming with no small amount of horror, for how she'd thought it out all wrong. "I didn't—"

Lachlan nodded as her shoulders slumped. One of the more fascinating features of Mari Sinclair's personality was her capacity to know and accept when she was beat. She didn't now come at him with some new argument to see her slapdash plan to fruition. He needed only to mention that she'd be putting those lads at a greater risk, and that was that.

Maintaining her disillusioned posture, she asked, "Will they be all right, Lachlan? Truly?"

He wouldn't lie to her now. She didn't deserve that. "I have to hope—to believe—that they will be."

She nodded at this and blew out a long breath from puffed cheeks. Mayhap she was trying to convince herself to believe as well.

"C'mon then," he said, moving the horse the last few steps to her, extending his hand.

Without further resistance, she stepped forward and he pulled her up onto the big black with him. He turned the steed around and began the trek back to Hawkmore, and neither of them spoke for several minutes.

"I'm sorry for all the...trouble I've caused you, Mari."

She nodded, the top of her head close to his chin. After a moment, long enough that he thought she might give no response, she said, "I am and I'm not."

He considered this, thought he might understand what she intimated, but then he decided he wanted her to say it. "You're going to need to clarify that."

Mari leaned back and met with his chest, turning her head to the side against him. Lachlan snaked his arm more closely around her middle.

But she only said, "I don't think I do. You know it already."

"Aye. I do."

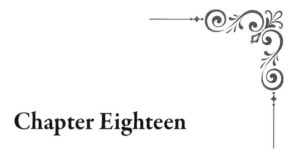

Chapter Eighteen

When they returned to Hawkmore, he gave Murdoch a nod, as he and several soldiers were gathered around a barrel fire near the barracks. Mari glanced their way but said nothing. They dismounted near the stables, leaving the steed to Rory's care, as he came running to collect the destrier. Inside, the hall was empty, and Lachlan followed Mari up to her chambers.

"You dinna want to eat first, lass?" He asked upon the stairs, two steps behind her.

"I don't."

Yet another clue revealing the current state of her mood, as Mari wasn't known for refusing a meal.

At the door, she turned to him and offered a wee parting smile, which was actually more of a grimace, and a woeful one at that, before slipping inside her chambers, closing the door behind her.

Lachlan visited his own chambers but did not much more than remove his plaid and sit near the cold hearth, his mind yet buzzing, recognizing the complete exhaustion he felt. After half an hour, he grumbled, "The hell with it," and left his chambers, once again standing in front of Mari's door.

He rapped lightly but did not wait for any call for entrance but pushed it open and stepped inside. She was abed, had sat up with his knock. She held the coverlet up and over the nightrail at her chest.

"I'll be staying here tonight, lass, make sure you dinna get any other foolish ideas in your head," he said as he closed the door, as answer to her unspoken question.

She said nothing to this, looked only as weary as he felt.

He loosened his belt, removed that and his sword and leaned them against the wall by the door. He stared at the fire for a moment, too drained to stir it to life, loosening the laces of his breastplate. This was lifted over his head and set near his sword. Approaching the bed, he said only, "Move over," before sitting on the edge to remove his boots. The mattress shifted behind him. The boots were left on the floor. He turned and laid down, on his side, one arm under his head, his left hand on her legs.

"Lachlan," her voice was tiny, barely hinting at a question.

"Lie down with me."

She hesitated, but did comply, turning onto her side as well, that they both faced the window and the dusky sky. Extending his arm fully across her, Lachlan pulled her up against him. She smelled of lavender and goodness. He buried his face in her hair for a moment, breathing deeply.

"Will you—"

"Let's no' talk, Mari. Nothing has changed. Just let me hold you." He closed his eyes.

Mari gave herself up to the fatigue of his voice and snuggled neatly against him, folding her legs along his, and laying her hand over his at her middle.

"I want to spend my last day at the beach," she whispered after many minutes.

"Aye."

HE WAS GONE WHEN SHE woke and Mari couldn't help but feel—but *know*—that last night, with him beside her had been a great missed opportunity. Yet, bone-numbing exhaustion and that ever-present hopelessness had determined that sleep was all they would have.

In the midst of dressing, she saw that the blue linen pouch was not as she had left it upon the cupboard, but was hanging on the pitcher, the thin drawstrings draped over the handle. Lachlan, she supposed, and affixed the strings to her rope belt, along with her sheath and knife.

She broke her fast with Florie and Edie in the kitchens while all three worked together, kneading so many pounds of dough for Marjorie's pork pies. Her friends were kind enough to make no mention of her upset yesterday. When they went off about their other household chores, Mari put off any other industry she might have found inside the keep and slipped through the door at the rear of the yard. She made her way down to the beach, giving gratitude to the heavens for the clear skies and calm sea. Not wanting to be discovered, to be denied this last bit of freedom, she did not remain in front of the castle but wandered further, to the spot where Lachlan had both thrilled her and broken her not so long ago.

The beach was a peculiar place. There wasn't much to do if one wasn't swimming or climbing into a boat for any greater purpose, and still she knew this might well remain her most favorite spot on earth. She filled her gifted drawstring bag with memories scavenged from the sand, and spent a good amount of time just sitting and staring out to the sea, so still that a small fox emerged from the dunes and skittered along the shore, in and out of the surf, undisturbed by her presence.

Yet, try as she might, she could not keep at bay the very fact that at this time tomorrow, she might well be gone from Hawkmore.

Diana was right; it was terrible luck to have been born a woman and not a man. For all the good and bad in her life, not any of it was her doing. Not her choices, not her decisions. She tried to recall if any person in all her life had ever asked her what *she* wanted, what she dreamed of, what she hoped for in life.

Shaking herself, chastising herself for wallowing in self-pity, she rose again and spied some very curious pieces of wood. They were far away from the water, at the edge of the flat sand near the bottom of the embankment. The wood was weathered and worn, pale and lifeless, arms of a tree at one time, she imagined. She lifted and inspected first one and then another, shrieking when she turned over the second piece as its underside was infested with ugly black and red bugs. She dropped it quickly and then startled when a shadow fell over her.

Turning with a start, she knew both relief and nervousness when she discovered Lachlan standing between her and the sea.

She could make no sense of his inscrutable gaze, but then saw no reason that she should not return his thorough regard. She decided, as they stood staring but shared no words, that they were only committing this to memory, the image of the other.

And Mari realized that all her life, her heart had ached for something unknown.

Until now.

Lachlan was what she dreamed of, what she had hoped for.

"Good heavens," she said, breathless with this new awareness.

The sound of her voice, the very fact that she'd spoken, seemed to have roused him from his brooding reverie.

Squaring her shoulders, a bold plan forming, Mari stepped closer to him, shortening the distance to only a few feet. "Lachlan, I need you to ask me what I want."

"Mari, I dinna come here—"

She stamped her bare foot in the packed sand. "Lachlan, for once can you just do as I ask? It's a fairly straightforward request. Ask me what I want."

"Fine." He threw up his hand. "Mari, what do you—"

She waved her hand, stopping him. She'd gotten ahead of herself. "No, wait. First, what is it actually called when a man and a"—she rolled her eyes at her own self, for being awkward now when so much was at stake, for the blush that came—"when a man and woman procreate, or whatever? The act? What's the act called? Oh, fornication, I just recalled the word. Never mind."

She was babbling and he was seriously confused, his eyes wide now. And she didn't care. She'd get it out *and* she'd get what she wanted! Refusing her was not an option.

She started again. "All right. Now ask me what I want."

Possibly, he appeared less befuddled now, mayhap slightly entertained. Honestly, she never could actually tell with him.

"Marianna Sinclair," he said, removing his belt and sword from his hips, "what is it that you want?"

She only allowed a small pleased smile for his compliance when he faced her again, so much of her concentration on what she was about to suggest, on the arguments she had literally just prepared. She said bravely, in a clear voice, "I want to fornicate with you." Immediately he looked about to argue. She hurried along. "You may *not* say no to me. Since the moment I met you, since the minute you kidnapped me, it has been about you and what you needed, why you kidnapped me, why you wouldn't even consider keeping me as yours. And we're done with that." He applied the toes of one foot to the heel of the other to remove his boots but paused to hold up his finger as if he might yet disagree. Mari wouldn't let him. "No, Lachlan, please hear me out. I want that with you, the fornication. I want it to be with you. I won't beg or cry for anything else. Just that."

"Mari—"

"Lachlan, I'm only asking for this one thing. Finish it with me, finish what you started. Just once, pretend..." she stopped, her shoulders slumping with a sigh. "Can you pretend that you love me? I promise I'll go quietly then."

He lifted his tunic over his head and dropped it next to his boots.

"Why would you refuse this, the only thing I've ever asked of you?" She felt as if she might cry. Or scream. He seemed interested only in swimming now. She didn't want to swim! She wanted him to love her. With greater passion, she accused, "You build these mammoth walls around you, comprised of your scars—of body and mind—but you've built them so tall only a crazy person would dare to climb over them."

Bare-chested and bare-footed, Lachlan came to her.

Nearly losing her train of thought at the sight of him, she finished weakly, "And yet, here I am." Oh, but he was so magnificent. "Crazy."

Standing in front of her, he lifted his hand and brushed the stray curls off her shoulder. "I was no' about to refuse you, lass. I sought you out now for exactly this. But I can no' have you running around using the word *fornication*." He turned her around and untied the ribbon that held her messy hair, dropping it to the ground. "It's called lovemaking, or making love, depending how you use it." He unlaced the gathered ties at the neck of her gown and turned her back around.

Mari was speechless.

"It would only ever be lovemaking, between you and me, lass. But I'll be needing to warn you," he said and touched his lips to her, but only for the barest of seconds. "Your husband will ken you've done this. You'll be ruined, Mari. No more untouched by any man."

Breathless now with his seeming assent, she spoke the lone truth she knew, "I only want you." She kept her gaze on his eyes as they moved with his intent.

He put his forefinger lightly into the hollow at the base of her throat and dragged the finger down until it reached the fabric of her gown. "There's often pain the first time." The loosened gown and kirtle bowed beneath his finger until it gaped over the top of her breasts.

"You would never hurt me." She watched his eyes still; his gaze lowered yet more. His hands followed, his fingers gathering sections of her gown and kirtle at her hips, raising it.

And now he looked her in the eye. "I will make love to you, Mari Sinclair. Maybe I've always known that we would. And aye, I'll pretend that I love you, just for now, just today, but you ken that it changes nothing come the morrow. It canna."

Mari nodded. She couldn't at this moment name one emotion that clogged her throat or twisted her heart or brought that heat between her legs. And she didn't care. There would be plenty of time to identify it all, but right now she just wanted to feel.

Lachlan began to lift the gown and kirtle higher and higher, inch by inch. He still held her gaze, his eyes darkened to that familiar aching need he'd shown her before. "And you'll pretend, too, lass, aye? You'll pretend that you love me as well?"

She smiled with some bittersweet heartbreak and shook her head. "I won't have to pretend, Lachlan."

His response was similar to hers, at once grateful and sad. "Nor I, love."

Chapter Nineteen

Lachlan lifted the nightrail up and over her head, dropped it to the ground, and let his gaze roam with abandon over her. His regard came with a bit of breathlessness, his and hers. But he did not touch her.

She felt exposed and then adored by his regard and finally understood what Lachlan had shown her the day of the river crossing, when she'd seen his naked chest for the first time, when he'd caught her staring: he'd been aroused and enlivened.

As was Mari right now.

Mari couldn't wait. She lifted her own hand, placing it on his chest with a great consciousness. For just a moment she closed her eyes, feeling him, so hard and warm beneath her hand. Opening her eyes, she raised and set her other hand upon him. He stood still, let her know him. She moved both hands, slowly and with great reverence, over his muscled body, traced one finger lightly over his nipple. Following with her eyes, she slid her hands upward, one on each shoulder, traced over the outline of him, measuring the breadth of this magnificent man.

Mari sketched a path all the way down to his hands, pausing there to glance up at him.

Squeezing her fingers, he pulled her near. When he lowered his head and his lips to her, she thought for sure she might weep, for his beauty, for his willingness, for this thing they would do.

I am in love with you.

His kiss was slow, as gentle as her hands had been upon him. She allowed it, trusting Lachlan to guide them. They stood, only their fingers and lips touching. And then his hands left hers, but his mouth remained. There was other movement that Mari soon realized was Lachlan doffing his breeches and drawers. He stopped kissing her, only to pull his legs up and out, leaving the garments in a heap beneath his feet.

Mari opened her eyes and showed no shyness, only enormous curiosity, letting her gaze wander over him. He was so very different from her; hard where she was soft, wearing as many scars as she did freckles; his hips were lean whereas hers flared; and between his legs, his manhood swelled, while between her own came a quivering response.

Lifting her gaze again found him staring, waiting, seeming to hold his breath. She recalled how he had taken her hand before and bade her touch him, and reached for him now. He'd been clothed then that she'd only rubbed her hand up and down him. This was different now, and she wasn't sure how to handle him so that she only touched her fingers to the tip of him. He drew in a breath and breathed out through his mouth but otherwise remained very still. Mari slid her fingers along his shaft, toward the base, and then back. Some instinct made her wrap her whole hand around him. She moved her gaze from his face to his erection, and back again, needing some sign this was acceptable, desired even. His eyes were dark and heated with that same intensity she'd noticed each time he touched her. He'd shown her previously the motion and she used that now, back and forth while his cock grew larger and stronger and pointed directly at her, it seemed.

Too soon, his fingers circled her wrist. The corner of his mouth lifted.

He said nothing, just dragged her to him, lifting her hand away from him, crashing his lips onto her again.

A great and exquisite unknown was met when their bodies touched, her naked breasts were pressed against his warm and bare chest, his erection throbbed against her belly. Mari pulled her hands from his, tipping her face up further to him, gliding her fingers into his hair, pulling him closer to her. Lachlan set his hands on her hips, not drawing her any nearer, though his fingers dug into her flesh.

She made the kiss wild, wanting to know and feel everything all at once, nearly climbing upon him, lifting herself up onto her toes. Some savage need gripped her, that she wanted to devour him, know his soul, that she needed to get there now.

The fingers at her hips pushed downward, kept her feet on the ground. He breathed against her mouth. "Mari, your passion is more than...it thrills me beyond anything. But lass, if we want the memory, we have to go slow."

"I want everything, all of you. I am...jittery and twisted inside with the need."

She saw only pleasure, enough to fill the sea, in his gaze. "You canna ken it yet," he said, surprising her with a sheepish chuckle, "but everything will be done right quickly if I canna control it."

"I feel like my lack of control is part of something bigger." Feeble kin, she supposed. She reached for his hand and placed it over her breast "But can you touch me please?" She closed her eyes just as he closed his fingers around her. "I want this," she whispered with a new breathlessness. "And I want your lips on me, here," she said, her hand covering his.

"Aye, love," he said, lowering his head. A vocal sigh emerged when his tongue flicked over her nipple. But then her legs threatened to give out, that she clung to him.

Lachlan's steady hand snaked around her waist. He moved her backward, toward the edge of the beach and lowered her onto the windswept sand, following her down, his mouth barely leaving her breast. He nipped with his teeth and laved with his tongue and suckled with his lips and Mari was undone, naught but pudding in his arms.

She wasn't sure how she could manage thought, let alone words, but she said to him, "How do I make you feel...like this? How do I touch you to make all this fire and swirling inside you?"

"The fire burns already, Mari," he said huskily.

Lachlan trailed a line of soft kisses along her skin, down to her navel and over her hips. He sat back then, on his haunches at her side. With their gazes locked, he placed the tip of one finger on her mound.

Her body and mind reacted, the flames expanding while she knew there was more to come, that everything he did to her would be glorious. A gleam sparked in Lachlan's eye as he moved his finger in through the dark curls to find her bud, the touch so whisper soft and tantalizing, Mari nearly came undone. He pressed on, two fingers now touching her, reaching more intimate places, one sliding further between her legs, swirling the wetness around her before pushing inside. Gasping, she clenched and arched, and Lachlan groaned and fell nearly on top of her, taking her mouth in a savage kiss. He began to move his finger inside her, and she moved against him, wordlessly begging for more. A second finger joined the first, moving in and out, igniting further sensation and moans.

She felt weightless, felt not her limbs or any part of her but where he stroked, as if every nerve inside her had raced to that place to receive this new touch. It was gone too soon, though, his fingers sliding out of her that Mari whimpered her distress. But then he came on top of her, slid from the side of her across her. "Open your legs more," he said, his breath hot and heavy at her cheek. They fell open, her legs, under the insistence of his. And his penis touched where his fingers had, and she moaned with this fresh excitement, knowing, understanding now that he would fill her and all that pleasure would return, and grow.

"Please," she pleaded against his lips, rising against his hardness, offering herself.

With excruciating slowness, Lachlan held himself on his elbows and pushed into her folds. While her body adjusted to this, while her hips still moved, he forged ahead only gradually, that she begged *please* once more. He surged forward then, embedding himself deep inside her, breaking her barrier.

Mari's eyes opened wide.

"Oh, bother," she groaned with some surprise. "It does hurt the first time. Lachlan...?"

He stilled. They breathed heavily against each other. "You trust me, aye, Mari mine?"

"Very much."

"The pain will fade. But aye, give me a second here."

"Does it hurt you as well?"

He shook his head and a husky chuckle followed. "Only hurt my pride," he said, "if I come too quickly."

"I don't know what that means."

"But you will, love." He shifted above her, bringing his nose to hers. "I'm going to show you. And you won't want to ever leave me when I do and I won't want to send you off, but I'm going to show you anyway."

"Because you love me?"

"Aye, lass."

He began to move inside her.

Mari was very still, waiting for pain to come again. But she felt only him, filling her, sliding in with exquisite slowness, withdrawing almost completely before he filled her again.

She closed her eyes, concentrated on that motion, put her mind in that place, the very core of her, where he reached so deep. The very intimacy of the act, the way Lachlan moved, how deep he penetrated, how her wet body received him and accommodated him, excited her.

A new sensation overtook her, drew all her attention. It began deep inside, where Lachlan reached. It was liquid heat and pulsing need and it became so strong that she flexed under him, moving her hips up and down, both an answer to his thrusts and a search for whatever beckoned her.

They moved together, hips pumping, languidly and then with greater need, faster and faster. She moaned and he grunted, rising up to set his hands on her hips. He bent his fingers into her flesh, held her to his hard thrusts, and sent her over the edge.

She cried out, joy and wonder and pleasure overwhelming her. She lifted her hands, digging her short nails into his sides, silently begging him to never stop. She didn't know its name, didn't know at all what it was, but it washed over her in waves. It shook her insides, quaked her limbs, and stole her breath. A sound erupted from Lachlan and she knew he'd found it, too. He slowed his thrusts, made them torturous and deliberate, drawing out the ecstasy. Intuitively, Mari squeezed herself around him and he groaned and shuddered, and she felt his release inside, felt the vibrations. She reveled in this, her joy immeasurable, believing he'd felt what she had, had known the same exquisite beauty of that joyous release.

Lachlan laid his head next to hers, his breath hot and fast on her neck.

She didn't ever want to move. She'd yet to open her eyes, was still feeling everything. But she held him close, her fingers in his hair, thought she might not ever let him leave the here and now.

"I love you, Lachlan."

SOME VERY LARGE PART of him knew—had known since he'd found her returned and had lain with her last night—that he wouldn't send her away. And that had been before she'd so adorably begged him to fornicate with her. Likely, the absolute pureness of her request, so innocently articulated and argued for, would be something he would cherish always.

Despite what he'd said to her, only minutes ago, that he would give her this and it would change nothing, he'd known inside that it was a lie.

It came as no surprise to him how selfless and giving she was while lovemaking. Her passion was new, the complete joy unknown to her before, and yet she'd wanted to be assured he felt as she did, knew each and every tingle of pleasure and every ripple of delight. And *Jesu*, how could he not? She was beyond exquisite, formed and fitted so clearly for only him, her body perfection, her passion mind-numbing. Every touch was love. His arms trembled, even now, with some insane desire to squeeze her so hard, never let her go.

So...to hell with the Ramsays. They were going to march back up to the keep right now—maybe not right now, not until he'd loved her once more—and he was going to tell Murdoch to begin moving the waiting army. They would borrow a tactic from the old MacBriar chief, wouldn't sit around waiting for some peace treaty that the Ramsays were unlikely to uphold. He would storm Gershouse and get his lads back, and he'd tell Walter Ramsay that Mari Sinclair was his, would always be his.

His breathing had mostly returned to normal. Lachlan lifted himself, finding her cheek with his lips, pressing a slow and thoughtful kiss there. "Mari mine, I'm going to need you to pretend a wee bit longer." She smiled, he felt it against his lips, felt her cheek move as her mouth stretched.

"Lachlan, I'm going to need you to do that—all of it—again with me."

He raised his face yet more, wanting to see love in her gaze.

Mari stiffened beneath him.

At the same time, Lachlan heard the low, ominous screech of Hawkmore's alarm, wailing across the sand and sea. With little finesse, he pulled himself from her and jumped to his feet, scanning the beach behind him. It was empty yet, no army come to call, nor any soldier come to fetch him. Lachlan reached for Mari, pulling her to her feet.

"It's a terrible end to a beautiful beginning, Mari mine," he said and kissed her worried lips. "But we need to make haste, get up to the keep."

She nodded without hesitation, raising no fuss for the hurried conclusion. They dressed quickly, with Mari tossing his tunic to him at one point. He hopped on one foot and then the other, donning his boots, and once Mari was dressed, they took off running, Lachlan holding her hand in one of his, his belt and sword in the other.

He knew, even before they'd reached the top of the slope at the rear of the castle, that this was no simple fire in the yard. The sound of the main gate being raised, the scrape and groan of metal and wood being lifted, came to him, and Lachlan just knew the Ramsays had come.

The yard was all a bustle, people scurrying to and fro. Lachlan dragged Mari with him to a crowd that had gathered near the now closed gate. Torquil and Edric and several others were just slamming the huge timber brace into place, securing the entrance.

He stepped between Murdoch and Utrid and saw a body on the ground. He noticed first the orange hair and thought it was Charles, but Mari pushed forward, crying, "Harman!" She fell to her knees at his side.

Christ, but the lad had been tortured, mercilessly, Lachlan saw. Blood, old and new covered so much of his skin and garments. He'd pissed himself, more than once, the stains on his trousers said. His eyes were nearly swollen shut, but he lifted one hand at the sound of his sister's voice. Two fingernails were missing completely, ripped from the nail bed, the blood there old and dried.

"Harman, my God," Mari cried, "what has happened?"

He said something unintelligible. Mari lowered her head, putting her ear to his face.

Murdoch said to Lachlan, "Rider came up, about midway across the field out front and dumped him. Just rode away then."

"Has he said anything?"

"Only that Ramsays were on their way."

"Did he mention Niel or Charles or Edmund?"

This question drew Mari's brother's attention. He moved his legs fitfully and cried out as he did, as one was bent at an unnatural angle.

Lachlan squatted next to Mari, who straightened and gave him a horrified look for the damage done to her brother. He spared her only a quick nod, having no idea what that might do for her, and questioned the agitated Harman. "What news of my soldiers?"

Harman groaned and squeaked and seemed wholly incapable of forming words that Lachlan wondered for the briefest of seconds if his tongue had been cut out. But no, he'd already given information to Murdoch. Finally, Harman managed, "They were in the cells. They hadn't started on them...weren't done with me."

"Why did Ramsay do this to you?" Lachlan wanted to know.

A great blubber of a sob preceded his answer. "Because I dinna keep my sister safe for him."

Murdoch hunched low then as well. "How many are coming, boy?"

He had to repeat this several times, as Harman was wailing, over and over, "I'm sorry, Mari. I'm sorry."

"Dammit, lad. How many?" Murdoch finally roared.

Flat on his back, unmoved as of yet, Harman shook his head against the gravel of the yard. "I dinna ken. Hundreds. Four. Five. I dinna ken." Every word was wept.

"When?" Lachlan asked.

"Now," Harman moaned. "They're just beyond the trees."

"Bluidy hell!" Murdoch cursed. He and Lachlan stood at the same time.

"Bring the litter!" Utrid called. He bent near Mari, where Lachlan had been. "We'll get him inside, lass. Make him comfortable."

He could do nothing for her now, Lachlan knew, and had no time for her brother. He'd let Utrid arrange his move. To Murdoch, he said, "Four or five hundred. Christ."

Murdoch's expression agreed. "Ours are all here, all who'd come at the call, expecting we were marching in the morn, but lad, that's only a few hundred."

Lachlan's mind had been spinning with each bit of information Harman had given them.

To the group growing around him, awaiting instructions, he began to bark out orders.

"I want a dozen to the village," he called to the general crowd, knowing the orders would be allocated appropriately. "Get every man, woman, and child away. Send them up to the caves in the Killen Hills." He swiveled his head, included all who listened attentively. "Ready the boats at the sea, the mistress and Mari and the household staff go off first sign of falling." He singled out young Rory, who hovered nearby. "Bring Oliver to me, now." To Murdoch, "Archers on the wall, fletcher and his lads bringing up the supplies. Have the stable lads begin boiling the pitch." Addressing the soldiers collectively once again, he stated, "At all costs the beach is *not* to be breached. We canna let them surround us." Hands on his hips, he scanned his brain. Aye, that was it for now. "Go on, then." They'd trained for this as well, every person who lived and worked inside the keep.

Murdoch was still at his side. "Send Diana and Mari off now, lad. Five hundred? We canna hold them off, not with those numbers."

"No," Lachlan said, watching the steward, Oliver, walking sedately toward him, his usual calm not marred by any heightened sense of fear or impending doom. "We can hold for a while, but no' for too many days," Lachlan agreed with Murdoch. To Oliver, now at his side, he instructed, "Send a boat down to Berriedale. Tell Iain McEwen I need his army," he paused and pointed at the steward, "use these words: a wee critical something."

"A wee critical something," Oliver repeated, not questioning the phrasing, as his laird—all chiefs—often used strange words and sentences in their missives for authenticity's sake. He bobbed his head and retreated into the keep.

To Murdoch, he wondered, "Dare we send off a unit to Gershouse? Get the lads now, while Ramsays' army is here?"

Murdoch nodded, lifting a brow. "They'd no suspect it, wouldn't think we'd give up any defense." With a shrug, he reasoned, "A dozen less here won't make a difference when he's got hundreds more already."

Lachlan had been thinking the same thing. "They can head north, undetected, and cut across at Coulmore Pass."

"Aye," Murdoch agreed. "I'll make that happen." And he took off, calling out names as he moved away.

The litter had finally arrived, but people were scrambling still, busy with orders that there weren't enough remaining to lift Harman. Lachlan pulled at Mari's arm, bringing her to her feet.

"Go on, Mari," he said. "Get inside. I'll get your—"

A missile caught his eye, a flaming arrow sailing through the sky, on a downward path. Lachlan yanked at Mari, pulling her out of the way, shielding her in his arms. The missile landed only feet from where she'd stood, harmlessly upon the dirt.

"Eyes up!" was called belatedly from the battlements, followed by a more hysterical call of, "Incoming!"

Lachlan cursed and began dragging Mari toward the stables, the closest cover. A quick glance over his shoulder showed more flaming missiles flying overhead and landing in the bailey. She fought him. "Lachlan, no! Harman!"

Utrid was already dragging the crying man by the shoulders along the ground, pulling him away from the open yard and into the stables as well, under the cover of those roofs. He deposited him none too gently into one of the empty stalls.

Lachlan pushed Mari down into the stall, next to her brother. "Mari," Lachlan said gruffly, drawing her gaze from Harman, "do not leave these stables, not for anything, not until I come for you."

She nodded shakily, seeming to have no fear of the looming battle, but only for her traitorous brother. She quickly put Lachlan from her mind, gathering straw from around her brother, uselessly, frantically pushing it onto the fresher spots of blood on Harman's body.

Assuming the task of trying to save her brother, which Lachlan thought improbable, would keep her well occupied, he charged from the stables, dodging the still flying projectiles and raced up to the battlements.

Surveying the great expanse of field before the castle showed only a few dozen archers lined up, hundreds of yards away. No other soldier of the Ramsay contingent was visible, must yet be concealed in the trees another few hundred yards beyond their archers.

"Longbowmen! Take them out!" Lachlan shouted, even as several men atop the wall, mostly archers at this stage of the siege, were already answering the Ramsay's fiery first strike with a returned barrage, minus the flames. He saw only one or two of Ramsays longbowmen drop initially. He cursed under his breath, fighting the urge to grab up a weapon himself and hurl one arrow after another until they all fell. Many dozens more flaming projectiles skittered across the sky into the yard and onto different sections of the roof inside Hawkmore before three more Ramsay archers fell from their mounts, then four, five, six.

There was little to celebrate, though, as those soldiers were quickly replaced by another unit of archers trotting out from the trees and positioning themselves near the lads running from man to man, with buckets of pitch and torch to light each arrow before it was sent.

Soldiers in the yard scrambled all around, chasing each fiery missile with buckets of water, to douse the flames as they met with wood and straw and grass.

"Take out the drudges with the tar!" Murdoch yelled, with an extreme amount of frustration that the Maitland longbowmen needed to be told this.

Seconds later, those six or seven young soldiers dropped, felled by Maitland arrows.

And all was quiet for a while.

Chapter Twenty

When blood began to dribble out of Harman's mouth, Mari knew there would be no saving him. She held his hand and told him everything would be all right.

She brushed back the coarse orange hair from his forehead and stayed with him, tucked safely inside the quiet of the stables while outside, soldiers and others moved here and there about the courtyard; occasionally she heard Lachlan's voice shouting orders, or Murdoch doing the same.

He settled after a while, lost all the twitchiness, that Mari wondered if he might be going beyond the pain even. She stayed with him and observed him calmly, always having supposed Harman must have received his looks from his own mother, bearing no resemblance at all to their shared father.

"Did Walter himself do all this to you?" She didn't want to see, to know, all the torture that had been inflicted, but she was so close she could not escape it.

"He's got a man...a demon, to do this. Walter would no' dirty his hands."

On her knees, she bent close to hear his soft words.

"Harman, is it true what's been supposed? That you've been pillaging and reiving about Aberdeen?"

"Aye," he answered, seemingly without shame. A full minute passed before he added, "Old Ramsay bade me do it, no other reason but to vex the Maitlands. Made no sense to me...but the coin was good."

Mari didn't have too much experience with death, but she had a vague notion that people, with their last breaths, sometimes displayed contrition for things they'd done or how they'd lived. She sensed none of this in Harman. He only relayed information, it seemed. His heart had no need or no desire to make amends, even with some pitiful last minute plea for salvation, she concluded.

He stopped breathing in the next minute, saying nothing else.

Mari was sorry that she felt so little, that she never truly knew her brother, though she did acknowledge some nebulous grief for the loss of this connection to her childhood, to that time when her dear mother had lived.

She turned and yanked down a horse blanket that was draped over the wood partition between this stall and the next and covered Harman's body. Disheartened, she leaned against the wall behind her, quiet for a moment with her thoughts.

"Mari!"

Turning her head against the wall, she saw Lachlan approach. He paused when he noticed the shrouded body. His expression then gave her yet more proof that he was a good man. He had no reason at all to feel anything over Harman's death, but he pursed his lips with some displeasure and the gaze he gave to her was etched with softness, his sorrow related only to his love for her.

"C'mon then, lass." He offered his hand to her.

Mari let him pull her to her feet. But he did more, pulled her into his arms, rubbed his hand up and down her back. "I'm sorry, Mari."

She nodded against his chest, both her arms folded between them, her eyes closed. Already, it felt as if days, weeks, months maybe, had passed since he'd made love so splendidly to her.

"It's quiet." She just realized this. "Is it done?"

"Nae, lass. But I want you inside the keep now."

He walked her briskly across the yard to the hall and closed the door behind him when they entered.

"Where is everyone?" She asked. She hadn't given it much consideration, but rather thought the household might be gathered in the hall.

"They'll be down in the chapel," Lachlan said, leading her toward the rear of the keep and through the dim passageways.

Mari had only twice been to Hawkmore's chapel, each time at the insistence of Diana. She'd not minded, but supposed it was obvious to any and all that she wasn't pious, had no relationship with the church or services, as it had not been a part of her life since her mother had died.

The chapel was on the ground floor, one floor below the hall and kitchens and larder. It was not a remarkable room, being low ceilinged and large enough for only seven pews in the nave, each of which might seat four or five people across. But the altar at the front of the chapel was set upon a raised platform and surrounded by carved wood walls and a surprisingly colorful tiled ceiling.

Many faces turned, anxious, when the door was pushed open by Lachlan. Diana set her hand to her heart and breathed some faint relief—for Lachlan's current well-being or for the fact that it was no intruder who'd entered, Mari could not say.

All of the regular household was here—Florie and Edie, and the kitchen lad, Robert; the steward, Oliver, and the mistress, of course; and Marjorie, the cook.

Diana waved her forward so that Lachlan pushed Mari down onto the pew next to his mother.

More than one questioning, hopeful gaze settled upon him that Lachlan informed them with some pity, "It's no' really begun yet." To his mother, specifically, "The boats will be kept at the ready. Use the tunnels if the time comes. Down to Berriedale, if needs must."

Florie whimpered while Diana nodded tightly at this instruction, wrapping her arm around Mari's shoulder. Diana reached for her son's hand, and he gave it, Diana squeezing tightly, so much said between mother and son just then.

He laid his other hand on Mari's shoulder. She bent her elbow and placed her hand over his. She did not look at him again but closed her eyes and felt him.

His hand slid away from her and he left.

The door closed behind him with a certain ominous thud.

"Set the brace now, lad," said Oliver softly.

Robert leapt quickly from his seat to lift the heavy timber into the waiting brackets, securing the door from within.

Quiet descended when Robert had taken his seat again next to Marjorie in the second pew.

It was interrupted not ten minutes later.

As one, all those within the chapel jumped in fright as a loud and dull crashing noise broke the silence. The sound was monstrous, and the pew trembled beneath Mari.

Oliver, whose hands were folded prayerfully and hanging over the pew in front of him, advised 'twas naught but the catapult being used, hurling huge rocks against the outer castle walls. "Generally ineffective," he said. "Makes no more than a dent or two in the stone." While Mari and the others looked unappeased by this news, he added unpleasantly, "Of course, if they're sending over anything on fire, well then, that usually makes a difference."

Florie and Edie simultaneously let out little squeaks of fright, which soon became larger shrieks when another loud boom was heard and felt from above.

Up until this moment, Mari had convinced herself that she was calm and that all would be well. She and Diana fastened hands, their knuckles white, and exchanged gazes meant to calm each other, stoic and tense. Nothing was assured, she realized. Her knowledge of warfare was decidedly limited—non-existent, actually—but even Mari understood that the victors would suffer losses, as well as the losers. She feared for the men on the front lines of defense, those atop the parapets and castle walls, those tucked into the crenellated rooftop to stave off the initial attack.

Mostly, though, she thought of Murdoch and Utrid and Torquil, and could not keep her mind at all, every other minute, from wondering if Lachlan were all right, and if he might stay that way.

"Have you done this before?" She asked softly of Diana.

"Not in this house," Diana said, her voice breaking. "But aye, I have."

Tearfully, Florie asked, "Will it last long?"

Diana considered all the faces, and all the fright. "There are no normal answers. Could be done in hours, might take days. Hundreds of casualties, or only a handful. Win, lose, stay, go. We'll get through it. We, us here now, have an out. If it comes to it, we'll slip through the tunnels behind the altar and emerge just near those boats on the beach. *We* will survive this, no matter what. Our prayers and our fears should be reserved for those above us, who must stay and fight, to protect us, to protect all of Hawkmore."

"THEY'RE BUT TOYING with us, it seems," Murdoch mentioned late in the evening.

Lachlan concurred. "I'm beginning to think they'd used those archers earlier only to test our capabilities." Since then, the Ramsays had employed the huge catapult, though had sent only a dozen boulders, which had little effect, the first few falling short of even the outer wall. One lucky toss had seen a huge rock crash into the roof over the bakehouse, caving in the front of that small building, and that had been the most damage inflicted as of yet.

Since then, they'd lined up hundreds of foot soldiers and cavalry, just beyond the reach of the Maitland longbowmen, but Lachlan thought these were not their complete numbers yet. And they hadn't moved in hours, made no push forward, that it only seemed they were waiting for something, though neither Lachlan nor Murdoch could guess what. Around dusk, he saw that a few tents had sprouted up within the Ramsay ranks, as if they had plans to camp for days, at least certainly had no plans to mount the bulk of their attack this night.

It was, then, a long night, fraught with little sleep and more anxiety about what the morrow would bring. He convinced himself not to visit Mari inside the keep. He needed to focus, needed to gather rage, and hold it tight for the battle to come, couldn't risk giving way to softness that must come with any look or touch from her. He had to remind himself of this again and again.

Lachlan remained on the battlements, catching rest where he could, as did every soldier inside these walls. The upper walkway along the parapets held now more than one hundred Maitland men, in constant vigil about all four sides of the castle. After one boat had left the beach yesterday, aimed for Berriedale, with Lachlan's request for aid, not another living soul had stepped foot on that sand.

The sun rose majestically over the sea, spilling light onto the walls of the castle and keep, and eventually across the wide expanse of brown and green in front of the watchful men atop the wall.

Shortly thereafter, Lachlan cursed roundly and with true dread when the trees beyond the meadow spit forth the exact numbers Ramsay had amassed and brought with him.

"Christ almighty," Murdoch said, standing beside Lachlan, seeing the same thing. From this distance, hundreds of yards away, further than the spot where their archers had set up so briefly, the full force of the Ramsays appeared only as army ants charging out of a hill, come at once and in droves, to wage their war. "That's more than four, five hundred."

"Closer to six, seven?"

"Aye."

"They've got to be mercenaries."

"Or free company," Murdoch supposed.

"No difference, when they're lining up in front of you."

Murdoch harrumphed. "Here's hoping they're better provided with daring than with arms."

Still, the Ramsays made no move to charge on Hawkmore.

Lachlan was bewildered, could only imagine the show of force, the stalling, was intended as naught but mental warfare, hoping to diminish whatever fighting spirit might be left after witnessing these numbers amass. Not much, he had to assume. Not a man here, watching that many enemy rallying outside their door, could have any inclination that he might yet be breathing by the end of the day.

Finally, shortly before midday, when several more hours had passed without a drop of blood spilled, a fine wagon, sporting two flags bearing the red boar's head on the gold background, rolled up into the meadow. Further confused by their methods and audacity, Lachlan watched as the wagon moved closer and closer to Hawkmore, being escorted by only two dark helmed soldiers. The driver circled and parked, halfway between the gate and the standing Ramsay army—well within range of the Maitland archers—and stopped so that the bed of the wagon was visible to all upon the wall.

Inside, semi-prone upon blankets and cushions of bright red and gold, sat an old man, so pale and feeble in contrast against his colorful bedclothes.

"Rannoch Ramsay," Murdoch guessed.

"What the—?" Lachlan was, now, beyond confused.

The old man began to speak. The distance was still great enough and his voice so frail, they couldn't hear a word he said.

Sometimes, with the advent of a coming terrific disaster, emotions were riled to severe incongruity, that Lachlan burst out laughing. The whole scene was just ridiculous.

Others followed suit, several lifting their hands behind their ears, pointing them forward to indicate they couldn't hear. After a moment, while the man appeared to still be speaking, the entire wall of soldiers began to laugh, loud and crudely.

"Is he fecking kidding me?" Murdoch groused. "Is this what we've been waiting on?"

One of Rannoch Ramsay's minions, upon a big black at the side of the cart, began to shout out the words of his chief. The wall barely settled, amused to distraction, that only snippets reached any who might have an interest in them.

Lachlan caught something about *one hundred years of acrimony* between the Ramsays and the Maitlands and *the time had come*....

Ignoring this babble, dismissing it as superfluous grandstanding, Lachlan said to Murdoch, "They're coming through, no matter what."

"Aye," Murdoch said, pursing his lips, "and that'll be that, lad. Too many for us to hold."

Lachlan nodded, sour about the whole affair, near distraught with this surety that he would have no more joy with Mari. He wasn't ready to die, had only just learned to live, had only just found hope for the future. He was sorry that all these good men would fall today.

Murdoch seethed, "When I get where I'm going—up or down, I dinna ken—I'll be having words for whoever thought it made any sense for the proud and mighty Maitlands to be taken out by the fecking Ramsays. Never met a more spindly-spined, belly-crawling blood pool of waste."

"Shite, I rather wish we'd gone by way of the English," said Torquil, nearby.

"Aye to that," Utrid chimed in.

"Dinna suppose you'd consider taking off with the boats?" Murdoch said to Lachlan.

Lachlan sent him a look that gave the answer Murdoch was already well aware of. It was tempting, to be sure, but he was not made like that, to run away.

While Rannoch still blathered and his henchman still called out the words to be heard, Lachlan said to those around him, "Archers, can you hand me one last boon and silence that old goat?" His voice was filled with cheer, his adrenalin rising, knowing his men needed to see fearlessness yet and still something positive—knowing as well that the request in essence would be the end of their levity, that it would bring the waiting army charging full force at them.

Plenty of laughter followed, interrupted by Murdoch demanding, "And get that one yapping at his side. He's wearing a fecking felt hat—who the bluidy hell does that?"

More laughter then. Archers knocked, away from the wall, so that when they lifted their bows over the top of the wall, they needed only a split second to aim. A barrage of arrows flew straight and fast, peppering the bodies of Rannoch Ramsay and the two mounted soldiers on either side of the cart.

And while the Maitland warriors shouted their liking of this, raising their fists and their swords and their bows into the air with a bloodcurdling war cry, Murdoch exchanged a bittersweet look with Lachlan, his eyes misty. "Aye, lad. You're a great man. It's been a privilege."

Lachlan wrapped up his captain in a huge bear hug. "You were—are—more of a father than I ever deserved."

Only seconds later, the entire horde of the Ramsays army moved from a half mile away, slowly at first, a shifting dark brown splotch upon the earth, undulating and springing forward, spreading out as they raced across the meadow.

Lachlan leaned over the inside wall, shouted loudly for the lad, Rory. He showed himself in seconds, emerging from the stables, his young face frightened and fierce at the same time.

"Go on now, get down to the chapel! Get them out on the boats right quick. You take them down to Berriedale."

The lad's relief was palpable, that he could leave here, escape the promise of death as signified by the thunderous pounding of hooves.

While his army prepared in earnest now to at least give a good fight, Lachlan called out to one and all. "It has been my great honor, lads, to have been your laird for these few years. I'll see you on the other side."

Murdoch raised his sword and called, over the thundering of the Ramsays and their paid militia racing toward Hawkmore, "If we're going to hell, lads, we might as well take 'em with us!"

The next war cry that followed was deafening, drowning out the noise of an army three times their numbers thundering toward their gate.

As soon as the Ramsays came into range, the Maitland archers let loose, one after another, in remarkably quick succession. They felled dozens, saw many more drop as horses began to trip and stumble over the downed persons and animals.

Just as the coming horde reached the castle walls, the remaining Ramsay archers set up in the middle of the field, behind the charging warriors and very near to the wagon and their dead chief. The missiles they shot now were aimed better, bent on taking out any man shown on the wall who might defend the keep. Lachlan glanced up to the highest tower inside the keep, saw arrows exiting from the two slim windows. Those men, who likely would be the last to die, had only one purpose, to take out the Ramsay archers that would wreak so much havoc.

Soon, the walls were met by the Ramsays, ladders were laid against the stone, soldiers were sent upward. This was answered from above with the heated pitch tossed down over them, sending them screaming and falling back to earth. Rocks, stacked in many piles around the battlements, were hurled as well, taking down others, as they kept coming. Torches, wrapped in linen and dipped in animal fat were dropped into the spilled tar, igniting large fires near the ladders.

Any Ramsay who did reach the top of the wall was met by a sword-wielding Maitland, keen to take off his head or send him plummeting backward to a sure death.

The bulk of the Maitland archers were now sent to the side walls, intent on keeping any Ramsay from gaining the beach around the side of the castle. They let loose continuously, mostly effective for the next quarter hour.

Screams and smoke and spurting blood filled the air. They'd inflicted a tremendous number of casualties in the first rush, but the numbers still favored the Ramsays and always would until the last Maitland fell.

After half an hour, thinking the wall was well-defended—for now—Lachlan raced down to the yard, where the gate was about to crash in. On the opposite side, the battering ram had arrived, equipped with an arched dome roof to protect the grunts underneath, making it difficult for the wall archers to dismantle that effort. They managed to kill a few, but these were quickly replaced each time by another foot soldier.

Pushing through the waiting soldiers, Lachlan stood at the fore, waiting for the horde to gain the yard. Someone near him, in this thick crowd of waiting Maitlands called out just as the gate was forced open, wood splintering, "Now it's a feast, lads!" As one the entire group charged forward, meeting the enemy at the gate.

Lachlan danced with one and then another Ramsay, dispatching them with ease. Any man defending his home would always bring more ferocity, more zeal, and more fervor into the fray than any paid mercenary. He swiped cleverly at one helmed soldier, purposefully missing, and then took to the stairs near the gatehouse, prompting the man to pursue. Upon the third step, he pivoted, and struck forcefully, catching the man just beneath his collarbone, sending him onto his back on the gravel. Lachlan held this position, wanting to keep any Ramsay from gaining the stairs.

Another came at him, they just kept coming. Kicking the body off his sword presently sent the ones behind tumbling down as well that Lachlan was afforded a moment to survey the carnage happening before his eyes.

It was then that he saw a mounted rider enter the yard, watched him tiptoe his horse over the shattered wood of the gate. The man astride the horse was unsoiled as of yet, his blade devoid of even one drop of blood and Lachlan immediately knew who this man was.

"Walter Ramsay!" He called above the clangs and grunts and cries.

A pale and thick face turned toward him from across twenty feet or so, over the grappling and fighting men in the yard.

"Your bride is dead!" Lachlan taunted.

Walter Ramsay curled his bright red lips with disgust and watched while Lachlan dispatched two more who charged up the steps. He'd made himself a target by addressing Ramsay and now there were plenty scrambling to have at him upon the stairs. When two enemies appeared at the top of the stairs, Lachlan leapt down off the side of the steps and was promptly surrounded.

He might have been instantly skewered but for Walter Ramsay's strident call.

"Do not touch him!" Walter screeched. "Bring him to me!"

Lachlan stilled, his chest rising and falling for all the combat and his efforts thus far, and considered his odds. Of course, he had no chance, as so many Ramsays now stood and fought inside the courtyard. He wiped his hand across his mouth, his gaze fixed on the toady Ramsay, and dropped his sword.

He was pleased when Ramsay called out shrilly, "Cease! Ramsays, hold!"

Giving himself up now would, at the very least, buy time for the boat to get further out to sea. Certainly, it would make for a slow and gruesome death, not the quick battle-born demise he'd hoped for, but at least Mari would be safe.

Hands grasped at him, clutching him under the arms, marching him forward to Walter Ramsay. The yard was littered with bodies and abandoned weapons, the gravel and wee bits of grass red with so much blood. Little by little, hearing Walter's command and sensing the posturing of these two men, the battle around them stalled.

Walter Ramsay dismounted and when he turned to face Lachlan, meeting him in the very middle of the yard, he wore a warped grin of evil delight.

There would be no honorable death, Lachlan realized.

Walter did not approach, stayed near his horse, taking his sweet time removing his immaculate gloves while looking over Lachlan.

Even far away, atop the wall and outside the gate, the entire fight seemed to have paused. All was quiet.

"It appears someone has already had some fun with you," Walter said, flapping his gloves toward Lachlan, indicating his scars. He tucked the gloves into his belt and promised, "Whatever that is, or was, it will seem like child's play by the time I'm done with you."

Bluidy hell, a preening little man who needed to prove his bravery by practicing torture.

Lachlan rolled his eyes, pretending a great disinterest, and moved his gaze away from Walter Ramsay, scanning the yard. The keep itself had been breached, the doors flung wide.

All the color drained from his face as his gaze swept past and then stopped at the door, as Mari herself came running out into the courtyard.

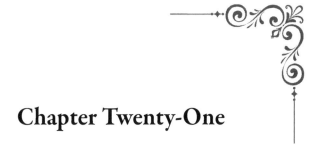

Chapter Twenty-One

"Lachlan!" She saw him straightaway and ran to him, about to throw herself at him. The bottom foot of her gown was wet; she'd gotten as far as the boat, it seemed, but had returned.

Ah, Mari, why? "No!" He roared as her arm was grabbed up by a Ramsay man, as her forward motion was stopped so suddenly as to drop her to the ground.

The entire yard stilled completely. Walter's head swiveled and his mouth gaped.

"Mari," he mouthed, catching sight of his betrothed.

Mari was held back, struggling to her feet, now detained by two Ramsay men, thirty feet from Lachlan. Her teary gaze held his.

Lachlan let her see all the anguish in his face, hid nothing from her.

"You dinna listen, lass," he said savagely, the cords in his neck bulging. His throat tightened, his eyes watered. Now she would see him die. *Ah, Mari. Why dinna you listen?* "You are the worst bluidy captive ever," he said, every bit of agony felt and known just now heard in his voice.

She tried again to reach him, was jerked back by strong arms.

"Mari?" Louder now.

She turned at Walter's voice, first left then right to locate him.

Ramsay stepped forward, away from his horse, bewildered yet by her actions and her tears, by Lachlan's words.

When she found her betrothed, she cried and begged of him, "Let him go. I'll do anything. I'll marry you, whatever you want. Just let him go."

His face just then, pasty and pale, looked exactly as if he'd just swallowed some meat or milk that was many days gone bad. "You would beg for his life?"

"I'll do anything. I'll beg. I'll grovel. I'll take his place. Walter, please."

"Mari," Lachlan called bitterly. When she faced him again, her cheeks streaked with her tears, Lachlan shook his head. "You'll no' beg for me, Mari mine."

She fell to her knees and sobbed then, the life ebbing from her.

Lachlan sagged as well, only kept upright by the hands that held him.

Walter, recovering, though still showing some furious astonishment, approached Mari and grabbed a fistful of her hair, bringing her to her feet. The goons holding her stepped away, releasing her to Walter Ramsay's unequivocal rage.

Lachlan surged forward but was hauled back swiftly, that he could only watch as Walter Ramsay made a grisly face at Mari and sneered at her.

"You low-born piece of shite. I was prepared to raise you out from the ditch you were born into. I had thought that you and I—"

Two things happened next—and within only seconds of each other—that changed the entire course of the day. Mari swung her arm out at Walter, appeared to only claw for her freedom as she was lifted by her hair to her feet, but he stopped talking so unexpectedly, and blood began to spurt from the neat slice in his neck that it was obvious that she had just slit his throat. For several seconds, while dozens of men inside the yard could only stare, shocked and confused, Mari did the same. Her fingers curled up near her mouth in horror, so shocked she possibly didn't realize she still held the blade, pointed now out toward her ear as it was held so close to her face. She squeaked and jumped back as Walter Ramsay crumbled to the ground at her feet, spitting blood from his mouth and neck.

She collapsed as well, in slow motion it seemed, destroyed and dropped by this awfulness. Lachlan never took his gaze from her, stunned as all the rest of the watchers were.

And just before all the fighting men inside the courtyard might have resumed the combat now, another thundering of hooves was heard, and another army—neither Ramsay nor Maitland—rode hellbent into the yard.

Lachlan spared them only a glance. The green and brown of the McEwen plaid shouted out that the cavalry was here.

As quickly as the fighting had stopped moments ago with Lachlan's surrender, so now did the battle resume, the McEwen war cry enlivening the remaining Maitlands.

Lachlan jerked his arm away from one soldier holding him and pushed his shoulder into the one on his other side, dropping to the ground as the man on his left stabbed his sword wildly, striking his own man on Lachlan's right. Lachlan crawled forward, grabbing up some dead man's sword and rolled onto his back, raising the sword just as the man from his left now stabbed at him. Lachlan's blade found him first. He used his foot to kick the man off his sword and scrambled to his feet and to Mari.

Reaching for her hand, he yanked her to her feet just as a horse reined in hard, its front legs lifting off the ground directly in front of them. Lachlan lifted his eyes and his sword, ready to defend yet more, but saw only Iain McEwen's battle-grim face.

"Get her inside," his friend said. "We've got this."

He might have cried, his relief then immeasurable. But he spared only a nod to the McEwen chief and rushed Mari in through the open doors.

The hall was not empty of persons, but the four or five strewn about were all dead, both Ramsays and Maitlands.

"Is the boat gone, then?" He asked, tugging her behind him.

"Aye," came her shaky reply.

He pulled her through the passageway and then the eerily vacant kitchen and out the back door, scolding her all the way. "When this is done, I'm going to fetch you and blister your arse for the fright you just gave me." There was so little fighting in the rear yard that Lachlan easily reached the postern gate and pushed Mari through it. "You won't sit for a week," he promised, his grip punishing around her wrist. "And I might yet lock you up in the bloody tower, one day for every bluidy year you took from my life just now." He turned left and strode briskly along the top of the embankment, until the trees thickened, sparing only a glance out to the beach and the sea to take note that the boat was gone, out of sight. "And when that's done," he barked yet more, "I might still invent more punishment." He stopped when they were deep into the trees, could see not the sea nor the castle walls, and spun around to face her.

She was crying still and covered in Walter Ramsay's blood. In her free hand, she still held her thin blade, her knuckles white around the hilt. Lachlan grunted and pulled her into his arms, trembling against her and breathing raggedly as the reality of what had just happened crashed down upon him. He held her tight, crushed her to him, and closed his eyes.

But he hadn't time for more.

Pushing her away, he pointed to the nearest tree. "Sit there! Dinna move a bluidy muscle. No' until I come for you."

She was panicked yet, shaking, but he hadn't time for her trauma, the trauma that came to every man after their first kill. Lachlan backed her up and pushed her down against the tree. He put the big bloodied sword across her drawn up knees. "Use that, if you need it."

And he left her. Turned to rejoin the battle, took many angry strides, and then cursed and retraced his steps, returning to her. He went to his knees before her and took her face in his hands and kissed the living daylights out of her.

When he left her again, he ran hard all the way back to the keep and the battle.

SHE SAT, STARING BLINDLY, and didn't move, not even when her legs began to fall asleep. Her hands covered the sword Lachlan had laid across her knees.

The sun moved further across the sky. She remained motionless against that tree. She tried to listen, but heard naught but the sea, didn't know if the battle raged yet or was done. The shivering had finally stopped.

She stared at her hands, unblinking, and absently considered the blood, dried now, red and brown. Part of a man's life, the one she'd taken. More blood upon the sword, more lives gone. Initially she was plagued by a certain notion that this was her fault. She had no reasoning to support this, just randomly thought she herself to blame. This stayed with her for quite some time, until other thoughts, logical ones, pervaded the fog that was her brain.

The Ramsays were at fault, for what they'd done to Harman and so many others because of his reiving, all in the name of some ancient feud between the families, as Harman had said, with no other objective but to irk the Maitlands. And it had been the Ramsays who'd come for war, who didn't wait for the peace accord; they'd brought all this death and destruction with them. While it was true Lachlan's kidnapping of her had possibly set off the spiraling of events that had brought them here, today, it was also true that he'd only wanted peace, that no one had been harmed by him until the Ramsays came.

When she thought her limbs might support her, when she thought surely hours had passed, she stood, holding the huge sword by its hilt, the blade pointed into the earth before her. Still, she remained at the tree, where Lachlan had left her. She thought it might be a long time, if not ever, before she disobeyed him again. Jumping out of the boat, in hindsight, had been both reckless and ill-advised. She hadn't helped, really, but to have killed Walter herself. That other army had arrived—Mari had no idea who they might be—and it was probable that Lachlan would have been spared by their entrance, despite the dire straits she'd found him in when she'd charged from the keep.

Shaking her head, determined not to relive it again, she turned toward the castle just as a sound spooked her. Because her hands were already around the hilt, Mari lifted the sword instinctively in front of her. Her arms shook with the weight of it.

She dropped the blade to the ground again when Lachlan appeared, jogging through the trees toward her. Mari dropped the sword completely and ran to him.

They crashed into each other. Lachlan circled his strong arms around her and pressed his lips to her hair while Mari sank her face into his chest and sobbed her relief.

"Oh, thank God," she cried.

"It's done now, Mari. Shh."

Eventually, Lachlan released her, pushed her away and collected the discarded sword, and found Mari's knife by the tree as well. He tucked the latter into his own belt and carried the sword, taking Mari's hand, leading her back to the castle.

"The battle is done, Mari," he said, walking ahead of her as there was no space in these trees wide enough to accommodate them side by side. "But we'll have plenty of work ahead of us. Just now, we've got dozens of wounded who need attention." He stopped at the rear gate, only a foot taller than him, and turned to her before he pulled it open. "Donal and Edric are gone, lass."

More tears, more grief. Mari lowered her head and trembled with this new awfulness.

"Murdoch and Utrid are in bad shape," he continued. "Murdoch'll be fine, mayhap, but Utrid....I dinna ken."

He told her all this with purpose, she thought, told her before she was thrust into it, wanted her to expose her sorrow and fear now before she saw them. He was asking her to be strong.

Swallowing, lifting her gaze to him, she nodded.

Lachlan opened the gate and passed her through.

The yard was devoid of all the bodies that had littered it so distressingly earlier, though the dirt and gravel and grass was bathed yet in varying shades of red, as if it had rained blood inside the bailey. Maitlands and soldiers of that green and brown plaid clan labored about the yard and upon the battlements, while a pall hung over the entire site of the massacre. Lachlan did not tarry but walked her quickly into the keep.

As soon as they entered the hall, Mari realized the room had been transformed into a dormitory for the wounded, the trestle tables employed as beds for some, the floor for others. A quick scan suggested possibly forty to fifty injured men waited or were receiving attention. She spotted Murdoch immediately, upon one of the tables, and let go of Lachlan's hand to rush forward to him.

He'd been divested of his tunic and shield that his big barrel chest was bare, and one shoulder was wrapped with linens, the linen showing a large dark stain of seeping blood. Another cut across his side had not been addressed, but appeared to be only a surface wound, a slice rather than a gouge.

"Murdoch?"

He opened his eyes. "Aye, there she is." Oh, but his voice was so weak, so tiny compared to his usual rich sounds.

Mari smiled down at him. She teased, "What have you gotten yourself into?"

"Ye ken I dinna like any to threaten me and mine," he said softly.

"I know," she said and kissed his grimy forehead. "What can I do for you?"

"No' for me, just now, lass. You go on, see to those who need the care."

She would, imagining any extra hands would be appreciated. "But you'll call if you need me?"

He nodded, his eyes closed again.

When Mari turned, she found Lachlan talking to the man who'd ridden in to their rescue earlier. They stood close yet, their voices low. Lachlan extended his hand to her, drawing her into their conversation.

"Mari Sinclair, meet Iain McEwen, of the Caithness Mackays."

She bobbed a curtsy, but did not rush it, as he deserved great respect for what he'd done.

"Lachlan Maitland has done a fine job," she said, "showing what an honorable man looks like, sir, but those Ramsays greatly challenged the concept outside of Hawkmore. I thank you for restoring my faith in humanity."

Iain McEwen was big and brawny, similar to Lachlan, though mayhap a bit narrower through the shoulders. His eyes were blue, much darker than Lachlan's mesmerizing gaze, and his skin was unmarred, though weathered, the lines near his eyes and bracketing his mouth creased with the day's dust. He grinned, appreciative of her comment, but he directed his reply to Lachlan. "This your wee critical something?"

Mari hadn't seen too much sheepishness in Lachlan Maitland, but his response to this was definitely so. He ducked his head to hide his grin. When he lifted his face, he stared at Mari, the grin softening.

"The greatest wee critical something," he answered.

Iain McEwen laughed and patted Lachlan neatly on the shoulder. "Good for you, Lach."

Like so much of Lachlan, there was a hardness to Iain McEwen, which was not dispelled with either laughter or smiles. He was efficient of movement and words, wasted not either; and the depth of his gaze, when he settled it upon Mari with solid appraisal, hinted at deeper shadows.

She excused herself then, leaving them to their discussion, wanting to be about the business of helping with the care of the injured.

Mari remained in the hall until late into the evening. Grisel, the healer, had been found and brought to Hawkmore. Elesbeth had come, the people of the village returned from the caves in which they'd hid. The pretty blonde cried out when she found Utrid, but he heard nothing, having not regained consciousness since he'd been laid upon the table many hours earlier. The gaping wound in his side had been the first Grisel had administered to, teaching Mari and Elesbeth, both anxious to learn, so much during just those spare minutes she'd afforded to Utrid's care.

Over the course of the next few hours, while Mari really wished Diana and Florie and Edie had returned already—Lachlan said it would be days, at the earliest—she was constantly at Grisel's side. She received a swift and abbreviated course in wound care, cleaning and sewing, and learned so much about poultices applied to stave off infection, and plants utilized to relieve pain.

Soldiers, those not injured, played a vital role as well, keeping the hall equipped with clean and heated water, and a never-ending stock of linen strips. Three men, Torquil among them, had emptied Grisel's cart into the hall, which contained most of her complete stock of wares and medicines, and had brought in another table from somewhere else inside the keep to serve as the healer's base of operation. So many other soldiers, accustomed to being afield and having to manage their own sustenance, took to the kitchen and prepared broths and soups and kept the hall well fueled with bread and bannocks and ale.

At one point, Torquil approached her to give her the happy news that Niel and Charles and Edmund had been recovered from Gershouse, "Roughed up, but no' so bad, lass," he'd relayed with some excitement.

Mari was overjoyed to receive this news, and hoped there were more occasions, and very soon, of good and positive things coming to Hawkmore.

"YOU'LL BE PLEASED TO ken," Iain McEwen said to Lachlan, "that your missive alone, wax seal unbroken and carried by the sea, would have had me moving right quick from Berriedale. But Lach, you start tossing around *a wee critical something*, and God's truth, we tore out of there as if the fires of hell were nipping at our backsides."

"Aye, but they were already here," Lachlan said.

He and Iain sat atop their mounts, in the middle of the wide field before Hawkmore. Men moved all around them, clearing the meadow of bodies and that damn wagon, with Rannoch Ramsay's remains inside.

"How'd we first use that?" He wondered of Iain. So many of the small memories of their time in captivity was hazy, or by now forgotten.

Iain grinned, showing little humor. "Alec started it, when he was trying to trap those mice. Thought they'd make for good eating. Remember? Him crouched in that dark corner, hours on end. I kept asking him what he was about. Finally, he turns—he was right pissed for my nagging, but Christ, what else had I to do?—and says, real surly, *I'm working on a wee critical something.*"

Lachlan recalled now. "They were not good eating," he said, upon reflection.

"But they were food."

"Aye." And then they'd taunted Alec mercilessly, attributing *a wee critical something* to so many things. It was the answer to every question for days, served as the only amusement, such as it was, that helped them stay sane, not give in, or give up. And when the old MacBriar had come to save them, his son, Alec, had supposed to Iain and Lachlan, *Aye now, we've just survived our own wee critical something.*

"You see him lately? Alec?" Lachlan asked of Iain.

"Not since that mess at Methven." Iain let out a large sigh. "He'd gone down to MacGregor at Inesfree then, kept company with them over the winter. I only ken this because Tess wrote my mother. Haven't heard of his whereabouts since spring."

"Mayhap he's back at Swordmair?"

"Could be."

"He's got more anger yet than I," Lachlan guessed, which meant that Alec's anger was beyond extraordinary.

"Aye."

Lachlan considered Iain. No scars were visible on his old friend, but he knew they were there. "You do well with it. Or at least give the appearance that you do."

Iain shrugged. "The latter," he acknowledged. "It's in the past, Lach. I try to leave it there." He grinned at Lachlan. "You ken these current wee critical somethings are powerful tools for pushing all that even further away."

THE DEPTHS OF HER SOUL

Lachlan lifted a brow at Iain, understanding he was being told that Iain had a lass in his life. He smiled at Iain, this one sincere. "Aye, they are at that."

Hours later, Lachlan returned to the keep. The McEwens would stay on for a few days, camping in and about the yard of Hawkmore and beyond. Iain had refused the offer of a bedchamber, choosing instead to bunk down with his men.

By now, Lachlan had learned the extent of their losses: sixty-seven Maitlands and twelve McEwens dead. The numbers were awful, heartbreaking, but he admitted to himself it could have been—he'd certainly expected—so much worse. 'Twas only that they'd remained inside the walls, that he'd not sent out a contingent to meet the warring Ramsays that had kept the numbers low. That, and Mari's arrival, her killing of Walter Ramsay, and then the coming of the McEwens, was what had saved them.

He found the hall settled, saw immediately that Mari sat yet with Murdoch. He knew her love for the old man was huge, knew as well that his captain favored her greatly, was beyond pleased for this circumstance. He was content to stand near the door and simply watch her.

She would never leave now. This came to him, struck him somewhere in his chest, and hope fluttered. The Ramsays were no more and she was his. He couldn't yet formulate any coherent judgment about what she'd done today. He only knew, or was reminded, that she was bonny and provocative, and then exasperating and so willing to be open, giving and receiving. And she was fierce, he knew now, she'd not lay down and let evil prevail; she would fight for what was in her heart, for those she loved.

Closing his eyes, he pictured the first time he saw her, when she'd turned those magnificent blue eyes upon him and had breathed, *Oh*. He'd been taken almost instantly, but had he known then what she would be? Was there any sense at that moment that she would be everything to him?

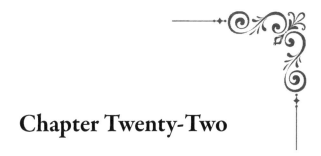

Chapter Twenty-Two

By midnight, Mari was sure she had visited or checked on each man at least twice—by now she'd counted thirty-seven injured—and Murdoch much more than that. Now, she sat on the bench near the table that served as his pallet and held his hand while he slept. The sword thrust through his shoulder had required stitching on both his front and his backside. Grisel had offered many opinions on the injuries of all these men during her many hours here, some grave and some encouraging, and Mari had happily latched onto her positive estimation that Murdoch would certainly survive this.

The hall was quiet now that Mari supposed she might fetch a few hours of sleep herself. Lachlan and Iain McEwen had left the hall hours ago, giving assistance out of doors, for repairs to the keep and yard, and the removal of bodies, and preparations for funerals that would take place on the morrow.

She let her gaze scan the hushed hall and was surprised to find Lachlan standing just inside the door. It seemed he'd been doing the same thing, taking in the whole of the hall, surveying what damage had been done to his Maitland men.

He came to her, said nothing initially, but passed his inscrutable gaze over Murdoch, pleased at least it seemed that his captain slept comfortably. He'd had a bath, possibly in the sea, his hair wet, his clothes fresh, all evidence of the day's horror washed away.

"I was just going up," Mari said when he looked at her, "thought I'd wash up and sleep for a wee bit."

Lachlan sent another glance around the whole room. "Plenty of able-bodied lads here, if anyone should have a need," he said, referring to all the uninjured soldiers who'd made their beds inside the hall as well. "Go on up. There's still water boiling, like as no'. I'll fetch a bath for you."

She wanted to deny this; he must be exhausted as well, in all likelihood more so, but a bath sounded heavenly so that she only nodded and retreated to her chambers.

Mari removed all her clothes except her linen undergarment, and sat on the side of the bed, working on the tangles in her hair. By now, she'd acquired her own soaps and linens for her baths, which sat on the cupboard, the soaps bunched in an oval pottery dish.

Lachlan was not long, entered her chambers with both the big wooden tub and the first large bucket of steaming water. He made two more trips, one more for another bucket of heated water and then for the cooler water from the rain barrel, to temper the heat.

When this was set up, he knelt and lit a fire in the hearth for her.

Mari combed her fingers through her unwound braids and the snarls and asked, "What is a *wee critical something*?"

The question caught him off guard. He turned with his elbow on his bent knee and considered her thoughtfully.

"The McEwen and I go way back," he said and shrugged. "It's just a phrase used once, years ago. We ken it, it's recognizable to us that if it's used in a missive or a call to help, it's authentic." He turned back to the task of making the room warmer.

"But he asked if I were a *wee critical something*."

"In essence, it means something very important, life-changing."

"Was Iain McEwen with you? When you were a prisoner of the English?"

He didn't answer immediately, put one more log onto the pile he'd made over the small burning flames, and then stood and faced her.

"He wears that same dark frown you do," she said, explaining the reasoning behind her evidently correct assumption. "Underneath his seeming good humor—which I cannot decide was genuine or effected by the battle itself, as I do not know him at all. But he has similar sorrow, the same guilt."

After a moment, he nodded. "Aye, he was there." He sat in the chair next to the hearth, his sword scraping on the floor, his body too big for the dainty piece of furniture.

She let her hands fall to her lap, abandoned the tangles in her hair. "How do you go on? How do you find joy ever when so many are lost?"

"That's the answer just there, Mari," he said, his voice mimicking the same dull tone of hers. "If you refuse it, any joy, it's all for naught. Think any of them that fell want to ken that all those who lived are only wretched ever after?"

"But it feels traitorous, to want to be in your arms, when…they're all gone. Why do we get to live, and they do not?"

He considered this, gravely it seemed, his expression dark and still. "I've struggled with exactly this for years, lass. All those men gone at the hands of the English when we were taken captive. Why did I get to live?" He rubbed his jaw, scratched a bit over the scarring on his right side. "Never did find the answer. Murdoch says it's the living—truly living well—that honors those dead. It dinna seem enough though. But then life happens, day by day, year after year—eating, sleeping, toiling, warring, everything...until you realize that's how you do it, one day at a time, the best you can." He shrugged, as if to say he didn't know any other way and shifted his gaze to the growing fire, lost for a moment in the dancing flames. "I'm no' a great man, Mari," he said, keeping his gaze inside the hearth, "but I try. I try to practice honor and truth and integrity. I fail repeatedly, too often, but I keep trying."

"And love? Do you practice love?"

He turned and met her curious gaze now, smiled vaguely. It didn't reach his eyes. Something sorrowful tinted his features.

"I canna say I dinna ever let myself love because I thought I dinna deserve it, because I lived, and they died. Like as no', I never considered it because of the scars...but then, that's no' living, no' honoring them at all, aye?" He shifted in the chair, thoughtful for a few minutes. "When they showed the strength of their force earlier—their full numbers—I knew I was bound to die this day. Believed it at the time, anyhow. My first thought then was no' sorrow that my life would end, or dread that death might be painful, or that the Maitlands would breathe no more." He let out a short, humorless chuckle. "My first thought was bitterness, that I'd only just found you, and hope, and love, but that I wouldn't get to ken any of it." Wryly, he said, "I was bluidy peeved about the whole thing."

She stood then and lifted her kirtle over her head, too exhausted to be shy about her nakedness just now. Lachlan sat just beside the tub, as he'd set the bath in front of the fire. She put her hand out to him and when he took it in his own, she used this for balance and climbed into the bath. She sighed with a wearied pleasure as she sank into the depth of the wonderfully warm water, closing her eyes.

"I think Lachlan Maitland is a very great man," she said softly, honestly.

"But would you want to spend all your life with this man?" He asked solemnly.

She did not open her eyes. "I would. I would like that above all else."

"He's snarly and overbearing at times, I ken."

"He is," Mari said. "And he's quick to anger and he practices kidnapping as well, I hear. But then he drapes a plaid over his hostage when she's sleeping and saves her from drowning and never raises a hand against her and doesn't lock her up because he knows that she doesn't ever want to leave him, not really. And his kisses are heavenly, and his heart is good, and she loves him beyond measure, beyond…anything." Mari opened her eyes, feeling him close.

"I am so in love with you." He was at her side, on his knees, soap and cloth in hand, his arms draped over the rim of the tub. He, too, was tired, exhausted in body and mind.

Mari smiled softly at him, her heart in her gaze. "And his fornicating is divine."

Lachlan's shoulders shook. "Now, lass, we've talked about this."

"The fornicating?"

He dunked the cloth and lathered the soap in it. "Aye, that very thing."

"Are we to have more discussion about fornication?"

His crooked grin remained. He lifted Mari's leg out of the bath, running the soapy linen up and down her thigh and calf. "You canna be running around using that word."

She tilted her head on the edge of the tub. "But how do I get you to..." she began, and he lifted a brow, a warning contained in his gaze, "make love to me again?"

Lachlan smiled. "You only need ask, Mari mine."

Her gaze misted and the small smile that came was bittersweet. "This is living, right, Lachlan? This is us, attempting to live well...?"

"Aye, lass. We'll just get to it, day by day." He set her leg down, let his arms sit on the rim again. "In my life, I've had some pretty formidable emotions. Feels like the strongest ones have always been negative—anger, injustice, grief and so on." He pursed his lips, stared only at the water of the bath. "What I feel for you" —he shook his head, coming to terms with it— "it's greater than any of those. But I dinna mind telling you, it's a wee bit frightening."

She considered this, did not downplay this admission. She pulled the cloth from his loose grip and washed her face and neck. And then she asked, "Does it help that I feel the same, that I'm not entirely sure our souls are not the same? That if you didn't love me, then nothing else would matter, not anything at all?"

Lachlan lifted his gaze to her. "Then you understand."

"I know that I love you and I know I'll be a better person for loving you, for being loved by you. I feel like that's all I need to understand just now."

He nodded and stood, pushing himself to his feet by his hands on the rim of the wooden tub. "C'mon then, Mari mine. Let's see about that fornicating."

"MURDOCH, YOU MIGHT have told me how difficult this actually was," Mari complained. She'd been about this rowing for nearly half an hour, and they'd not moved very far from the shore. Her arms ached and she wasn't sure she'd not have blisters on her hands from these oars.

Sitting comfortably in the bow of the boat, upon blankets and plaids thick enough to make a good cushion, Murdoch grinned up at her. His good arm rested over the top of the side rail, and his injured arm, well healed by now with the siege more than two weeks behind them, yet bandaged still, stayed close to his side.

"You're no' listening, lass. Move them at the same time, in the same way, if you want to move straight forward."

"Well, that's easier said than done," she argued. "The oars are heavy."

"It's the water that's heavy and would be heavier still if you bothered to slice those oars properly through it."

Mari made a face at him. "Would that you had two good arms just now, Murdoch."

"Let it be, lass," Murdoch suggested. "Sitting and floating is just as nice."

She didn't need to be told twice, letting the oars drift aimlessly in the near placid water. They sat quietly then, both watching the goings on along the beach, which was not far at all from where they sat. As many as thirty or forty people crowded the shoreline, split into different groups. The smallest group was Diana and Florie and Edie, on the sidelines, watching the play. Utrid and Elesbeth were with them as well, the former recovered agreeably and the latter having barely left his side, which pleased Mari to no end. Utrid had shyly asked her only this morning what words he might use to beg Elesbeth's hand. Oh, but he was a dear, thinking any words uttered could possibly be wrong, which was exactly what she'd told him.

The others running all about the beach were separated into two teams of twelve each, all shirtless soldiers. Even the young lads, Rory and Robert, were bare-chested as well. Earlier, several men had scraped out with their feet a long rectangle and had used driftwood to mark two similar boxes at each end. Every player carried a shiny, well-hewn stick with a curved and clubbed end, which they used to poke around a leather covered ball. Follow the ball seemed to be a great part of the game, chunks of persons descending upon it when it was forwarded and sent through the air or over the ground.

"What's it called again?" Mari asked of Murdoch.

"*Camanachd*, properly" Murdoch told her once more, "but ye just say shinty, lass."

"Shinty," she repeated. "What's the point, though?"

"Get that ball past that man in the goal, the one inside that driftwood box."

"Why?"

Murdoch frowned at her. "What ye mean, *why*? Ye get a point each time you get the ball past there. The team with the most points wins."

"Wins what?"

"The game," Murdoch said, his tone hinting that he might suspect she was daft.

"Is there a prize?"

"Winning is the prize, lass."

Now Mari frowned. Seemed an awful lot of work if there were no treat or boon to be awarded. They should have some sweet bread or cakes waiting for the winners. "Why are they wearing those red flags about their middles?" She saw that only some of them did, Lachlan included. The red flag was simply a linen strip, tied around the waist of mayhap half the men.

"That's one team, the red team," Murdoch said. "The others are called the skins."

Mari saw Lachlan send his shoulder into Torquil's chest, bumping him out of the way as he made for the ball. He chased it with his stick, swatting at it so it skittered across the sand and was taken and moved by Niel, who wore a red linen tie as well. She decided she might only enjoy this game for the benefit it provided her, watching a shirtless Lachlan moving with such fluid beauty around the field of play. He laughed often, she heard, as did many.

"Games are good," she decided, understanding now the release it possibly offered, from heartache and sadness, and even the mundane of labor and tedium.

"Aye, gotta have fun, lass."

Mari sighed wistfully. "I don't ever want to leave Hawkmore," she said, rather out of the blue. At Murdoch's kindly grin of understanding, she added, "Being kidnapped is the best thing that ever happened to me. Isn't that silly?"

"Nae, it's a good landing, lass. And ye ken, we're happy to have ye, every person here."

Utrid's earlier question had put something in Mari's head that she'd not dared to voice, not even inside her head, not once. "I want to be by his side always." She was watching Lachlan, as of yet still bemused by the good fortune that had thrown her into his path. They'd talked of forever-ish things that night of the siege, but not since. She hadn't given it much thought, truly, until just now, that she wanted more with him, wanted a permanency.

"That'll need a wedding, then," Murdoch said, sounding not at all displeased by the idea.

Meeting Murdoch's gaze, interpreting the lifted brow, she said, "I guess it's up to me to do the asking."

"Now, that's no' how these things are done. He'll get around to it, I've no doubt."

"Murdoch, you do understand that for all his strength and all his fearlessness, that he needs prodding often in all the feeble kin matters."

He chuckled outright now. "And I bet you're just the one to do the prodding."

Mari shrugged, grinning like a fool. "If I have to...."

She watched more of the game on the beach. The ball moved around from man to man, the red-flagged group having control, until Niel sent it off through the air, past the flailing goalkeeper. Half the men on the field cheered, and Lachlan gave a shout of joy, wrapping up Niel in a bear hug, the rest of their team dancing around them. And that was the game, she supposed, as sticks were dropped and at least half the players charged into the sea for relief, washing away the sweat and sand.

Lachlan dove expertly into the surf and emerged very close to the boat, while others stayed nearer the shore. He swam the rest of the way and lifted himself up against the boat, hanging one arm over the side, teasing Murdoch with a handful of water sprayed at him.

"You take up with Grisel yourself, you get this bandage wet," Murdoch threatened. "You dinna want to mess with her, trust me."

Lachlan only grinned and sent more water up and over the boat.

He considered Mari then, giving her a wink while Murdoch groused.

"You dinna get very far, lass."

"Rowing and I do not agree," she admitted without shame. "And you can clearly see that he's no help," she teased and sent a saucy grin to Murdoch.

"Lass better stick with being bonny," Murdoch said with a disgruntled sniff that wrinkled his nose. "The rowing's no' for her."

"So, it's up to you," Mari said to Lachlan, "either pull us in or get in here and take control of these ridiculous oars, which are more likely to obey your direction than mine."

"I was thinking I'd adopt a similar circumstance as Murdoch, let you row us around the sea."

"That is not going to happen," she promised, scrunching up her face.

He hoisted himself up, his arms rippling gorgeously with the effort, bringing himself up high enough to swing his leg over. The boat tilted, Mari hung on, Murdoch growled something, and then Lachlan stood in the middle, facing Mari. "I suppose now you'll be wanting to sit alongside the old man and let me take you two all about."

She moved quick enough, her grin coming swiftly, that he might have guessed that was exactly what she'd hoped for. She stood and hung onto Lachlan's wet body as she worked her way around him, then used the siderails to make her way to Murdoch. The old man smiled, lifting his good arm a bit, that Mari sat and settled in under his shoulder, wedged into the bow next to him.

She held Murdoch's hand near her collar. "Row away, sir."

Murdoch cackled and added, "Nice and slow, if you please. I feel a good midday nap coming on."

Lachlan sat, taking up the oars, and shook his head at the pair, then sent his gaze behind, to gauge their direction, and make sure no others had swum this far.

"Ah, this is perfect," Mari said.

"You've got all the best ideas, lass," Murdoch concurred.

"I know." She sighed happily. "Should we tell him about my other idea?"

"The one we just discussed?" Murdoch wondered, his eyes closed, his head turned up to the sun. "Nae, lass, ye probably wanna present 'em slow, one at a time."

"Aye, you're right of course."

She peeked through a narrow slit in her own closed eyes, and found Lachlan still grinning at them, not perturbed at all by his present circumstance.

LATER THAT NIGHT, AS Lachlan met her in her chambers, he said evenly, seeming only to make conversation. "Looked like some serious conversation you were having with Utrid this morn."

"He's very silly," Mari said. "Wondered if I had any advice on how, exactly, he might ask Elesbeth if she would wed with him."

He asked no other question about that but gave Mari a grin for Utrid's complete lack of self-confidence. He stirred the fire, as he did every night in this room, this now seeming to be their room as he'd shared it each night since the siege on Hawkmore. The only change he'd made was replacing the dainty chair beside the hearth with a larger and sturdier one, culled from where, Mari hadn't asked.

He sat there now, removing his boots. Setting them aside, he leaned back and ran his hands up and down his thighs. "What did you tell him?"

Mari turned from the small cupboard, where she'd been cleaning her face and teeth. Her hair was held yet in its usual ribbon tie, falling over her shoulder as she pivoted. "Tell who?"

"Utrid."

Tilting her head at him, for his query coming so many minutes after her previous answer, she said, "I told him any request for her hand should come from his heart, and that there likely wasn't a wrong way to ask."

"So, a simple *lass, will you be my wife* should suffice?"

She might not have caught on, but that his gaze was unusually intense, set so remarkably upon her, while at the same time showing an uncertainty that seemed endearingly boyish.

She shrugged, and played along, her heart bursting. Softly, slowly, she said, "Aye, that might do...for some. Others, say a lass with a powerful love for her man, might wish something a little more...emotive. Maybe heartfelt."

"Aye, but what if the man has an even greater love for the lass?"

Mari set down the cloth next to the basin and crossed the room to him. She lifted his hands away from his thighs and set them on her hips. Lachlan sunk his fingers into her and stared up at her. He pulled her forward, wedged his knee between hers and then tugged further, so that she sat, and straddled him.

"Then I suppose he should lead with that," Mari said and kissed his forehead. "He might want to wax poetic about stars in his eyes and fires in his heart"—she kissed his cheek—"and speak of how truly wonderful she is"—she kissed his other cheek—"tell her he cannot breathe without her"—she kissed his mouth—"or...he can show her, with his lips and his hands and his body, and perhaps an occasional heart-melting grin, how much he loves her. I'm fairly certain that might work."

Lachlan kissed her, showed her just the beginning of his adoration with that kiss. "I think I understand. I'm no' sure about Utrid, but I've got an idea what I should do." He stood, bringing Mari with him, his hands under her legs while she clung to his neck. "Show her, aye? Sounds like fornication if I'm not mistaken." He pecked her lips again, and laid her on the bed, following closely, his hand finding her breast immediately. "Fornication, I ken."

"I don't want you running around using that word, love," she said on a sigh and his lips found hers again.

Epilogue

Lachlan Maitland waited until everyone within the hall was seated. When they were and quieted all at once, he stood and pulled the tankard in front of him closer, though did not lift it yet. He glanced to his right at the empty chair beside him, deliberately bringing attention to Mari's absence.

"Unlike her to miss a meal," Murdoch called out from Lachlan's left. The captain was relaxed, leaning back in his chair, content in his role which hadn't included giving any speech or toast in almost a year.

The general assembly shouted out agreeable laughter; this had been truer than ever in the last few months.

Between Lach and Murdoch, Diana grinned as well. Her delight this day was unmatched in recent history. Even now, she felt she might weep with her joy. She staved off the tears, gazed adoringly up at her son. Most of her elation resided just here, with him. It had been so very long since her son had known joy. He'd earned every bit of it and to her further delight, embraced it well. He didn't fight it, didn't live in the past anymore. She knew she owed her gratitude to Mari for that. That girl was everything she'd feared—emotional and without a clue how to go about in a great manor, and forever prone to mishaps and missteps—but then she was also everything Diana had hoped—stalwart and loyal, so deeply in love with Lachlan, and so very perfect for him. She couldn't have asked for a better daughter, couldn't have asked for a better person to love her son.

When the hall quieted again, Lachlan said in his deep and sure voice, "Your mistress has given us a son this day." He'd barely finished the sentence before the room erupted in good cheer. He smiled at their happiness, hardly able to contain his own, Diana was pleased to see. "Now, you all ken the lass as well as I. She bore it well, with true Maitland grit, and only threatened to emasculate me twice through the entire ordeal." More laughter answered this, so many smiling faces thrilled by this happy news. "Some of you ken I wanted to name my first born son Robert after our great king and my own grandsire, but aye, the lass had her mind set on Christian. Folks, I'm pleased to announce that we reached a grand compromise and the lad will be called Christian." Murdoch's loud chortle next to him nearly drowned out all the other laughter about the room.

Serious then, likely feeling the agreeable weight of so many emotions tighten his chest, Lachlan said, "I'll no' lie to any one of you—and you can ask the captain—I cried like a babe at the sight of my own."

"Aye, he did," Murdoch called out, "was almost embarrassing, but that I was weeping a bit myself."

Lachlan smiled, many did. He included his mother in his moving gaze. "I can only wish, for each and every one of you, to have this, to ken this—this is joy, pure and simple. Mari...is joy. My son now is joy." He fisted his hand over his heart and then he raised his tankard.

"To the newest joy at Hawkmore! To Christian Maitland!"

This roused the room once again to a thunderous cheer.

When he sat, Diana placed her hand over his. "Happiness was a long time coming, Lach."

His good mood continued, and he kissed his mother's cheek. "More than worth the wait."

WHEN LACHLAN RETURNED to their chambers that night, he found his wife asleep. He dismissed a watching Florie with a smile, giving his thanks for keeping company with Mari. He was content then, to sit at her side and stare at her, sharing his regard with his new son, cradled so close to his mother. Mari was on her side, her son next to her, her hand lying lightly over the swaddled newborn. It seemed she had only been staring at the babe, mayhap had fallen asleep doing so. He thought he was gentle and quiet, removing his sword and climbing into the bed next to her, the babe between them. But Mari opened her sleepy eyes, smiling instantly at her husband.

"Look what you've done, Marianna Maitland," he said, keeping his voice low. "Look at this wee perfect human you've created."

"I know," she cried, giving her husband no credit at all. And then, waking more, and with a bit of a panic, "Lachlan, we must absolutely shower him with love. He must never, not for one minute, ever have any cause to doubt. A person should not live like that."

His eyes welled up. *Jesu, this lass.*

"Mari, we must keep him safe as well," he said. "He should never ken pain or fear or hopelessness."

She concurred heartily. "Yes, yes. Oh, the poor wee lad. His parents are going to smother him."

"Aye, they are."

Mari lifted her teary gaze to her husband. "You are very much in love with me, are you not?"

"Aye, lass. Very much." If you'd told him a year ago that he'd love her more tomorrow, and more the day after and the week after and tenfold in the next month, he'd have said you lied, would have said it was impossible. How ignorant he'd been.

"Very good. Lachlan, he's lovely, of course, but please don't forget that you love me, too."

"More?" He suggested helpfully, so rarely not entertained by how Mari's mind worked.

His little wife winced. "No, that doesn't sound fair to him. Maybe" —she sent her teary gaze to her husband once more— "maybe just differently." She was rethinking this, he could very well see. "Actually, *more* would be all right, but you mustn't ever tell him."

"Nae, I never would, lass," he said gravely, holding back his grin but then was completely pleased to befuddle her. "Aye, lass, and we willna tell the poor boy that his mother loves his father more than him."

"Lachlan, I can't love you more than this sweet babe—look at him."

Lachlan didn't bother to hold back his laughter now. "You are, sweet wife, still and always, the worst prisoner I've ever taken."

She wasn't listening, was instead cooing, "Oh, you've woken him," showing no upset at all. Eagerly, she sat up, and pulled her son into her arms.

Lachlan followed, sitting up next to her against the headboard. Christian Maitland was content to only flutter his eyes and scrunch up his face, to the delight of his new parents, and then settled again into sleep.

Mari turned her head toward Lachlan. "Thank you for my son."

"I ken all that fornicating would result in something other than those big smiles we wore."

Mari laughed out loud, didn't seem to care that it was noisy and roused the babe again.

This was his favorite laugh from Mari, the one that caught her by surprise, the one that gushed merrily from her, that highlighted her dimples and every freckle.

She set her hand onto his scarred cheek and matched her gaze to the words that followed. "Oh, Lachlan, I do love you so."

The End

The Highlander Heroes Series
The Touch of Her Hand
The Memory of Her Kiss
The Shadow of Her Smile
The Depths of Her Soul
The Truth of Her Heart
The Love of Her Life
Highlander Heroes Collection, Books 1-3
Highlander Heroes Collection, Books 4-6

Other Books by Rebecca Ruger
Highlander: The Legends
The Beast of Lismore Abbey
The Lion of Blacklaw Tower
The Scoundrel of Beauly Glen
The Wolf of Carnoch Cross

Far From Home: A Scottish Time-Travel Romance
And Be My Love
Eternal Summer
Crazy In Love
Beyond Dreams
Only The Brave
When & Where

Heart of a Highlander Series
Heart of Shadows
Heart of Stone

Heart of Fire
Heart of Iron
Heart of Winter
Heart of Ice

rebeccaruger.com

Printed in Great Britain
by Amazon

57846123R00193